THE
WOLF
AND THE
CROWN
OF
BLOOD

THE WOLF AND THE CROWN OF BLOOD

ELIZABETH MAY

An Aria Book

This edition first published in the US in 2026 by Head of Zeus,
part of Bloomsbury Publishing

First published in the UK in 2026 by Daphne Press

Copyright © Elizabeth May, 2026

The moral right of Elizabeth May to be identified
as the author of this work has been asserted in accordance with
the Copyright, Designs and Patents Act of 1988.

All rights reserved. No part of this publication may be: i) reproduced or transmitted in any form, electronic or mechanical, including photocopying, recording or by means of any information storage or retrieval system without prior permission in writing from the publishers; or ii) used or reproduced in any way for the training, development or operation of artificial intelligence (AI) technologies, including generative AI technologies. The rights holders expressly reserve this publication from the text and data mining exception as per Article 4(3) of the Digital Single Market Directive (EU) 2019/790.

This is a work of fiction. All characters, organizations, and events portrayed
in this novel are either products of the author's imagination or are used fictitiously.

9 7 5 3 1 2 4 6 8

A catalogue record for this book is available from the British Library.

ISBN (standard HB): 9781035925551; ISBN (special edition HB): 9781035912896
ISBN (XPB): 9781035926084; ISBN (eBook): 9781035912926

Cover design: Simon Michele
Typeset by Siliconchips Services Ltd UK

Printed and bound in Great Britain by Clays Ltd, Elcograf S.p.A.

Bloomsbury Publishing Plc
50 Bedford Square, London, WC1B 3DP, UK
Bloomsbury Publishing Ireland Limited,
29 Earlsfort Terrace, Dublin 2, D02 AY28, Ireland

HEAD OF ZEUS LTD
5–8 Hardwick Street
London, EC1R 4RG

To find out more about our authors and books
visit www.headofzeus.com
For product safety–related questions contact productsafety@bloomsbury.com

For those who have always pondered the question:
If villain bad, why villain hot?

A NOTE FROM THE AUTHOR

A glossary of terms can be found at the end of the book.

The Wolf and the Crown of Blood is a dark fantasy romance. It has more mature themes, strong language, sexually explicit scenes, and graphic content than my previous books. It is not intended for those under the age of eighteen.

Evander, the main male protagonist, is a morally black bastard who does terrible things. If you're looking for a hero, you won't find it here.

Bryony, the main female protagonist, comes from a family bound to divine ritual sacrifice. Readers sensitive to depictions of self-harm, ritual suicide, suicidal ideation, and familial violence should approach with caution.

Additional content warnings for:
Graphic violence with extreme gore and body horror
Trauma and PTSD
War crimes and massacres
Substance abuse
Mention of sexual assault.
The relationship depicted is a dark romance, with content warnings for:
Emotional manipulation
Dominance and submission
Rough play
Power dynamics that blur ethical lines
Darker intimate content with dubious consent, blood play, knife play, breath control, impact play (spanking), primal play, and consensual pain/bruising.
As always, a full list of content notes can be found on my website.

ETERNALS OF SCILLARI

Alexios—God of Storms
Also known as: Storm; Eternal of Asteria
(the Court of Storms)
Primary powers: weather manipulation, control over lightning, some psychic abilities

Severin—God of Death
Also known as: the Dark King; Wraith; Eternal of Nyholm
(the Dark Court)
Primary powers: necromancy, death touch

Evander—God of Light
Also known as: the Wolf
Primary powers: light shaping and manipulation, control over fire, healing

Bastien—God of Shadows
Also known as: the Blade
Primary powers: shadow manipulation, psychic influence, control over metal

Prologue

THE PRINCESS AND the god met in the ashes of a broken city and made a pact in blood and sacrifice.

War creates strange alliances—no one emerges unscathed when death leaves its mark. Humans turn savage. Gods become monsters. And there's a moment when the dead outnumber the living and everything you've ever loved lies in ruins at your feet that you're left with only two choices.

You either bury your pride or you die choking on it.

So Amalthea Devaliant, the last daughter of her family's dynasty, sought the enemy king. "I want to make a deal."

Alexios, Eternal of Asteria, God of Storms, had been alive long before humans dreamed of empires. He'd fought battles that had aged him more than seven thousand years ever could, and of all the wars he'd survived, this one had scarred him deepest. If the princess wanted peace, she'd have to prove it and pay the price.

And Alexios only traded in blood.

He drew a dagger from between his crimson and black wings, pressing the hilt to Amalthea's palm. "There are worse things than being tired of war," he said.

"Like what?"

"Being hungry for it."

She couldn't argue with that. They had a hundred reasons to hate each other, but hatred takes something from you, and neither had anything left to give. Just two broken realms and pyres stacked high with enough bodies to block out the sun for days. A conflict with no end in sight.

Unless *she* ended it.

The princess shut her eyes and raised the knife. It felt wrong somehow—too delicate for sacrifice, too cruel for salvation. But a bargain is a bargain, and the God of Storms wasn't known for changing his mind. So she pressed the weapon to her chest.

Breathe in. Hold. Let go.

This is how you save a world.

She plunged the blade in.

It hit her all at once—metal scraping bone, blood spilling over her fingers, her legs giving out. Then falling, hitting the ground hard. Amalthea stared up at a sky she couldn't quite focus on as numbness crept through her limbs.

It's worth it. It'll all be worth it.

Alexios kneeled beside her and cut open his palms, mingling his blood with hers. He spoke the ancient rites that would bind them. When the last syllable fell from his lips, a ripple went through the world. Starlight and iridescent color spread over the mountains—a veil separating the god and human realms. A Shroud held in place by a promise. A lineage. An Accord carved into every temple altar in Vartena, written in stone, in blood, in memory.

And with its birth, the war gasped its final breath.

The humans rebuilt and recovered. Their recollections of those dark days were worn smooth by time, and eventually, all who fought and survived that horrific era were gone. Their descendants remained in blissful ignorance.

But the gods? They lived with the terrible clarity of immortal memory. They couldn't erase the taste of ashes, the sight of the pyres, the trauma of losing children and lovers and family.

This story is about what comes after, when promises are stretched thin and treaties wear down until they break. This is about what happens when humans forget that peace is paid for in blood.

This is what happens when everything goes to shit.

PART ONE

BLOOD AND BEAUTIFUL THINGS

1

BRYONY

Three hundred years later

DEATH WEARS A beautiful face, and he's come to collect a soul.

I take my morning walk through the palace woods, counting my steps like always, when a strange pressure builds in the air. Like before a storm rolls in and the world seems to hold its breath. A sparrow's trill cuts off mid-note. The breeze dies. It all just…

Stops.

"Help me."

A man staggers from behind a tree. One look, and I know he's not supposed to be here. He's not a guard, not a servant, and definitely not a noble. Just an intruder caked in days' worth of dirt who somehow slipped past walls and sentries meant to keep him out.

"Hide me," he says, lunging forward to seize my arm. "*Please.*"

That's when I see it: seared into the skin of his inner wrist is a closed eye slashed through.

Oathbreaker.

The power saturating the forest, the unnatural charge—it's a god. And this man is what it wants.

"I'm sorry, but I *can't.*"

I pull against him, but the stranger is desperate, and desperate men are strong. Dangerous. He's panting in uneven little gasps, his hold tightening. The palace is right beyond those trees. Guards patrol these paths. If I run—

"Let her go. Now."

The words drop like stones into a still pond.

The stranger and I freeze. My heart gives a painful lurch as that stormy pressure from before suddenly shoves hard against me.

Shit.

Slowly, I turn.

The god is beautiful in that alluring way of predators. Tall, dark-haired, wearing gleaming golden armor that leaves his muscular arms bare. He has a face more suited to a work of art than a death dealer. Like all gods, his skin shimmers in the light, but his wings are unique. *Singular.* Pure gold feathers from ridge to tip, as if they've been dipped in molten metal.

He flexes them slightly, an unmistakable warning in the small movement. *Don't touch.*

Don't even think about it.

I'd know him anywhere. No one grows up in Vartena without hearing stories about the golden assassin who serves as Alexios' right hand. I've seen the murals on the temple walls painted with images of this god and the carnage he leaves behind.

The Wolf.

And I'm standing between him and his prey.

My eyes meet his, and I go cold. Not because of the bright, unnatural color—gilt and amber—but the way they pin me in place with the flat, dead glare of a hunter deciding which category of problem I fall into: nuisance or inconvenience.

"*Please.*"

The whimper yanks me back to the oathbreaker. He collapses to his knees, pressing his forehead to the ground. Poor bastard. Begging won't soften a creature who has murdered thousands without remorse. The Wolf's probably played out this exact scene every time—watched these desperate, weeping victims try to appeal to a sense of compassion that doesn't exist.

To feel compassion, he'd have to have a heart. And the Wolf of Asteria is a soulless monster. Everyone knows it.

"Mercy." The oathbreaker's voice cracks. "*Please.*"

But the Wolf is still staring at me. I shiver as he takes in my walking dress, the waist-length braid of silver-white hair resting over my shoulder. Lingering on my features, my violet-colored eyes, and the gleaming skin that's not quite as ethereal as his but suggests a demigod in my ancestry. My skin is as unusual as his wings—it tells him exactly who I am before the gold cuff on my wrist confirms it.

Bryony Devaliant. Princess of the Blood. The youngest Anchor of the Shroud.

In other words, I'm not a human he can fuck with.

The Wolf's mouth curves into a mocking smile as if he plucked the thought from my head. His hand drifts up almost lazily and curls around the sword sheathed between his wings.

"Five seconds, Devaliant." His voice is smooth and deep. Resonant.

I blink. "What?"

"You get five seconds. I want you to close your eyes and count for me, nice and slow. Then keep them closed."

It takes me a moment to grasp what he's offering. Is he... seriously giving me an out? Some twisted courtesy so I don't have to witness him butcher an oathbreaker?

I hesitate. What might he do the second I look away? But his expression darkens in a warning that reminds me I'm in no position to refuse. So I let my eyes fall shut.

"One."

My nails dig into my palms.

"Two."

My pulse roars in my ears, nearly drowning out the man's whimper.

"Three."

Every muscle tenses as I brace myself.

"Fou—"

A whisper of steel cuts the air, and something wet and warm splashes across my face—*blood*. My stomach lurches, but I force the bile back down my throat.

Thump. The sound of a corpse hitting the dirt is its own particular horror.

"F-five," I gasp.

My eyes fly open. The Wolf is close—*too* close—and still holding his dripping sword. Near enough that I can see the flecks of amber and bronze in his irises. Neither of us moves. Neither of us speaks.

Then he reaches his free hand out and skims the pad of his thumb along my cheek. Smearing my skin with the dead man's blood. "What did I say about keeping those pretty eyes closed?" There's wry humor in his voice that's all wrong for this moment. Like this is a game we're playing. "It was a simple instruction."

I let out a slow exhale, resisting the urge to turn out of his touch. "You said I got *five* seconds. That wasn't even four. But I suppose Death finishes his work fast."

"Death is still here, Devaliant. I haven't gone anywhere."

"Hard to miss that fact when you're finger-painting your handiwork on my face." I can't hold back the slight tremor that goes through me.

He drops his hand, and some of the pressure eases from my chest. "Most humans can barely string two words together around me unless one of them is *please*. Yet here you are, running that smart mouth."

Every instinct is screaming at me to run. But what's the point? There's nothing he can do to me that hasn't already been done hundreds of times over.

"You know what I am," I say, forcing calm into my tone. "I spend half my life on an altar. You're just another kind of knife."

His gaze falls to my wrist. Hidden beneath the cuff is a brand seared magically into my skin that marks me as the protected human property of his monstrous king. I'm one of Alexios' Claimed. The Wolf could murder me in seconds, but there would be consequences for him if he damaged the goods.

His eyes snap back to mine. "Never give me a reason to come for you. I'd be so fucking eager to put another Devaliant in the Void for good."

My eyebrows pull together. Not a *human*—my family specifically. Did he hunt them before the Accords? Did he kill my ancestors?

The question burns on my tongue, but different words come out instead. "Then I want to make a deal."

He blinks at that. "Excuse me?"

Too late now. *In for a broken drachma, in for an aurelii*, as they say. Death is the one thing this monster and I have in common; we're two sides of the same bloody coin.

"If Alexios ever decides I've outlived my usefulness and sends you to take me out"—I gesture to the body cooling in the dirt—"I want a better end than that."

"That sounds a lot like a demand." There's a strange glint in his eye—something feral and almost hungry peeking out from behind the killer's mask. "I didn't realize we were on demand-making terms."

With a jolt, I realize what that look is: *interest*. Eternal save me, I've caught the attention of the god-king's Wolf.

I swallow hard. "You only come to this realm when you need to murder someone. I'm using this as a chance to negotiate. Just in case."

"Just in case," he mutters with a short laugh. "Unbelievable. And what makes you think you've earned the right to negotiate shit with me?"

"House Devaliant bleeds out every fourteen days to keep your king's precious Shroud intact. Be as eager as you want to kill me, but I want to choose how I go. Let me have that much."

No flicker of empathy at the reminder of what I endure for his king, not even a twitch of emotion. The Wolf just studies me in that unnerving way of his, then leans forward and taps my cuff. "You get this conversation because of what's under here. Never forget that. It's the only thing standing between your neck and my blade."

My thoughts are shouting. *Shut up and go. Just nod and walk away.*

But an image flashes of the temple altar slick with my blood, the ceremonial knife opening me up over and over and over. After all that, I've damn well earned some basic courtesy.

"I haven't forgotten. Will you bargain or not?"

He shrugs. "Tell me what you want."

I nearly gag when he leans down and casually wipes his blade on the dead man's clothes before sheathing it between his wings.

"Let me guess," he says when I don't answer, his sharp stare settling on me again. "A string quartet playing your favorite song while I butcher you? Some pretty flowers to brighten up the proceedings? Want me to tell you how *special* you are?"

What an asshole. I should've known the monster from the murals would be an unbearable prick.

I glare at him. "Leave my guts where they belong and my head attached to my body. Don't steal any trophies for whatever murder collection I'm sure you keep. Sound fair?"

"It *sounds* like you've given this an alarming amount of thought."

"When you die as often as I do, you think about the permanent version."

"Clearly." Now he just looks bored, as if I've somehow disappointed him. "Anything else?"

"Treat me like an equal," I tell him, just to see what he'll do. "Or should I lower the bar even more?"

That finally gets something out of him. "Bury it in the ground if that's what you expect." His lip curls in disgust. "You're not my equal."

Right. Seeing humans as insects scraped off the bottom of his shoe is probably how he justifies his daily slaughter quota before he goes to bed at night.

Well, fuck him.

"Pretend for one occasion," I snap.

His eyes narrow. Just when I think he'll declare he'd rather eat glass, he says, "Only if you don't make me hunt your ass down. Chasing my targets is irritating."

I snort. "Like there's anywhere I could go that you wouldn't find me."

The Wolf doesn't disagree. "One more thing." His smile is sharp. "I want eye contact the whole time you're bleeding out."

I cringe. Good gods, he's vile. I'd heard the Wolf was part feral, like a toddler with a knife and the skill to use it, but I always thought those were exaggerations meant to terrify children into good behavior. Of course, I had to go and negotiate with Alexios' most unhinged Enforcer.

Too late to take it back now.

"Fine. Uninterrupted eye contact until my last breath." *You heartless bastard.* "Sound good?"

"Deal. If it comes down to it, I'll make it a good death." Those gold eyes rake over me one last time. "See you around, Devaliant."

Then he spreads those massive golden wings and leaps into the air, disappearing over the canopy in seconds.

Leaving me to deal with the corpse.

2

BRYONY

Two years later

THE CROWD ROARS beyond the gates as Theodora and I step out of the palace. My older sister and I wear matching gold gowns shot through with crimson, rubies glinting at our throats and earlobes. Our gaudy temple regalia as Princesses of the Blood.

Another day, another death.

The city sprawls past the royal square. Hellevig is a patchwork of ancient ruins and buildings constructed after the Godkiller Crusades, when the war between humans and gods nearly wiped this place off the map. During the rebuilding, House Devaliant's colors became the dominant palette. Red spires. Red domes. Red pillars. Red arches. Red, red, red. There's a reason the capital of Luceni is called "the city that bleeds," not just because of what my ancestress did with that blade, but because you can't escape the color of Amalthea's sacrifice.

Theodora's nails dig into my wrist, jolting me to the present. To the crowd clamoring for our attention.

"Smile," she tells me. She tucks an errant curl of copper hair behind her ear. "They're all watching."

No one could accuse me of being anything but well-trained, so I plaster on a smile and follow her toward the carriage waiting in the drive.

The portcullis groans as the servants heave it open.

"Princess Bryony!"

A girl darts under a guard's arms before he can grab her, skidding to a halt in front of me.

My bodyguard tenses, but I wave a dismissive hand. "Stand down, Silas. She's six, not an assassin. Just give her a minute."

The last thing I need is an overenthusiastic member of my security pulling a sword on a child in view of a few hundred spectators. The broadsheets would have a field day.

I crouch down, my skirts pooling around me. "Hi there. What's your name?"

"Ara." She sticks out her small hand. "May I have your blessing?"

For a moment, I'm sure I misheard her. But no, those words definitely fell out of her tiny mouth, hanging between us like an accusation. Theodora goes rigid beside me. We both know blessings are the Eternal's purview, not mine.

I bend and kiss her knuckles. "May Eternal Alexios protect you always."

A standard non-answer. But the girl isn't having it. Her grip tightens, nails biting at my Claim cuff. "Please, Princess. A blessing from *you*."

Theodora's lips press into a thin line, her expression hardening. *No. Don't you dare give that girl what she wants.*

So I kiss the girl's head and say the most neutral thing I can. "Fortune keep you, little one. Now get back to your mother before she worries."

Silas scoops her up and deposits her behind the gates with a scowl darkening his face.

I smile and wave at the rest of the spectators, blowing a few kisses. "Remember to visit the temple and offer your tithes!" I call out. "Eternal bless you!"

I'm signaling our procession onward when a voice shouts, "*The Princess will lead us to ruin! Alexios' butchers will come for us all!*"

My head snaps up, but I can't see anything past the sea of faces. A ripple goes through the crowd as confusion gives way to anger. It looks like a fight might break out.

"Time to go, Bry." Theodora's grip on my elbow is firm as she guides me to the carriage.

The door slams shut, muffling the chaos outside. I stare out the window, watching as the guards attempt to calm down the masses and clear the road. Some people are still shouting.

"It's always a delight joining you on temple day." Theodora settles across from me and arranges her skirts. "I never know if I'm going to see a brawl or a parade in your honor."

I glare at her. "Hilarious."

The famous Devaliant skin is the only thing that marks my sister and me as related. Our father once told me that Theodora got her looks from our mother, who died giving birth to me, while I inherited features from a dead grandmother. Where my hair is nearly white, hers is a rich, glossy red, spilling over her shoulders in loose curls. Her bone structure is elegant, with a willowy physique that resembles a dancer's. Mine is more petite. The Hellevig broadsheets often remark that we're equally beautiful, but Theodora has an austere face that comes across as aloof. Remote. *Cold*.

People call her *the ice princess* when they're being kind.

Frigid bitch, when they're not.

"Should we take bets on when they build you a shrine?" Theo asks me. "Ten aurelii says it's up by next week. Twenty says someone tries to steal a lock of your hair for a holy relic."

"People are literally screaming about divine wrath, and you're making jokes?"

"What else am I supposed to do? Uncle's too busy drowning in wine and women lately to listen about the crowds outside our gates. Last week, he face-planted in his soup before I could even finish a sentence."

I slump against the seat with a sigh. When the emperor spirals like this, it never ends well. Last time, he vanished for half a year, hopping on our family's private train to screw his way across the empire while Theo kept the capital from crumbling.

Not that I could blame Idris much, to be honest. It's tempting to throw yourself into any random vice when your life revolves around scheduled ritual sacrifice. That's the price House Devaliant paid when we brokered peace with the gods three hundred years ago. Meanwhile, every other citizen gets off easy with a fingerprick and a single drop of blood for their tithe.

I trace the notches I carved on my inner elbow—five cuts, five steps to resurrection. *Breathe. Feel. Name. Present. Real.* To remind me that I exist and that I'm more than just a vessel.

Outside, gravel crunches under the carriage wheels as the vehicle makes a turn. Silas bellows at someone in the crowd who strayed too close, "Back the fuck off before I remove your head!"

I wince. "Could Uncle not find me a bodyguard who's less... threatening? He made three children cry yesterday."

"Listen, that man might have a brain like a rusted bear trap and the personality of a hostile brick wall, but he's very large and enjoys hurting people who come near you." Theodora taps her fingers against her armrest. "Which, given current events, makes him more useful than our wine-soaked excuse for an emperor."

"At least Uncle isn't riding with us."

"Oh yes, I'll miss his lectures on our many failings." She mimics Idris' voice, slurring slightly. "'Theodora, you empty-headed waste of space. Probably dropped you on your head as a baby.' Like he has any right to criticize when his idea of leadership is bellowing at people until his face turns red."

Laughing, I peer out at the streets rolling by, at the stone towers and their massive stained glass windows. Every pane depicts some Devaliant sacrifice in revolting detail. You can't walk ten feet in Hellevig without seeing our family's offerings commemorated somewhere. They've made our deaths into decoration, our suffering into architecture.

And perched on the hill in the center of the city, with spires piercing the low-hanging clouds, stands the temple where I've been summoned for my tithe. Alexios' holy building is the only structure built entirely of pale marble, probably because blood shows up better on white, and the God of Storms enjoys watching us all bleed from wherever he is in Scillari. The facade comprises multiple twisting steeples that loom over the landscape like jagged teeth.

I hate that damn place.

Theo's hand finds my knee. "You okay?"

"Fine. Thanks for coming with me today. You didn't have to."

"Please. I'd crawl through broken glass to escape the palace. Made the stupid mistake of smiling at the new footman, and now he thinks we're destined for true love."

"Is he the one who's been leaving flowers at your door?"

"Flowers, poems, and yesterday, a note comparing my eyes to 'emerald pools of eternal longing.'" She shudders. "There are only so many times I can hide in the library before it gets pathetic."

"And here I thought you came for moral support."

"Well, that too." Theo sits back. "Speaking of support, I'll tell you my new coping mechanism for when the Oracles shove that blade in."

"Do I have a choice?"

"Of course not." A wicked grin spreads across my sister's face. "I think of all the filthy things I'm going to have Kas do to me when I wake up. Really takes the edge off dying when I know I'll be riding my guard's cock within the hour."

I choke on air. "Theo!"

"What? It's practical. Strategic." She lets out a satisfied sigh. "I ride that man before the carriage even leaves the temple grounds. You wouldn't believe how hard he gets when I'm still covered in blood from the ceremony. Something about seeing me come back to life really does it for him."

The noise I make is something between a retch and a whimper. "Stop. Stop right there." I hold up both hands. "I don't need the visual. I don't *want* the visual. The visual is burned into my brain. What in the Eternal's name is *wrong* with you?"

"So many things. Want the list alphabetically or by order of moral depravity? We've got time before we reach the temple."

"I'd rather throw myself in front of a train."

"Maybe save that move for after your wedding. And remember, if you need to plot your new husband's tragic end, I know people who know people."

I elect to ignore that in favor of hunching in my seat. The last thing I want to dwell on is my wedding to Markus von Reding tomorrow. I've only met him three times, and I don't think he's ever bothered looking above my breasts. But I suppose that doesn't matter. The marriage is purely transactional to get me pregnant. Devaliants are only good for two things—dying and breeding more Devaliants to die.

The carriage makes a hard turn. The road is closed to all but our procession, with storefronts shuttered until after we finish. Even the temple has been emptied to prepare for our arrival.

We stop along the rounded royal entryway, where a statue of Alexios glares down at us. The sculptor caught the striking lines of his face, every feather of his wings. He's seated on a throne with one hand holding his sword and the other reaching down. I can't tell if it's meant to look like he's blessing me or threatening me, but maybe that's the point.

The wind lashes my cheeks as we climb the steps and push open the doors. The smell hits me first, the heavy incense barely masking the strong, coppery scent of centuries of blood coating the holy stones.

The candles in the alcoves illuminate the reliefs painted on the walls. In one, Alexios sits in judgment while a human grovels at his feet. In another, he flies into battle with his sword held high, and his red and black wings spread.

And in the next panel is the Devaliant princess who changed the realms. *Amalthea.* Offering her life to anchor the Shroud, seal the Accords, and end the war that nearly brought both worlds to ruin.

At the end of the naos rises the altar stone, a simple slab of rust-stained white marble. Three dark-robed Oracles stand around its base, their faces obscured behind gauzy veils. I see them every fourteen days for the ceremony, but we're not on friendly terms. It's difficult to establish a cordial relationship with the women who've held you down and shoved a knife in your chest since childhood. You don't look so fondly on them after that.

I dip my chin in a curt greeting. "Good morning."

The Head Oracle steps forward, her vestments shimmering. "Princess Bryony, the Eternal sent word that your tithe isn't welcome."

Theodora freezes, her breath catching in her throat.

I'm certain I've misunderstood. The incense fumes must be causing me to hallucinate. "I'm sorry. It sounded like you said—"

"You heard her correctly," the second Oracle says. "There will be no anchoring ceremony today. Your tithe is no longer required."

No longer required. The words make no sense. *No longer required, no longer required, no longer—*

All my life, I've been *necessary*. I've played my preordained role, a linchpin of the Shroud. One of Alexios' Anchors in the mortal realm. I've bled for him since I could walk. Died for him again and again and again. I'd say it's almost impressive how thoroughly I've debased myself.

And now I'm no longer *required*?

"I don't understand," Theodora says. "Has my sister offended him?"

The Oracle's head turns toward my sister. "The Eternal's will isn't for mortals to question."

It takes every scrap of courtly training I possess not to lunge across the altar and throttle the Oracle with her veil.

"Two weeks ago, I was indispensable. Now I'm nothing," I say, my voice calm despite my pounding heart. "Did Alexios share his reasons, or does he prefer to keep us guessing?"

The third Oracle answers. "You live and die by the Eternal's mercy, and he's revoked it. There's nothing more to be said."

Mercy. How precious.

"Unrevoke it," Theodora says sharply. "My sister is ready to make the tithe and do her duty." She rakes them with the glare that earned her the *frigid bitch* moniker. "It's your obligation to take her blood."

"You're not regent anymore, Princess," the Head Oracle says. "You have no authority here."

Theodora flinches, and I see the barb hit home. She swallows hard at the reminder of everything she's lost.

"Ah, yes," I say. "I'd forgotten that obedience is a requirement of Alexios' faithful. Tell me, do you gain your position only by being the bastard children of demigods and humans, or is there a test you have to pass for sycophantic devotion? Does he screen for a lack of individuality? I'm curious how that works."

The Oracles gasp. I think one of them might be choking on her own spit behind that veil.

"Bry," Theodora says. "Come on. We're going."

I'm reaching for Theo's arm when the third Oracle says, "If you doubt our words, Princess, look at your Claim."

I turn back. "What did you just say?"

The Oracle points at my wrist—at the golden cuff that's been there for as long as I can remember. "See for yourself."

I fumble with the clasp, my breaths growing shorter. This has to be a mistake. Some sort of sick, ritualized humiliation.

The cuff falls away, and branded on my inner wrist is a slash through the eye of Alexios' mark. The same sigil that's declared me his Claimed since the day I was born and given the drop of his blood like every other infant in Luceni. Only now, the eye is closed.

And I'm marked for death.

3

BRYONY

A TINY MARK. That's all it takes to destroy a life.

All these years, I've bled for the Shroud—died hundreds of deaths for it. Laid myself on that altar, over and over, and felt my heart stop long before I even understood the meaning of *sacrifice*.

Memories flicker of a little girl, confused and terrified, tears streaming down her cheeks as she pleads with them to stop. Begs them not to hurt her again. But the ceremonial blade splits her skin, the world goes dark at the edges, and the Void rises to claim her. No one listens. No one cares.

The gods don't answer prayers. Monsters seldom do.

"I've never missed a tithe," I say faintly, staring down at that damning symbol. "Not once."

The Head Oracle regards me in silence. "For months, the people in this city have been tossing roses at your feet instead of spilling their blood for the Eternal. He's given them more grace than most. These are the consequences."

My face heats. I never asked for their worship. I only ever did what Theodora needed me to do—put on a united front when our uncle abandoned the throne. Offered the public some small reassurance that House Devaliant wasn't crumbling.

But I watched their tentative questions turn to admiration and then twist into something far more dangerous: reverence. Every offering and prayer whispered in my name gave the Eternal more reasons to despise me. I should have recognized the warning signs when the crowds swelled outside the palace walls.

The child today begged for my *blessing*.

"You can't be serious," Theodora says, eyes blazing. "They love her because she *dies* for them. Because she's the one out there showing them we give a damn. Maybe if Alexios dragged his ass across the Shroud to reassure *his* Claimed instead of sending his rabid dogs to slaughter the masses, people wouldn't be so damned eager to break their oaths."

Scandalized gasps rise from the cluster of Oracles.

"Watch that mouth, girl," the Head Oracle hisses. "Or the Eternal might decide your tongue would look better decorating his wall."

Theo steps forward. "Then he can come down here and cut it out himself."

I have to fix this. He can't just mark me for execution after a life of service. "Let me make the offering now. There's still time—"

"No." The Head Oracle cuts me off. "The Eternal's judgment is final. It won't be overturned by an arrogant girl who doesn't know her place."

And there it is. I'm nothing. Worse than an Unclaimed. Someone to be shunned, hunted down, and butchered in the streets. Because since when have the gods been fair to those they subjugate? Those they *own*? I'm only a tool that's outlived its use.

My hands shake as I slide my cuff on my wrist and cover up the mark. I turn and stride out of the temple, Theodora and Silas falling into step behind me. My guard shoots a furtive glance my way. I wonder what he's thinking, knowing the princess he's sworn to protect is a pariah.

It doesn't matter, I suppose. When the Enforcers come, his opinion will be less than worthless.

The courtyard sunlight is too bright. I pause before the largest statue of Alexios, studying the perfect features of the god who sentenced me to death. He towers over us in obsidian and marble, with red gems glinting in the carved folds of his raiment, meant to depict droplets of blood.

"Bry." Theodora's voice is soft. "What are you doing?"

"Just having a moment with my executioner." I blink back the sting of tears. "Seems only polite."

My gaze catches on the fresco painted across the back wall of the courtyard. It illustrates Alexios' six Enforcers soaring above the smoke and rubble of a broken city, their swords bared and their wings spread wide. Savage and terrifying. Beautiful and cruel.

And *him*.

The Wolf is front and center. His gilded armor is splashed with gore, his irises blazing like molten gold. I remember the weight of his stare. The suffocating pressure of his power, old and unfathomably vast.

Never give me a reason to come for you.

Well. Here we are. I guess he'll be collecting soon.

I should give him no cause. Let him look me in the face and know this isn't my fault.

"Silas." I extend my palm without looking away from the painting. "Let me borrow your knife."

A beat. "Princess?"

"That pretty blade you love so much. Hand it over."

I can see him wondering if his charge has finally cracked. If I've given in to the madness that runs in Devaliant blood like a bomb waiting for the right moment to detonate.

It's not an unreasonable fear. My family isn't exactly known for our sterling mental health after dying and coming back so often. We hide it well by staging the deaths and changing the stories, but suicide has become something of a family tradition.

"I'm not going to off myself," I mutter, my lips twisting. "Not permanently, anyway."

Another moment of hesitation. Then he draws the weapon from his belt and places it in my palm. Such a paltry thing to wager against a god's wrath, but it'll have to do.

"Tell me you're not about to do what I think you are," Theo hisses. "Tell me you aren't about to defy the Eternal's direct orders at his *own temple*."

"I'm just performing a Devaliant's duty," I say with a shrug. "One last tithe for old times' sake."

"This isn't the altar, you reckless idiot. They can't resurrect you if you bleed out here!"

"Alexios' power flows through every inch of this sanctum. So either he accepts this offering and gives me back my Claim, or he sends his dogs to finish me off. I'll give him something to chew on while he mulls it over."

The Eternal bound our lineage to the Shroud, with the blood of citizens across Vartena as a sympathetic link. But he never said *where* on the temple grounds we had to bleed. Let's see how he likes that little loophole.

Theo's mouth tightens, and she jerks her chin. "Fine. Lie down."

I move to the base of the steps and settle on my back on the warm flagstones. It's now or never.

"Your Highness," Silas says, "I don't think you should—"

"Quiet," Theodora tells him, her voice brooking no argument. "Go get the Oracles."

Silas curses under his breath, but he spins on his heel, hurrying toward the temple entrance. Probably trying to figure out how to salvage this mess.

I'd pity him if I had any left to spare. But monstrous kings and sacrifices don't deal in tender mercies. We barter in the hard currencies of blood.

Theodora sinks to her knees beside me. "Want me to do the honors?"

Forcing a smile, I tell her, "Tempting, but no. I'll see to my own stabbing today."

I focus on the knife, on the hammering of my heart against my ribs, on the sick swoop of my stomach as I raise the blade. I inhale through my nose. Hold it.

And slam six inches of steel through my chest.

Pain explodes through me. I can't breathe. Can't scream. Every muscle locks up.

How do you like this tithe, you bastard? I think as my gaze finds Alexios' stone face once more. *Is it sweet enough for you? Loud enough? I hope you choke on it.*

Someone screams—the Oracles are here. Tugging, pulling at me. A veiled face blocks my view of the statue. "What have you done, you foolish child?" she snarls. Ah, the Head Oracle.

I laugh—or try to. "I thought... it was... obvious. I'm making... a fucking point."

"Bring her back." Theodora's voice cracks out. Through my dimming vision, I see her grab the Head Oracle's arm. "The instant her heart stops, you'll perform the rite, or I swear by all the gods, I'll have my loyalists sack this temple and tear you apart with their bare hands."

Darkness spreads, reaching for me, eager to drag me down into the Void. Strange how after so many deaths, I still manage to forget this part—the inexorable slide into the abyss, the helpless feeling of being pulled against my will as all the light fades. *Under, under, under.* No air, no sound, just a crushing pressure like I'm being buried alive.

In those final, fading moments, my thoughts drift to the Wolf. When I come back, I wonder if this will work or if Alexios will send him to hunt me down and finish what Silas' knife started. If he does, I hope my blood stains the Wolf's hands, his wings, his soul, if he even has one. I hope I haunt him.

The shadows claim me. They always do.

Then the Shroud's power wraps around my soul and *pulls*, dragging me upward. Hauling me through the suffocating blackness. The pressure shatters, and the Void spits me out.

I gasp awake, choking on air, my fingers already scrambling at my sleeve to find the scars.

One. Breathe.

Two. There's a breeze on my face and the warm flagstones beneath me.

Three. My name is Bryony.

Four. I'm at Alexios' temple.

Five. This is real.

I open my eyes, blinking against the harsh sunlight. When

I look down, there's no trace of the wound that killed me—only the sticky, cold residue of Alexios' blood smeared on me from the revival bowl.

"Get up." The Head Oracle's sharp voice cuts through the fog. "And get out. Don't come back."

No gentle words to ease the transition. Just a perfunctory ritual, the minimum required to pull my soul from the Void. The message is clear: they don't give a shit about me. I'm not protected by my service to the Shroud.

I'm *no longer required.*

It takes two tries to stand even with Theo's help. Resurrection never gets easier—my body always aches after, like it's been broken apart and stuck back together wrong.

Silas hovers behind the Oracles, looking like he'd rather be anywhere else. Jumping into the Rionese Sea, perhaps. Or taking a walk off the palace battlements. Honestly, that makes two of us.

I return his knife, and he takes it without a word, probably wishing he'd never handed it over.

"You okay?" Theodora asks quietly as she leads me down the temple steps. "They didn't do the aftercare."

"Fine." The word comes out flat. "As fine as I can be."

She helps me into the carriage. I stare out of the window as the vehicle starts toward the palace. For years, this route has defined my existence—palace to temple, temple to palace, over and over again. A life shaped by orders and duty. I've given up this body to a god for so long that I can barely remember what it was like to be mine.

And I won't ever have that again.

Theodora grasps my hand. "We'll fix this. Just keep up appearances for now, and don't take that cuff off."

"Right. Play my part tomorrow night, too?" My lips twist. "Spread my legs for my new husband like a good little princess?"

"One crisis at a time, Bry."

I nod. It's not that I don't trust my sister's plans. It's that deep down, I'm already preparing for the Wolf.

4

EVANDER

THE STENCH FILLS my lungs, one I've encountered a thousand times before: mortality combined with power that doesn't belong to a human.

The man is unaware he's being hunted. I first caught his scent after an execution in Montorosa, the capital of Havenridge. Then I followed him on the train to Valchek, and watched as he went about his business for the last week. Patiently biding my time. Other than the scent, there's nothing noteworthy about him. Unremarkable face, average body, *boring* life. He wears Alexios' Claim, but that won't save him—he's going to be another tally on my centuries-old kill count. Yesterday, I watched him clip his toenails at the dinner table, gather them in the tobacco tin, and eat one. Honestly, I'm doing the realm a favor by killing him.

After he leads me where I want.

He walks the dark street with his shoulders hunched and his hands in his pockets. I follow from the rooftops, feet soundless. Windows across the city glow as I leap from building to building. Smoke curls from chimneys, and the occasional burst of chatter drifts up from the roads below. My wings tense as I land on another roof, but I keep them tight against my back. No need to announce my presence yet.

He turns onto a narrow lane just off the main road, pausing in front of a shitty little apothecary shop with a faded wooden sign creaking in the wind.

Roots & Remedies. How quaint.

My target knocks on the door, and something dark clenches in my gut at the familiar pattern, the sign I've been waiting for: *quick-quick-quick, slow-slow*—the code of fleshtraders.

The door cracks open. "Yeah?"

"Here for the Butcher."

The doorman grunts and opens the door wide. "Inside."

I drop to street level, wrapping myself in invisibility before slipping in after them. The shop looks innocuous enough. Dried plants hang from the ceiling rafters alongside bones and animal hides. Shelves groan under the weight of colored glass jars, their contents floating in murky liquids and oils. Roots and leaves fill the tiny cabinets built into the wall behind the counter.

But it's for show, a cheap veneer of legitimacy hiding the real merchandise in the back.

My nostrils flare as the apothecary worker's scent wafts over me. I narrow my eyes at the tall, thin man. He's been indulging. And if the strength is anything to go by, he's been on dust for years.

Humans can't seem to help themselves.

I trail after them as they head down the hall. They stop at a door, and the apothecary fumbles with an oversized ring of keys.

"In here." He jerks his head, flipping on the light. "Special stock."

The air inside is cold and tinged with the stink of preservatives. Shelves are packed with my realm's spoils—books, scrolls, trinkets, and oddities. Stone carvings of Scillarian beasts are perched alongside busts displaying jewelry our demis wore into battle. Beside that sit precious gems in open velvet boxes, infused with god power that glows from within. The plunder of thousands of destroyed lives, stolen from corpses and homes during the human occupation of my realm.

Magic rises with my anger, the heat of it sliding across my skin, but I shove it down before it betrays my presence.

Not yet.

The apothecary approaches an ornate wooden cabinet, pulling out a silk-wrapped parcel.

Something stirs in me—a resonance, like plucking a string and feeling another vibrate in harmony. Power recognizing power. I know what's in that bundle before he opens it.

No. Not here. Not like this.

"Just got these in," he says, laying it on the table and unfolding it carefully. "Found in an old war cache. These came right off some ascended prince's back."

He flips back the fabric to reveal four dark feathers sparkling with starlight. *Bastien's* feathers.

I'm going to rip their throats out.

Memories flash of my brother shackled to the wall of a filthy cell, with his blood pooled on the floor and his wings hacked off. There's a reason my people call that war the *Devouring*.

"Beautiful, aren't they?" I watch as the apothecary strokes a feather, picturing myself cutting off his fingers. "Grind these up, and you've got pure power. Most just want the high—like swallowing stars. But if you take enough and let it build up in your system? The magic becomes yours."

Fuck.

I figured the forbidden knowledge still circulated in some corners of the mortal world—it's what started the war and left gods trafficked for parts. But I haven't heard it spoken aloud in years. I've worked with Alexios and his other Enforcers to eliminate every trace of that information from mortal memories and any documents we could find.

The buyer plucks a feather from the cloth. He holds it up to the light, turning it this way and that, watching the stardust glitter. "They're old, though. Won't that affect the potency?"

"Not from an Eternal. You want a taste? First pinch is free."

At the buyer's nod, the apothecary reaches beneath the counter to retrieve a silver tray with a tiny pinch of dark powder in the center. My target shoves his sweaty black hair out of his face and bends to snort the dust. When he straightens, his mouth is slack with pleasure, skin pulsing with the glow of stolen Eternal magic.

This. *This* is what my people broke ourselves trying to stop. What countless demis died fighting.

"Holy fuck," he gasps. "That's... That's..."

"Unreal, right?" The apothecary grins and gestures with his fingers. "Go on, try the power. Just focus a little, and you'll feel the pull. See what you get."

The buyer closes his eyes, brows furrowed in concentration. I watch as all the shadows in the room detach, writhing and curling around him like tendrils of smoke. Waiting for his command. Bastien's magic—the ability to bend and manipulate darkness to his will—flows through this human, diminished but unmistakable.

Just as quickly, the shadows dissipate and settle.

"Shit," the buyer pants, wiping some of the sweat from his forehead. "It didn't last."

"Takes more than a pinch to keep it stable at first," the apothecary explains. "But that rush? That'll last a few days. Still feeling it?"

"Yeah." A jerky nod. "Fuck yeah. I'll take them all."

"Two thousand aurelii."

"Two thousand?" The buyer shakes his head and curses under his breath. "That's robbery. I can go to the docks and get twice the product for half that."

The apothecary scowls, expression darkening with impatience. "You can't compare the demi parts at the docks to the power of an Eternal. I've got another buyer who'd kill for this." He jabs a finger at the feathers. "You want these? Pay up. Eternals don't exactly grow on trees these days."

The other man swallows hard, hesitating, but then he reaches for his pocket and pulls out a sweaty wad of folded-up aurelii.

And now it's time to add some red to my ledger.

With a lunge, I seize the apothecary by the neck and slam him into the wall. The buyer bolts for the door, but a flick of my power freezes him in place.

"*Stay*," I snarl. He'll wait there obediently until I'm ready to deal with him.

The apothecary claws at my wrist, and it's like watching a fish flopping on the end of a hook. Only in this case, the hook is a pissed-off god he can't see, and I'm this close to snapping his damn neck. But that would be a waste.

"Where did you get the feathers?" I growl.

"I-It wasn't—"

"Did you know," I interrupt in a soft, conversational tone, "that there are fourteen major bones in the human face? And over forty-two muscles working in tandem to create those delightful micro-expressions you humans are so fond of. The one you're wearing right now is that special expression that says 'I'm about to lie to the angry god holding me.'" I squeeze hard enough to make him gag. "So let's try this again. Where the fuck did you get the feathers?"

"Collectors," he wheezes. "People who scavenge the war zones. Sometimes, they find valuable things."

"Have more Eternal parts changed hands?"

The apothecary bucks against my hold. Stolen power crackles through him, searing my skin where we touch. He's devoured our essence for so long that magic saturates his entire body. But it won't save him from me. I'm more powerful than whoever he's been consuming—an Eternal. *An ascended prince.*

"Get fucked," he says, still struggling. He scratches at my arm, nails digging in. "I've got Alexios' protection."

This smug prick thinks he's untouchable. He's got no clue who I am. *What* I am.

"Seems you're confused about who has you pinned to the wall. Let's have an introduction, shall we?"

My invisibility drops, and I let him get a good look—my gold wings, the wrath burning in my eyes, the promise of a painful, messy end. His breathing quickens, and he releases a pathetic whimper.

Ah, there it is. I love that sound.

"Yeah, you recognize me, don't you?" I glance at the buyer

frozen by the door, smirking as a dark stain spreads across the front of his trousers. "Your friend over there's already pissed himself. Want to see if you can do better? Tell me where you got those feathers, and I may be moved to mercy."

I never am, but he doesn't need to know that yet.

His body shakes against mine. It takes him a few tries to speak. "The m-market. Silk Street, beneath the old tannery in Hellevig." He lets out a sob. "That's all I know, I swear. Please—"

"Shhh sh shh." I tap his lips with a finger. "That wasn't so hard, was it? But there's still one more thing I need to do."

I mentally reach for the tether that binds me to Alexios—a shimmer at the edges of my consciousness. When I pluck gently, his attention sharpens.

What is it, Wolf?

I need you to burn two Claims, I tell him.

Why?

Alexios will do it without hesitation, but he likes to remind me that for all my power, he's the one who holds my chain.

Because these sick fucks have been trafficking Eternal parts. They have Bastien's feathers.

His silence has a weight that crushes. The tension in my skull swells as his power gathers, dark and dense as a singularity.

Show me.

My will becomes subsumed by his. I'm helpless as he forces his way in, peeling back my eyes and flooding my senses. He feels the apothecary's body pinned against the wall. Sees the buyer cowering by the door. He turns us to the till's table where the four feathers rest, each one a damning indictment of all he's built and bled for.

Destroy them. Make it slow. Make it painful.

With pleasure, I say.

I wrench the apothecary's wrist up and watch as a slash cuts through the Claim. And then the eye in the center of the triangle winks shut.

"No," the apothecary whimpers, sobbing now. "No—"

I hush him again. "Quiet. It's time to revisit your chat about getting acquainted with an Eternal's power. I'd hate to leave you unsatisfied." I graze my thumb over his throat. "Few humans know what we can do with these pretty feathers on our wings once we become Eternals. Want me to show you?"

His eyes bulge. "Please, I—"

I unfurl my wings with a snap, and the razored edge of my primary feathers slices through his shoulder to the bone beneath. Quick and clean as a scalpel.

The apothecary's severed arm drops to the floor with a thud.

He gives a choked gurgle, gaping at the bleeding stump where his arm used to be in silent shock.

"Not so amusing now, is it?" I ask mildly. "Being vivisected for parts?"

I take my time dismembering him.

The apothecary's screams ring out, but I don't let him die. He'll feel it all—every cut parting skin from muscle, muscle from bone. I carve my fury into his body and paint sigils in his blood. Killing him is *art*. Each wound tells the story of how he died, why he deserved it, and what drove the Wolf of Asteria to visit this shitty little shop in Valchek. I break him so badly that he weeps for his mother like a fucking baby at the end.

When his whimpers fade to noiseless twitches, I finally end him. My magic unclenches, and his head topples from his shoulders.

It's almost anticlimactic.

My focus snaps to the buyer still held in place by my power. His breath saws in and out, panicked.

"And then there was one," I say with a grin. "Want to tell me about those docks you mentioned earlier?"

I don't play in this one's guts. But I do get him to sing for me, and he babbles about the docks in Valchek getting shipments, but he doesn't know from where, doesn't know the suppliers—just knows where to go when he needs a fix. So I torture him a little more to make sure he's being honest. By the time my flames start burning his lungs, he's whimpering that he doesn't *know*, and that's my sign to finally put this bastard down. He combusts from the inside out in a blaze of my burning power, skin melting off and bones blackening. His screams echo long after his lungs collapse to ash.

When it's done, blood drips from my wings and pools at my feet. Something in me settles. Quiets. I want to etch this into my bones as fuel for the hunts to come. For all the deaths I'll grant the oathbreakers, the fleshtraders, any buyer who sets aurelii down for god parts to consume like we're animals.

I collect Bastien's feathers and tuck them into my armor to burn later. There's still something I need to do here first.

I shut my eyes and gather my magic, letting it rise until my skin heats. And then I release it in a searing wave that crashes over the room.

When I open my eyes, nothing in the shop is left but drifting motes of ash and the crackle of super-heated stone. I stride into the waiting night. The cobbles steam in my wake, puddles flash-boiling to vapor. Passersby scramble out of my path.

Good. Let them remember what happens to fleshtraders in this city.

Alexios' voice slides into my thoughts, as cold as a blade. *If you're finished playing with your food, I need you at my palace. I have another throat for you to slit.*

5

EVANDER

NOTHING BEATS THE first flight after a kill. The knowledge of a job well done is better than ichor wine. Better than sex.

Well, sometimes. Depends on the job, depends on the fuck.

The Shroud shimmers ahead, a veil of starlight over the jagged peaks of the Duehavn Ridge. I slice through it, magic sparking across my skin as the protection wards flare and recognize me. Reality splinters, and Vartena disintegrates until I'm nowhere, suspended in that terrifying emptiness until—

The world snaps back together.

Scillari's forests spread out below, broken by the ruins of old territories jutting up through the dense canopy. Trees emerge through crumbling throne rooms, towers are snared in the crush of vines, and ancient palaces of long-dead Eternals lie vacant and dilapidated. Nature is patient. Doesn't matter how grand your territory—give her enough time, and she'll turn your monuments to rubble.

Rivers of starlight snake through the valleys of Asteria, Alexios' territory. And past that, water thunders down a massive cliff face, misting the Osbu Sea's glassy surface.

I ride an updraft toward the Tokle Mountains. Sheer walls of granite and basalt rear up to meet me, their flanks shrouded in fog. Alexios' palace resembles a crown of black glass nestled in the crags. It's a sprawling complex of spires and bridges, barracks and pleasure gardens. Every part is built from dark opalescent stone native to Asteria. During the day, when the sun hits just right, all that black rock glows with red and orange inner light.

The palace is one of only two Eternal strongholds still standing. It survived because of its position—too high for human armies to reach, and too well defended if they tried. For a time, it served as a refuge for demis who had lost everything but the clothes on their backs. But now it's back to housing the elite in the Court of Storms, the assembled descendants of past Eternals who live alongside the reigning god-king.

The garden stretches across the front of the property. In summer, it blazes with colorful blooms visible for miles. But now, during winter, only pale blossoms and glittering frost remain.

I close the remaining distance to the landing plaza, wings spreading wide as I land in a crouch.

Upended chalices and abandoned garments litter the grass—telltale signs of a revel. Not even the cold is a deterrent when the court wants to party. When I inhale, the scent of ichor wine hits me, mingled with the musk of sex and sweat.

"About time you showed up," comes Elias' familiar voice. "We were starting to think you'd found yourself a different group of degenerates."

I turn to find the king's other Enforcers in various states of undress and sobriety. Elias lounges against the fountain's edge, white wings spread beneath him, shirt long gone. Gabriel stands with his typical stern expression. I swear, it's like someone shoved a stick up his ass and he's determined to keep it there out of spite. Arcadia casually tosses one of her knives, silver wings rustling behind her as she snatches it from the air. And Vespera... she just watches me with shadows coiled around her fingers.

"You'd all die of boredom if I weren't here to keep things interesting." I kick at a discarded silk robe with my boot. "Starting the orgy without me, though? That's rude."

Arcadia's face scrunches. "You smell like an abattoir fucked a sewer. Clean it off, and I might consider extending an invitation next time. No one here wants to use blood as a lubricant. We have standards."

"Standards are overrated. Just ask Elias."

Elias laughs. "Ignore her. I think the whole 'savage beast fresh from a kill' look works for you."

His power brushes my skin in a subtle tendril of lust. Warm. Insistent. Not unpleasant, if I'm honest, but after centuries of this shit, I've built up a tolerance.

"Cute," I say, shaking it off. "Save it for someone who hasn't seen your dick." A rumble of thunder draws my attention to the palace proper, where storm clouds are gathering above the highest spires. That can't be good. "Do I want to ask what crawled up the king's ass and died? He says he wants me to kill someone."

Gabriel rubs at the bridge of his nose. "No idea. Nearly took my hand off earlier when I tried to give him my report on the border patrols. Apparently, we're all incompetent children who couldn't find our own asses with both hands and a map."

"Any volunteers to go in with me?"

Elias barks out a laugh. "Pass. I like my face the way it is. You're on your own with this one."

Everyone agrees.

"Cowards," I say.

Their voices chase me across the plaza. Elias shouts something about kissing my mangled corpse. Arcadia and Vespera place bets on which gate would look best adorned with my severed head—the west gate has a certain dramatic flair, but you can't beat the east gate at sunrise.

The ladies have taste, I'll give them that.

I've barely crossed into the foyer when Alexios' power slams into me. Dark. Turbulent. Like facing down a hurricane. I breathe it in, letting that electric bite sear my throat.

The palace buzzes with noise. Everywhere, clusters of demis draped in silk and jewels block my way. Snippets of gossip whisper past me, slipping between languages—Gaufian and Uruk, the singsong cadence of Fér. I track the noise to the central atrium and step onto the balcony. A hundred pairs of eyes lock on me at once. There's a collective intake of breath.

What can I say? I make an entrance. All artists sign their work; blood is just my signature.

Their whispers trail me as I descend the grand staircase.

"... blood everywhere, *all over his hands and wings. Looks like he bathed in...*"

"*Tore through an entire village, I heard. Ripped them apart with his teeth.*"

I flash the scandalized speaker a lazy smile. "If you ask nicely, I'll demonstrate."

The demigod shrinks back as if I might rip his throat out. Which I wouldn't. It's poor form to kill guests in the throne room. The thing is, though—they've got the basic facts right. There's always a village that won't be showing up on any maps anymore. Plenty of them over the years, actually.

Death is my craft, and I'm nothing if not a master artisan.

Alexios lounges on his throne at the far end of the chamber. His massive, dark wings stretch almost lazily, red feathers catching in the light. His chin is propped in his hand, shoulder-length black hair loose and framing a face that rivals Elias' for beauty. The Eternal of Asteria has cultivated the appearance of a bored, pleasure-seeking king. But when his scarlet eyes find mine through the press of bodies...

There he is. The predator beneath the facade—a god shaped for battle, ready to eat the world whole and pick his teeth with the bones. That look right there is the difference between a king and a demi in this realm.

We don't build dynasties on birthright in Scillari. Power isn't passed to whichever squalling infant is pushed out of the right cunt. You want to rule here? Better be prepared to bleed for it. To kill for it. To have the realm crawl inside you like a parasite, working its way into your bones until you either ascend or die trying. I was five hundred when it chose me. The youngest ever blessed with the magic of an Eternal—and it nearly killed me.

Alexios is far older. That time, the realm selected a ruthless, calculating monster. And it picked well. When everything went to shit during the war, he and the Dark King were the only reason Scillari didn't fall to human armies.

"Clear the room," he says, voice soft but carrying to every corner of the chamber.

The courtiers move swiftly at the king's command. Within minutes, it's just the two of us, the silence shattered by the boom of thunder outside.

Alexios studies me. "I see you enjoyed yourself today, Wolf."

"I did. They didn't." I give him a smirk. "Funny how often it shakes out that way."

"Anything useful?"

The stench of the shop wafts through my memory. The piss-reeking heap of offal that had once been the proprietor.

"Got an address from the apothecary before I cut his throat. Silk Street, beneath the old tannery in Hellevig. Could be nothing, could be a solid lead. The buyer also mentioned fleshtraders working the docks."

His jaw tightens. "Which docks?"

"Valchek. But they were sourced from elsewhere. I'll brief Zephyr on what I managed to torture out of him and have her keep an ear to the ground while I handle Silk Street," I say, referring to Alexios' spymaster. "It's urgent."

"Define urgent."

I take a breath. This is the part that's going to make him lose his shit. "The apothecary knew that consuming our kind gives mortals temporary access to our abilities. He wasn't just pushing demi parts as a high. He had a whole setup—back room, display cases, regular buyers. Professional operation. If he knew, the network knows."

Alexios stares at me. But I feel the storm building—that pressure change right before lightning strikes.

Then his power detonates.

Lightning tears through the chamber. It ricochets off the marble walls and shatters a column to my left, leaving smoking black trails across stone that has survived centuries of immortal tantrums. The stink of ozone floods my nose, sharp and metallic, mixing with the smell of burnt stone.

Then, as suddenly as it started, it stops.

Alexios uncurls his fingers from the throne. "Did you find anything else?" he asks, the words soft. Like he hadn't just lost control. "Any other relics?"

My gut twists. I know what he's asking. What he's been driving himself half-mad hunting for.

He wants to know if I found his sister.

"No. There was nothing else. I'm sorry."

And I am. I understand his grief as intimately as my own. I still wake up sometimes thinking I'm back three hundred years, desperately digging through the ruins of my homeland, searching for bodies.

That kind of wound doesn't heal. Not really. Might scab over if you're lucky, but underneath? The rot keeps spreading. Working deeper. Eating you alive from the inside until one day, it finally reaches your heart.

When Alexios speaks again, his voice is flat. "Keep me updated." He stands, his wings flaring wide. "Walk with me. This involves Hellevig. I have something to show you."

He guides me through the palace corridors to the great Eternium vault—god-steel, they call it. The bones of immortals broken and reforged into an impenetrable shell. Whorls and runes of power score its face, the metal seeming to drink the light. Ancient wards burst to life beneath his touch. With a groan, the vault opens to reveal the Eternal's private sanctum.

And there, at the chamber's heart, is a pool.

We stop at the edge. My reflection stares back, and then the surface changes, settling on the interior of the temple in Hellevig. But something is wrong. The marble altar stands bare and neglected—and most damning of all, the offering channels are dry.

The breath leaves me in a rush. "So they're not making the tithe." I glance up at him. "Want me to decorate the walls with their insides? Rip out a few spines? Between this and the possible fleshmarket in their capital, seems they need a reminder about honoring agreements."

"Not yet," Alexios says, shaking his head. "Destroying Hellevig would damage the Shroud beyond repair. I can redistribute the remaining tithes as a temporary measure, but the foundation is already compromised." His fingers drum against the pool's rim. "The problem is their youngest. The masses worship Bryony Devaliant. Get rid of her before we deal with the fleshtrade."

My head snaps up. Fragments of memory flood in: violet eyes, the blood from my thumbprint stark against her pale skin, her voice steady.

Treat me like an equal.

"She's your Anchor, Alexios. I can't fly into Hellevig and take her head without a damn good reason."

If all three Devaliants die, the Shroud falls. No barrier means no protection. No protection means Scillari is wide open to fleshtraders.

The god-king's expression goes colder. "I forbade the princess from making her tithe yesterday. She was an oathbreaker the moment she left the temple. And you know what we do to oathbreakers, don't you, Wolf?"

I raise my brows. "You manufactured a violation of the Accords? That's impressively cold, even for you."

"I used the tools available to me," he corrects, like that makes it any better. "The Accords prevent me from direct interference in Devaliant rule—Amalthea made sure of that. If I'd had my way, you'd be perched in their throne room, ensuring they govern with a bare minimum of competence. But this?" He gestures to the pool, mouth twisting. "The Claim is all the leverage I have left. It's mine to give and take away through whatever loopholes I had the foresight to hide in that agreement."

"And killing her for being too popular seems like the best use of that loophole?" I try a different angle. "Idris is supposed to enforce the tithes. If you're looking for someone to punish, he's—"

"She's being worshipped." Alexios cuts me off with a sharp look. "Do you have any idea what that's like inside my skull? Thousands of voices chanting her name? The combination of oathbreakers and Shroud rot? Punishing Idris won't change the fact that the veil is failing because people exalt her above the duty that keeps our realms stable. The risk of keeping her alive far outweighs the potential consequences of eliminating her." Lightning dances between his fingers. Thunder booms beyond the windows, responding to his emotions. "So the girl dies, or I'll remind you exactly how tight I can pull your leash."

I clench my jaw at the reminder. "Send Bastien. He's been dying to put a Devaliant in the ground for centuries. Let him have this one."

"Bastien has the subtlety and restraint of a battle-axe. I want a surgeon for this, not a butcher."

And for better or worse, I'm a god of my word. I made the girl a promise.

If it comes down to it, I'll make it a good death.

"I'll handle it," I tell him.

Lightning arcs over the ceiling. Alexios smiles. "Good. Don't disappoint me."

The pool's surface ripples a final time. I swear I see Bryony Devaliant's violet eyes before the water goes dark.

6

BRYONY

THE SERVANTS BUSTLE through the palace gardens, arranging the decorations for my wedding. Dozens of tables are scattered around the central pavilion, covered in cloth stitched with gilt thread. Crystal goblets glint from each place setting. Each bears our family crest—a serpent eating its own heart.

How fitting.

I trail my fingertips over the centerpieces. Nobles from every kingdom in Vartena have flocked here to witness the Lucinian emperor's niece finally shackle herself to the marriage bed. The tables all pay homage to each country, their trade and culture honored with each item.

The Brevig tables feature vases overflowing with blue flowers draped in pearls and shells. Ollestad's winter is captured in frosted evergreen boughs and blown glass sculptures resembling snowflakes. And Havenridge, with its nightshade berries and raven feathers, is a study in gothic elegance. Polished amber gleams between each centerpiece, glowing in the light like—

Like the Wolf's eyes.

My hand jerks back so fast that I nearly knock over a vase. I can't help seeing his face every time I blink. It's been two years, but I still recall everything with perfect clarity. The exact shade of his irises, the sunlight glinting across his wings, his mocking smile. The way he stared right through me.

Chasing my targets is irritating.

Digging my nails into my palm, I focus on the last

centerpiece—a dedication to Ostavika. Burnished apples are heaped in bowls alongside sheaves of wheat tied with crimson ribbons, a reminder of the fields and hills of my betrothed's homeland.

I wonder how Markus von Reding would respond if he knew about my mark. What do they say about oathbreakers in Ostavika? That we're lower than dirt and fouler than shit? That our shadows blight the earth and spoil the crops?

Probably. That hatred runs deep in every corner of Vartena. I'd be disappointed if his people lacked the creativity to put their own spin on it.

A burst of laughter draws my attention. A group of children darts between the servants, playing some game. The oldest, a boy with a wild tangle of dark curls, leans toward his captive audience. He can't be more than seven, all skinned knees and missing teeth.

"They say the Dark King gobbles up the souls of wicked little children. He'll snatch you out of your bed and crunch your bones between his teeth if you don't behave!"

The younger ones gasp. One girl looks like she's about to cry.

Oh, for the love of—

Apparently, adult supervision has fucked off to get sloshed on wine.

I sigh. "That's enough," I call out as I approach. "Let's not scare your friends with made-up tales."

"But it's true, Princess Bryony!" the boy insists. "My father says so!"

Great. This is what happens when nobles have too much time on their hands and start making up wild tales to keep their rebellious children in line.

I drop into a crouch, meeting the boy's gaze. "Oh really? And I bet the Dark King loves pickled children's toes, too, right?"

He blinks at me. "Umm. I don't think so? Maybe?"

"Well, who am I to question a god's taste?" I shrug with a hint of a smile to let him know I'm playing along. "But I have it on good authority that the Dark King prefers his wicked children braised, not pickled. Something about the marrow going all gelatinous." That startles a giggle out of one of the younger girls, and I flash her a quick grin before sobering. "Jokes aside, the Dark King may be an Eternal, but the Accords bind him like the rest of us. Do you remember what that means?"

"It means…" His brow furrows in thought. "It means he won't snatch us out of our beds. Not unless we break the rules first."

"That's right." I tap the eye on his wrist. "You have Alexios' Claim. He gave us this after Amalthea's sacrifice to keep us safe from the other gods. That was the deal to end the war. So long as we pay our tithes and spill our blood for the Shroud, you have his protection. And I promise you, the Dark King won't challenge Alexios. He has no interest in snacking on children. Not their bones, not their toes, and certainly not their hearts."

I omit the part of my speech where Alexios revoked *my* protection for imagined slights. No need to shatter the boy's illusions.

The uncertainty fades from his face. "Swear it? Cross your heart, the Dark King won't drag me from my bed and gnaw on my toes?"

"Cross my heart." I make an exaggerated X over my chest. "Now go find a better game to play. I don't want to hear about you scaring your cousins with stories about the Dark King, okay?"

He flashes me that gap-toothed grin again and scampers off, his little band trailing after him.

I envy them, to be honest. Even when I was that age, I wasn't that… innocent. You grow up so quickly when you're a ritual sacrifice. We're vessels first, Devaliants second, and *people* a very distant third. And now I'm just tarnished goods.

"Good gods, those children are getting more morbid with each year." I look over to see Theodora picking her way across the path, wiping sculpting clay off her hands with a cloth. "Should I speak with the nobles about not traumatizing them before bedtime?"

"Please do," I say. "Last week, I caught Lady Umber's daughter building salt circles in her bedroom. Apparently, she's convinced Nyholmian wraiths are living under her bed." I nod at the residual clay on her fingers. "Sculpt anything worth seeing today?"

"I haven't sculpted anything worth seeing in years," she says, shoving the cloth into her frock pocket. "Why do you think I stopped inviting you into my studio? It's full of garbage."

"You've always been your harshest critic."

Theodora snorts. There's a tightness around her eyes as she surveys the staff and all the decorations coloring the garden.

"How are you holding up?" she asks quietly.

I shrug. "I thought I might appreciate the finer things in life. Like wondering: is it better to marry a nobleman who can't even tie his own boots or have an Enforcer separate my head from my shoulders?"

"Nice. Nothing screams 'living life to the fullest' like picturing gruesome deaths and disastrous marriages."

"Maybe I should get drunk before the consummation."

"Don't do that. Passing out in a puddle of your own vomit before Markus pounds you into the mattress is no way to begin a marriage."

I stare down at my cuff, fidgeting with the clasp. "I just don't want to think about it. Is that terrible of me? To spend what might be my last hours pretending none of this is happening? That tonight I won't be shackled to Markus for the remainder of my likely short, miserable life?"

"I'm working on it." She gives me a tight smile. "Uncle's looking for you."

"Lovely. Can't wait for the lecture on smiling as I'm shoved onto my husband's co—"

"Bryony. Theodora."

I turn to face the emperor, steeling myself. *He looks like our father*, I think. The same features, the same blond hair and blue eyes. But where Father had a gentleness to him, Idris is nothing but edges.

As he draws closer, his scent hits me. He reeks of soap and wine, with that unmistakable after-sex smell. The same overindulgence that once drove him into seclusion after his daughter and my father took their lives. Theodora ruled for ten months while Uncle tried to drink and fuck away his grief.

Idris crosses his arms, and I'm struck by how the famous Devaliant skin—that pearlescent, glittering sheen—highlights the harsh angles of his face.

"Uncle," Theodora says.

He ignores her, fixing that icy stare on me. "I heard there was an incident at the temple yesterday."

I should have known better than to trust in my guard's discretion. Silas probably ran straight to Idris this morning.

I unfasten my bracelet and thrust my arm out, baring the slash carved through Alexios' Claim. "You mean *this* incident?"

His fingers close around my wrist, bruising. "What did you do?"

I've bled for that Shroud my whole life. Died for it over and over. I refuse to be shamed for this.

"Bryony didn't *do* anything," Theodora snaps. "Alexios revoked her Claim because Hellevig hasn't been diligent about the tithes. He's scapegoating her. It's vindictive."

"Mind your tone, Theodora." A muscle jumps in Idris' jaw. "The Eternal's word is law. If Alexios decided Bryony's responsible, it's not our place to question why."

"Don't you dare lecture me on my *tone*. Not when I'm the one who sat on that throne and held this kingdom together while its emperor was off drinking and fucking his way through every brothel from here to the Red Wastes."

She's treading dangerous ground, but I can't bring myself to stop her. She *did* pick up the pieces when Idris was gone. And what was her reward? To be cast aside the moment he slunk back from whatever gutter he'd crawled into. Expected to step down without protest.

A fact my sister has never let him forget.

"Bryony wouldn't be in this position," she continues, "if

you'd spared more than a passing thought for your duty beyond what best serves *you*. Reminding the people about the tithe is the most basic tenet of statecraft. Is it any wonder Alexios is losing patience with our house? When you can't even be bothered to uphold your end of the Accords?"

Idris' hand twitches toward the dagger at his belt. For a moment, I'm certain he's going to draw it. That today will be the day he finally makes good on his threats to carve the insolence from my sister's hide.

But then he notices the servants. They're eyeing us discreetly, listening hard.

Idris slowly leans in, switching to Lybräian, the formal tongue of Vartenan nobility—a language that the staff aren't permitted to learn.

"That's rich coming from you, Theodora. Still fucking every guard who looks your way?"

Theodora's cheeks flush, but she doesn't flinch.

Idris' lip curls. "The only reason you ever warmed that throne was the Accords' requirement for a Devaliant ass in the seat. I'd rather let Silas' horse sit there than see you sully it again." He gestures at me. "Bryony will wed Markus as planned. Tonight. Whatever mess she's made, we'll sort it after."

"I'm right here," I snap, the cadence of Lybräian sharp on my tongue. "And in case it's slipped your notice, I have a death warrant on my skin. I may not live long enough to see my wedding, let alone sort anything after."

"You won't be executed immediately. We have a few days, enough time to smooth things over."

"You don't know that." My nails bite into my palms. "I doubt the Enforcers will be inclined to rearrange their busy murder schedule on your whim."

Idris' gaze slides to the servants. They're no longer pretending they aren't riveted by the scene unfolding before them. They might not understand the heated Lybräian spilling from our lips, but they know good gossip fodder when they see it.

"We'll go back to the temple tomorrow and send word to

Alexios," he says. "Highlight the position he'll put himself in if he insists on killing one of his only living Anchors."

As long as a Devaliant is alive in Hellevig, the Shroud holds. But our family tree withers more each year, pruned by disease, bad luck, and rampant rates of madness and suicide. Dying and coming back over and over breaks us all. Two years ago, shortly after my encounter with the Wolf, my father fell on his blade in the palace forest. Sixteen months ago, Idris' daughter jumped from a balcony.

Only the three of us remain.

"How noble," I say. "That you're fighting so much to make sure I'm shackled to both the altar and my husband's bed."

"Spare me the dramatics," he says, rolling his eyes. "You're not the only one who dies for the Accords." He scoops up my discarded bracelet, turning it over in his hands. "You'd better pray Alexios can be persuaded to mercy. Now get inside and make yourself pretty for your groom."

7

BRYONY

DEFT FINGERS PLUCK and prod at my hair. The maids twist the pale mass into an elaborate style with loops and curls studded with gems, gossiping about my coming nuptials.

"... heard the Redorans brought three entire rail cars just for the bridal gifts!" one whispers as she wrestles another pin into place. "Spices from Havenridge and enough silk to dress the court twice over."

Theodora used to tell me a story about a songbird that lived in a golden cage. The nobles who kept it would decorate its wings with jewels until their "gifts" made flying impossible. They called it kindness, devotion. *Love.*

I think about that damn bird a lot lately.

"Her Highness is so fortunate," Marigold sighs. "Lord von Reding is gorgeous. I hear he's very skilled with his—"

"*Marigold!*" The eldest maid cuts her off with a scandalized hiss.

The maids are putting the finishing touches on my hair and cosmetics when familiar footsteps approach. I glance up to see my sister stride into the room, resplendent in the traditional red silks of a Lucinian wedding ceremony. Scarlet for the guests, silver for the bride—the colors meant to symbolize the blood we give and the Shroud itself.

She pauses on the threshold. "You're not dressed yet? I thought Idris wanted the ceremony to begin at moonrise."

I switch to Lybräian so the servants won't follow our

conversation. "He wants me to make an entrance after the guests are drunk enough to appreciate whatever spectacle he has planned."

Theodora drifts closer, green eyes sweeping over the organized chaos of combs and cosmetics that litter the vanity's surface. "And what did Idris decide you're wearing?"

"My gown is designed to tear away with a yank. A thoughtful addition from the couturier at Idris' request. He called it a 'marital aid.'"

"He. *What.*"

"Mmhm. I won't be surprised if von Reding starts pawing at me before we've even left the altar." I pause, biting my lip. "Theo. Did you know Idris plans to marry you off by the year's end?"

Her hand clenches into a fist, nails digging into her palm.

"I heard him arranging it with Lord Dunne," I continue, watching her face darken. "The plan is to chain you to some inbred nobleman from Brevig to secure a new trade deal. He says there's no excuse for you to still be unmarried without children at twenty-three."

"That bastard," she hisses under her breath.

The maids begin lacing me into my wedding dress, pulling the stays so tight I can barely breathe. When they finally release me from their clutches, I'm cinched into a gown of silver shot through with a webwork of shimmering rubies. A heavy choker rests against my collarbones—deliberately placed to hide the scar on my throat.

"It's perfect, Highness!" Marigold gushes. "Wait until Lord von Reding sees you!"

"Here's hoping he's struck dead on the spot," I say cheerfully. The maids titter before making their exit.

The instant the door clicks shut, Theodora rounds on me. "I can't marry. There are... things I need to figure out first. I don't think I can have children. Not yet."

"I don't want to either, but—"

"No." She grabs my hand. "Listen to me. I dream about it.

I keep seeing Odessa's body at the bottom of the tower, over and over and over."

My lungs seize. The memory hits me—Theodora stumbling into my room, dress smeared with blood not her own. She'd been the one to find our cousin after Odessa threw herself from the Celestine Tower. Another Devaliant who couldn't bear the weight anymore.

No one in my family has made it past the age of fifty since the Godkiller Crusades ended and the Accords were signed. We're not built to last.

We're just born to die.

"After each resurrection, it gets worse." She turns away to stare out of the window. "For days, I'm... not here. Like I'm floating above myself, watching some stranger wear my skin. Nothing feels real. Not the palace, not my art. Not even when I—" She stops and bites her lip. "Not even when I let the guards into my bed. Nothing makes me feel alive anymore."

I study my sister's profile, wondering when her face became a stranger's. How did I miss it?

Everyone calls her the ice princess. They think it's because she's cold and untouchable, but they don't understand that it's armor meant to freeze out everything that hurts. I've watched her perfect the art of burying pain beneath duty for so long that I started to believe the lie myself. But now? She's shattering right in front of me.

"So we delay it," I tell her, taking her hand. "I'll cause a scene tonight. Show everyone my mark. It'll buy you some time while they're all distancing themselves from the disgraced Anchor."

Her brow furrows. "If you do that, the other kings and queens might—"

"What will they do that's worse than what's coming?" I give a harsh laugh. "I'm dead, anyway. Might as well make it count."

"Don't say that." Her fingers squeeze mine. "You're not dead."

Yes, I am. But I swallow the words back.

Other rulers get off easy with blood offerings—the same fingerprick as every other citizen. But we Devaliants give pieces of our souls, and what has it earned us? Earned *me*? An appointment with the business end of an Enforcer's blade and my life snuffed out at the whim of a god. I have nothing left to lose except my sister.

"When I give the signal, follow my lead," I tell her.

I take my place beside Markus at the garden's altar.

The drums take up a rhythm, each sonorous beat reverberating through my chest. The weight of hundreds of stares settles on me as the wedding guests crane their necks for a better view of the spectacle.

Theodora places a steadying hand at my elbow and leans in close. To everyone watching, it would seem like she's comforting a nervous bride. "Almost time. Ready?"

I nod curtly, meeting Markus' stare.

He's handsome enough, I suppose. Blond, blue-eyed, athletic, with the typical arrogance of a man with money and status. When his proprietary gaze slides over me, it resembles someone evaluating an acquisition. He paid for me—virginity intact. I'm sure he's imagining how I'll look splayed beneath him, spilling my blood on his cock.

Funny how much this feels like another anchoring ritual. Same incense, same blood, different altar. Servants move through the throng in diaphanous scarlet veils, bearing trays of tiny cordials, candied rose petals, and dishes of pomegranate seeds. All styled in homage to the tithe I'll make tonight in the marriage bed.

At some unseen signal, the crowd ripples, silences, and parts. My uncle emerges from the palace in a gem-encrusted greatcoat that's ostentatious, bordering on vulgar, but Idris has never been a man burdened by an overabundance of taste. His golden hair is a mess. He's swaying enough to tell me he's already several glasses deep in his cups.

Idris barely glances at me as he takes his place to perform the ceremony. His eyes say what his lips won't: *Play your part. Smile nicely for the guests.*

He faces the audience. "Friends, honored guests. We're gathered here this evening to celebrate the marriage of my niece, Her Royal Highness Bryony Devaliant, Princess of the Blood, to Lord Markus von Reding, Captain of the Thirteenth Legion."

Everyone erupts into applause, peppered with more ribald cheers from some drunker lords. Someone bellows for Markus to "break her in proper-like" amid hoots and guffaws from his companions.

I grit my teeth so hard I swear I hear my molars crack.

Idris turns to my groom. "If you would join hands with your bride?"

Markus' fingers close around my own and squeeze too hard. I fight down the panic.

"Bryony," my uncle says. "Repeat after me…"

His words fade with the rushing of my pulse in my ears. I'm expected to recite all the practiced words—the *lies*—by heart. The vows written by someone else's hand, spat out by rote.

They're all watching me now. Waiting. Expecting me to be a good girl and stand here meek and compliant while they give me away to a man who'll use me however he sees fit. And why shouldn't they? I've spent twenty-one years doing everything I was supposed to, letting them hold me down on altars and kill me. Never fought or questioned anything. I just took it.

Not anymore.

I catch Theodora's gaze. My sister gives me a small, almost imperceptible nod. I nod back—our agreed signal to light the match—and pull my hand from Markus' grasp.

Inhale. Exhale. Brace for impact.

"Actually," I announce, "I have something I need to say."

Idris' head whips toward me. "*Bryony.* Now is not the—"

"I had my vows all memorized." I raise my voice to be heard over the growing swell of confused mutters. "All about gratitude and honor and how eager I am to fulfill my duty."

I sweep my gaze over the crowd. Their expressions crack a little more with each passing second, lips thinning and eyes narrowing, whispers rising. Good. Let them talk.

"But that would have been a lie," I continue. "How many of you would be so happy to cheer for this marriage if you knew what I am?"

"*Bryony.*" Idris' fingers close hard around my arm. "That's *enough.*"

I wrench free of his grip, yanking off my gold cuff—my last flimsy shield ripped away. I hold up my wrist. Hundreds of eyes stare at the brand seared into my flesh, its lines stark and unflinching in the garden's light, glowing like a beacon. As if it's calling an Enforcer right to me.

"The truth is, there's no honor here," I say into the silence. "Only a princess marked for death."

No one moves. The collective intake of breath seems to suck all the air from the garden—and then the shouting begins. Chairs scrape against the flagstones as guests surge to their feet. Demands for answers mingle with prayers and frenzied accusations, while others turn to their neighbors in frantic whispers. I see Lord Dunne's face go ashen, while Lady Moretti clutches her daughter to her chest, backing away. The word "oathbreaker" ripples through the garden.

"*She's marked!*"

"*The emperor allowed this?*"

"*... doomed us all...*"

Markus recoils from me so violently, you'd think I'd drawn a blade on him. "You—You let me touch you. You're..."

He spits on the ground between us.

I almost laugh. Five minutes ago, he planned to do much more than touch me, but so much for marital devotion.

Idris' grip returns, fingers digging in hard enough to leave bruises. "You think this is funny?" He jerks me forward, then rounds on Theodora. "And you—I know your fingerprints are all over this disaster. We'll discuss your involvement thoroughly."

He drags me down from the altar. I don't fight as he hauls me across the garden into the palace. What's left to save? The mark on my wrist has done what I wanted—destroyed any chance of this marriage happening.

I've burned it all down.

Idris flings open the door to my bedchamber and shoves me inside. "I'll clean up your mess. Tomorrow, we'll visit the temple. They'll help me decide what to do with you." His lip curls. "And fuck you very much, Bryony."

The door slams shut behind him.

8

BRYONY

THE BLADE AGAINST my throat jolts me awake.

As I struggle to make sense of the intrusion, lips graze my ear. Then a whisper: "Time for that memorable death, Devaliant."

It's been two years since I last heard that voice, but I'd recognize it anywhere.

I open my eyes to find the Wolf staring at me. His irises glow, shifting from gold to bronze to copper, with the barest hint of blue that resembles the center of a flame. Those beautiful golden wings fan behind him as he leans in, dark hair falling across his forehead.

"Wolf," I say softly in greeting.

A part of me is… resigned, almost. If there's one lesson every Devaliant understands, it's that we die badly. We always do. Choosing my death while I'm sane enough to appreciate it is why I made that deal with him in the first place.

"Devaliant," he says. He bites his lower lip and releases it slowly in a cruel, mocking grin. "I heard you've been a bad girl."

He's enjoying my unease. Savoring his damn dagger being one twitch away from splitting me open.

"I wish I'd been worse," I tell him. "I think you know I haven't earned this."

"Alexios doesn't care what you think you've earned. And frankly, neither do I."

Right. Since when have gods ever concerned themselves with *fairness*?

He pushes the blade forward slightly, not breaking the skin, but closer. Letting me feel it.

"You seem eager," I say, holding back a flinch. "Should I be honored?"

"Honored. Flattered. Maybe even terrified, if you've any sense at all." His grin widens as he looks me over, murmuring to himself, "Now, how should we pass the time before I kill you?"

I imagine how I must appear to him. Sleep-mussed and vulnerable, my hair tangled against the sheets. My nightgown has slipped off one shoulder, baring a long stretch of skin. I'd wager there's no lovelier canvas for an artist of death.

"I'm not in the mood to pass the time with you," I say coldly.

He makes a dismissive noise, as if my opinion doesn't rank on his list of considerations. Then his attention falls to my throat, and his expression hardens. A gasp leaves me as his fingertips trace over—

My scar, I realize. He's noticed my scar.

"Someone tried to steal your death from me." His voice is deeper now, a lash of heated power scorching the air.

I suppose I shouldn't be surprised he's angry. He *did* tell me he was eager to put another Devaliant in the Void for good, and the man who gave me my scar nearly succeeded before the Wolf got the chance.

"A year ago," I say, pushing down the memory. "Clearly, he failed. I want to—"

I inhale sharply as he bends his head to nose at the curve of my neck. To... scent me? Unnerve me more? I'm suddenly enveloped by the aroma of soap, citrus, and evergreen. *Him.*

"I want to remind you about our terms," I finish breathlessly.

"Uninterrupted eye contact as you die." His breath is warm against my skin.

Naturally, he'd remember his *own* insane demand first.

"That was *your* condition, Wolf. Not mine."

"Then refresh my memory." His lips graze my scar, and I get the sense that he's *playing* with me. Batting me around between his paws before he rips me open. "Pretend I'm distractible."

"No decapitation. No flaying. No disembowelment." He grunts when I sink my nails into his arm. I tip my chin up, pressing into the blade's bite. If I'm going to die tonight, I won't do it screaming. I have some dignity. "You promised you'd *pretend* to treat me like an equal."

"Seems a shame to limit me." He trails the knife lower, scratching over my collarbone, raising goosebumps. "Maybe I'd like to make you a masterpiece."

His masterpiece. Of course, a soulless monster like the Wolf sees brutality as an art.

"Why?" I ask him bitterly. "Because I'm an Anchor, or because I'm the only human who's ever decided to waste precious breath negotiating with you?"

"Because I've waited three hundred years to have another Devaliant impaled on my knife, and some clumsy asshole"—he taps my scar—"tried to take you from me. I'm going to savor you."

I clench my jaw. "No."

He arches a brow. Oh, he's enjoying this. Because I'm prey who bites back, even if it's an exercise in futility. I know it. He knows it. The Wolf lowers the dagger, tracing the swell of my breast through the thin silk, as if he's testing me. Seeing what I'll do.

I don't even twitch.

"What do you want then, Devaliant? For me to kiss you before I end you?" Then his eyes flick up to mine as he whispers, "Hard or soft?"

I seize his wrist. "I'd rather die with your blood on my hands."

For a beat, I think he'll slash me open after all. But then he smiles slowly, pulling away to stand. He shakes out his wings with a rasp of feathers. "Then get up," he orders, sheathing his blade.

"What?"

"I won't ask twice."

I get out of bed, watching him reach for the fastenings of his breastplate. He unbuckles the clasps with deft fingers and drops it to the floor with a muted clank. My breath catches as he strips off the undershirt fastened between his gold wings, baring a torso of taut muscle and gleaming skin. There isn't anything soft about this god. His body is as much a weapon as his dagger.

My mouth goes dry. "What are you doing?"

"Playing with my food before eating it," he says with a smirk.

Everything in me freezes. His promise to give me a good death wasn't a pact made in blood. No contract, no divine obligations. If he wanted, he could make this as slow and painful as possible.

"So I'm a mouse to your cat?"

"Mouse? No." The Wolf wraps his hand around my throat. Not squeezing, but a warning that he *could*. "Mice are smart enough not to dictate terms to cats. They know better."

My pulse flutters against his grip. "What am I, then?"

"The daughter of an arrogant house who should be grateful I'm humoring her instead of slitting her throat and calling it a night."

He reaches behind his back, drawing a smaller dagger from a hidden sheath between his shoulder blades. Power thrums through the metal—there's a god's magic embedded in that knife.

"Turpori craftsmanship," he says, watching me. "The only metal that can make an Eternal bleed." He seizes my hand, places the hilt in my palm, and curls my fingers around it. "I meant what I said before. You and I aren't equals. I'm a god, and you're just a doomed girl living on time I let you borrow. But since you didn't earn my execution, I'll give you your dying wish. Take this blade and carve yourself a death so memorable, I'll carry it for eternity."

I blink. "Is this a trick?"

He scowls at me. "I never *trick* when it comes to spilling blood. It's the only thing I hold sacred."

It has to be a trap—a cruel game. But when I search his face, I find no trace of deceit. Only a dark sort of anticipation. "Why? Why let me do this?"

"I'm bored. And you're interesting. So congratulations, you get to be tonight's diversion. I'm giving you a real chance to deserve your death—no tricks. No traps. Just you, me, and this knife." His lips brush my ear as he whispers, "Wherever you want to put it, Devaliant. I'm all yours."

"*Wherever?*"

"That's what I said. So take it or get on with dying. Your choice."

My hand shakes as I study the blade. A maelstrom of emotions rises in me—a lifetime's worth of smothered fury clamoring for release. "What if I'm tired of being a god's toy?"

His indulgent mood vanishes in an instant. "Oh, *poor baby*," he sneers. "What a shit hand you've been dealt, huh? The princess cutting herself open every other week like a good little sacrifice. Letting all that helpless anger fester."

Images strobe in my mind. *The Oracles pin me down. The altar is cold against my back. The knife settles against my chest, and the Head Oracle gives a sharp command—no empathy or regret.*

Stay still, Princess. Stop squirming.

My fingers tighten on the dagger's hilt.

"This execution is the one thing you think you can control," the Wolf mocks, jarring me from the memory. "Your last-ditch attempt to salvage some paltry scrap of dignity before the end. Because it kills you, doesn't it? Knowing that no matter how earnestly you tithed or bravely you negotiated, you'll just be another carcass rotting at my feet."

I didn't know it was possible to hate anyone this much. Some self-destructive impulse wants me to goad him. To see how far I can push.

"Maybe I should bury this blade in your throat and watch you die choking on it," I say, baring my teeth.

"Points for ambition, but I'm not a demigod. It takes more than a Turpori dagger to kill an Eternal." He gives a little laugh. "But I'll let you in on a secret. A bit of wisdom from a god who's seen more killing than most: we're all just walking corpses in different stages of decay, waiting for the end. The only difference is how much of the world we take with us when we finally lie down. So accept what I'm giving you. It's more than a Devaliant deserves."

The air thickens. Something feral scorches through my veins, snarling, *Hurt him. Hurt him like they've hurt you.*

He must see it—that dark emotion building inside me, all my anger and repressed violence ready to spill out between us. His next words shudder through me, smoky and intimate. "Where do you want me? Where do you want to sink in your claws and teeth and *tear?*"

Before I can think better of it, I'm shoving him. He smirks as the backs of his knees hit the bed, and then the Wolf settles on my rumpled sheets like he belongs there.

Like he *owns* this space. Owns me.

This close, I can't help but study the ring of molten gold limning his irises, the way his lashes cut stark shadows over his cheekbones. His skin has the luster of crushed diamonds.

I hate him. I hate him so much for the beauty that speaks to some base, primitive part of my hindbrain that looks at the monster and thinks, *yes, please*, instead of running.

I step between his parted thighs, reaching out until my fingers hover over his wing. I toy with the idea of seeing what sounds he might make if I tugged until those gold feathers came away bloody. "Everywhere is fair game? Even—"

His hand shoots out, and he seizes my wrist, giving me a stern look. "Let me clarify. No one touches a god's wings. Not even pretty little sacrifices."

"So it's a universal law? Not a human restriction?"

His grip tightens. "Inviolable. For *everyone.*" Then he releases his hold and reclines on his elbows—an ancient god awaiting worship. "Well? Put that dagger to good use."

I bring the knife up and lay the edge against his shoulder.

"Make me bleed for you, vicious girl," he says.

And that? *That's* my undoing. The last thread of my control snapping.

I slash the blade down in a shallow cut that's more blood than pain. His breath hisses through his teeth, and his hands fist at his sides, but he doesn't move. The sight of crimson welling against that glittering skin makes something fierce and hungry unfurl behind my ribs. Is this what power feels like? This dizzying, swooping sensation? This dark and covetous thing?

"That's it." His head tips back. "Let me feel it. Let me choke on your rage."

A part of me screams to stop. *This is wrong. This is madness.* But that part is drowned out by the rush of my pulse in my ears, the savage joy clawing up my throat.

With a snarl, I lunge and straddle his hips, opening a matching line across his chest. He grunts at the impact. His hands close around my thighs, gripping me as I carve my anguish into him. My helpless fury at every injustice ever done to me in the name of sacrifice.

It's power and depravity. Sacrilege. This body is a temple, and I am defiling it with greedy hands. Violating him. Claiming him. Marking him as mine. A profane consummation in steel instead of skin, a black mass spoken in the language of shared brutality. The hilt grows slippery in my grip, and my breathing goes ragged, but I don't stop. I *can't*.

My teeth ache with the need to bite. To rend and tear and mark in a way no immortal flesh can heal. To take all that monstrous grace and beauty and make it a ruin, because with every slash and visceral jolt of the blade sinking in, everything inside me quiets. The memories and the smothered screams. The swallowed grief and violence over all the times everyone told me that princesses can't say *no*, can't be angry, can't fight back. We just lie down and take it.

"More," he says. "*Harder.*"

I've spent so long hiding this hunger. This need to hit something, to hurt something. Images flash. *The altar. The knife. The Void. Waking up to the numb reality of a life that isn't really living.* I'm sick of being the thing that breaks—a woman who climbs up onto a slab of rock and dutifully, *prettily* dies every two weeks.

And it's like he sees it. Sees down into the rotting bedrock of me, the parts that the altar blade keeps chipping at with each death. The Wolf's burning gaze never looks away. It devours me, memorizing my snarls and quick, uneven breaths. He watches me as if this is rapture, revelation. As if he wants to crawl into the wildness of me and revel in my unmaking. The veneer of Devaliant royalty stripped to this animal wearing her skin.

I shove the knife into his side. It sinks through flesh and muscle until it scrapes bone. He groans but holds still, gripping my thighs hard enough to bruise. Letting me take and take and *take*. And I'm so ravenous. Like I could eat the fucking world and crave more.

He must sense it, the flat dissatisfaction twisting my mouth. The grief. He reaches up to cup my face in his palms, smoothing his thumbs over my cheeks to catch the tears that spill down. I sob soundlessly as I watch his wounds knit back together. His skin glows with all that Eternal power as every mark and hurt I made disappears. Because even this brutal mastery—this fleeting dominion over a god—is as empty as an altar rite.

I'm still just a sacrifice. Still chained to the altar.

And he's still the one who gets to kill me.

"It's not enough, is it?" he asks, low and too-knowing. "All that fury, and you'll go to your grave still starving."

This is a joke to him. An obligation. He gets to fly away and wash his hands of me, go back to his life in Scillari, and celebrate a promise kept and a Devaliant killed. He'll never understand what it's like to be powerless.

"You want to know what I loathe about you?" I say. "You're untouchable in a way I'll never be. Powerful. Immortal." I lean down until our noses brush. "And you *squander* it all on meaningless shit like this. It's pathetic."

A muscle tics in his jaw. Then he leans in and brushes his lips over mine. It's not a kiss—not really. Just a meeting of mouths, cold and perfunctory. Like he's mocking me.

It makes me want to *bite*.

"Show me," he murmurs against my mouth. "Show me how much you hate me. Let me taste it."

Fuck you.

With a growl, I surge against him and sink my teeth into his bottom lip until I taste copper. We're panting into each other, sharing breath and blood. His hands twist in my hair.

His expression is almost tender as he yanks the dagger out of his side and angles the point over my thundering heart. "Let me see all that loathing in your face as you die. Any final words? I'll be sure to carve them on your tomb."

I lean into the blade, giving him the eye contact he bargained for. "*Here lies Bryony Devaliant,*" I sneer. "*The stupid woman who still gave one last tithe against the Eternal's orders when she should have spat in his face.*"

He blinks. "You did what?"

"Sank the knife into my own chest on the temple grounds. Figured I'd try to reverse his decision. Clearly, it didn't work."

And then, to my shock, the Wolf laughs. "That's either the bravest or stupidest thing I've ever heard." He returns his dagger to its sheath between his wings. "But I can't help but appreciate a mortal finding a loophole to a god's loophole. Guess I can't fault you, considering. But now you're not an oathbreaker."

That's not comforting. The Wolf of Asteria is not someone who just walks away from an execution on a technicality.

"I don't like that this amuses you."

"You shouldn't. Means I get to play with you longer. You've done an admirable job holding my interest tonight." His hands clamp around my waist, hauling me closer. His magic lashes against my skin in a wave of heat. "Here's what you're going to do. I want you to go scrub off the blood. When you come out, these sheets will be clean, and this room will be empty. You'll put your head on your pillow and remember this as nothing more than a hazy dream until the next time I visit to fuck with you."

Next time. Is he insane?

The command vibrates through my skull, surging into my limbs and compelling me to obey. I strain against the thrall of his power, the inexorable pull of it. "But if I'm not an oathbreaker," I pant, "then I'm Unclaimed. Fair game to kill right now without consequences. Are you seriously risking your king's wrath and granting me a stay of execution because you're *bored*?"

The Wolf stares at me for a long moment, his brow creased in confusion. As if he doesn't understand why he's making this decision, either. "I don't always like listening to the king when he yanks my leash a little too hard. Keeps him on his toes. Reminds him who I am." His gaze drops to my lips. "And I want another taste of your rage. Next time, if you're very lucky, maybe I'll let you sample mine."

Then his magic crashes over me in a tidal wave of light.

And the world goes black.

9

BRYONY

My bedroom door bursts open.

A jolt goes through me as Theodora storms in, coppery curls all mussed, dark circles under her eyes. She heads for my armoire and starts flinging drawers wide.

"On your feet, Bry. We need to get you dressed. I've been up all night trying to menace and bribe someone in the palace to drive us to the temple without alerting Uncle." She pulls out a heap of clothes. "This place is full of spineless idiots."

I push myself up on my elbows. "Theo, what—"

"After what happened last night, I don't trust Idris with your safety." She dumps the bundle of fabric on my mattress, already turning to rummage through another drawer. "I'll threaten the Head Oracle into contacting Alexios and negotiate with him myself."

I shiver as I swing my legs over the side of the bed and—*Wait.* Different nightgown. Gray silk, little vine pattern. When did I put this on?

A dream returns in snatches—those amber eyes, hot skin beneath my palms, lips against my ear.

Where do you want me? Where would you like to sink in your claws and teeth and tear?

Stupid. If the Wolf had been in my room, he'd have slit my throat and whistled while the blood pooled.

"*Bry.*" Theodora's sharp voice cuts through my spiraling thoughts. "Get that nightgown off. We need to move."

I scramble to tug the shift off. Theodora lobs a chemise at me, followed by stockings. I yank them on, my hands trembling so badly I can barely work the buttons.

"How do you know Alexios will even bother to bargain?"

"He did it with Amalthea, didn't he? I'll be convincing." She spins me around and tugs a soft muslin dress over my head. "I've seen an Enforcer come to collect. I won't let that happen to you."

My breath catches. I never spoke with Theo about that day in the palace woods two years ago—how quickly the Wolf killed. The way his power had pressed down on me. His words, low and intent.

Don't ever give me a reason to come for you.

I swallow past the sudden dryness in my mouth. "Which did you see? The Wolf?"

"The Blade. The one without proper wings. His are like... living shadow spilling down his back." She laces up my bodice, fingers deft. "I saw him when Aldgate stopped tithing and Uncle abandoned us. I went to speak with the village elders and remind them that nowhere is too isolated for a god's notice. A lesson they all learned."

"He killed them?"

"Yes. Every single one." A shudder rolls through her. "By the time I reached the village, he was standing on a pile of corpses admiring his handiwork. I've never seen that much death."

Watching the Wolf kill an oathbreaker was bad enough. I've heard his brother is worse. The Blade isn't known for efficient kills; he just shows up for a massacre and makes it as bloody and brutal as possible.

"You spoke to him?" I ask, swallowing hard.

"You might say that. I got up in his face and insulted him."

A strangled laugh escapes me. "Theo, you didn't!"

"What was he going to do? Killing an Anchor breaks the Accords, and even an immortal attack dog has limits."

Before I can respond, heavy footsteps thunder down the corridor. A moment later, Idris' broad frame fills the doorway, and he scowls as he takes in my half-laced gown. "Whatever you're planning, forget it."

"I'm taking her to the temple myself," Theodora tells him, finishing with my laces. "Right now, I don't trust you to navigate your way off a toilet, much less with Bryony's safety."

Idris glares at her. "You take one step toward those gates with her, and I'll have you dragged back by the hair." He jerks his head at me. "Let's go, Bryony."

"Let her put shoes on," Theodora snaps. "And don't manhandle her in front of the servants. Grant her that small dignity."

"Dignity?" He stalks to my dressing room, voice rising to a bellow. "She pissed that away the moment she bared her traitor's brand to half the empire's nobles and every royal family from here to the Southern Reaches."

Idris storms out with a pair of my slippers. He chucks them at my feet, lip curled in a sneer. "Put those on."

I slip into the shoes and tie up the ribbons.

Theodora grabs a cloak, settles it over my shoulders, and gently works the clasps. "Let me ride with Bryony. She shouldn't be alone for this."

Alone with you, she means.

"Absolutely not. Stay behind and keep the nobles calm."

"You honestly expect me to play hostess after they all saw their princess show off an oathbreaker's mark?"

"You're a clever girl, Theodora. If those lords give you trouble, do what you always do and fuck them into compliance."

Idris seizes my arm and hauls me toward the door. Panic claws up my throat. I twist around, searching for Theo's face. She looks at me—angry, scared, her hands shaking.

"I love you," she says.

"I love you, too."

Idris yanks me away.

The servants won't look at me. As my uncle drags me down the palace colonnade, everyone averts their eyes as if the sight of an oathbreaker might taint them. A few of the younger maids turn their backs.

Well. Guess I'm poison.

It's funny, in a bleak sort of way. These same people used to fall all over themselves for a scrap of the Princess of the Blood's attention, and now they avoid me like I'm a plague carrier. Typical. Once a god judges you, everyone's quick to throw you to the wolves.

"Keep up," Idris barks, tugging at my arm.

My teeth grind together, but I lengthen my stride. He wrenches the carriage door open, shoves me inside, and clambers in after me.

The interior presses in from all sides. My chest constricts. Some distant part of my mind registers the first stirrings of panic.

"Stop that," Idris says sharply.

I blink. "Stop what?"

"The dramatics. There's no use for it."

Right. Silly me. How dare I have an inconvenient feeling about the Eternal completely screwing me over.

"Let's go!" Idris bangs twice on the roof.

With a sudden lurch and a grinding of wheels, the carriage moves over the cobblestones. I watch the palace walls slide past, the ground still littered with crushed flower petals and muddy ribbons from my ruined wedding. What a waste.

Idris folds his arms and leans back, tapping the toe of his boot against the floorboards in a restless beat as the carriage rattles through the streets. Despite the early morning, crowds have already amassed along our route.

Princess Bryony! Princess!

"What if Alexios doesn't agree to undo my mark?" I ask, keeping my face hidden behind the curtain.

Idris lets out a rough sigh. "We'll handle it, whatever it takes. The empire is bigger than one girl's mistakes."

My mistakes?

"I'm being punished for *your* failures," I say.

And there it is. That look. The one that says he'd like nothing more than to wrap his hands around my neck and squeeze until I stop making noise.

"I don't want to discuss this with you, Bryony. Clearly, the Eternal thinks you hold some responsibility."

"Theo tried warning you, but you didn't listen. You *never* listen. You're always too busy pouring more wine down your throat."

A muscle flickers in his jaw. "You and your sister have no idea what I do for the Accords. How many dead Devaliants do you think I've had to arrange? How many bodies I've dressed and posed so our citizens don't see our family's decline?"

I flinch, my breath too quick and shallow.

"If you knew how many lies I've told, how much shit I've eaten to keep up the front that we're just a tragedy-prone family..." His lips twist as he gestures to the crowds along the road. "You can't hold an empire if they all know you're rotting."

I flash back to that terrible morning in the forest when they discovered Father's body. Idris was pale, his hands shaking as he brushed my hair from my face.

Don't look, he'd said.

He'd seemed... small. Diminished. And beneath the shock, there'd been a flicker of something bleak and resigned.

Take her inside, he'd ordered my sister, his voice distant. *And don't let her see.*

The court had whispered. What had caused Emperor Titus' sad end? They theorized, of course. Ugly rumors about his mental decline and even uglier whispers that maybe Idris had killed his brother for power.

My uncle acted quickly. A tragic hunting accident, he'd told the broadsheets. The emperor's horse had spooked and thrown him against a tree. If people speculated after that, they did so privately. But in public, Luceni had accepted it as another Devaliant tragedy.

The shouting crowd draws my attention. The guards line the road, pushing everyone back.

Princess Bryony! Princess!

I force a smile and wave. A father hoists his daughter on his shoulders for a better look, and I blow her a kiss. It's what

Theodora would advise. *Act normal. Don't let them think anything is wrong.*

Idris gives a bitter chuckle. "Even with your life going to shit, you still show up for them. That's why they love you. Odessa had that gift, too, remember? That ability to wrap people around her finger."

Tears sting my eyes. It's been a year since Idris' daughter stepped off the palace balcony.

"I'm showing them we care," I say. "You might want to try it sometime. Wouldn't your daughter want you to?"

His lips flatten. "You don't know what it's like to outlive your child and lie about her death. So spare me the accusations and the judgment. I've done more than enough. Maybe you should have done less."

"I never asked for them to love me."

A silence descends between us, punctuated by the clatter of wheels and the shouts from outside. Then Idris sighs. "That's the edge we walk, isn't it? Give them nothing, and they'll despise you. Give them everything, and they'll destroy you. Either way, we bleed. The most we can hope for is a cut that kills us quickly."

He reaches out to tap my knee. As if that awkward touch can somehow encompass the breadth and depth of what we don't say. All the hollow spaces the dead leave behind.

Our driver stops the horses at the base of the temple steps. Idris climbs out and takes my hand, half dragging me inside. It's still too early for tithes to begin, and the inner sanctum is empty. The only sounds are the rasp of my exhales, the erratic thud of my pulse, the echo of our footsteps.

"Just breathe," Idris mutters.

He leads me down the corridor, and we duck through a low doorway into a cramped room cluttered with old books and wingback chairs. The space is windowless, lit only by guttering candles. The Head Oracle is reading at a table, face hidden by the black veil.

"That girl is not welcome again in this temple," she says,

snapping the book shut. Her veil flutters with an agitated breath. "Get out."

Idris grips my arm harder as if to prevent me from bolting. "I'm your emperor. When I give you a command, you do it. I want you to contact Alexios about my niece's mark."

Not so much as a twitch from the Oracle. "Sit." I can't tell who she's addressing until she crooks a finger in my direction. "Here. Now."

I sink into the chair.

The Oracle seizes my wrist and yanks my arm closer. I'm frozen, watching as she traces her finger over the ugly gash cutting Alexios' mark in half. Inspecting her god's handiwork.

And then I feel it—a foreign presence slithering into my mind. The Oracle. She shoves past my flimsy mental walls like they're nothing.

Memories flash: the child asking for my blessing, the crowds outside the palace gates, the offerings they threw at my feet instead of visiting the temple. Echoing chants, the roar of blood in my ears. Smothering. Hungry. All those voices calling my name. Then—

Emptiness. Alone in my head again, the connection severed.

The Oracle hums, a slow, considering noise. Speaking with Alexios, probably. Figuring out exactly how worthless I am to him now.

"Well?" Idris taps his fingers against his thigh. "Can it be undone?"

She shakes her head. "No. Once Eternal Alexios makes a judgment, he won't be swayed. Your niece's fate was sealed the moment the masses decided a Princess of the Blood was more deserving of their devotion. Her life belongs to him. It always has."

Her words knock the wind out of me. I've been abandoned by the god who was supposed to protect me. The god my family has served for generations. The god I bled and died for. I knew, of course. But hearing it out loud is a different thing entirely.

"There has to be something." Idris paces the room. "A tithe. A sacrifice. Tell him to name his price."

The Oracle slaps her palm against the table, rattling the candlesticks. "I'm not one of your courtiers or bootlicking lords, so don't presume to command me. I'm the Head Oracle of Hellevig. My bloodline traces to an Eternal who walked these realms before Alexios drew breath."

"Killing her would destabilize the city," he says, running his hands through his hair. "The people adore her—they'd riot in the streets!"

"Gods grow weary of empires." The Oracle shrugs. "They rise, they fall. Alexios will be alive long after your pitiful empire is dust and memory."

I can't breathe. My lungs won't work. I can barely focus on their words through the roar of my heartbeat.

Idris pauses, giving me a considering look. "He'll accept Bryony's death as recompense?" he asks the Oracle, keeping his stare on me. "Swear it."

"Oh, I'm sure he'll do more than accept it. He might even reward you for such a display of devotion. Slide the knife in, and he'll measure your faith in the spill of her blood."

No. No, no, no.

The truth of it settles like a stone in my gut. The Wolf's bargain, my promised end—all of it will be snatched away, and my uncle will do the job. He won't know how to make it painless, how to make it quick.

Something wild thrashes in my chest, battering my ribs. I need to move. Now.

I lurch out of my chair and rush out of the room.

"Bryony."

My slippers skid as I careen down the twisting halls. I have no idea where I'm going, just away, away, *away—*

The sanctum opens up ahead, and I stumble in, knees hitting the marble floor as my body revolts. I heave out the contents of my stomach behind the altar.

Footsteps sound at my back. Idris wrenches me up by the elbow, fingers digging in. "Done with your tantrum?"

I twist against his grip. "Don't touch me."

"You think running will change anything?"

"Let. *Go*."

"For fuck's sake."

He shoves me. I slam into the altar stone and go down hard, my skull cracking against the floor. Pain explodes behind my eyes—blinding, vicious.

"Fuck," he mutters. "Look what you made me do." His voice comes from far away as his hands slide under me. "Why can't you ever make things easy? Always fighting. Always causing problems."

He lifts me, and my head lolls against his chest as he carries me.

I must lose consciousness, because when I open my eyes again, we're in the carriage, and it's moving. My head throbs. I touch my temple, and my fingers come away red.

"Where—" My tongue feels thick. I blink away the darkness overwhelming my sight. "Are we going to the palace?"

Idris doesn't answer right away, his focus on some distant point out the window. When he finally speaks, his voice is flat. Cold. "We're going up the Duehavn."

Five little words that tighten around my throat like a noose.

The Duehavn Ridge is a crooked spine of rock and snow—a landscape pared down to its rawest elements. On the high slopes, everything is still. Quiet. The peaks glitter in the afternoon light, the low-angled sun catching on the icy crags. Nothing green softens its harsh edges. Nothing lives, nothing thrives. It's the kind of place where things end.

A fitting backdrop for what's coming.

I press my forehead to the window. Maybe if I close them, this will all melt away and reveal itself to be another resurrection nightmare dredged up from the silt of memory and trauma. Something I imagined after hitting my head on the temple floor. But the cut stopped bleeding thirty minutes ago, and I'm wide awake now.

My fingertips find the crook of my elbow, tracing the upraised lines carved into my flesh.

One notch. *Breathe.*

Two notches. *I feel the velvet seat beneath me. Hear the rattle of the wheels.*

Three. *My name is Bryony Devaliant.*

Four. *I'm on the Duehavn Ridge, and my uncle is planning to kill me.*

Five. *Real.*

Still here. Still rattling up the road to my murder.

I suck in a shaking breath. The air in the carriage feels too thick, and I want out, out, *out*—

There's a shimmer in my periphery—the Shroud catching the sunlight. It hangs above the peaks, a veil of starlight that ripples and dances like a living thing.

Colors bloom over its surface in pinks and shimmering golds, indigo and red, bleeding into each other across the snowy slopes. The mountain glitters everywhere the light touches.

"Cruel, isn't it?" I murmur. "How something so exquisite can demand such a brutal price."

Idris' lips press together in a grimace. "The gods' creations often do."

Nausea grips my stomach. I swallow it down and meet his eyes. "You're going to do it, aren't you? What the Oracle said."

"For Vartena."

Two words. As if they encompass the beginning and end of all things.

I choke back a bitter laugh. Of course he's going to do it. The Eternal's favor is worth a hundred oathbreaking princesses. A thousand. To him, I'm less than nothing, just a carcass to be dumped in some shallow grave. Another doomed woman murdered and discarded.

Murdered.

It feels important to name it. To acknowledge the truth of what's about to happen.

The rage is sudden. Incandescent. It fills my head with a roaring static, narrowing everything down to the drum of my pulse, to my spiraling thoughts. What has Vartena given me? Nothing but a life spent shackled to the altar. I think of every cut, every dagger shoved into me at the Eternal's command. And for *what*?

My fingers curl into fists. What would happen if I let all this fury explode out of me for once? If I turned on everyone, made them bleed the way they make me bleed?

I think about the Wolf in the forest clearing. Those amber eyes searing into mine, bright with a vicious sort of interest. At least he was honest about his work. At least he was quick.

Treat me like an equal.

"I can't believe I'm saying this, but I'd rather die by the Wolf's hand than yours." I stand, steadying myself against the seat, and pound against the roof. "Stop the carriage!" I shout to the driver.

"Sit down, Bryony."

"I said stop."

"And I said *sit*."

Fuck this.

The carriage slows just enough. I wrench at the door handle and jump onto the road, the sharp rocks skittering under my slippers.

Idris grabs me before I can take a step. I lash out with my fist and hit something soft. He grunts, but his grip on my arm tightens, bruising now.

"Let go!" I thrash. "Get off me, you miserable bastard—"

He slams me into the dirt, his weight pinning me down and driving the air out of my lungs until I'm gasping. He shoves his knee into my sternum.

"Get off me."

I buck, putting every scrap of my strength behind it. Clawing at everything in reach. But Idris only pushes his knee harder and wraps a hand around my throat, squeezing, cutting off my air until bright sparks swarm my vision. Until that roaring static drowns out everything else.

Movement catches my eye. The driver. He's watching us with his mouth hanging open as if he's uncertain whether to intervene.

"Get back to the carriage," Idris tells the other man without looking away from me. His thumb presses into my windpipe. "This girl is an oathbreaker."

The driver's mouth snaps shut. He looks at me again, and I see it—the moment he decides I'm not worth it. I'm nothing. He turns and walks to his seat like I'm not dying ten feet away.

Abandoning me to my fate.

"Please," I rasp to Idris. Grasping, desperate. I force the words out through my narrowing airway. "Please, just let me—"

"No." Idris' free hand moves to his coat, and he draws out his jeweled dagger. "The Eternal wants you dead, and you heard the Oracle. Better I do this myself before he sets his sights on me."

I bare my teeth. The fury inside me lunges against my ribs. "Fuck the Eternal. Fuck Vartena, and *fuck you*."

He meets my gaze. Holds it.

And then he sinks the blade into my stomach.

He plunges the weapon in again and again, grunting with effort. It happens so fast. I don't even feel it when he twists and rips the blade free one last time. Everything is so numb, so cold. I taste blood.

Through the black haze coating my vision, I see him crouched over me, silhouetted against the sun.

"I'd take you back for a pyre," he says, wiping the knife clean on his pants, "but I'd rather not incite a riot on top of everything else."

His fingers twist in the ruined tatters of my gown. With a few brutal slices, he cuts the blood-soaked fabric away. Leaving me in nothing but my cloak, naked and splayed open like an offering.

"But this will have to do for proof." He straightens and stares down at me again, clutching that bloodied dress. "I'll make it a good story, Bryony. I'll say you were brave. That you didn't beg when the Wolf came for you."

His jaw tics, and for a moment, he almost looks sorry.

Almost.

Then he climbs into the carriage and leaves me to bleed out in the dirt.

Memories flicker.

I'm an infant, receiving my first drop of Alexios' blood in the temple to form the Claim that binds me to him.

Five, when the childhood fingerpricks on the altar change to the dagger in my chest.

Sixteen, when I cut notches into my skin after an anchoring ceremony makes me feel so untethered and adrift that I lose grip on what's real.

Nineteen, watching Idris drag my father's body out of the palace woods.

Twenty, when he stumbles into my bedchamber, reeking of wine. "Odessa fell. We'll tell them it was an accident. Off the Celestine Tower."

Twenty-one, the last time I die.

I'm ageless as I sink into my memories. They layer over each other: every knife's sting, every death, every resurrection. Every time I counted my five notches and understood this was all real. An eternity compressed behind my eyes, played out again and again and *again*.

Not the death I bargained for. But then, I suppose that was another lie I told myself. A sacrifice, bartering for dignity like a starving dog groveling for table scraps. Begging for the right to choose, even if the only choice was in how I met the knife.

We're all just walking corpses in different stages of decay, the Wolf had said. *The only difference is how much of the world we take with us when we finally lie down.*

Everything hurts, and at the same time, nothing does. Ice and fire, a strange, floating numbness spreading through me as my surroundings go soft and gray at the edges.

There are worse ends, maybe. Crueler ones.

But as the Void reaches up to claim me, I think this is a particular kind of cruelty, too.

To be left to the dark and the cold. Alone and unmourned.

Already forgotten.

10

EVANDER

I LAND ON a narrow ledge along the Duehavn Ridge, kicking up flurries of snow.

Alexios doesn't turn at my approach. His red and black wings flare wide against the night sky as he places a boot on the object at his feet—a body. Well, more a broken pile of limbs and torn feathers. Guess someone pissed him off.

That's about to make two of us.

"Been entertaining yourself, I see," I say.

The leather jerkin he wears is worn at the edges—something he trains in, not his usual formal attire. It leaves his arms bare and his tattoos on full display. I recognize the celestial constellations inked onto his biceps, but the script flowing up his forearms is a language that's been dead longer than I've been alive.

The shimmering veil of the Shroud stretches before us. The colors ripple and churn, ribbons of emerald and amethyst threading through fading starlight. But all I notice are the holes. The places where the Vartenan landscape across the divide is visible when it shouldn't be.

"You didn't deal with the princess," Alexios says.

I suppose kings and killers don't need to waste their breath on pleasantries.

Just like that, I'm in the Devaliant's bedchamber, with her thighs bracketing my hips and her body arched against mine as she raged. There was no artifice in it. Just the purity of all that pain and anger unleashed, as if she'd wanted to swallow my heart whole.

You're untouchable in a way I'll never be. Powerful. Immortal. And you squander *it all on meaningless shit like this. It's pathetic.*

What the fuck does she know about the prices I've paid? She's only a doomed sacrifice paying the well-deserved penance for her family's brutality. So why do I still feel her weight on me? The heat of her skin?

Why am I so eager to go back and see how all that hatred and rage looks when she comes on my cock?

"You promised me an oathbreaker," I say, dragging my attention back to the god-king. "I didn't find one."

Alexios pivots to face me, his red eyes glowing as his power lashes out and slams into me so hard that it rattles my teeth. "She never bled on the altar. I didn't feel her blood hit the collection channels."

"The Accords never stated an offering had to be given on the altar. She tithed on the temple grounds. Ergo, not an oathbreaker. Ergo, no bloody smear on my pretty knife. Your Anchor found the loophole to your loophole. You should appreciate the irony."

I'm baiting him when he's already primed for violence. But this delicate push-pull is a path we've walked many times over the centuries, and fuck if I don't get a thrill every time I remind him that his leash isn't as tight as he thinks.

Those tattoos of his flare red. "Did you honestly believe that pathetic excuse would hold? Even if she's not an oathbreaker, she's Unclaimed. Nothing stops you from opening her throat."

I tilt my head, considering. "That needs a second order, then, doesn't it?"

The air changes. Electricity crawls across his skin, blue-white sparks jumping between his fingertips. Thunder rumbles in the distance. "I would tread very, very carefully, Wolf. If you disobeyed me to be contrary, it's pointless now." He reaches for a scrap of fabric on the ground and flings it at me. "This was left on Hellevig's temple altar, and I felt my Claim fade. Bryony Devaliant is dead."

I rub the bloody muslin between my fingers. The scent hits me instantly—jasmine, lilac, wisteria. *Her.* Some strange, nameless emotion stirs behind my ribs. "Who carved her up? Her uncle? Sister? Some noble licking your boots?"

"Does it matter? Killing her lanced the infection before it could spread."

I don't know why I should care. She'd leaned into my knife and dared to judge *me*. She was an arrogant mortal who believed she could dictate terms to a god.

But I made her a promise, and I've never broken my word.

I wonder if she thought of me in those final moments—of the death she'd bargained for and the god who failed to deliver.

It shouldn't cut so deep. I've sent countless people to their deaths. Pretty faces, pretty girls, all of them blurring together. She was a Devaliant, and that made her more worthy of a brutal death than anyone else.

It shouldn't matter. It *doesn't* matter. I just don't like leaving debts unpaid. I'd abandoned her to be hacked apart by vermin who didn't give her the execution she earned after cutting me open. Her dying breaths belonged to *me*.

"Anything else?" I keep my voice controlled, bored. As if I don't care if he gives me another order or tells me to get fucked. "More throats to cut? Bodies to bury?"

"Find what's left of the princess." He says it like he's asking me to fetch his boots. "My Claim snapped when she died, but traces of my magic will cling to her. The worthless idiot who gutted her was too much of a coward to bring me the body." The tattoos on his arms pulse again, and more lightning crackles between his fingers. "I want a public pyre for the Devaliant bitch. Everyone in Hellevig needs to see her burn and understand that not even Anchors are spared my wrath."

Something twists in my chest, sharp and unwelcome, as I picture it. Her corpse. Violet eyes now dull and empty, the heart that beat so fiercely against mine entirely still. All that vibrant emotion snuffed out on a king's orders.

I blink, keeping my expression neutral. "Now?"

"After." He gestures to the crumpled demi on the ground. "Watch me finish playing with this one."

A runed collar winks at the hollow of the captive's throat, the glyphs flaring as they siphon away his strength. My brother, Bastien, etched the shackles with magic to keep prisoners immobilized while Alexios plays.

I let out a whistle. "Must be quite the prisoner to get the royal treatment. What'd he do? Piss in your wine?"

"He's a traitor. One old enough to remember the war"—he aims a brutal kick at the male's side, earning a wet gasp—"and stupid enough to want to resurrect it. A scouting party found Turpori steel on him during the arrest."

My head snaps up. "Where did he get it?"

Bastien's blades are infused with his unique power signature. They were his gift and legacy to our realm—before humans learned that consuming our flesh would transfer our power temporarily. That our bodies were another resource to be exploited, carved up, and devoured. Now, the godkillers are permitted to be carried only by a few, but there's a bustling black market for them. Every time some fleshbuyer gets their hands on Bastien's feathers, they can use his magic to make Turpori steel. We keep having to track them down.

"I couldn't torture an answer out of him," he says. "Someone scrubbed the memories. But never forget how many of our own were complicit in the slaughter."

He reaches down and wrenches the demigod up by his hair. "Maybe you've forgotten the screams of our dead. Or maybe you're pissed off that the Eternals of Asteria and Nyholm are all that's left. Is that it? Loyalty to a murdered Eternal?"

The demigod stirs with a rattling cough and gathers the remaining dregs of his defiance to spit a glob of bloodied saliva onto Alexios' boots.

For a long moment, Alexios and I stare at each other, and I see my own grief reflected in his gaze. My own need to repay humanity's sins. A part of me regrets him ever signing the Accords that prevented me from slaughtering every last one of them.

I think he knows that. I think he feels it, too. Understands precisely how deep this poison runs. This ugly, symbiotic rot that we'll never get rid of.

"Just... kill me..." the captive says between choking gasps. "I welcome it..."

"Oh, I will," Alexios says. "But first, I'm going to tear you apart until you're a drooling, shitting husk." His fingers squeeze around the demi's throat. "Maybe I should have the Wolf put you back together so you're lucid when I carve out your insides and feed them to you."

I watch, saying nothing, as Alexios' power burrows inside the prisoner's chest and *wrenches*. The male makes a noise somewhere between a scream and a whimper as something in him gives with an audible snap.

The king winds his magic deeper. Wet pops fill the air as organs rupture. Blood gushes from the demigod's gaping mouth, splattering Alexios' hands and face.

He doesn't so much as flinch.

"What do you think, Wolf?" Alexios' voice is light. Conversational. "Want to dust off that healing ability? Should I start with feeding him his intestines or save that particular delight for the finale?"

"Depends. How long are you planning to stretch this out? I have a nice wine waiting for me at home."

"Hmm, valid point." He drops the body to the ground with a thud. "I'm leaving his corpse here," Alexios says, wiping flecks of blood from his cheek with the back of his hand. "Let it be a reminder to anyone who foolishly mistakes my restraint for weakness."

"You know for sure there are others?"

His smile is bleak. "There are *always* others willing to ally with the filth who cracked open our brothers and sisters and ate them raw, no matter how many carcasses I leave in my wake. That's why we can't ever show mercy."

My mouth twists in a grim smile. "I know."

"Yes, you do," Alexios murmurs, and for a moment, it almost sounds like understanding. Like kinship.

Maybe that's why he kept Bastien and me around. Saw the empty space where most people keep a conscience and figured he'd found the perfect killers, loyal not because we love him but because he's the only one who can give our grief *purpose*.

After all, Alexios knows intimately what it's like to watch your whole world burn.

He steps over the demi's body and plucks the muslin from my hands. "Final offering from the princess. Let's put it to good use, shall we?"

The Shroud pulses. The colors have leached away, leaving only faded hues that are shot through with veins of necrotic black. Beyond the fraying weave, Vartena peeks through, the mortal realm little more than a heat haze.

I smell the stagnation and slow rot.

"This damage. Was it from—"

"From the Devaliant's cult members?" Alexios' lip peels back from his teeth. "Yes."

He extends a hand and crooks his fingers, and the blood seems to sing in answer. It lifts from the fabric in ribbons, curling through the air as it pools above his upturned palm. The droplets dance, strung together by threads of power.

With a percussive snap of magic, Alexios flings his arm out in a sweeping arc. The blood streaks toward the Shroud in a glimmering spray. The veil ripples where it strikes, crimson tearing through the rot. Devouring. Cleansing. Slowly, new wards flicker to life in glittering veins of ruby and obsidian.

It's a temporary measure—a scab over a festering wound. But it buys us time.

Alexios' magic fades. He sways on his feet, a tremor running through him. Even an Eternal has limits.

"You're burning too hot," I murmur. "You need rest. If you keep pouring yourself into the Shroud at this rate—"

He gives a mirthless laugh. "I *need* a bottle of Black Ember and a good hard fuck, not necessarily in that order. But this barrier isn't going to maintain itself."

He turns to me, the dying light throwing the harsh planes of his face into stark relief. Deep bruises smudge the skin beneath his eyes, and I'm struck by how exhausted he looks. Less the untouchable god-king and more the battle-weary soldier.

"I'm at the end of my patience with mortals." His words are flat, emotionless, and that's when he's at his most unpredictable. His most dangerous. "The Vartenans are complacent, and I can't keep spreading tithes thin over the Shroud whenever some little princess distracts the idiots on the other side. If those sheep can't manage themselves, and the Accords prevent me from interfering in their rule, then they need reminders of their place."

"You want me to make an example of the oathbreakers?"

"Brutality is an art in times like these. No more half measures, no more clean kills for traitors and oathbreakers. When the masses grow lazy, it's our duty to deliver a lesson."

I incline my head. "Any other orders?"

Alexios goes motionless in the way of a predator poised to lunge. Slowly, deliberately, he leans in until his lips hover above mine and I can taste the spice of his breath.

"One more thing," he says, lethally soft. "Don't think I've forgotten or forgiven you for ignoring a direct command."

I lift my stare to meet his. "Disobedience is part of my charm."

"You're right," he murmurs. "Insolence is one of your more attractive qualities. I've always enjoyed how this mouth gets you into trouble."

Alexios pushes his lips against mine, kissing me deep and filthy. There's no tenderness in it. No real affection or desire. With the God of Storms, everything is about control. About the dizzying, destructive push-pull of power—who wields it and who bends to its whims. He's not kissing me because he wants to.

He's kissing me because he likes to fuck with my head.

Alexios breaks the kiss to run his lips over my jaw. "But I can't help but wonder..." His tongue laves along my neck before his teeth clamp down punishingly hard. I swallow a hiss. "If you didn't kill the princess as I ordered, what exactly *did* you do?"

"Played with her. Let her get a taste of my blade."

"Mm. What was she wearing? Paint me a picture."

Unbidden, the memory of the princess surges to the surface. Perched astride my hips in nothing but that bloodstained nightgown. Luminous skin and tousled hair and eyes bright with murderous intent. For a few minutes, I let myself forget all the reasons I should hate her.

"White silk," I rasp out. "Hardly covered all the interesting bits. It looked even better soaked through red."

He growls, a burst of breath shuddering against me, and his hands dig into my shoulders, demanding. Asserting his claim even as he makes me recount how I defied him. Still fucking with me.

"Tell me about your game." He grazes his teeth down my neck, ending the movement in a kiss. "What did you play?"

I know what he's doing; he's reminding me that I let a Devaliant walk away. That I had my knife against her heart and chose entertainment over duty. He's playing with me the way I played with her.

But I'm not a pretty little Anchor on your altar.

"A game where she cuts me open," I say roughly. I tip my head back, baring more of my throat to his mouth. A silent *fuck you*. "And I take her measure. Decide if she's amusing enough to keep around for another night before finishing the job."

"Was she?" he asks, kissing along my collarbone. "Amusing?"

"Vicious. Spitting mad. The kind of girl who goes straight for the throat and shakes until something snaps. Prettiest damn thing I've seen in centuries."

Intended to provoke. To irritate.

His lips skim the shell of my ear. "Did you beg her to hurt you a little deeper?"

And a little harder.

"I enjoy seeing how violence brings out the beast in sweet things. I decided she deserved an encore performance before her final bow."

For a few moments, cradled between my body and the blade, the princess had burned *incandescent*. She'd wanted to make someone—anyone—choke on her agony. A girl like that, with a mouth made for sin and a heart like a black hole…

I'd wanted to see how far she went until she broke.

Alexios chuckles and presses his lips hard to mine again, whispering, "I hope your little indulgence was worth it."

Then his power lashes and clamps tightly around my throat. Crushing. Choking. Dark spots swarm my vision, my lungs burn, and my senses dull until the roaring tide of my pulse drowns out all else.

"I warned you that if you disappointed me again, I'd remind you what happens when my leash becomes a noose." He skims his thumb over my cheekbone. "Disobedient subordinates get put down. And liars? *Liars* get their tongues ripped out."

His grip tightens as he forces my head back. His other hand digs between my lips and pries my jaw wide. Then he pins my tongue between his fingers.

And draws his dagger.

I feel the sharp edge of the Turpori steel, the blooming sting as he cuts off my tongue. I taste metal and blood as it gushes over my chin. The pain is distant, drowned out by the thunder of my heartbeat and the throbbing pressure of the king's power.

He shoves my severed tongue down my throat and slaps his palm over my mouth.

"Swallow it," he hisses against my cheek.

Fuck you.

I glare up at him even as black spots crowd my vision, my bones creaking beneath the crush of his will.

"*Swallow. It.*"

Alexios' collar keeps my strength leashed to half what it is naturally—without it, we'd be equals. One day, I'll sever it. And when I do, it's not bones I'll settle for breaking. It's the base of his fucking spine.

But today isn't that day.

So I swallow.

Alexios releases me, and I crumple to my knees.

"By the time that tongue grows back," he says coldly, "I hope you'll learn to use it more wisely. I'd hate to take your wings next."

11

BRYONY

"You're alive." A woman's voice cuts through the static. Gentle but firm. "Just breathe through it."

I try to focus on her, but everything feels distant and hazy as if I'm deep underwater. My body hurts. The sort of pain that makes you wish for death—except I *was* dead. Wasn't I?

My fingers move on instinct, shoving past the cloak to trace the scars on my inner elbow. Each one is a tether pulling me back from the brink.

I feel for the first notch. *Breathe. You're breathing.*

Two notches. *Feel the jagged rock beneath you, the bite of the cold.*

Three. *Your name is Bryony Devaliant.*

Four. *You're on the Duehavn Ridge, where your uncle tried to kill you.*

Five. *This is real. You survived when you shouldn't have.*

I crack my eyes open. Blurry wings fill my vision, charcoal dark feathers with violet undertones that shimmer in the light. A demigoddess stares down at me with pale irises that are almost colorless save for the darker flecks of blue. She's slender and fine-boned, with a heart-shaped face and shoulder-length lavender-colored hair. Her lips press into a line as she looks me over.

"I spotted you when I was flying over the Osbu Sea." She lightly taps my stomach, where bandages peek out from under the cloak. "Good thing I know some field medicine because you were dead for about half a minute there."

"Thank you," I say hoarsely.

"Don't thank me yet. You're still pretty fucked up." She tugs my cloak tighter around my nakedness. She's brusque but gentle with me, the way you get when you're used to handling broken things. "I noticed an oathbreaker's mark on your wrist before the Void took you. This an Enforcer's work? They usually go for cleaner kills."

My heart stops when I see my bare wrist. Alexios' Claim is gone, with no sign of his judgment. It's the first time I've ever seen my skin there without the glow of his symbol. I'm Unclaimed now, defenseless—anyone's for the taking.

"It was my uncle," I manage. "Emperor Idris. An offering to the Eternal."

She snorts. "Never seen a precious Royal of the Blood marked for death." Rising, she stretches those massive wings. "We need to get you somewhere warm before shock sets in. Can you stand?"

The world slips and slides, refusing to stay put. My vision won't settle. "No."

With an exasperated sigh, she unbuckles her belt and loops it around my cloak, cinching the fabric tight over the bandages. "There. That ought to keep you decent for the trip. One of my wings is weaker than the other, so it won't be a smooth ride carrying you. If you throw up on me, I'm dropping you into the sea. Are we clear?"

I give a feeble nod, lacking the energy to say anything else.

She leans down and gathers me into her arms, and then we're airborne. The ground falls away with dizzying speed. My stomach lurches as she banks hard left to avoid a jagged outcropping. I feel the strain in her shoulders, the flex and bunch of muscles working to hold us aloft.

I make the mistake of glancing down and immediately slam my eyes shut again. Blackness drags me down and pulls me under.

This time, I let it sweep me into the dark.

"Hey. Wake up. We're here."

I open my heavy eyelids to find the demigoddess looking me over, her pale purple hair dancing along her cheek. Past her is an arch of trees. A hot breeze rustles the leaves, thick and humid, prickling my skin with an unfamiliar energy.

"Where?" I manage.

"Somewhere I figured could handle the mess you're in."

I turn my head and blink to clear my vision. There's nothing but a misty forest extending in all directions, not a trace of civilization in sight—until a dark shape emerges from the fog.

At first, it looks like a lone spire knifing up from the ground. But then the haze shifts to reveal towers—*plural*—in a sprawling mass of black stone. Some are thin and tall, and others are shorter and wider, linked by arched bridges and winding paths to one primary edifice that stands the tallest.

And roses. Thousands and *thousands* of red climbing roses with branch-thick stems that twist carelessly around everything, as if the owner couldn't be bothered to prune or tame them. No part of the building is spared from the foliage—even the front walkway is framed in briars bristling with glowing scarlet roses and thorns as long as fingers. They crawl up the walls, tangling together until the masonry disappears beneath them in places. They look less like they're climbing and more like they're *strangling*.

Dread turns my muscles to water as I catalog it all: the unnatural glow of the flowers, the structure of that building, the luminous quality of the plants, the heavy pressure in the air that I now recognize as magic.

I'm in Scillari. She took me through the Shroud.

Oh, gods.

Fear washes over me. Pain shunted aside in favor of something worse—blind panic. My thoughts narrow to a single, pulsing imperative: *I have to get out.*

"Fly me back." I claw at her shoulders, ignoring the agony ripping through me. "I don't care where you leave me, just—"

She sets me on my feet with a huff of irritation. "Sure thing, Princess. I'll take you right back. And when you bleed out somewhere over the Azureian Sea, I'll give your corpse a proper send-off. Maybe a touching eulogy about your great decision-making skills."

Hysteria claws up my throat. "It's *illegal* for me to be here—"

"I'm aware. And blood loss is making you hysterical, so I'll keep this simple. You're going to drag your ass over to that door, and when the asshole on the other side answers, tell him Amara sent you. Think you can handle that?"

"But the Accords—"

"Won't mean anything if you're dead." She nudges me forward and then, with a snap of her wings, launches into the air. "Door. Knock. Amara sent you," she calls over her shoulder. "Good luck."

I watch, frozen, as she fucks off and leaves me there. Just like that, I'm alone, and my thoughts are shouting.

I need to run as far as I can. Maybe I'll get lucky, and it'll end fast when my body gives out.

But some stubborn part of me that's kept going through all those deaths on the altar whispers: Not yet. Just a little longer. I've died too many times to give up now. Theodora needs to know I'm alive.

I limp through the trees to the tower, gritting my teeth against the pain stabbing into me with each step. *Keep moving. One foot in front of the other.* The briar claws at me as I push through it to the front door. There's a huge knocker shaped like a wolf's head with its jaws open in a snarl.

My hand trembles as I reach for it. Glowing sigils flare in shifting patterns across the wood, and the door swings inward. Beneath the pervasive thrum of magic, spice and incense tickle my nose.

I lurch over the threshold. The light stabs my eyes as the atrium swims into focus. There are roses everywhere in here, too. Crawling up the walls, around the pillars, and looping up the staircase. The wildness contrasts with the ostentatious architecture. Tall, arched windows frame the entire hall, at least twenty feet high, curving up to a vaulted ceiling covered in black and gold filigree.

Plush couches are shoved together haphazardly alongside dark wood tables filled with books and candles. Despite its grand decor, the space has a cozy, lived-in feel. There are odd little statues poking out from the chaos, objects used to track the stars, and random nicknacks I couldn't even begin to guess the purpose of.

There's no mistaking the message it all screams: someone important lives here. Someone with power and money and way too much of both.

That's when I hear it. A voice, slicing through the hush like a weapon unsheathing.

"Now *this* is interesting."

Oh no. Oh no, no, no.

I know that voice. Smoky and resonant, a lovely accent curling around those syllables.

I squeeze my eyes shut, willing the universe to fold in on itself. To swallow me down and remake itself into a shape where this isn't happening, where I'm not—

"Alexios told me you were dead, Devaliant."

This is a nightmare, right? I'm about to wake up any moment. *Right?*

"Yet here you stand," he continues, closer now. "Mostly intact, though you look like a stiff breeze could do you in."

I finally gather the courage to open my eyes and turn.

The Wolf lounges against a pillar a few feet away. His head tilts as he studies me, golden eyes gleaming and a smirk of amusement on his lips like he's trying not to laugh at me. His gold feathers catch in the light falling through the glass dome overhead. The bastard is perfectly at ease, as if he's been waiting for me to stumble in and ruin his day.

Damn my life. Of course this is where I'd end up, injured and barely conscious. Trapped in the home of the most lethal, depraved creature I've ever had the misfortune to meet.

"Amara knew." My voice comes out flat as I grit my teeth through a new flare of pain. "She knew exactly who she was dumping me with, didn't she?"

The Wolf chuckles. "*Amara* brought you here? Oh, she knew. I guess she decided she'd send me a gift. Wasn't that thoughtful of her?" He pushes off the pillar. "So. Who was it?"

I blink, struggling to concentrate past the spots dancing in my vision. "Who... what?"

The Wolf steps closer, closer, until only an inch remains between us. His smell invades my senses—rain, smoke, a hint of citrus. A lure that urges me to approach and let down my guard even as rational instinct shouts at me to flee.

His eyes flick to my throat, catching on my scar and what I'm sure is an impressive ring of bruises Idris left on my neck. "We'll come back to that scar," he says, "and whoever got close enough to give it to you. But first, let's focus on the piece of shit who bloodied you and took your clothes to the temple. I want a name."

His expression makes me go very, very still. The amusement is gone, replaced by a cold and merciless stare. I picture myself throwing Uncle to this monster and letting him do his worst.

But no. Idris is mine. At least, he will be if I can get out of this.

"It's my score to settle," I say, forcing my voice to stay steady. "Are you about to kill me?"

If I'm going to die, I'll do it on my feet.

"You and I talked about this before," the Wolf says with a smirk, "but I made you forget. Want it back?"

His power slams into me. A deluge of images sears through my mind, fractured sense-memories tumbling over each other: his skin under my hands, slick with blood. The copper taste of his lip between my teeth. His voice at my ear, telling me to hurt him harder.

Make me bleed for you, vicious girl.

"Oh."

"Yeah," the Wolf drawls with a smile. "*Oh.*"

Heat stains my cheeks. But before I can tuck my shame out of sight, his hands land on my hips and keep me pinned, preventing retreat. He's back to watching me with the interest of a predator toying with his prey.

My heart stumbles in my chest. "Wolf—"

"Wolf, what? Let me guess, 'Wolf, please spare me'? 'Wolf, please have mercy'?" He leans closer, whispering, "Or maybe 'Wolf, please let's do it again'?"

"Wolf, go… fuck yourself," I gasp, catching myself before I sway.

He grins. "Every night, sometimes twice if I'm ambitious." His hold tightens a fraction. "Here's the thing, Devaliant. Your family and I don't have a glowing history, and Alexios wants me to deliver your corpse. He was *very specific* about the corpse part. But I'm thinking…" His eyes rake over me. Slow. Deliberate. "I'll take my time with you. Really plan it out. I want to enjoy every second before I watch those pretty eyes go dark."

Sick bastard. My fingers curl into fists as I fight to keep standing. I can't believe I survived getting stabbed by my uncle only to end up here.

"Then can I rest while you… plan?" The room won't stop spinning.

Something in his expression shifts. Sharpens. I brace myself for the blazing onslaught of his power.

Instead, he exhales on a controlled breath. "Down the corridor on your right, there's a bedchamber beneath the tapestry of a white hart. Get some rest. Don't touch my shit. I'll decide what to do with you later."

I nod, my throat tight.

Without responding, he releases my hips, wings tucked close to his back as he walks away.

"Why did you want a name?" I call after him. "The one who hurt me."

The Wolf pauses. "Because I accepted your execution terms. I get to choose how you die. No one else."

Then he's gone, stalking down the hall in a streak of gold feathers.

12

EVANDER

AMARA IS LATE, and I'm left with nothing to do but pace my garden and stew in my own restlessness.

I've never been a patient male. Waiting is an unlatched window inviting memories to come slinking out of the dark. And doesn't that sum up the entirety of my existence these days? A former Prince of Turpori and future god-king of Scillari demoted to a wolf for the Eternal of Asteria. Waiting for orders. For *permission*. Like a dog.

Sit. Stay. Heel.

Unruly subordinates get put down. And liars? Liars *get their tongues ripped out.*

And now I have the girl Alexios wants killed in my possession. The irony would be hilarious if it weren't so damning. When I saw Bryony Devaliant standing there in my foyer, my initial instinct wasn't to rip her throat out. It wasn't even rage.

It was relief. I do not feel *relief* over one inconsequential mortal not being dead. A hunter doesn't hesitate when wounded prey is delivered to its den. It lunges. It devours. So why haven't I?

You're going soft, a voice that sounds suspiciously like my brother's whispers. *Have you forgotten what the Devaliants did to us?*

I haven't forgotten. I never will. So why is it that when I looked down into the Devaliant's face, I didn't think, *I'm going to break her.*

No, it was a traitorous whisper. Insidious.

I want to taste her again.

The east wing windows have been dark since she went in. I can't help but picture her in my guest bedroom, touching my things. Lying down on my bed, all that silver hair stark against my black sheets. I'd smelled blood all over her cloak earlier. Some pathetic, disgusting part of me keeps thinking I should go in there and check on her.

I tell myself it's because I don't enjoy playing with broken toys. It's not actual concern. I tell myself that her getting my dick hard is just a normal response to being near attractive, forbidden human pussy. I haven't fucked a mortal in six centuries. It's practically a novelty again.

Honestly, I tell myself a lot of things.

"I can hear you growling from here." Amara's voice cuts through my spiraling thoughts. "So either you're choking on a live rodent, or I've stumbled on one of your brooding sessions."

I turn as she drops out of the sky, wings spread wide. Moonlight catches on the violet sheen of her feathers as she lands on the garden path. Her eyes are more purple than blue in the darkness.

"You're late."

"Wow." She flicks a feather from her shoulder. "Not even a 'thank fuck you're alive' or 'so glad you didn't die on the way here'?"

I stalk over to her. "I'm so glad you didn't die on the way here because then I wouldn't get to do the honors myself for the *shit* you just pulled."

"So you got my gift," she says with a slow grin.

For a moment, I can only stare at her. The sheer audacity…

"*Gift* implies some consent from the recipient. What *you* did was risk setting off every ward in the Shroud to dump a half-dead human on my doorstep like a cat dropping a mangled bird at its master's feet, then fly off into the sunset." My hands curl into fists at my sides. "Do you have any idea what happens if Alexios finds her here? I'm supposed to be delivering her for a public pyre, not hosting her for tea. I had my tongue ripped out this morning over that girl." I lean in closer. "Next time, he'll probably make me choke on my own dick."

"That's pretty dramatic if you ask me."

"I didn't." I rake a hand through my hair. "How did you even get her into Scillari without the Border Watch finding out?"

"Please. I may not be an *Eternal*, but I know my way around Alexios' security measures. They're easy to avoid if one knows where to look. I'd be happy to pass on a few pointers to the Watch, assuming you don't murder the captain for incompetence first."

I don't bother mentioning that I've already made mental notes to hunt down every bastard stationed at a Shroud checkpoint and nail their balls to the palace wall as a teaching aid. That particular fantasy has been keeping me warm for the past few hours.

We're all works in progress.

"Why did you risk it?" I demand. "You could've signaled me to meet you at the border if you wanted an execution."

She glances at my tower and shrugs. "I thought you deserved the chance to take what you're owed in private."

She understands exactly what kind of festering hurts she's prodding at here. Revenge and I have a long history. Like a trusty knife, it's dulled but still hungry for blood. I just need an excuse to let it loose, and thanks to Amara, I've got a living, breathing symbol of every hurt and loss trussed up like a sacrifice in my home.

What a gift. What a neat, tidy box to cram all my hate into. How *thoughtful*.

"She came to me smelling like blood. How bad off is she?" I'm proud of how controlled I sound.

Amara hesitates, studying my face. "I counted four stab wounds. She died on the ridge before I got her heart beating again. She wasn't going to last much longer where I found her on the Duehavn."

Something twists sharply in my gut. I ignore it. Push it down deep where all the other inconvenient feelings go to die.

If she passed into the Void on that ridge, it would have broken the magic tying her to Alexios and the Shroud. He won't be able to sense she's still alive. Thank fuck for that, at least. I wouldn't want to test how many body parts I can regenerate in one go.

"But you managed to stabilize her?" I say, dragging my focus back to Amara. "She was upright and talking when I saw her."

"I patched her up. The divine blood polluting the Devaliant line probably did the rest."

As if I could forget what flows in that girl's veins. As if the reminder of her heritage isn't a deliberate twist of the knife.

The thing in my stomach wrenches tighter. Uglier. I bury it under old hatred. Tried and true. So much safer than the alternative and infinitely more satisfying.

"Devaliants have a talent for lingering longer than they should," I say. "I need you to bring me something for her to wear. I can't have my usual servants at the tower while I've got her here, and she needs clothes."

She blinks. "Wait. You're going to *heal* her? I brought her to *kill*. Not to adopt as a pet."

Oh, I'll heal her. But not out of kindness. I want another chance to make Bryony Devaliant hurt the way I hurt. One more opportunity to break someone from that family into pieces. Immortality, combined with the horror of war, tends to breed a particular type of unhinged madness.

I still want to see her hatred when I bite into her.

"I can't kill her when she's likely lying in a mangled heap in my guest room. It's unsporting."

"That," Amara says slowly, "sounded dangerously close to an actual feeling."

"Don't be ridiculous. I'm going to stitch her up, watch her squirm and snap at me, and then I'll make her wish I'd killed her quickly. I've never had a Devaliant for a toy."

It doesn't matter that she woke something up when I touched her. It'll pass.

Amara looks like she wants to argue. Like she can see right through my flimsy justifications.

Then she's stepping back, wings flaring. "Fine, whatever." She rolls her eyes. "I'll bring her a dress. I hope you know what you're doing."

13

BRYONY

THE DOOR OF the Wolf's chamber thuds shut behind me. The room is lavishly appointed, with leather chairs and polished dark wood furniture, complete with bookshelves nearly reaching the vaulted ceiling. A killer's lair dressed up as a gentleman's sanctuary. At the far end is a four-poster bed with black silk sheets—the perfect place to lie down and die.

But I only manage three steps before my legs give out.

I crumple to the floor and curl onto my side, pulling my knees up to my chest to protect the vulnerable softness of my center. Darkness bleeds into my periphery. Breathing is excruciating.

I anchor myself in my old ritual—the raised scars I carved into my flesh, my fingertips mapping each ridge.

One jagged line. *Breathe. Remember how your lungs expand and contract, how air flows in and out.*

Two furrows. *Feel. The carpet beneath your cheek, the chill of the floor.*

Three gashes. *Name. Bryony. No one can take it from you.*

Four grooves. *Present. You're in Scillari.*

Five scars. *Agony means this is real.*

I don't know how long I lie there, counting scars and heartbeats. Hours, I think. Eventually, I register the soft snick of the door opening. Careful footfalls stalk closer.

The Wolf has returned to toy with his prey.

The footsteps halt. I sense his stare on me, as crushing and inexorable as his power. Shame scalds through me at the thought of how I must appear—curled up in a pathetic little ball, baring my teeth in a silent snarl even as furious tears burn my eyes.

I brace myself for brutality. For the bruising grip of his hands. For the bite of a blade against my throat, finishing what my uncle started.

It doesn't come.

Instead, strong arms slip under me, scooping my limp body up and cradling me against a broad chest. His scent envelops me—citrus and evergreen.

"You should have told me how injured you were," the Wolf says as he sets me on his bed.

I lick my cracked lips and rasp, "Find... another toy. This one's broken."

"*Devaliant*. Look at me."

I drag my stare up to meet his. The hall light gilds his face and illuminates those amber eyes. Once, I thought the stories of his beauty were exaggerated. The reality is so much worse.

"Listen very carefully," the Wolf says. "Can you do that for a minute?"

I nod.

"Good." Warm fingers graze my cheek, and I can't help but flinch. He gentles his touch but doesn't pull away, the pad of his thumb skating over my cheekbone in an absent caress. "You've got two options. Option one: I use my power to knit you together, and we resume negotiating your death. Option two: I pour myself a drink and watch your demise in a disappointing conclusion. Take a guess which I'd prefer."

Is he seriously asking me if I'd rather slowly bleed out here or let him murder me in the future? Those are my choices?

"*Bastard*," I hiss.

Genuine laughter rumbles through him. "That was lacking in creativity or sting. The woman who called me *pathetic* can do better. What do you say? Am I healing you or letting you die?"

It's so easy, isn't it? To give in and live on whatever borrowed time he deigns to give me. But, on second thought, it would serve him right to be robbed of his shiny new plaything mere hours after acquiring it. I'm spiteful enough to deprive him of the joy of shattering me at his leisure.

"What if I want it to end?" I ask him.

Fury darkens his features. "You're telling me that's it? The Devaliant who had the spine to bargain with me for an ending on her terms is just going to quit?" He scoffs, disgusted. "Fuck me, that's pitiful."

I flinch as if he's slapped me. Somehow, disappointing a god is worse than angering him.

But he's not done. "So, is that your final answer? Please let me know if I should *squander* my time on shit like this or if you still want me to choke on your wrath."

My own words flung at me as a challenge. I cut him open and demanded an end worthy of my rage, and now he wants the rest—the whole feast.

I could ask for other things. The chance to deal with Idris personally, for an opportunity to say goodbye to Theo. Things he might be willing to grant if I make it worth his while.

So I set my jaw. "Get on with it, then."

Satisfaction flares. "There you are. I knew you wouldn't bore me." He reaches out and hooks a finger under my chin to tip my face up to his. "You're the very best sort of nemesis. The kind with teeth."

His hand drops to Amara's belt at my waist. One sharp tug and the fabric parts, leaving me bare and exposed. Panic claws up my throat. I've never been naked in front of a man.

My hands lift to cover my breasts, but he bats them away with an impatient noise.

"Don't," he warns. "I have to assess the damage."

My eyes slam shut. That's almost worse, the not seeing. It amplifies everything—the hum through my body, the drag of his stare over every hurt and scar and flaw.

He carefully removes Amara's bandages. With his other hand, his fingertips graze the puckered slash across my neck. I feel the weight of the Wolf's gaze as it moves lower, taking in the stab wounds next—the chronicle of what I've endured. Of men and kings who sought to pour me into the narrow confines of *sacred Anchor* and *oathbreaker* and *sacrifice*, as if the whole of me could ever fit inside those tidy boxes.

"*Devla svaust*," he mutters. "Even a butcher knows the value of a sharp knife and a steady hand. Only a hack takes dull steel to his work and abandons a pretty woman to bleed out on a mountain."

His touch is gentle as he probes the gash on my ribs. I have to force down a pained moan at the fresh burst of agony.

"Red roses," I gasp out.

He gives me a questioning look. "What?"

"When we're... finished. The flowers in your atrium remind me of funeral roses... back home. Put them on my pyre. So you'll remember me."

His slow, devastating smile steals my breath.

Then he ruins it by opening his mouth.

"Don't worry, Devaliant. When I end you, it will be a reckoning to echo through eternity. I'll carve a monument to our mutual ruination from your bones and build you an altar worthy of the ages."

He is an absolute *lunatic*.

I'm struck by the sudden, visceral certainty that this creature could swallow me whole. That he *wants* to. That when he's wrung all the entertainment value he can from me, he'll sink his teeth in and devour me.

"Anyone ever tell you that you're deranged?" I ask.

"Endlessly. I'd be concerned if they didn't."

The Wolf splays his hands over my abdomen, his touch intimate. Strangely reverent. There's an unnatural heat to his skin, his power a current humming between us, suddenly sinking hooks into me like *claws*.

I suck in a sharp, pained hiss.

He gentles, power easing until it's barely there. "I know it hurts. But I need contact with your body to set you to rights. As it stands, this will take multiple sessions. It won't be pleasant, so hold your breath and think of something else. Can you manage that for me?"

I squeeze my eyes shut as I fight for composure. Then I nod curtly.

"Brave girl," he says, so softly I almost don't catch it.

His power unfurls again. It laps at the ragged edges of the deepest wound, building and building until my nerve endings sing, and then it plunges in, in, *in*, coaxing torn flesh to knit, stitching perforated organs and severed vessels. Heat suffuses my veins as the pain ebbs. I sigh as the burn of agony eases, and the warmth of his power turns strangely comforting.

His hands continue their explorations, touch sure and firm. Certain.

"You have the hands of an artist," I murmur. "All that power in those clever fingers, and you use them to unmake instead of create."

He hums. "Butchers and artists aren't so different. We both understand the beauty in rearranging pieces."

"But you're an executioner with a healer's power. Funny, that."

"Life has a sense of humor. Trust me, I've ripped apart more bodies than I've put back together." His fingers press against my ribs, checking something. "The internal bleeding's stopped. Any more tonight, and your body will shut down. I haven't used this power in a long time."

"How long?"

The silence stretches between us. Then: "Since the war."

Three simple words, and in the negative space between them, the truth he doesn't voice—centuries of disuse. Of letting this magic wither until he had to excavate it from some dark, disused corner of himself, dredged up and dusted off for the likes of me.

Realizing he's revealed too much, the Wolf blinks, and his jaw clenches. "You look like something I might have found broken and bleeding on a battlefield," he continues with deliberate cruelty. "You would have fit right in with all the hopeless humans I tore into."

My equilibrium is unraveling. Everything I've survived suddenly crashes over me, and it's too much. All at once, I'm viscerally aware of my nakedness, his hands, my vulnerability, all this blood everywhere. Everything is *too much and too close and too raw*. The room is shrinking, black eating at the edges of my vision as my lungs constrict.

I need to not have blood on my skin. I need—

"I need to be clean," I gasp. "I need—"

"*Breathe.*" His voice is crisp and commanding. "We're going to breathe first, yeah? Nice and slow, in and out. Focus on me."

I struggle to obey, to suck air past the pressure crushing my ribs. Gradually, the roaring static recedes to a low hum. The bands constricting my chest loosen.

"Good." The Wolf pulls back to study my face. "I'm going to dress what's still unhealed. Then we'll get you in a bath." He retrieves a box from a nearby table and draws out a length of soft fabric. "This will hold up in water," he says as he winds it around my midsection. "I'll remove it tomorrow when I heal the rest. Think you can manage if I help you to the tub?"

"Yes."

He scoops me into his arms. I brace for the swell of revulsion, the animal panic. But it doesn't come. There's only the solid heat of him as he carries me into the bathing chamber.

Extravagant is my first impression—all cool marble and gilt fixtures. A large sunken tub dominates the space, able to accommodate his wings. Plush towels and an array of colored glass bottles line the counter.

He sets me down in a chair at the tub's edge and spins a few taps. To my astonishment, a panel opens, and a small waterfall fills the basin. Not like the pipes back in Hellevig—a real, natural waterfall. The room quickly saturates with a lovely, citrusy scent. After a few minutes, he twists the knob to close the panel, and the flow cuts off.

I hold my breath as he helps me into the bath, and a moan catches behind my teeth as I sink in.

He moves away, collecting bottles and unfolding towels. And

then, to my shock, he kneels beside the tub. Subservient, almost. He flicks a sponge into the water and reaches for me slowly enough that I could stop him if I wanted. I don't.

"What are you doing?" I ask as he draws it across the knobs of my spine.

"You can barely sit upright. I'm helping." His ministrations don't falter, each swipe of the sponge hypnotic. "I've never met anyone who inspired this stupid impulse before. The verdict's still out on whether I like it."

I rest my temple against the cool lip of the tub. "Do you have a lot of impulses?"

"Can't say I've ever been accused of being rational."

Exhaustion is settling into my limbs, dragging me into the warm dark. I fight it, clinging to consciousness. There's one thing I need to know.

"Tell me your name. Your real one," I say, barely loud enough to be heard over the drip and plink of the water.

He goes still. Then, as if the admission is being dragged out of him: "Evander."

"Evander," I whisper, letting my eyes drift closed. I turn the shape of it over. Tasting the sounds. "Pretty name for a monster."

Pretty name. For such an ugly thing.

"Monsters aren't born." He smooths the sponge over my neck. "We're made. Some of us in pointless, brutal wars. Now go to sleep. I'll dry you off and put you in bed."

I'm weightless, drifting, surrendering to the dark. "You won't hurt me, will you?"

"Not tonight."

14

BRYONY

I WAS FIVE the first time they killed me.

The Eternal has rules about these things. Alexios says our souls can't take the trauma of dying when we're babies, so Devaliant children prick their fingers, the same as every other Claimed human. Just a tiny drop of blood in the temple collection channels.

Until your fifth nameday.

No one prepares you for the altar. No one is allowed to hold your hand and whisper reassurances. And every moment before and after the knife isn't some hazy, half-formed nightmare you shake off: you're old enough to remember. When most children are figuring out how to tie their boots, I was finding out what it feels like to die.

"It's okay," Theo whispered to me that day. Two years of deaths had hardened her into someone who could lie convincingly. "It'll be okay."

The Head Oracle didn't even look at her when she spoke to my father. "Take her outside. She's distracting the child."

I can still hear Theo shouting as Father dragged her away.

Three Oracles surrounded me. One grabbed my arms and lifted me onto the altar, another locked my legs down.

And one held the blade.

I screamed when I died that first time. The Oracle with the blade slapped her palm over my mouth until I stopped making noise. When I came back from the Void, I didn't scream again—not until Idris sliced me open on the Duehavn.

That's the thing with trauma: it doesn't heal like skin. It doesn't stay buried. It nests inside you, patient as a snare, waiting to wake up. And when you're trapped between sleep and waking, between nightmares and reality, where the world is black ice—that's when ugly memories come slithering out of the dark. I thought that five-year-old girl died for good when the Void swallowed her. That it spat out some unrecognizable creature wearing her face.

Then I dreamed about her, and the dream went like this:

Soft morning sun on my cheeks. The aroma of freshly baked bread and sausage. I'm a little girl again, stretching awake to breakfast in bed on temple day. Before the blood. Before the blades. Before the hand over my mouth—

Shut up. Stop thrashing. Hold still.

I jerk upright, gulping air. Sun slants over the stone floor, the rugs with golden threads, the bookshelves. Not my room in Hellevig.

The Wolf's tower.

By the window is a silver tray piled high with covered dishes. The competing scents of food hit me again, threatening to unbury the memories.

I force myself out of bed. Folded fabric sits next to the tray—a gown. The blue silk is so sheer it's almost transparent, adorned with lace trim and pearls alongside yellow gemstones on the bodice. This isn't a garment that lasts through multiple wears. Neither are the underthings it came with—those are the kind meant to be admired by a lover before he tears them off.

Heat floods my face, thinking of the Wolf picking out each scrap of silk. Picturing how it would cling.

How it would tear.

Theodora's voice echoes in my mind. *You need clothes, Bry. You can't walk around in a tattered cloak with nothing underneath. Now get dressed.*

So I do. I shove into the ridiculous underthings and yank the gown over my head. Of course, it fits perfectly, hugging close to my body in all the places he'd want to stare at.

I manage to stab the last tiny pearl button through its loop before the walls start closing in, before my lungs turn to stone and the room tilts and blurs, and I'm drowning in air and *I can't breathe can't think can't stay here another second.*

I run. The corridor stretches until—*there.*

Windows ahead, a burst of green past the glass. I push through the doors, heaving air into my constricted lungs. *In. Out. In. Out.* Letting the perfume of roses fill my senses.

Finally, when I manage to return my breathing to normal, I look up. The garden spreads wild and free, nothing like Hellevig's sharp-cut hedges. Climbing roses choke the walkways and twist around every tree trunk and branch, every crumbling statue and fountain. Beneath it all is a faint electric hum that prickles my skin—magic.

The Wolf's magic.

For a reckless moment, I consider running. Trying to get to Theo—

Stop. My bare wrist is a mocking reminder that I'm a human illegally in Scillari and stripped of the only thing that might offer some security.

No mark. No protection. Just meat for the taking.

A snarl tears from my throat. "*Fuck.*"

I kneel in the middle of the roses, scrabbling my hands in the dirt. I have to grab onto something. I need to *hurt* something. Thorns gouge my palms as I tear at the weeds, fistful after fistful. Blood slicks my hands, vines tangle around my wrists, but I keep going. I can't stop—

"Most people rest when they're injured." The Wolf's words cut through my spiraling thoughts, equal parts amused and annoyed. "You didn't touch your breakfast. Not hungry? Or are you too determined to rip up my garden to bother?"

I stare down at my shredded palms. "Why do you care?"

"I'm trying to decide if you're an ungrateful brat or working to earn that execution I promised you."

I don't answer. "Did you need something?"

"As a matter of fact, yes. I need you to stop spattering your blood all over my roses. It upsets them."

An incredulous laugh leaves me. He can't be serious. But no, there's no trace of humor in his voice.

"Keep going the way you are, and those roses will tear you apart before I do," he adds.

Heat crawls up my neck as I realize what a mess I am. Panting like an animal, gown ripped to shreds, caked in filth and blood. Tearing up his garden as if I could unearth the rot in me if I dig deep enough.

"Look at me." A quiet command. "At my face, not the dirt."

Finally, I drag my gaze up to his. It's a mistake to look at the Wolf directly. At those golden wings gleaming in the sunlight, at the dark hair falling over his brow as if I'd somehow disturbed his rest. He gives me a searching look, lingering on my hands. On my broken, muddy fingernails and the scrapes from the thorns.

"I didn't piece this body back together just so you could damage it again," he says, almost gently.

For a moment, the Wolf is gone, and it's the male staring at me. If I didn't know any better, I'd almost call the expression on his face concern. But I *do* know better. This has nothing to do with me; he's probably worried that his toy might be too damaged to entertain him.

I shove to my feet. "Take me to Vartena. I need—there are things I have to do. People who need to pay."

It's as close to begging as I'll ever get.

The Wolf tucks in his wings and studies me once more—assessing the destruction, the obvious signs of my unraveling. I hate that I've let him see me this weak.

"I'll *consider* it," he says. "After."

"After what?"

"After," he repeats slowly, "we go inside, and I finish stitching you back together without you bleeding all over my property."

"I didn't agree to be your prisoner," I snap. "That wasn't in our negotiation last night."

"Tough shit. I'm not negotiating with you right now. You don't even have clothes that you haven't destroyed."

My teeth clench. I glance down at myself again, taking in the ruin I've made of the gown. "I don't want silks," I say flatly.

His attention rakes over me. "Amara's the one who picked out the dress. If I'd known you planned on mutilating my roses, I would have asked her to bring you something more…" He waves a hand. "Durable."

"I'd like something *practical*."

"You're full of demands today, aren't you? *Heal me, clothe me, send me home.*" He snaps his wings in irritation. "Do you dictate terms to every god generous enough not to gut you, or am I special?"

"If you want me to be your nemesis in this sick game, I have needs."

He stares at me, head tilted. Surprised. As if I've caught him off guard.

I wait for him to put me in my place. To snarl that I'm nothing, that I'm only a human destroying his property with no right to make demands. That he'll grind me under his boot until I remember what I am. What I am not.

But instead, he steps closer. "Let's pretend I give in to this little tantrum and send you back right now like you asked. No weapons, no preparation. Not even a decent pair of shoes. Where will you go? What's your plan?"

I glare at him. "I'll stay alive long enough for you to get what you want out of this. Don't fuss."

"Consider me fussed. I'm invested. And I protect my investments until I'm finished with them."

It takes every ounce of self-control not to spit in his face.

The Wolf makes a low sound. His fingers skim my jaw, tilting my chin up. "Who stabbed you? Your uncle? Another gutless noble? Vengeance and justice make a fine pair, Devaliant. Give me a name, and I'll give you their corpse for trying to steal your death from me." His head dips, lips grazing my cheek as he breathes, "Who do I hurt, vicious girl?"

It would be easy to give him a name. To let him unsheathe those lovely, lethal claws and ruin everyone who's ever wronged me. There is violence in his voice, in the too-careful way he holds himself. He would make such a glorious carnage of all my enemies.

But that's not what I want.

I curl my fingers around his wrist, noticing the way his pulse jumps against my palm. "No."

He raises an eyebrow. "No?"

"I won't give you a name. You don't get to claim my revenge. I'll take back everything they stole from me with my own hands, in my own time."

Slowly, his lips curve into a smile. "One day, you're going to set entire realms ablaze with the force of all that fury. And I want to be there to watch them burn."

"You'd have to let me live long enough to see it through," I say, caught in his gravity. In this strange, violent kinship.

And I realize that my death on the Duehavn changed me just like that first one at age five. I woke up different. This time, as someone with a purpose, and that purpose is to make the world bleed. And the Wolf? He's the perfect god to draw out every dark thing that came back with me from the Void and expose all my ugly, snarling pieces to the light. To shape me into a monster as hungry and vicious as he is.

"I suppose I would, wouldn't I?" he murmurs. "Shame you're a Devaliant."

The Wolf drops his hand and steps away.

"Don't stay out here too long." He nods toward the tower. "Bathe. Eat some food before your stomach tries to claw itself out of your body. Then come to me so I can finish healing you."

15

EVANDER

THE STUDY DOOR creaks open. I keep my eyes fixed on my book as the Devaliant steps into the room, but I track her all the same—the rustle of fabric, the sweet, wild scent of jasmine and rain and soap from the bath.

"Hello, Wolf."

"Hello, nemesis," I say, flipping a page. Not reading a damn word.

Her feet whisper across the carpet. "I'm surprised someone as important as you doesn't have an army of servants. I probably aged a year wandering these halls searching for you."

"I had to tell them not to come when a mortal princess landed on my doorstep."

"You're more than welcome to take me back to Vartena."

"Still mulling that over. Deciding if it fits in with my plans for you."

She heaves a sigh. "I need to go home. I told you I have unfinished business."

I don't reply to that. Instead, I snap my book shut and toss it aside, pinning her with the full weight of my attention. Her silver-white hair is mussed, cheeks still flushed from the bath. She's wearing the shirt I left out for her. It hits mid-thigh, barely decent, the barest hint of cleavage. My gaze drags over her legs, snagging on the angry welts and scratches marring her luminous skin—souvenirs from her tussle with my roses.

"Come here," I say, patting my thigh.

A flush crawls up her neck. "You can't be serious. I'm not sitting on your lap."

"No?" I give her a smirk. "You had no problem straddling me when I let you play with my knife."

"That was different."

Was it? As far as I can tell, the only thing that's changed is our location. She's still looking at me like she wants to bathe her hands in my blood. I'm still picturing how she'd feel on my cock.

"I need contact for my power to work. So unless you'd prefer me to lay you on the rug…" I pat my thigh again. "Sit."

For a moment, I'm sure she'll tell me to go fuck myself. I practically see the battle waging behind her eyes, the swift calculation of her rapidly dwindling options.

Then, as if the concession is being dragged out of her, she steps forward and settles across my thighs as if she's lowering herself onto hot coals. "Happy now?"

"Ecstatic." I reach for the buttons on her borrowed shirt. "Let's see what damage is left."

Her hand shoots out, fingers wrapping around my wrist. "Don't get any ideas."

I arch a brow. "About what? Healing you? Or the fact that you're about to be naked in my lap?"

"Both. Neither." She blows out a frustrated breath. "Just… behave."

"I always behave. I just have my own definition of good behavior."

After a second of hesitation, she slowly releases me.

I take my time with the buttons, each slip of fabric a slow reveal. The delicate hollows of her collarbones, the smoothness of her sternum, the lush swell of her breasts. Her nipples pebble in the cool air, and I bite back a groan. *Devla svaust*, the stars made my nemesis pretty.

She tracks each movement, a faint tremor running through her. As if it's taking every scrap of self-control not to bolt. Not to snarl and snap.

Good. If she didn't have the sense to be afraid of me, I'd be questioning her intelligence.

"Relax," I murmur. "I won't bite unless you ask me to."

"That's not as reassuring as you think it is."

My hands find her waist as I unwind the bandage with careful fingers. Her breath hitches when the wrap falls away, exposing what remains of her wounds: some slight bruising, some cuts not yet fully healed, her new injuries from my garden. Yesterday had been about keeping her from slipping into the Void, mending all the internal damage. Today is for the rest. The small agonies.

I flatten my palms against her ribs and carefully channel my magic into her. Not too much—just the faintest lick of warmth chased by a whisper of pleasure.

"What—" Her voice breaks on a gasp. "What are you doing?"

"Healing you. Unless you'd prefer I stop?"

A shiver rolls through her as another pulse of power sinks in. Her spine arches, those long lashes fluttering against her cheeks. The scent of her arousal blooms in the air, rich and heady, and when her eyes open, she looks perturbed. Irritated.

I hold back a laugh. The Devaliant wants to fuck me—and she hates herself for it.

"Doing okay there?" I ask, all innocence.

I'm a bastard. A killer. I'm going to ruin this girl's life. But I'm not quite cruel enough to point out that I feel the slick heat of her pussy through my trousers, not when she's this close to bolting.

She gives her head a small shake as if to dislodge an unpleasant thought. "It feels… different from before. The pain is less."

I hum thoughtfully, letting my touch skim over the delicate ladder of her ribs, the sharp jut of her hips. So many lovely bones. "I was out of practice yesterday and kept it brief so I didn't accidentally do any damage. But this gift wasn't for the battlefield. It was meant for worship." I pause, meeting her gaze. "For giving pleasure as well as mending."

Her thighs clench around my hips and her ass squirms right over my cock. I grit my teeth, shifting her back so she doesn't feel how hard I am. If she keeps moving like that, this is about to get uncomfortable fast.

"Let's keep things strictly clinical, shall we?" she says tightly. An attempt to reestablish boundaries eroded by proximity and sensation.

"If you insist," I say, shrugging. As if I'm not aroused just from having her here.

I gentle my touch and keep the contact chaste as I work. She swallows, glancing away to focus on the roses snaking up the chamber walls and nearly covering the ceiling.

"Your roses are lovely. The way you talked about them before, it was almost as if..." She pauses, careful. Deliberate. "As if you spoke to them."

Something tightens in my chest—some wounded thing I buried three hundred years ago. My hands flex against her waist before I can stop them, an aborted flinch. I'm tempted to remind her of her place. Show her the cost of prodding at old scars.

Instead, I shove down all those inconvenient thoughts and say, "The realm granted me the power of an Eternal. It recognizes me as part of itself. Sometimes, it speaks. Sometimes I listen."

"And what does it say?"

And *this* is the side of her I don't know what to do with. Always pushing, pushing, pushing. Seeking out the ugly, squirming bits and holding them up as if to say, *Look what I found. Aren't you curious? Aren't you dying to unearth all the broken pieces of yourself?*

No, vicious girl. You don't get to see. You don't get to pluck out all my ugliest secrets and pin them to the wall for your perusal.

The roses creep and curl along the stones of my tower, an ever-present reminder of my failings. Of the king I refuse to be. And each year, the branches grow thicker, the blooms more suffocating. The realm's wordless message grows louder.

You're abandoning your responsibilities. You're wasting all that power I gifted you.

I lean in and whisper, "It says you ask too many fucking questions."

She snorts. "I hope it scolds you for being a neglectful gardener. The weeds are staging a revolt. Your roses are strangling your tower."

"My duties keep me away," I say curtly. "You're very chatty and judgmental for someone at my mercy."

"You're awfully defensive about some roses. Maybe I want to know more about the male who's going to kill me. Is that so strange?"

"Strange? No. Foolish? Absolutely. The more you know about the monster, the harder it becomes to despise him."

"Bold of you to assume I could ever stop despising you."

I glare at her and shove another pulse of magic into her body, watching her eyes flutter shut. A low moan catches between her teeth as the last injuries knit closed without a mark left behind.

"You're as mended as you'll ever be." I run careful fingers over the smooth skin. "Not even a scar. See? I'm very talented."

Emotions flicker over her features as she takes in the flawless expanse of her torso. "It's like it never happened."

Something in me gentles. "The worst ones never really go away. No power in either realm can heal those."

Those are carved into the soul, knotted up and gnarled in all the black spaces. The holes where something precious used to live before it was ripped out at the root.

My attention snags on her arm—on the ladder of neat marks scoring her flesh on the inside crease of her elbow. Deliberate. I trace the outer ridge with my finger with a barely there graze. "These aren't from a fight."

They're too precise. Each notch is the same depth and width, five of them lined up like little soldiers.

A sudden tension thrums through her. "No. Those are private."

"And this?" I shift to the mark slashed across her throat, a brutal seam of scar. It was a killing stroke. "Is this private?"

The Devaliant clears her throat, shrugging back into my shirt. "It was given to me," she says, doing up the buttons, covering up all that flawless skin again. She makes no move to dislodge herself from my lap. "By a nobleman who thought he was entitled to take whatever he wanted. When I refused him, he decided if he couldn't have me, no one would."

A quiet rage simmers through my veins. What sort of cowardly piece of shit tries to murder a woman over saying no?

"Give me his name." I can't keep the anger out of my command.

The beginnings of a slow, savage smile tugs at her mouth—a glimpse of the creature she could become if given enough time and the right incentive. "He's already dead. The palace guards saw to it."

Some of my bloodlust banks. "Then where are his remains?"

The amusement stays. I love that expression on her, the way her face lights up. "Planning to decorate your garden with a rotting corpse, Wolf?"

"Don't be crass. I'd get you a courting gift first. Carve his spine into twin hunting knives and present them to you on a bed of his viscera as an early deathday present."

Because nothing says budding nemesis-ship like the desecrated corpse of her would-be murderer. I'm thoughtful when I put my mind to it.

For a moment, she just stares at me as if trying to parse whether I'm joking.

I'm really, really not.

But slowly, impossibly, the corner of her lips twitch—and then I hear it. A short burst of laughter. A fragile thing, barely there and gone too fast, but real.

My chest squeezes. *Do it again*, I almost command. *Do it until I get sick of it.*

"Corpse mutilation is a waste of your talents," she says, still smiling. "Sweet thought, though. In a disturbing, deranged sort of way."

"I have my moments." I trace the shape of her scar again in a leisurely drag that makes her breath catch. I want to memorize every bump and ridge, every mark and hollow. To paint the patterns of her pain with my fingertips until I'm able to recall them blind." "He went for your throat like a craven because he knew that's where he could steal your voice."

Where he could leave her silent and small. The kind of woman who bargains death with a god deserves better than cowardice.

The Devaliant's face shutters, all that lovely amusement fading. "Yes. The healers did their best, but…" She trails off with a half-shrug. "My voice was never quite the same after."

I curve my palm around her nape, fingers sinking into her hair. Power unspools from me in slow, pulsing waves, and the Devaliant tenses at the first electric lick of it over her skin. The instinctive flinch of prey.

"Name all your enemies," I say. "Everyone who might hurt you."

A considering pause. "Well, there's you. Obviously."

This fucking girl.

"Someone other than me. I want to know who might think to snatch you off the board before I've finished playing with you." I tighten my grip, relishing her sharp inhale. "Give me names."

"I hardly think it matters at this point."

"It matters," I growl, "because now you're an Unclaimed Devaliant." I tap her bare wrist where Alexios' mark used to glow. "Which makes you a prize. Every human and demi in the realms will be salivating at the chance to collar you." *To rip you open and rearrange all the messy bits into a shape that pleases them.*

She looks away. "Look, just take me back to Vartena and let me deal with the person who tried to kill me on my own terms. Give me time to say goodbye to my sister. I'm sure you'll get your piece of flesh from me before anyone else."

"Tell me you're not completely helpless, at least." I duck my head to meet her gaze. "That you can use a blade. Anything that might make me believe you won't be dead within an hour of crossing the Shroud."

The Devaliant's expression shutters. "I'm a Princess of the Blood. We don't fight. We bleed."

Of course. Of *course*, they taught her jack shit. They wanted her soft and yielding. Built for the altar, for bearing little Devaliant brats to continue the line of Anchors.

I can keep Alexios and Bastien off her scent until I hunt her down. But whoever dumped her on that ridge and left her to bleed out in the cold? Any other filth who sees the Devaliant and feels entitled to her?

Too many variables. Too many opportunities for someone to steal her. She wouldn't last a day.

"Change of terms," I say on impulse.

The Devaliant stills. "Sorry?"

"I'm not taking you back yet. You're staying here."

"No." She jerks away, nearly falling off my lap. "You can't—you're not Claiming me, are you? After what Alexios did—"

I catch her wrist, squeezing. "Would you shut up for five seconds? I don't want a Claim, you impossible creature." Her pulse hammers against my fingers. So fragile. So damn breakable. "How exactly do you plan to get revenge? I'm betting the person who put you on the Duehavn has guards, right? Protection detail you'd have to get through? And the only blades you've handled are the ones you've used on yourself and whatever butter knife they trusted you with at dinner."

Her jaw clenches. I've struck a nerve. "Then teach me to fight."

I don't hesitate. "Done."

Her eyebrows shoot up. She wasn't expecting that—probably assumed I'd laugh at her. "Just like that? I thought you detested me."

"Oh, I fucking loathe you." It's important she understands this, that every mercy and moment of kindness are gifts I grant for my own amusement. "I hate everything about your family. The sound of your name makes me want to tear out your throat. But I have no intention of letting anyone else kill you. Nothing that's mine gets broken unless I'm the one to break it."

"How generous of you."

"I'm a giver."

Silence stretches. I let it linger, let her consider my offer, watching emotions chase across her face as she weighs her options.

"Wait." She shifts on my lap. "I thought Alexios wanted my corpse."

I shrug. "Alexios will get what's left when I'm done. As far as he needs to know, scavengers got to you first. They would have if Amara hadn't found you."

"And what price am I expected to pay for this?" she asks with a scowl. "What do you get out of it?"

I stroke my knuckles down her cheek. "I'm not doing this out of the goodness of my heart. If it hasn't escaped your notice, I'm prone to destructive behavior in my boredom, and you're the worst idea I've had in centuries. I'm curious to see what sort of monster I can shape you into, given time and a blade."

Her brows knit together in indecision. She's so easy to read, even as she tries to lock herself down and bury all her soft places behind a facade of fire and thorns and defiance.

"Here's my negotiation," I continue, almost gently. "You can crawl back to Vartena and spend your numbered days trying not to get eaten alive. Or you can stay here and be my temporary entertainment. The more interesting you are, the longer you live. So take what I'm offering, extend this short mortal life with me a little more, and walk out my door ready to claim your retribution." My hands stroke down her sides, fingertips dragging over each ridge of her ribs. "But remember this. Your death is *mine*. It's always been mine. And when I get bored and you stop being fun?" I wrap my fingers around her throat. "I'll hunt you across both realms and through the Shroud itself. And when I find you, I'll rip you open and eat your heart while it's still beating."

Some dark and ravenous emotion flickers in the Devaliant's face. "Maybe I'll get good enough to carve out yours first."

Laughter rumbles out of me. Oh, she's going to be so much fun to conquer. I can't wait to see what she looks like by the time I'm through with her. "I'm counting on you trying."

She inhales a shuddering breath. I watch her piece herself

together, shore up her crumbling walls, attempting to hide all that human vulnerability. It's cute.

"When I'm ready—when *I* say I'm ready—you'll take me to Vartena and give me a three-day head start to settle my business. And you won't ever Claim me. Promise."

I study her face. Something about her makes me want to push until she pushes back. "Worried I might keep you?"

"Swear it."

My mouth curves into a slow smile. "You have my word. No Claims. Just an agreement between a god and his new toy."

Her eyes flare. She holds my gaze like she's planning the ways she might try to kill me. She'd fail, but I'd admire the attempt. "I'll stay if you never call me that again."

I squeeze her throat slightly as a reminder that I'm being merciful enough to let her negotiate when I can rip her apart. "You'll stay because you need my mercy more than I need your entertainment." I lean in close, whispering, "So I'll call you whatever the fuck I want. *Toy. Pet. Mine.* Still interested?"

Her lip curls in a little snarl at that. "Fine. Deal."

And just like that, I've got myself a Devaliant to play with.

PART TWO

THE NATURE OF UNMAKING

16

EVANDER

FUCK, I LOVE sunsets.

There's something savage about that final blaze of color spilling across the horizon—the way the gold burns into red before the dark swallows it up. Night always wins in the end. It's nature's daily execution.

I breathe deep, filling my lungs with salt and brine and the hint of a coming storm. Below, the waves of the Rionese Sea crash against the rocks. The village of Keksa sprawls along the coast, its quaint cottages and winding cobbled streets still peaceful. Indigo and pink flowers spill from window boxes. Linens flap in the wind on laundry lines strung between buildings. Gulls wheel above me, their cries piercing the air.

Pretty little place. Shame I have to tear it apart.

Wolf. Alexios' voice lashes through my mind, impatient. *Stop fucking around and finish the job.*

My wings rustle with irritation. *I'm enjoying the view first. Taking in the ambiance.*

I want the village destroyed by moonrise, Alexios says, his displeasure crackling along my nerves.

The mind-link severs with a vicious twist that leaves copper flooding my mouth. My tongue probes the split flesh of my cheek. Alexios has always been a dramatic bastard who likes to punctuate his orders with gratuitous violence. Three hundred years of this shit, and he still thinks pain is an effective motivator.

I sweep my gaze over Keksa again. All that charm, and

tomorrow it'll be wiped off the map because of that age-old human weakness: hubris. In this case, a mass quantity of it—this entire village chose to abandon their local temple and stop tithing. They'd *voted* on it, the arrogant pricks.

That's the problem with these remote communities. They hardly ever see gods, if at all. We might as well be a bedtime story, a myth to scare children into giving a drop of blood into the collection channels. The elders who witnessed the war that tore Vartena apart are long gone, and their descendants are soft. Lazy. They never see any bloodshed except for a bimonthly fingerprick, and they start thinking, "What's this for?" Because peace has been there since the day they were shoved out of the womb, and none of them realizes that the price for it was paid in blood. Their ancestors', my mother's, my brother's, *mine*.

Like too many Vartenans, they've forgotten what it's like to stare death in the face.

When the oathbreaker marks appeared on their wrists, they finally got it through their thick skulls that they weren't beneath Alexios' notice. No one is. Some tried to make a run for it, but I tracked them down days ago. It's almost a mercy that I'm here to reap the rest. Dread is its own kind of dying.

Feathers rustle above me, and Amara drops from the sky with a flap of charcoal wings. The sunset bleeds through her hair, dying the light purple strands in streaks of scarlet.

"What do you want this time?" she asks, voice sharp with annoyance. "I thought I told you not to bother me again unless the realms were ending."

I don't look at her. "Yet here you are. Always showing up. Do you miss me? Is that it?"

She scoffs. "Arrogance is even less appealing on you than bloodstains and grave dirt. I don't know how you stand yourself."

Amusement kindles despite myself. "Even villains get tired of their own reflections," I say wryly. "I'll make this quick before Alexios joins us. I'd hate for him to catch you. It's about the girl."

Amara laces her fingers together, interest sparking. "Did she fight back when you killed her, or did she just lie there like a good little sacrifice? Do I get a thank you for bringing you a Devaliant to slaughter after three centuries of being forbidden to touch them?"

"The Devaliant is staying at the tower."

Her mouth hangs open. "*What?* For how long?"

I shrug. "The foreseeable."

"The *foresee*—" Amara stares at me like she's trying to pinpoint the exact moment I lost my sanity. Then she grabs the front of my shirt. "I did *not*," she hisses, "almost get caught dragging the princess' half-dead ass across the Shroud so you could adopt her like a stray cat and make her your personal cock warmer."

I catch her wrist in a bruising grip. "You've got three seconds to get your hand off me before I remove it permanently."

She wrenches free. "Tell me you're not Claiming the Devaliant. Tell me you're not that stupid."

"I'm not Claiming anyone."

Yet all I've been able to think about for hours is the weight of her in my lap, all that bare skin like a blank canvas begging to be marked. But I am not a thing that wants, and she is not a thing to be possessed.

"You despise mortals," Amara says. "Especially Devaliants. You told me you were going to stitch her up and make her wish you'd killed her quickly. And now you're letting her live? Are you that desperate for company in your creepy murder tower?"

"Don't be ridiculous." I roll my eyes. "The Devaliant lacks even the most basic combat skills. She's never held a blade she didn't shove in her own heart. They raised her soft and breakable for the altar. "

"And? What's that got to do with anything?"

"So"—I smile pleasantly—"I want you to train her."

Silence stretches between us, filled with the cry of gulls and the distant crash of waves against the cliffs.

Then, "You've lost it. You've finally cracked."

Well.

It's not untrue. I left the best parts of my sanity somewhere amid the corpses in Turpori and abandoned it completely when I lost my family. But that's neither here nor there.

"I want her proficient in every weapon she can lift," I say, as if she hadn't spoken. "Any style she shows an aptitude for. She needs to be able to incapacitate a male three times her size in under sixty seconds. She's got business to settle in Vartena, and she has to survive long enough to make it interesting when I end her."

She looks at me in annoyance. "Train her yourself if you're so obsessed with turning a Princess of the Blood into a killer for your amusement."

"I've never been much for honing delicate things. And you owe me, Amara. For services rendered."

"*Services rend—*" she sputters. "Blackmail isn't a *service*, Wolf. It's coercion. You're holding my secrets over my head to get me to do your bidding."

My smile doesn't waver. "It's generous discretion between friends. A favor for a favor. Because if you don't agree to it, I'll tell Alexios where you are. How happy do you think he'll be when he finds you, hmm? When he realizes you've been lying to him?"

All it would take is a few whispers in Alexios' ear to watch her burn. I won't actually do that, though. Probably. Unless she irritates me.

Amara's lips flatten. "Fuck you."

"Not interested. Are you doing this for me, or am I telling him?"

She crosses her arms. "Who exactly is the princess planning to kill? Just her attempted murderer or every idiot guard who ever glanced at her tits? What kind of training are we talking about?"

No, don't like that. I don't like the idea of anyone else's hands on the Devaliant or someone other than me looking at her tits. From this moment on, she's mine. Those tits are mine, that body is mine, her remaining days are mine.

Her death is all fucking *mine*.

"I don't care if it's anyone who's looked at her wrong, touched her wrong, opened their big mouth to degrade her, or breathed wrong in her general direction," I say, ticking off the options on my fingers. "That's her business. I just want to ensure my prey can give me a good chase before I rip her throat out."

Amara studies me, probably comparing this current unhinged me to the god she's known for hundreds of years. "You know what your problem is?" she finally says.

Fuck's sake.

"By all means, enlighten me with your pearls of wisdom."

"You used to have some glimmer of control. But I think you've spent too long bathing in entrails. Between that and the isolation at your little hermit tower, your few remaining virtues have shriveled up and died."

"Are you done with the character assessment?" I ask with a sigh. "Because I have a village to slaughter, and you're cutting into my murder time. Do we have a deal?"

Amara's gaze drifts over Keksa, studying the meandering lanes strewn with flowers. I wonder if she's picturing how it will look when I'm finished.

"Fine. I'll do it. But you don't get to hold this over me again. Swear it."

"You have my word." I pause, considering. "When you train her, aim for the soft spots. I want the kill instinct hammered into her skull. It'll make things more interesting."

Amara shakes out her wings, getting ready to take off. "You're a sick bastard, you know that?" Her lips twist. "I'll come to your tower at first light."

"Wait. One more thing."

She looks over her shoulder. "What now? Need tips on proper pet care? A manual for keeping princesses in captivity?"

I hesitate, searching for the right words. This will require a delicate touch. "The girl was whining about clothes earlier. Basic shit. *Necessities.*"

"I fail to see why this concerns me."

"Well, that got me thinking. What's the opposite? Of necessities?"

She squints at me. "Is this your addled attempt to ask me what gifts you should get for your pet mortal? Because that's adorable in a demented, unhinged way."

I'm about to break every bone in her wings, possibly twice. "It's not a gift. I'm curious to see what she does."

With softness. With things she's never been allowed to have.

"Let me get this straight." She pinches the bridge of her nose. "You want me to help you spoil the girl you're planning on murdering?"

"Less commentary, more answers."

"Sweets," she says after a considering pause. "The more decadent, the better." She shakes her head. "Why do I feel like I'll regret telling you that?"

I ignore that, my mind already making plans. Miniature ambrosia cakes. Fruits drizzled with honey. I'll hand-feed them to the Devaliant, a bite at a time—a nice interlude before I kill her.

"What else?" I ask, dragging myself from the edge of distraction.

"Let her lead. Something tells me agency and autonomy have been in short supply for a Princess of the Blood." Amara's wings rustle. "Maybe if you give her a little freedom, she'll bite back harder. Show you what she's made of."

Yes, that's good. The Devaliant has been an Anchor for the Shroud her entire life, her choices stripped away. She seemed to enjoy being in control when she cut me up with my dagger.

"A word of advice." Amara gives me a look of distaste. "When you go to her later, try not to be covered in human guts, you savage."

Then she's flying off with a sharp flap of her wings.

Well, then.

I turn back to the village and take in another breath of the sharp air, admiring those quaint cottages before they're rubble.

Time to get to work.

Power ignites within me, and with a downward thrust of my wings, I launch into the sky. Screams erupt as I tear into a building. Someone tries to run past me, but I catch them by the throat and squeeze until something snaps.

The first death is always the hardest. After that, I become the monster they made me into.

There's an art to carnage. A poetry in the way bones break and flesh yields. *You have the hands of an artist*, the Devaliant said, and she was right. I'm a masterful painter, and tonight, this settlement is my canvas—a masterpiece of violence. The blood against the red hues of the fading light, the rubble silhouetted in lines of teal, the stars glittering above the slaughter.

I paint the world in my fury.

A whisper echoes through my thoughts, the ghost of my mother's voice: *Destruction is easy, son. Any beast can tear something apart.*

"Shut up," I mutter, crushing another windpipe. "Just shut the fuck up."

Some human tries begging me, but I barely even hear it over the buzzing in my head as a deluge of memories batter at me. Images flash of the decimated cities in Scillari, all our dead, the pyres stacked high. These people squandered the peace we paid for with our lives and sanity.

Three hundred years isn't enough to forget. Vengeance is a cruel master, and it never lets me rest.

By the time the last body hits the ground, my ears ring in the silence. I'm drenched in gore, my clothes barely visible. The stink of death is overwhelming. I straighten and take a slow measure of the devastation I've wrought—a once thriving settlement is nothing more than rubble and dust.

There's always a strange stillness after a slaughter, a sound unique to each place. Here, it's the lapping of distant waves and the rhythmic grind of sea rocks, the coo of a bird in the distance. And in that hush come the too-loud thoughts.

I want a drink.

I want my brother from before the war.

Remember when you were more? When you wore a crown instead of a collar?

I shove the images down where they belong, into the locked box in my chest where I keep all my weaknesses. There's no place for sentiment in this line of work.

A figure moves in the wreckage. I walk through the rubble to the remains of what was probably a charming little town hall twenty minutes ago. A woman huddles there, hunched and shaking, and in her arms is a man. I know a corpse when I see one, and he is firmly, emphatically dead—and I'm his murderer.

I stare at the woman curled over her deceased love, the oathbreaker's mark glimmering on her wrist. A declaration of her guilt. She swore her life to the Accords, and she reneged. She failed in her duty.

I should finish this. Put her out of her misery and call it a night. It'd be a mercy, and the stars know I'm not in the business of being merciful, but...

There's something hypnotic about her grief. She's lost everything in the space of a single night, her entire world reduced to ashes, and it's like being confronted with a mirror image—horribly, viscerally familiar.

But centuries of loss and duty have carved out all my soft places, everything in me that should have been the king Scillari chose me to be. Now, I look at this woman, and images fill my head of golden spires crumbling to dust. The air in Turpori stinking of bodies. My brother, broken and bleeding against my side as we staggered through the streets humans tore apart with stolen power.

A rustle of wings jars me from the memory. I don't turn. I'd know that aura anywhere, cold enough to numb.

"You missed one," Alexios says.

I keep my attention fixed on the woman. "Didn't realize you were keeping such close tabs on me."

"Someone has to." He moves to stand beside me, wings settling. His irises glow in the dim light—the same color as the blood on my clothes. "Especially when you hesitate over simple executions." His breath ghosts across my ear as he leans in. "Did that little princess fuck with your head and get too deep under your skin? Is that what this is?"

My hand shoots out, wrapping around his wrist. "Don't."

"Or what?" His smile is mocking.

"*Don't*," I repeat, very softly. "No games. Not tonight."

His expression falls with a sudden understanding. "You're thinking about Turpori."

It's not a question. He understands me too well, knows all my scars like they're his own. After all, he found me in the aftermath and offered me purpose when all I wanted was for the realms to bleed the way I did.

I nod.

"Put those memories back in their box." His voice is almost gentle. "Lock them away."

I can't help but watch the woman again. Some strange heaviness settles in the pit of my stomach as the screams echo from the lockbox of my memories. "Ever consider trying mercy? Change things up?"

Alexios jerks his head toward me, eyes blazing with inner light. "You can't be serious."

"Thought exercise."

"Don't start that *thought exercise* shit with me. One human skips their tithe? Fine. But then another follows, and another, and soon I'm drowning under the pressure of a thousand broken vows. So don't stand there and preach to me about mercy when you don't carry what I carry."

At this moment, he's not Eternal of Asteria. He's a male buckling under his burdens—the Shroud, the neglected tithes, two realms balanced on his shoulders.

"If you feel so bad for her"—he gestures to the woman—"go on and Claim her. See how long your compassion lasts when you've got her every thought bleeding into your skull and her constant existence pressing against yours."

I hesitate. There's a feverish light in his eyes I don't like, a manic energy thrumming beneath his skin. He's fraying, and I'm not sure I want to be around to witness the shape of what's left when he finally loses it.

"This isn't working," I say, picking my way through the

minefield of his mood. "Beating them into obedience isn't a solution. The Vartenans already hate us, and someday, we'll have another war on our hands."

"Then give me an alternative to the blood and the tithes." He spreads his arms. "Tell me how else we keep the realms at peace and maintain the Shroud without sacrifice. Come on, enlighten me."

"You could try showing yourself once a century. Attract the crowds, speak to them. It wouldn't go against the Accord's clause about interfering with Devaliant rule if you—"

"I can't," he says through his teeth.

That pulls me up short. "What do you mean *can't*?"

"Their voices get too loud." He taps his temple. "I don't hear them when they're dead, which is why I prefer to visit their corpses."

I knew he could sense his Claimed and sometimes hear their thoughts. I hadn't realized proximity sharpened the connection until it was physically agonizing for him. But then, no god in history has Claimed as many as Alexios. No god has held an entire realm barrier together with their power alone.

"You came to me full of vengeance once," he continues with a sigh, "determined to make the humans pay for what they did to our people. You understood why this was our only option. So if you want mercy for her, what are you willing to trade?"

I swallow down a surge of bitterness at how easily he wields our shared past like a dagger poised over my chest. "You never bargain for human lives."

He gives a sharp, mirthless laugh. "That's because I'm still choking on the last deal I made with one. It's currently splitting my skull in two. Be grateful I'm making an exception for my favorite Wolf."

"So, those are my options? Save her or kill her?"

"Yes," he says simply. "Choose."

He makes it sound so simple, as if he's not asking me to crack my ribcage open, pry out a shard of this woman's soul, and stake it to mine. "My mother taught me it was obscene to Claim someone without soulbonding with them. It's sacred. For Chosen only."

For those who earn the right to touch your wings, to share your breath and know your soul. To soulbond is to bare your jugular to someone's teeth and say, *Here, this is where I'm softest. This is where I break.* I won't Claim anyone I'm not willing to soulbond with.

"Well, your mother's dead, along with everyone else who believed in sacred anything. This is what's left. These are the choices we make now." He jerks his head at the woman again. "Choose. Kill her clean, or I'll make it last. You know I will."

So I obey because I'm his Wolf—his weapon. And a weapon doesn't get to choose, not really. It simply cuts.

The woman clutches her dead lover tighter. "Please," she whispers. "Please."

"Shh," I say.

My hand closes around her throat, and her pulse flutters against my palm like a trapped bird. With a sharp jerk of my hand, I snap her spine and drop her to the ground.

Alexios watches me. "Don't ever ask me for mercy again." He turns to leave, then pauses. "One last thing. The princess' body—did you find it?"

I keep my face blank. "Not yet. Scavengers probably got to it. I'll get her for you."

Once I'm finished with her.

"You better."

Something dangerous flickers in his expression, a warning of what he'll do if her corpse isn't found. Thunder rolls across the sky and lightning flashes, painting everything in harsh white light—the broken buildings, the scattered bodies, the blood turning black on the ground. Alexios' mood making itself known. His wings rustle as he walks away in dismissal.

"Clean yourself up," he says over his shoulder. "You smell like a slaughterhouse."

17

EVANDER

THE FLOATING ISLANDS of Caelestis dot the horizon like a string of pearls.

Often called the crown jewel of Asteria, the city is a breathtaking expanse of crystal spires set against patches of lush greenery. Elaborate sky gardens float overhead, loaded with hanging vines and luminous flowers. The pools of starlight scattered across the landscape are connected by bridges between the islands, ending in waterfalls that cascade over the sheer cliffs and into the sea below.

I veer west to the smallest island in the chain. Zephyr's home dominates the cliff face, an elegant spire with glowing blue wards winding around every pillar and arched window—a warning to anyone uninvited to back off. But I've known Alexios' spymaster since I was an infant, and she's one of maybe seven gods I trust. Well, trust is a strong word—let's call it confident apathy. I doubt she'll stab me without a good reason.

Probably.

I drop onto the landing platform, my boots leaving bloody prints behind. The smell of metal and leather thickens as I stride toward the smaller building just off her sky garden.

Zephyr's workshop is a cozy space with vaulted ceilings and marble columns inlaid with runes to enhance her magic. Workbenches and tables are pushed up along every wall, littered with half-finished works—the flowing fabric of a formal gown, leather armor, some training garments. Zephyr makes any wearable for the right price.

"You're dripping on my floor, you degenerate."

I huff out a laugh as I turn.

Zephyr stands in the doorway, her black wings tucked against her back. She's all lean muscle and sharp edges, always buttoned up and proper, with her dark hair pulled tightly in a braid. Her light brown skin glitters in the runelight. She has an elegant face that's the kind of pretty that doesn't stick overlong in your mind—until you see her eyes. One black, one silver. No other god in the realm shares those irises.

"Funny," I say. "I thought you'd be used to blood by now."

"On the battlefield? Yes. In my home? Absolutely not. I ought to take you out back and shove you in my pool."

"I'll send you a cleaning crew."

She crosses her arms over her chest, and a tattoo peeks out from under her collar—angular marks, each representing a campaign during the war, back when she led armies instead of trading secrets. Whether she has tattoos other than those, I couldn't say. I've never seen Zephyr in anything but her high-collared uniform.

"Why are you here, Wolf? I'm on a schedule."

"I need clothes."

"You're wearing clothes," she says dryly. "Granted, they're more blood than fabric at this point, but I didn't think that bothered you. Unless you've suddenly developed standards?"

Hilarious.

"Not for me. For a female."

That gets a raised eyebrow from her. "I thought you preferred your lovers wearing as little as possible. Did you actually find one who gets off on bloodshed as much as you do?"

If she only knew.

I can't help but picture the Devaliant in my lap, blade in hand. The look on her face after she cut me up, all that anger turning into something darker. Hungrier. I can't wait to feed all that rage.

"She needs a functional wardrobe," I say, ignoring her question. "Clothes that can hold up in a fight or on rough terrain."

Zephyr is quiet for a long moment, just staring at me. I stare right back, daring her to ask.

"This girl," she finally says, "must be special if you're asking me to dress her."

"She's a means to an end."

"Well, whatever the end, she'll need to come in for measurements."

"I have them memorized."

And then I'm speaking, spilling numbers like secrets. The architecture of *her*. The flare of her hips and the dip of her waist. The delicate circumference of her wrists, ankles, and throat. I map the Devaliant in digits and degrees, charting her body as one might the stars.

The air thickens as Zephyr's magic unfurls. She perches on her workbench, liquid shadows spilling from her fingertips to pool on the floor. Her loom rises from the darkness. It's an ancient-looking thing made of black metal and gleaming filaments. Honestly, I can't explain where it comes from when she pulls it up out of nothing. Zephyr's power is singular in Scillari—the magic of creation, the ability to pull from the realm at will.

She begins to weave.

It's mesmerizing to watch her work. Shadows gather in her palms, becoming solid and real. Piece by piece, armor takes shape—leather molded to invisible curves, scaled and segmented for ease of movement. The hide is soft yet reinforced, lined with silk for comfort against bare skin. Metal follows, but not the crude stuff of mortal forges. This forms a mesh so fine it might as well be liquid. It reinforces vital areas without adding bulk or weight. Perfect for someone small who needs to move fast.

Someone like my nemesis.

There are a hundred little details I wouldn't have thought to include. The precise flare of a vambrace, the cant of a shoulder piece, the slight thickness of the chest piece for protection. It's so clearly made for a woman as petite as the Devaliant. I can already picture how it will cling—the perfect mix of allure and armor.

"No fastenings for wings," I instruct. "Closed at the back."

Zephyr's hands go still. Her stare digs into me as if she's trying to pry open my skull and peek inside. I know how it must look, commissioning armor without consideration for wings. Plenty of demis lost their wings in the war, but it means losing status—being permanently ground-bound and barred from battle.

But she only nods and keeps her questions to herself. Her fingers twitch and pull more shadows from the air. They twist between her knuckles while bits of starlight cling to her skin. I've seen her kill a man with those same gentle movements.

"It needs to be tight. Make it cling," I add, just to see her scowl. She doesn't.

She turns, reaches again into the heart of the loom, and tosses a garment at me. I catch it, glaring down at the scrap of clothing in my hand.

It's a nightgown. Black silk and lace, a swooping V-neckline that plunges to the navel, and cobweb-fine silver embroidery that gleams in the workshop's low light.

My mind blanks out to images. The Devaliant laid out across my bed, breasts straining against the fabric, the juncture of her thighs a shadowed tease. Tearing it off with my teeth and fucking her in scraps of starlight.

I swallow hard, my throat tight. Then I lift my gaze to Zephyr's. "This isn't what I asked for."

The demigoddess has the audacity to look amused. Like she knows every filthy, depraved thing I just pictured. "No, but I'd bet my best blade it's what you *wanted*." She leans back and raises an eyebrow. "Will there be anything else?"

I exhale slowly through my nose. I'm not about to engage in a verbal sparring match with Alexios' spymaster. "Someone told me to get her sweets. Good advice or no?"

"Decent," she says with a shrug. She turns and rummages through a chest behind the workbench, pulling out a silver box. "I was saving these for myself, but go ahead and take them." She flips the lid, revealing rows of confections wrapped in parchment. "Ambrosial clusters. Roasted nuts and dried fireplums drizzled in nectar and rolled in edible gold. Useful for your purposes?"

"Perfect." I take the box from her and tuck it into the bundle of clothes. "Thank you." I turn to leave, then hesitate on the threshold. "This stays between us."

She's closer to Alexios than anyone in the realms. I trust her with my life and my secrets, but I also don't pretend to understand the complexities of her bond with the king, the way her eyes follow him when she thinks no one's watching.

Her mouth thins. "Keep it from becoming a problem, and he won't hear anything from me."

Oh, Zephyr. It became a problem when I didn't cut her throat.

Bathwater runs down my spine and drips from my wings as I give them a hard shake. I'm toweling off when *her* scent crashes into me.

"Fuck," I mutter, my eyes slamming shut. *Not now.*

It's everywhere, clouding my thoughts—jasmine and lilac, the sweet floral fragrance of my guestroom soap. I tug on my pants and shove a few of Zephyr's treats into my pocket, heading up the stairs.

And there she is, the bane of my existence, wandering my halls.

My shirt. That's all she's got on. The hem skims her thighs, one sleeve slipping down to bare the curve of her shoulder. So much skin begging to be touched, to be bitten. Her silver hair is a messy tumble down her back, and I want to grab it. To twist the strands around my fist and *yank* until her throat is bared to my teeth.

Get it together.

I fade out of sight, wrapping myself in invisibility. Some dark, depraved part of me gets off on the idea of stalking her through these halls and waiting until the right moment to snatch her up, pin her down, and—

And then what? the last vestige of sanity mocks. *Fuck her or kill her?*

The Devaliant goes rigid. As if she can feel my stare and sense all the violent, filthy things I long to do to her.

She whirls to face my direction. "Wolf. I know you're there."

I stay silent as I circle her, letting my power brush down the elegant line of her spine, then the dip of her waist and the curve of her hip. She shivers.

I lean in close, still unseen, my breath teasing her ear. "You like me watching?"

She scowls. "Have the courtesy to do it to my face or leave me alone."

With a chuckle, I let the invisibility bleed away. Her gaze rakes over me, taking in my bare torso, the black trousers riding low on my hips. I flex my wings a little for show.

Her eyes snap up to mine accusingly.

I just flash a grin. "You're far from the guest room. Lost your way?"

"Can't sleep."

I wait for more, for all those messy human feelings to come spilling out. But she keeps her expression smooth and unruffled. The Devaliant mask firmly in place.

"You never told me which parts of the tower were off limits," she adds. "I'd hate to stumble somewhere I'm not wanted."

I'm not fooled by the innocent act; this girl is always looking for lines to scuff out. Any excuse to disobey. It's in her blood.

"There aren't any locked doors here," I say. "No forbidden wings or chains rattling in the attic. I'm not your jailer."

"Really." Before I can stop her, she's reaching for the handle to her left. "Then why don't I start with—"

No.

I slap my palm against the door to keep it shut. She blinks up at me, startled.

"Correction," I say, shoving down all the memories threatening to bubble to the surface. *Stay the fuck down.* "See this obsidian seal right here?" I tap the carved symbol on the wood for emphasis. "Memorize it. Burn it into your brain. Consider it the one hard line in this whole fucked up arrangement. If I *ever* catch you opening this door, that's it, Devaliant. Your stay of execution ends, and I'll make you wish you'd died on that mountain."

She snorts. "That reminds me of an old story in Vartena about a naïve bride who gets the keys to her new husband's castle. He tells her she can explore anywhere she likes except that one special room. No explanation, just a command. Want to guess what she found when she finally looked?"

"Let me think." I back her up against the door. "Rotting corpses? The bones of all the other stupid girls who couldn't follow simple instructions?"

"Close enough. So what's in this room? The remains of dead princesses who bored you?"

The memories begin shoving at the box, screams echoing from hundreds of years ago.

Stay. The fuck. Down.

"Everyone has rooms they keep shut tight," I say, dragging my focus to her. "Where we put the ugliest parts of ourselves. I'd bet even a perfect princess has hallways she keeps locked down, doors she doesn't want anyone going through." I press my palms to the wall on either side of her head, leaning in. "Could be real fun picking those locks and digging up all those things you think you're hiding. That appeal at all? Or you want to tell me to fuck off?"

Anger sparks in her eyes. But beneath that…

Fear.

Good, I think. *You should be afraid of me.*

"Thing is, Devaliant," I continue, "I don't need to hide what I am behind closed doors. You know *exactly* what kind of sick bastard you're dealing with. I get off on violence. I get hard when I hurt people. I've killed more humans than you've had hot dinners, and I'd do it again in a heartbeat. And yet here you are, strolling around wearing only my shirt like you want me to bend you over and show you how monsters fuck."

Her mouth parts slightly, and a breath gusts past her lips.

But she doesn't back down or retreat. "The alternative was strolling around naked," she snaps, as if I'm being particularly dense.

"Doesn't sound like a problem from where I'm standing. Toys can be clothed or unclothed, depending on my mood."

Her scowl deepens. "If you wanted a naked toy, you should have bargained for one."

"I suppose I should have," I say with a smirk, reaching into my pocket. "Maybe one day, we'll renegotiate your wardrobe. Let's try something else tonight." I pull one of Zephyr's sugar clusters from my pocket and hold it between us.

"What's that?"

"Me being generous."

She looks at the treat like it might grow fangs. "Prove it's safe."

"Doubting my good intentions?"

"Why in the realms would I trust your intentions?"

Fair enough.

I bring the sweet to my mouth and sink my teeth in. Decadence explodes on my tongue—ambrosial honey and succulent fruits, toasted nuts, and the decadent crunch of edible gold leaf. Exquisite.

Holding her gaze, I slowly lick the honey off my finger. "That do it for you?"

She's staring at my mouth. "I guess so."

I peel the wrapping off another cluster, and she tries to take it from me, but I push her hand away. "No. Toys get hand-fed when I want." I press the sweet to the seam of her lips. "Open up. Think twice before biting."

"Or what?"

"Or I'll bite back."

Her eyes flash. *Do it*, they seem to say. *Push me until I push back and make you bleed.*

"Behave," I murmur.

Her lip curls like she's holding back a snarl, but she leans and takes the candy delicately between her teeth. I swear the world stops. The noise she makes shoots straight to my cock—a low, throaty moan that has no business existing outside a bedroom.

I am going to devour this woman whole.

I'll lay kingdoms at Zephyr's feet. Shower her in the corpses of her enemies—any gruesome offering her spiteful heart desires—because Bryony Devaliant is licking honey from my fingers, and I'm about to lose my damned mind.

"Thought you might like that," I say roughly.

She rolls her eyes. "Don't sound so smug. Why did you bring these?"

"Maybe I wanted to see what you'd do with something that exists purely for pleasure. No purpose, no greater meaning. Just…" I trail off as her tongue darts out to wet her lips. "Indulgence."

"And what's the catch?" She bites down gently on my thumb. "Are you hoping to earn my trust with sugar?"

"Your trust is worthless to me. I want to watch you come undone and know I'm the reason."

"Such lofty ambitions." Another scrape of teeth. "You're not even subtle."

"I've been guilty of far worse crimes than ambition, and subtlety is for courtiers and grifters. For little boys who don't know how to take what they want. I prefer the direct approach."

"So do I."

Quick as a snake strike, she buries her hand in my hair and wrenches my head back with a strength that surprises me. Pain lights up my scalp, sharp and immediate, and a strange, giddy amusement stirs in my chest.

Fuck yes. This is what I wanted.

"Tell me why you *really* brought me this," she hisses. "A test? A trap? What game are we playing right now?"

For a moment, all I can do is stare at her—this wild, reckless creature who sees the monster in me and snarls right back. "The same game we've been playing since you got here. Move, countermove. Disarm, attack. You draw blood, I draw more."

Do it. Hurt me. Make me feel it.

She releases me with a disgusted sound and shoves at my chest. "The *toy* is going to bed. Enjoy your brooding, or lurking, or whatever it is demented gods do to pass the time."

It's too abrupt. Too much like a retreat. I want to keep poking at this woman and seeing what snarls out of her, finding hard lines and all the little things she craved when she was bleeding on the altar. I tell myself this is how monsters deal with any prey they toy with. They find weaknesses. They make it hurt.

My hand closes around her wrist. "Wait."

A frown tugs at her lips. I can practically see her pondering all the ways she could break my hold.

"Let me show you the library."

What the fuck? I want to swallow the words back. Pretend they never happened, because why would I be stupid enough to invite her there?

The Devaliant blinks. "What?"

"The library," I grit out, because apparently my mind and mouth have decided to mutiny. "I want you to see it."

There. I've committed now.

Dumbass.

Emotions flicker across her features. I tense, waiting for her to laugh in my face. To throw my offer back at me with a sneer.

But then—

"Okay," she breathes. "I'd like that very much."

I can't look at her. Can't breathe through whatever this is cracking open behind my ribs. I need to dig it out.

But instead, I just turn and lead her down the hall. I feel her stare between my shoulder blades as I push the library doors open.

She steps inside and sucks in a sharp breath, taking in the high arched ceilings, stained glass throwing color everywhere. A staircase circles up and up, railings wrapped in glowing roses. And the books. Hundreds of thousands of leather-bound tomes, scrolls, and stone tablets in a thousand dead tongues.

It's one of my most prized possessions, this library. The only surviving piece of my life *Before*—a repository of my people's history. Our language, our craft, the legacy of our magic before the war ripped my mother's territory apart. Turpori is now temporarily split between Asteria and Nyholm until my brother and I reclaim it.

And I let a human pass the threshold. A Devaliant. The last woman in the realms who should ever see this sanctuary.

Amara's right. I'm out of my mind.

"It's incredible," the Devaliant breathes. "I've never seen anything so beautiful."

She tips her head to take in the tiered balconies and the domed skylights, reverence softening her features. This is the first time something of mine has moved her to awe. I want to trap that expression beneath glass just so I can keep it.

In truth, my library is a rather modest collection by Asterian standards—a few hundred thousand volumes as opposed to the millions that line the archives of Alexios' palace. But to mortal eyes, I imagine it seems vast.

The Devaliant runs light fingers over the spines. "I can feel the power in each one," she murmurs. "Like a current. It's almost alive."

I go still, a sudden wariness tightening my muscles. "Magic leaves a mark. In the right hands, a drop of power can rewrite reality."

And in the wrong ones, it can raze entire cities.

If she hears the catch in my voice, she doesn't let on. "I've never seen so many books. How old are they? How old are *you*?"

"A few are as ancient as the first Eternals, before our realms divided. Others are more recent acquisitions from the fallen libraries of Scillari in the aftermath of the war." I flash her a smile. "As for my age—I'm a thousand. Old enough to have collected plenty of perverse pastimes." I lean in, breathing my next words into her ear. "And young enough still to enjoy them."

She shivers. "And luring wayward Vartenan royalty to their doom? Is that a recent hobby?"

"What can I say? I'm always in the mood for new experiences."

The laugh that startles out of her is effervescent, and it sends a shrapnel burst through my withered excuse for a heart. What a lovely sound, her amusement. Musical.

She moves deeper into the stacks. I follow her, never more than a half-step behind, waiting for the inevitable moment when realization sinks in and her survival instincts roar to life. Remembering what I am, what she is.

But she doesn't. The Devaliant has forgotten herself.

"There are more books here than in the entire palace in Hellevig. My sister, Theodora, would weep at the sight of it. Burst into flame out of pure, rapturous bibliophilia."

I snort. "The scent of charred princess would be difficult to air out."

That earns me another smile, this time more wistful. "Could you... send word to Theo? To let her know I'm okay?"

I *should* play gatekeeper. Should twist the knife until she understands exactly what it means to be at a monster's mercy. And yet...

I'm not your jailer, I'd told her. And I meant it.

"Tomorrow," I say gruffly.

The Devaliant gives me a grateful grin. "How do you have volumes from before the realms divided?" she asks as she continues down the stacks. "I thought all the records from that era were lost to the Great Burning when the Urnian Archives fell to human soldiers."

"Not all. Some were smuggled out in the years leading up to the border wars between Asteria and Vartena when tensions were escalating."

She pauses. "You fought in the war."

Memories batter against the inside of my skull. The taste of ash, the screaming. My brother's blood-slick hand clutching mine as his face twists in agony.

End it. Please. It hurts.

A blink, and I wrench myself back to the here and now. "Yes," I say flatly. "I fought."

"There aren't many surviving books about the war in Hellevig."

Her voice goes soft, careful. "I heard Amalthea ordered most of them destroyed as part of her bargain with Alexios. But the ones we do have only tell the Vartenan side." She fidgets, throwing me an apologetic look. "They say paying a tithe to the Eternal was better than losing more of our own. Alexios and the Dark King were killing us in large numbers, and nearly all of my family died before Amalthea…"

She notices my expression, the words dying on her lips. She must sense it—the sudden crackle of my power shivering through the air, the sparks of heat.

But the reckless creature barrels on.

"None of those accounts even mention what Vartenans did during the Godkiller Crusades—"

"Never call it that," I cut her off, the words bitten out between my teeth. "Not to a god. Not if you want to keep breathing."

I don't tell her what we call it in Scillari. *The Devouring.* As if mere language could encompass the scope of that devastation, the breadth of all we lost. Everything they stole.

She swallows hard. "What should I call it?"

My smile is a dead thing, empty of warmth or mirth. "The war. The purge. The culling. Take your pick. But call it a *crusade* again, and we're going to have a problem."

"I wasn't thinking." Her voice drops to a whisper. "I'm sorry."

Sorry.

She's fucking *sorry.*

Would she still be sorry if she knew? If she could see inside me, all the broken bits that used to be a brother, a son, a god meant to rule. Everything her family took from me.

I should tear into the fragile offering of her remorse and rip it to shreds. Even a creature like me can recognize the danger in it. The deadly, disarming lure.

"Be careful," I warn her. "Compassion is a poisoned chalice to offer a beast."

Because she doesn't know. She *can't* know what it costs me to let her live. To let her stand here and pretend to give a shit about my dead.

I turn and walk back to the door before I do something I'll regret. "Lessons start tomorrow at dawn," I call over my shoulder. "The northern garden. You'll be training with Amara. Don't be late."

The doors boom shut behind me. I lean against the wood and exhale, slow and controlled.

There are a thousand reasons immortals go mad, a gradual rot that eats you from the inside out. So we seek our own destruction, chasing the welcome dark at the bottom of blood-glutted seas.

Even monsters grow weary with the weight of memory.

18

BRYONY

THE WOLF ACTUALLY listened. I said I didn't want silks, and he brought me the wardrobe of a soldier: sturdy leathers, practical boots, loose trousers. Garments meant for movement. For action.

I run my fingers over the material, tracing the fabric so different from my Lucinian dresses. As I lift one of the shirts, a scrap of black flutters to the floor. Heat crawls up my neck when I snatch it up and realize what it is. To call it a nightgown would be generous. It's the thinnest silk and lace, designed to frame rather than cover.

Right. So there it is—the retaliation to my request. The mocking challenge.

Move, countermove. Disarm, attack.

And I can picture it with devastating clarity—his hands ripping this off my body. Golden wings spreading wide as he pins me down. The scrape of teeth along my throat as he—

"*Stop*," I snarl, squeezing my eyes shut. My skin feels too tight, too hot.

I stuff the nightgown under the stack of clothes. If he thinks I'm going to prance around in that shred of nothing, he's delusional. I'll strangle him with it first.

Jaw clenched, I yank on the leathers. Everything fits perfectly, which is both impressive and unsettling. I wrench open my door—and nearly miss the note pinned to the wood with a long rose thorn. Beneath it, a blade in an ornate sheath dangles from another thorn.

Dear Nemesis,

The kitchen is open to you. Eat after training, and don't ruin my floors with your bleeding. I just had them cleaned. The dagger is for practice. If you try to keep it, it'll be the knife I kill you with.

Wolf

"Prick," I mutter, yanking the note free.

I storm into my room and grab a pen from the writing desk to scrawl a message below his.

Go to Hellevig and tell my sister I'm alive, or I'll bleed all over your precious stonework. Her balcony is the biggest on the east tower. Don't be rude.

B

P.S. Your roses need pruning. Maybe start with the ones you used to stab notes on my door.

I push the thorn back through the paper and pin it to the door.

The morning air is frigid when I step outside. A breeze stirs my hair, and I breathe in deeply. It smells different here than in Hellevig—the fragrant perfume of roses, other growing things, magic. His power saturates the entire property.

"Still breathing, I see."

I turn at that cool, sardonic voice. Amara lands in a crouch, her dark wings settling against her back. The sunlight filtering through the leaves makes the violet undertones in her feathers shimmer.

"Don't sound so disappointed," I say, crossing my arms.

"How's he treating you?" She tilts her head, studying me with those pale blue eyes. "Has he tried to eat you yet?"

"Not yet. Though you wouldn't care if he did, considering you dumped me here like garbage."

She shrugs. "He handles oathbreakers. I handle my own shit. I was working with limited options since you were busy dying on a mountain when I found you. You're welcome, by the way."

"If he's supposed to be handling me, why are you here?"

"Blackmail." She smirks. "It's a time-honored tradition between the Wolf and me. If he tried to train you himself, he'd snap you in half in under a minute." Her attention drops to the blade at my hip. "Word of advice? Don't get too eager to draw that. You need to learn how to make your body into a weapon first." She rolls her shoulders, loosening her muscles. "Lesson one. Knock me on my ass. I'm real curious to see you try."

I'm self-aware enough to know she's trying to rile me up—but some contrary part of me rises to it anyway, snarling. As if it's been waiting for an excuse to punch something until my knuckles split.

"Come on," Amara says. "I'm not here to socialize. Hit me."

I set my stance, trying to remember the way the palace guards stood when they sparred with each other. *Breathe in, breathe out.* My fingers curl into my palms, and I throw myself into the blow—

And strike nothing but air as Amara weaves out of reach.

The crack of her palm against my cheek steals the breath from my lungs. My vision tunnels, the world lurching sideways as I stagger. I never even saw her move.

"Pathetic," she spits. "Is this all you've got? This is what I'm supposed to work with? No wonder your uncle thought he could gut you like a fish."

I stand there, clutching my burning cheek, trying to process what just happened.

"Again," she barks. "Move your ass!"

I lunge for her. She grabs my wrist, uses my momentum against me, and sends me flying. I hit the ground hard and roll, gravel tearing into my hands as I skid across the dirt. I force myself up onto my knees before she can kick my ribs in.

"You're holding back." Amara steps over me, planting her foot between my shoulder blades and shoving me down. My teeth clack together with the impact. "All that rage and hurt, and you're too craven to use it. Get up and make me feel it. Show me why he's keeping a Devaliant around instead of mounting your head on his wall."

I spit out a mouthful of blood. "Fuck you."

She just laughs. "Oh, Princess. You couldn't handle me even if I let you. Did they breed the fight out of your bloodline along with your dignity?"

I grab for her again, but Amara's next vicious blow sends me sprawling. Stars burst behind my eyes.

"Aw, did I hurt your feelings?" She crouches over me and grabs me by my hair, wrenching my head back. "Poor baby. Maybe I should fly your ass to the Duehavn and leave you there for the crows. Would've saved us both the trouble if I'd let you die like Alexios wanted."

I wrench away from her, growling through my teeth, but she shoves her knee against my spine and slams me down.

"Did you really think it would be that easy? That you'd waltz in here and suddenly become a warrior? You're so weak you can't even handle a warm-up." She pushes my face into the dirt, her grip on my hair hard enough to sting. "The world has been itching for the chance to tear you apart since the second you crawled out of your mother's cunt with that special Devaliant blood. Tell me, Princess. What will you give up to keep breathing one more day? Your pride? Your dignity? Maybe if you're real lucky, you'll only have to get on your knees and suck the Wolf's c—"

Something in me *snaps*.

It's a dam breaking, years of suppressed rage flooding me all at once. Every hurt, every humiliation, every time I had to *lie there and fucking take it.*

Later, I'll wonder what it says about me. How eager I was to turn to violence the moment I tasted freedom. How right it felt to finally draw blood that wasn't mine, to make something else hurt.

But in that instant, none of that matters.

I yank out of her hold and slam my head backward into Amara's nose. Light bursts in my vision at the impact, but I hardly feel it over the vicious rush of satisfaction as her grip loosens and she reels back.

"That's more like it," she snarls. "Come on, Princess. Show me what you're made of."

I leap on her with a snarl, and we crash to the ground. Some distant part of me shrieks that she'll tear me apart. That I should know better than to attack a demigoddess. But the rest of me revels in it. Revels in this chance to fight for my right to exist with something other than a bared throat.

So I punch and kick and claw, fighting dirty. Fighting *mean*. Messy and desperate and real. Amara gives as good as she gets. Her elbow cracks into my cheek, and her knuckles split my lip, my cheekbone, and the arch of my brow. But I don't stop. I can't stop. Because stopping means giving up, and I've already bled too much to let it be for nothing.

My fingers find her hair and yank hard. She hisses, retaliating with a knee to my ribs. We roll across the ground, each struggling for dominance, leaving blood and skin in the dirt.

Somehow, I gain the upper hand and wrench her arm up behind her back, shoving her down. We're both panting and sweaty, chests heaving.

"There it is," Amara says with a breathless laugh, and there's a warmth in her voice that sounds like approval. "Fuck, I knew you had bite."

"You let me win," I say.

"Obviously." She turns her head to grin at me. "But you needed to know what winning feels like. Needed to taste it. How else will you learn to crave it?"

I roll to the side, every inch of me screaming in protest. Amara pushes herself up on her elbows, looking more exhilarated than anything else.

"Oh, come on. Don't look so pissed. That was a damn good showing for your first real fight."

"You're insane."

"Probably." Amara grabs my hand and drags me to my feet. "But I'm the insane bitch who's going to keep you alive long enough to entertain the Wolf. You're welcome." She jerks her chin toward the tower. "Go get cleaned up, little sister. And if the Wolf has any complaints about the condition of his new toy, tell him he can shove them up his ass."

Little sister. The words strike like a blade to the chest. For a second, I'm back in Hellevig, in the palace gardens with Theo, giggling over something stupid. It feels like another lifetime, a grainy memory belonging to someone else. Someone softer.

I shake my head hard, locking it away. "Why did you call me that?"

Amara glances up. "What?"

"Little sister. Why did you say that?"

She opens her mouth, then closes it. For the first time since I've met her, she looks almost… uncertain. "It's just something trainers say," she finally says, but it sounds like a lie. "Don't read into it." She studies me, taking in the damage. I'm struggling to breathe through my nose, and my left eye is swelling shut. "Pain is an excellent teacher," she says softly. "The most efficient, if not the kindest. Those bruises? That blood? You earned them. Wear them with pride."

My senses are scraped raw, as if she peeled back my skin and exposed the angry mess beneath. Reached right into my chest and wrapped her fingers around all my soft, vulnerable places.

And it's the most alive I've felt in years.

19

EVANDER

BLACK MOURNING BANNERS drape nearly every building in Hellevig. Wilted rose petals litter the roads, trampled under countless boots, and the pavement is smeared with the wax of a thousand burnt-out vigils. The entire city is grieving the loss of its princess.

I've seen my share of grief. Too much, truthfully. In wartime Scillari, when the bodies stacked up faster than we could burn them, our funerals became public events—thousands of vessels floating into the sky, each containing the ash of demis being returned to the stars. You couldn't escape it.

The "death" of Bryony Devaliant reminds me of those ceremonies—the scents, the shrines on every street. Some deaths leave marks.

I fly unseen above the masses gathered at the palace gates. Hundreds of bodies are packed together, a sea of black fabric and red veils marking a royal passing. It's a credit to Bryony's status among her people that they've come at all. By now, rumors must have spread that she was an oathbreaker—and traitors don't get a public mourning. They don't get grief. But her? They're screaming for her.

"Where's the body? Where's the princess' body?"

"Murderers!"

"Princess Bryony lives!"

She's alive, all right. Wearing my shirts, wandering my tower like she owns the place. My personal plague.

I follow the curve of the Araxes River toward my destination. The wealth of Hellevig's center gives way to seedier districts as you move outward. Silk Street sits at the border between old money and new poverty, where respectable merchants rub shoulders with criminals.

I land at the old tannery, the only lead I have on the bastards peddling demigod flesh. The stench of smoke and leather hangs heavy in the air as I push through the sagging doorway into what's left of the building's interior.

It's been gutted. Shattered beams drip char onto the floor, and glass litters the ground from the blown-out windows. The debris is minimal, which means the building was stripped before they destroyed it.

Silk Street's a bust, I tell Alexios, bracing for the brutal crush of his presence. *They burned it all.*

His consciousness slams into mine. *Keep looking anyway. I want a lead. Rip that place apart if you have to.*

I crouch next to an overturned table, running my fingers over the gouges in the wood. The kind of marks you get from hacking over and over, really putting your back into it. Just the right size for a big Turpori blade made for chopping through bone.

And underneath the scent of fire and charred wood, I sense it. That ancient energy soaked right into the surface—demigod power. The *fresh* kind. The dying kind.

Bile stings my throat. An image flashes of bodies strapped to this table, naked and split open. They'd have started at the top of the wings, splintering through cartilage and ligament.

Fuck. Fuck, fuck, fuck.

We've got a problem, I tell Alexios. *These fuckers aren't just scavenging battlefields anymore. Someone's been funneling them fresh kills. There were demis held here within the last week. I can smell it.*

Shit. The pressure in my head builds with his anger. *All right, I'll have Zephyr ask around to see where any demis have gone missing.*

I turn over a broken crate with my boot and do one last sweep of the building. *I've found all there is to find here. Should we involve the Dark King?*

Let's wait for Zephyr's report. Severin might want peace as much as we do, but I'd rather eat nails than deal with him. The pain in my skull escalates to white-hot agony. *One more thing, if you're done. Circle Hellevig on your way back, and make sure they see you. The city is getting bold without the princess' corpse to weep over. Remind them why they should fear you.*

Then he's gone, the link snapping closed. The pain vanishes in an instant.

With a sigh of relief, I conjure my invisibility and slip out into the daylight. As I wing toward the palace gates, new mourners have amassed by the hundreds, choking the main thoroughfare.

Landing on the public-facing balcony, I spread my wings and let my magic fall away. The throng gapes up at me. It takes a few seconds for it to register—for them to understand what they're seeing. *Who* they're seeing.

Then the panic hits.

Gasps and shrieks echo across the square. People recoil in horror, stumbling over each other in their haste to flee.

I can't help but grin. *Yeah, that's right. Get a good, long look.*

With a strong flap of my wings, I take to the sky again and circle the palace. I hope the image of me is seared into their worthless skulls.

Once the street empties, I land on the large balcony along the palace's eastern spire. The air reeks of incense and perfume, the balustrade lined with half-melted candles and petals. Someone has left a shrine. A miniature portrait of my Devaliant sits wreathed in black ribbon and roses.

I pick it up, studying the delicate brushstrokes. They've captured her physical beauty well enough—the silvery hair, the luminous skin, those violet irises. But it's missing all the ways she snarls and snaps. The painting shows a porcelain doll; I have the real thing—messy and breathing and full of rage.

"Put it down." The voice at my back is cool and clipped.

"Princess Theodora, I assume?" I say pleasantly, still

examining the portrait. "You know, this doesn't look a thing like your sister. Too perfect. Too pristine. The thing that struck me the first time I saw her was how hungry she looked. A bit like a cornered animal still pretending to be civilized. And this?" I flick a dismissive finger against the painted surface. "It's dull. Boring. You should burn it, to be honest. It's offensive."

"I said put it down. Or I'll shove it down your fucking throat."

I turn slowly. Theodora Devaliant looks about two seconds from tearing out my jugular. Her red hair is all tangled, her green eyes flashing. The physical resemblance to her sister is there—a similarity in the features, if not the coloring. But where my girl runs hot, all restless energy and burning need, this one is cold down to her core. Even the way she holds herself is different—tightly leashed. In control.

I like seeing the contrast, knowing that my Devaliant is the wild one.

"Hasn't anyone ever taught you it's stupid to threaten gods?" I ask her.

Don't be rude, my Devaliant said in her note. I have the feeling her sister will make that difficult.

"You aren't the first arrogant prick from Scillari I've told to go fuck himself. Just ask your brother. He's had the pleasure."

Of course, Bastien would have crossed paths with Theodora Devaliant during his duties. I wonder if he saw the same thing I do now—that complete absence of fear that would be admirable if it weren't so foolish. Fucking Devaliants. Challenging monsters everywhere they go.

She takes another step. "Did you come to gloat, or do you get off on tormenting grieving families?"

Huh. I set down the portrait and give her my attention. Let's see how this plays out. "What exactly am I meant to be gloating over? Be specific."

"You murdered my sister." There's a waver in her voice, a crack in that icy composure. "Hunted her down like an animal and left her to bleed out on the Duehavn. *Alone.*"

For a moment, I can only stare at her. So this is the tale

Hellevig has spun for itself? Me as the black-hearted villain who slaughtered their precious princess? They won't be wrong, but it's a little obnoxious that they're bleating about it when they haven't even seen my actual work yet.

"She lived and died in service to Alexios," Theodora continues. "And she was branded an oathbreaker for crimes she didn't commit. What have you done with her body?" When I just raise an eyebrow at her—because honestly, she's a lot right now—she grabs the front of my shirt. "*Answer me.* I don't give a damn about that mark on her wrist, Bryony's ashes belong in the crypt with her family. She deserves to have a public pyre."

I try to remind myself that this woman thinks she's lost her sister. If I hurt her for the presumption, my Devaliant would never let me hear the end of it. I enjoy her fury, but not that much.

"Be careful," I say, almost gently. "You aren't my target today, but I can always make an exception."

Her fingers tighten. There's anger in this one, too. No hint of fear. Only fury and grief and something sharper, more bitter. Hate, perhaps. Runs in the bloodline or maybe in the circumstances.

"If you don't—"

"You'll what? Cry at me? Make threats?" I pry her grip loose. "Here's the problem with your tragic little story. If I'd been the one to kill your sister, I wouldn't have been so sloppy about it. Executing Devaliants is a rare treat these days. I like to take my time. She's simply misplaced."

"Misplaced," she repeats slowly. Processing my words. "Where?"

"Somewhere safe. And rather conveniently out of reach, as it happens."

She drags in a slow, rattling breath and blinks away the moisture in her eyes. "Is she with you?"

"She's where she chooses to be. I've agreed to deliver the news."

Theodora's eyebrows shoot up. "Since when did the Wolf of Asteria become a human's glorified carrier pigeon?"

Damn me, I wish I knew. "Since the human in question became my new favorite distraction," I snap. What is it with these Devaliant girls? Why do they ask so many questions? "And it might interest you to know she was *found* bleeding out on the Duehavn. And placed in my care."

Understanding flashes across her features, quickly masked—but not quick enough. She knows exactly who tried to murder her sister.

"I see," is all she says.

I could press her for answers. Demand a name. But I want to hear it from my Devaliant's lips.

"Good." I leap onto the balcony's edge. "And while I'm playing *carrier pigeon*, you might want to do something about the rabid mob at your gates. I've scared them off for now, but Alexios is getting real tired of their neglected tithes. And when the Eternal loses his patience?" I cast a cold smile over my shoulder. "People tend to die screaming."

"Wolf. Tell her…" She clears her throat. "Tell Bryony I love her, would you?"

I incline my head. And then I'm tipping back into the open air, wings stretching as I fly toward the horizon.

Snow falls over the tower as I descend.

I land in the courtyard, the ice collapsing under my boots with a muted crunch. Frost-covered trees crack and groan in the hush, and in the distance, the waves of the Osbu Sea crash against the shore. My wings settle against my back as I head down the garden path.

Then I see her, standing under an arch of branches with her head tipped back. Bryony Devaliant has a gift for demanding my attention without saying a word.

"You know, Devaliant," I say, approaching her, "there are quicker ways to die than exposure. Easier, too. If that's what you're going for."

She doesn't startle at my voice, just keeps her focus on the cloudy sky as snowflakes settle in her hair like a crown of crushed stars.

"I've never seen snowfall before," she says, soft and wondering.

It's such a small admission, inconsequential in the grand scheme of things. But it knocks the breath from my lungs—because how can this woman who moves through life like she was born to conquer the realms still have pieces of herself untouched by it?

"No snow in Hellevig?" I ask.

She shakes her head. "The magic that anchors the Shroud traps heat in the city. Even with how close we are to the Duehavn, it's never cold enough." Her laugh is so bitter it sends a painful jolt through my chest. "Not that I could leave to see it, anyway. A Devaliant has to stay in Hellevig to keep the Shroud anchored, and I was the convenient choice. No ruling duties. No diplomatic missions. So I never left the city."

"Never?"

"No." She wraps her arms around herself. "I used to stare at the mountains from my window. Press my face to the glass and imagine how snow would feel, how it would taste. You have no idea how often I thought about sneaking to the train station and running away. Pathetic, right?"

"It's not pathetic at all." The words emerge rougher than I intend.

I picture this wild, feral creature pacing the length of her enclosure. Craving freedom. Hungry to feel something—*anything*—besides the slow suffocation of a life unlived. I know what it's like to desire that so viscerally you feel it like an ache. Like a scream building in the back of your throat that you can never release.

The notion of Bryony Devaliant being caged is obscene. She wasn't meant for staying still.

"Is it what you imagined?" I ask. "Worth all that wanting?"

She lifts her hand, letting the snowflakes fall onto her palm. "It's different than I thought it would be. Sharper, somehow." She pauses, searching for words. "But softer, too. Like the realm's gone quiet. Like it's… holding its breath."

Like you, I think. *The contradictions of you. Sharp enough to cut, soft enough to break.*

"It'll melt by morning," I tell her.

She hums and drops her hand. "If it lasted forever, we wouldn't stop to admire it."

When she finally turns to face me, I freeze at the sight of her. Her face is shattered. One eye is blackened and swollen shut, her bottom lip is split down the center, and the arch of her cheekbone is fractured.

"I see Amara didn't pull her punches during training today," I say flatly.

The Devaliant goes still, as if she's only now registering the pain. As if the hurt is some distant thing. And isn't that just like her, to be so divorced from her own relative fragility that she doesn't even notice when she's broken.

"What's wrong, Wolf?" Her voice is mocking. "Isn't this exactly what you wanted? For Amara to beat the weakness out of me? Or are you pissed she marked up your toy before you got the chance?"

"Oh, I've no compunctions about blood in the pursuit of excellence. But this?" I gesture to her injuries. "This is inelegant. There are better ways to shatter a thing and make it stronger with a far defter hand." I lower myself onto the crumbling stone bench flanking the garden path, spreading my legs wide. "Come here. Tell me what lesson was worth Amara destroying that pretty face."

She doesn't move. Just watches me with that one good eye as if she's trying to figure out my angle.

"*Come here*, Devaliant. Unless you want to explain to Amara tomorrow why you can't train because you're still fucked up."

That gets her moving. She walks over slowly, each step careful, like she's approaching a wild animal. I wrap an arm around her waist and tug her into my lap, ignoring her sharp intake of breath.

"The lesson," I prompt, settling her more firmly against me. "What was it?"

Her jaw clenches. "That no matter how strong I get, someone will always be there to remind me exactly what I am and where I belong. In the dirt, under someone's boot."

Ah, so that's what Amara was doing. Reminding the Devaliant of her position in the grand hierarchy—a mouse can draw all the blood it likes, but it's never going to be a hawk. It's a brutally effective tactic. I'd bet Amara picked it up during her time in the fighting pits.

"Can't even savor your first snowfall without someone grinding your face in, huh?" I splay my hands over her hips. "Close your eyes. I'll keep you warm."

She hesitates, but then her eyelids flutter shut.

My fingers dip under the hem of her shirt to brush her bare skin. "I could make this feel good," I tell her, letting my magic flare against her just enough to make her gasp. "Make you feel it right between your thighs until you beg for things you don't even know you want yet."

"No." The answer is almost sharp. "Just… fix it."

The Devaliant is not a creature built for begging, but one day, I'll make an art of it.

Mend her first. Conquer her later. Stars grant me patience, because if you grant me strength, I will absolutely do something regrettable with it.

I slide my power across her body to take stock of her injuries: shattered cheekbone, burst vessels, broken nose, two fractured ribs. Amara was clearly making sure the lesson stuck without doing enough harm to kill her.

"This will hurt," I warn her. "Especially the ribs. They need to be forced back into alignment. Try to keep still for me."

At her nod, I reach for the deep well of magic inside me and let it spark along my veins. I temper the blaze into a controlled burn, sinking it into the damage, knitting bone and smoothing flesh. Her body is a grimoire, a history of violence and brutality inscribed in a lovely, fuckable package.

There's something intimate about sliding under her skin like this. About giving her the closest thing to worship these killer's hands know. I watch her closely, seeing how she responds when I drag my magic over her. Which parts make her clutch my shoulders. Which ones make her thighs squeeze mine.

Then the Devaliant's breath hitches. Slowly, so slowly, she leans into my palm and turns into the heat. And it's all I can do not to—

Consume.

But I've learned patience. She's going to yield to me, but it won't be tonight.

When I finally get to her ribs, she tenses. A soft gasp of pain leaves her. I coast a soothing hand across her shoulder blades and begin to hum. It's an old song from a home that no longer exists, from a life purged and hollowed out. My mother used to sing it to me when I was a demi—still a child learning to control my power. The lullaby helped me concentrate, gave me something to focus on as I struggled not to incinerate everything within reach. A song meant to soothe. To steady.

The Devaliant inches closer as I sink into her on a cellular level, finding all the pockets of pooling blood and splintered bone, refusing to miss a single scrape or bruise. The shattered architecture of her reassembles until only perfection remains. A blank canvas scraped clean and re-primed.

"There," I say, unable to stop myself from ghosting my lips over her jaw, her cheek, her temple. "Good as new."

I ease back and let the healing glow flicker and fade until we're just two bodies embracing beneath the falling snow. Snowflakes catch on her lashes and melt against her lips, and I'm tempted to kiss each one.

"What were you humming?"

"It's an old song," I say, reaching up to tuck a stray curl behind her ear. "From a city that's nothing but rubble now."

"Will you teach it to me?"

She asks it so simply, so without guile. As if she isn't requesting I crack open my ribs and offer her my heart on a platter.

"Maybe." I tap her on the nose, smirking when she wrinkles it at me. "If you're very, very good for me."

The Devaliant opens her eyes to glare at me. "Did you go to my sister today?"

"Yeah." I dip my head to scent her. She smells of frost and evergreen and my magic. "She told me to tell you she loves you."

She relaxes on a shuddery exhale. As if she's been braced for a blow, and now that she knows it's not coming, she can finally let herself crumple a little. She tucks her face into the hollow of my throat and breathes. I jolt with surprise when hot tears splash against my skin.

The long-neglected voice of my conscience—one that sounds too much like my mother's—says, *Stop behaving as if you were raised by wolves and comfort her.*

Slowly, tentatively, I stroke a palm down her spine. She doesn't flinch away. It feels like a victory.

"Will you..." She swallows. "Will you deliver letters to Theo for me? If I write them?"

My hand stills on her back. The request hangs in the air between us.

Say no. Tell her she gets nothing. Tell her she's lucky you're letting her breathe.

But her tears are still wet on my skin, and she's soft and trusting in my arms, and I'm apparently weak when it comes to her.

"I'll think about it," I mutter, hating myself.

Silence stretches. The crackle of branches echoes through the garden as a breeze rustles the trees. The snow falls harder.

"Can I tell you a secret?" she whispers.

I resume stroking her back. "Tell me all of them."

"No. Just one." She says it firmly, a reminder that I'm entitled to precisely nothing more than what she's willing to give. "Being yanked back from the Void hurts. It's the worst pain you can imagine—worse than the blade. The world doesn't feel real after because a part of you is still trapped in that nothing between your last breath and your first. Every time you die, you lose more pieces of yourself. And it drives every Anchor mad."

There's a sudden twinge behind my ribs, a terrible squeezing. I brace for her next words.

"Let me send Theo letters," she says, and it's as close to begging as I've ever heard from her. "So she's holding something real before she loses me for good."

Fuck. This girl and her goddamn feelings.

I haven't been burdened by sentiment in a long time. I'd almost forgotten the shape of it, that sharp wrench of emotion that leaves a hollow ache. With a few words, she's twisted me up, and the rational part of me is shouting that I shouldn't care. She's just the human I'm using. Her sister called me a *glorified carrier pigeon*.

"Fine," I hear myself say. "If you write, I'll deliver your letters."

Oh, you stupid fuck.

"Thank you."

Two small words that shouldn't feel so consequential. Why do they? Why? *Why?* She's just entertainment. I'll grow bored—I always do. But I think when I get her out of my system, she's going to take a piece of me with her.

I let out a bitter laugh.

"What's funny?" she asks.

"You could have the entire realms in the palm of your hand, couldn't you?" I tilt her chin up, staring into those violet eyes. "A girl like you takes what she wants. How much would satisfy you?"

She goes still, pulse spiking. "All of it," she whispers.

"All of it, huh? Including me?" I slide my hands down her thighs. "*All* of me?"

I've revealed too much. Given her a weapon shaped like my wanting, and placed it right in her vengeful little hands.

Something constricts in her features, an emotion I have no name for. No frame of reference. And then it's like a door slams shut.

"Stop."

"What?" I ask, blinking at her.

She slides off my lap, putting space between us. "We're not

doing this. Don't talk to me or touch me like you care what I want," she says calmly, almost cold. "Just be honest about what this is."

Pull yourself together, asshole.

My face hardens into a mask of cold detachment, a lifetime's practice of cruelty and distance. She's given me the perfect opportunity to reestablish lines and cut all the emerging sentiment out of me. Cauterize it like an infected wound.

"Truth, then?" I ask her softly. "If you think you can worm past my defenses into some soft, weak place, that's not going to happen. I'm sweet on you now because it amuses me, but don't mistake my amusement for affection. Don't think for one second that I care if you live or die beyond how much entertainment I can wring out of you first."

There's a terrible sort of knowing in her expression. "Thank you for reminding me you're not any different from Alexios. You're just another Eternal using me up before you finish me off."

She disappears into the tower and slams the door shut.

The snow keeps falling, silent and relentless, and I think about impermanence. About things that melt with the dawn.

About the life I had before her family took it from me.

20

BRYONY

THE WEEKS PASS in a blur. I wake up sore and aching, train with Amara until my vision blurs, the Wolf heals me, and then I do it again.

Shatter. Rebuild. Repeat.

When you're raised for the altar, fury lives under your skin with nowhere to go. Nothing to sink its teeth into. Nothing to push against. A body's just a vessel, and an Anchor's body always breaks. Now, I'm learning that my body can be a weapon.

I've never felt it grow strong, never experienced the rush of letting all that wrath out and pushing past limits I didn't know existed. So I seek it out—the control, the rage, the cuts, the bruises. Calluses harden my palms from clutching hilts and handles. I have muscles where there used to be softness.

And the Wolf watches me. There's something about being the sole focus of a god's attention that makes your blood run hot, even when you despise him.

Especially when you despise him.

I haven't spoken to him since that night in the snow, and I'm savoring every second of his frustration. Every ignored attempt at conversation. Every time I walk by him like he's furniture. Like he's nothing.

The hallway encounters are my favorite. The way his jaw clenches and his wings flare slightly, instinctively trying to block my path. I brush past without acknowledging him. He's used to humans crawling on their bellies for him, and I want him to taste what it's like to want what he can't have. Right now, his damaged pride is what's keeping me alive.

He'll want to conquer me before he kills me.

"Get up." Amara's wings block out the sun as she looms over me. "Lying there won't save your ass in a real fight."

"I could play dead," I mutter, pushing myself up. "If I get good enough at it."

She snorts. "Adorable. What's the first rule?"

"Keep my weight on the balls of my feet. Stay fluid. Be ready to move."

"Then why are you standing there like you're posing for a portrait?"

She lunges, but this time I'm prepared. My blade meets hers with an impact that rattles my teeth.

"Better." She eases back, something almost proud in her expression. "But you're still in your head too much. Real combat is in your blood. Either you feel it, or you die. A god is stronger, faster, and powered by actual magic."

"I only need to survive three days in Vartena," I say. "Get through the guards, gut my uncle, and maybe damage the Wolf as petty revenge before he finishes me. I'm not trying to take on every demi in Scillari."

"I don't do things by halves, and you never know what might happen. You live longer if you keep him interested, right? Nothing interests a god that deranged more than a challenge. So if you're going to fight, make it worth watching. Stop overthinking your footwork."

I wipe the blood from my split lip. "And what happened to all that talk about proper form?"

She rolls her eyes. "Form is just the foundation, and you already know that. Now you learn how to cheat. It'll keep the Wolf on his toes. Gods are arrogant bastards who expect humans to cower and beg. Use that."

"What if they expect resistance?" I ask.

"Then give them submission until you're close enough to slip steel between their ribs."

★

The Wolf always comes at night.

I'm perched on the bed wearing only my shift, counting the new bruises and scrapes scattered over my skin, when he appears in my doorway. No knock. He doesn't ask permission.

He tosses a folded letter onto the mattress beside me. "From your sister."

I offer him the barest nod—the only acknowledgment he's gotten from me for three weeks. I write to Theo, he delivers the letters, she writes back, and he brings them when he comes to heal me. That's it. That's all he gets.

He settles against the pillows next to me. "Come here."

I let him pull me into his lap without protest. This is a dance we've perfected. His hands find my skin under my chemise, and that now-familiar heat sinks in, soothing away the day's damage.

"The silent princess act is beneath you." He says this a lot, as if it'll irritate me into speaking. His thumb traces the curve of my shoulder. "It's starting to piss me off. How much longer are we going to play this game? It's been nearly a month, Devaliant."

I stare at the wall, my jaw clenched. His power pulses through me, and I press my teeth together to keep from moaning. The bastard's learning my tells. He knows exactly how to brush and drag his magic against every part of me in a caress of warmth and light intended to make me crave things I shouldn't. As if every nerve ending is being kissed awake.

I count the cracks in the ceiling. *One. Two. Three.*

"Look at me."

Four. Five.

"*Look at me.*" His voice is dangerous now. Hungry. His grip on my waist tightens. "Say you hate me. Say you want me dead."

I shift my focus to the roses creeping across my chamber walls. They've been spreading for weeks, as if his magic can't help but bleed into every corner of this space, making it his. Making it ours.

"Are you *trying* to bore me?" he snaps. "Trust me when I say you won't enjoy what comes next."

I finally meet his eyes. *Then finish me*, I say with my glare. *Do it.*

A muscle in his jaw twitches. "I get it. You're provoking me, aren't you?" His mouth curves into a cruel smile. "Baiting the god into throwing away his new toy?"

Toy. Something dark must show in my expression because his face sparks with triumph.

Got you, that look says.

"That's it," he murmurs, skimming his touch over my ribs. "I've been thinking about it. Toys don't speak, do they? They just…" His palm grazes the underside of my breast. "They just sit still and let themselves be played with. They take what they're given."

His fingers inch higher, brushing my nipple through the fabric. I seize his wrist, digging crescents into his skin.

"Problem?" His eyebrow arches. When I don't answer, his other hand wraps around my throat. "I said, do you have a problem with my hands on you, *toy*?"

When I do nothing but scowl at him, he shoves another pulse of power into me. Harder. A tidal wave of sensation that sends a lick of heat and white-hot pleasure between my thighs—designed to get me to submit. I bite my lip against a whimper.

"Maybe I *should* Claim you." His breath ghosts over my ear. "I could make you do whatever I wanted if I did. I could have you on your knees, crawling at my feet and thanking me for the privilege."

That's it. I've *had* it.

I shove him down, plant my palms against the mattress on either side of his head, and say my first words to him in weeks. "If you want some proxy to take your anger out on, there are thousands of Unclaimed humans in Vartena you could torment without breaking the Accords. Some must have ancestors who fought in Scillari during the war. You told me you have a history with Devaliants, so what did my family do to make you hate us? What made you focus on me?"

His irises flash with inner flame, and his hands flex as if he's fighting for control, holding himself back from murdering me.

But he doesn't move. Doesn't speak.

"Right," I say quietly. "You only want my voice when you know you'll like what it says. When it doesn't ask inconvenient questions." I push off his lap, putting space between us even as my skin hums with the memory of his touch. "If you *ever* threaten to Claim me again, I'll walk out that door and let Amara gut me herself. Now get out."

Three days later, I'm getting my ass kicked again.

"Who taught you to fight like this?" I ask Amara.

For a long moment, she's silent. Then, "My brother. Without his lessons, I'd be dead a dozen times over."

"During the war? Is that when you hurt your wing?"

"No." The word is sharp, final. A door slamming shut.

Before I can apologize, Amara comes at me fast. I block, the impact jarring up my arm, but I'm learning. I attack, putting everything I have into it. Our blades collide. She sidesteps, but I'm already adjusting, already moving. It feels natural now.

Advance. Retreat. Pivot.

Dance.

We trade more blows, the clash of metal punctuated by our harsh breathing. I clench my teeth and push through the burning in my muscles. She spins lightning-quick and cracks the flat of her blade against my wrist. My weapon goes flying.

I don't even think—just move. But she's already there, sweeping my legs out from under me. The breath leaves my lungs in a rush as my back slams into the ground.

Amara's boot lands on my chest, pinning me. The tip of her dagger kisses the hollow of my throat. "And you're dead. You yield?"

"Yield."

She sheaths her blade and extends a hand. I let her haul me up, trying not to wince at the fresh constellation of bruises blooming beneath my skin.

"Not bad. We'll keep working on your stamina," Amara says, brushing dirt from her clothes. "But you need to remember the three rules of fighting gods: hurt them from a distance, run fast, and hide well. Getting close enough for them to grab you? That's the end. You have to focus on—"

Her eyes flicker over my shoulder, and a wry smile twists her lips.

With a slow, dreadful certainty, I turn.

The Wolf lounges against the archway. The last rays of the dying sun paint his wings in shades of amber and russet, each feather edged in light until he glows.

Something clenches in my chest—a snarl of emotion too tangled to unravel. He leaves me off-balance, as exposed as an open wound.

You're just another Eternal using me up before you finish me off.

And he is. He's evaluating me. Taking inventory of his weapon, checking for damage, making sure his toy still works properly. That's all this is.

I shove down the mess of feelings and lock them away, turning to Amara.

"Thanks for today," I tell Amara, forcing my voice to stay steady. "Same time tomorrow?"

"Yeah." She glances between us, and her smirk widens. "Your girl needs throwing knives, Wolf."

He lifts a brow, keeping that burning gaze on me as if I'm the only thing in the world worth watching. "Does she?"

"You wanted her trained. She needs to be able to throw fast and hit what she's aiming at every time."

The Wolf makes a considering sound. His eyes travel over my sweaty skin, lingering over the cut on my arm and the bruises darkening my collarbones. My chest rises and falls as my breath quickens. It feels like being touched, that stare. Intimate and possessive. Claiming me without laying a finger on me.

"I want her kitted with at least four throwers," Amara

continues, either oblivious to the rising tension or content to ignore it. "Good ones."

The Wolf blinks and looks away. "I'll consider it. If she proves she's worth four Turpori blades."

Then he's gone, pushing off the wall and disappearing into the tower. The air seems lighter without him. Easier to breathe.

Amara leans in close. "Did you see the look on his face? That's a male trying real hard to pretend he doesn't want the one thing he shouldn't touch. That's power, little human. Use it before he uses *you*."

21

EVANDER

THREE HUNDRED YEARS ago, I realized the Vartenan fleshtrade was so vast that it covered the entire realm.

Traders had their systems down to an art—networks of buyers and sellers in every major city, bribes to grease the right palms, secret knocks and codes passed in whispers. It wasn't only parts of us for sale, either. In some places, gods were caged up, beaten, and used in blood sports for human entertainment. Humans bet a lot of aurelii to watch us fight to the death.

But black markets have vulnerabilities, and all it takes is one addict running his mouth and mentioning demi parts being sold at the docks.

I haven't forgotten about that prick in Valchek last month. Zephyr's been doing some digging while investigating the missing demis held on Silk Street, and while there's no information on the victims, she picked up a trail. We're here to see where it leads.

My wings rustle as I roll my shoulders, loosening up my limbs. Ready for anything. I'm with Elias and Arcadia on a roof opposite a run-down warehouse on the outskirts of Hellevig—a possible source for the operation in Valchek. My magic spreads over us, twisting the light to make us invisible.

What's the situation from your end, Zephyr? I ask into the mind-link Alexios is keeping open between my team.

Zephyr walks the perimeter down at street level, her black wings melting her into the shadows. *Nothing moving inside that I can see.* Zephyr's mental voice is cool and composed, as always. *Not much in the way of visible security. Either they're cocky, or this is a trap.*

I scan the building again. It's thick stonework with a flat roof and a couple of small windows dotted across the facade. The side has faded paint that reads, *J. Smith & Co. Medicinal Supplies.* The door on the east wall looks promising for entry.

Any specific intel on who owns this shithole? I ask her.

No. My contacts flagged some unusual shipping patterns from here over the past few months. Someone was trying to obscure cargo manifests and cover tracks, but I followed a financial trail to Valchek. It wasn't easy.

"Fuckers," Arcadia mutters.

"They always slip up, eventually." Elias taps his finger impatiently against his thigh. "I haven't seen dust demand this high since right before the Devouring. Fleshtraders are getting bold again."

Dust. Human slang for the remains of our dead. Wings are worth the most—a higher concentration of magic—then come the bones and organs, desiccated and ground up for easy consumption.

Alexios cuts in, his presence flooding the mind-link from his throne in Asteria. *Get this done fast and clean,* he says. *Take prisoners for interrogation. Pull out any survivors.* Then, to Zephyr alone: *No risks, Whisper.*

Sometimes, I wonder if he even realizes how his voice changes when he speaks to her. If anything ever happened to his spymaster, Alexios would tear the realms apart twice over.

Hold the perimeter, I tell Zephyr. *Signal if you spot trouble.*

I jump off the roof with Arcadia and Elias right behind me. We touch down in the alley, and I kick the door in, wood splintering around my boot. A chemical stink hits me, sharp enough to make my eyes water. Beneath that is the heavy thrum of magic. *Fresh* magic.

Shelves line the walls, filled with various herbs and medicines. To my left is a large wooden icebox to control the room's temperature—typical of chop shops. Rows of ceramic, tin, and glass containers fill the rest of the space.

Elias examines the cases, making a slow circuit. "Old apothecary cold storage is an ideal front for a chop shop when you think about it. Formaldehyde and surgical spirits mask a lot."

Arcadia cracks open a lid and gags. "Like putting a slaughterhouse in a perfumery."

I take stock of entries and exits for any potential hiding places. If these fleshtraders are consuming god parts, that means they have enough power at their disposal to put them on par with a demi. They could harm or even kill my team if we're not careful.

"Spread out," I say. "Clear the building room by room. Watch for traps."

Elias and Arcadia go right while I cover the left. The whole place groans and settles around us. Other than that, it's quiet. My magic buzzes under my skin, ready to let loose.

Arcadia's voice sounds in my head. *Wait. Do you hear that?*

Yeah, I do—a rhythmic noise filtering through the walls.

Tick-tick-tick.

Tick-tick-tick.

Detonators clicking down.

And under the ticking, buried beneath the stink of chemicals—

"Get out!" I snarl. "I smell powdered Turpori steel!"

I spin, running to the others and grabbing Arcadia, practically throwing her at the busted door. Elias ducks under my arm and clears the threshold in seconds.

Wolf! Zephyr's shout. *Get your ass out of there!*

I'm already mentally mapping out the blast radius. A structure like this will have all the load-bearing supports rigged with enough charges to reduce it to rubble. Even trace amounts of powdered Turpori steel will sear a demi's lungs, but the concentration I smell lacing the ordnance? It'll punch right through our healing and might actually slaughter my team if they don't get far enough from the explosion.

But for an Eternal, it will only hurt like a bitch.

I'm going to shield the blast, I say. *I'll see if there are any survivors.*

I pound down the stairs. The lower level opens into a corridor, and I make a sharp left, winding my way deeper until I hit a reinforced steel door pocked with rust. I kick it open with my boot.

The stench slams into me. I'm suddenly thrown back to the war, to my last raid, all the memories overlapping with the present.

Uneven stone walls rise on all sides. Viscera clots the gaps between the flagstones, gone nearly black. Manacles dangle overhead, the chains thick with rust and bits of flesh, and spattered across every surface is blood. Liters of it. A table dominates the floor, crosshatched with deep gouges—a dissection slab. And splayed on that platform...

Carnage. Mangled limbs and organs. And the feathers—jet, red, purple, gold—ripped out and heaped in piles.

But this isn't centuries ago. It's now, and it's happening again.

You never really leave the war behind, my brother once told me. *No matter how much time or distance you put between yourself and the killing fields.*

None of us ever climbed out of those trenches. The war keeps following us, sinking in its teeth and claws and dragging us down again.

"Fuck," I breathe.

Three dead, I relay to the others, grabbing a fistful of blood-matted feathers and tucking them into my armor to bring back for identification. *No survivors or signs of any fleshtraders. They must have caught wind of us and bailed. Stay away while I deal with the blast.*

I don't wait for a response. My power is already building. I cast out my senses, mapping every charge as I sink to my knees. My wings flare wide as fire roars through me, searing paths of heat beneath my skin as I shape the energy into a shield.

Everything goes white.

The detonations rip through the warehouse. Stone pulverizes

to dust, support beams shatter, and wood sprays like shrapnel. Blood trickles down my face—the Turpori steel burning my skin as I hold the shield.

I take the destruction and give it *focus*, shaping the explosion with my will and super-heating the rubble until the stone glows red and there's nothing left of the butchered demis. Sublevels collapse in a controlled implosion, directing the devastation down, down, down...

Until all that's left is settling debris and smoke, the crackle of embers, and the groan of a building gutted to its bones. The neighboring buildings remain intact without so much as a cracked window. But in the epicenter? There's only a crater with smoldering detritus.

I let the shield fall away and rise from the wreckage. My shirt hangs in bloody tatters, wounds weeping as flesh knits back together. I'll be sore for hours, but I've survived worse.

I sweep my gaze over the rubble a final time. A flash of something under a half-burnt chunk of wood snags my attention—a little book, somehow still in one piece, even with everything blasted to shit around it. I yank it out and shove it into my jacket, launching skyward.

The others are waiting in the alley when I drop down.

Elias gives me a once-over. "You look like shit warmed over."

"Fuck you very much," I snap, shooting him a withering glare.

"Did you find anything?" Arcadia asks.

I pull out the charred book and hold it out to Zephyr. "Most of it's torched."

She takes it from me, fingers gentle as she flips open the cover and scans the blackened page. "Looks like a ledger. *Full set of primaries. Previous asking price doubled.*"

An image crashes through my mind of wings cut off and plumage matted with blood.

She turns the page, continuing grimly, "*Marrow and viscera potency tested. Delivery arranged via blind drop. Rhosyn delivered. Twice confirmed with BC contact, ready for processing—*"

Ice crystallizes in my veins. "BC. The Bloody Court?"

Elias swears under his breath. "Someone's resurrecting the pits."

Where demigods were made to hack each other apart for the amusement of humans. Where my brother spent weeks being tortured and violated while I searched for him. Amara, even longer.

"Does Rhosyn mean anything to you?" I ask Zephyr, forcing the words past the lump in my throat. "Some kind of code?"

She stares at the page as she thinks. "Maybe. Or a name? Whatever it means, they're getting the shipment of dust."

I think of broken wings. Desecrated flesh. Survivors on killing room floors, waiting for death or worse. A familiar hatred shudders through me—the need to slaughter, to make every fucker who did this pay for it.

Clenching my jaw, I carefully pull the feathers out of my armor. "For identification and funerals."

Zephyr handles them reverently. "I'll give Alexios my report. I'm still following leads on more missing demis. If I have any new information, we may need to act fast. They'll be more careful after this. Elias? With me." She glances at me and Arcadia, her expression softening a fraction. "Get some rest."

Arcadia and I watch them launch into the sky. Their silhouettes shine against the stars for a moment before they disappear into the night.

"Are you okay?" she asks, silver wings rustling.

"I'll heal."

"Not what I meant."

There's worry in those mercury eyes. Understanding. Arcadia lost her brothers in the Devouring; she knows how it feels to lose part of yourself. We all do.

"No," I say quietly. "I'm really fucking not."

Her hand finds my forearm. "What do you need?"

You, I want to say. *Make me feel something.*

Arcadia would let me lose myself in her if I asked. I could stay at the palace and fuck her until my thoughts go quiet—I've done it a hundred times before. I know how to shatter her and put her back together, how to make her scream in pleasure. It would be easy to let her numb the hurt for a little while.

But when I picture the female beneath me in my bed, it's not Arcadia I see.

It's the Devaliant, staring up at me with those defiant violet eyes. *Her* silvery hair spread across my sheets. *Her* body moving against mine.

And she's a reminder of every damn thing that happened to my realm.

I'm so disgusted with myself that I can't even look at Arcadia. "Go home. I'll deal with it."

Memories batter against the inside of my mind as I stride down the hall of my tower.

Butchered bodies. Feathers removed and stacked. Rhosyn delivered. Twice confirmed with BC contact.

Turning the corner, I jerk to a halt. *No. Fuck, no.*

The Devaliant lingers outside the one door I warned her never to approach. Her fingertips ghost over the obsidian seal in the center, tracing the edges gone soft with age.

I move in a blink, slamming my hands against the wood on either side of her, my lips at her ear. "Devaliant. I believe I made myself crystal fucking clear about this door. *It. Stays. Shut.*"

She inhales sharply, a subtle tremor rolling through her. "I wasn't going to open it. I was just… curious."

"Well, fuck me, she speaks," I say with a bitter laugh. "A whole damn month of the silent treatment, and now she's found her voice."

A muscle tics in her jaw. Oh, I've pissed her off now. Good. She can give me exactly what I need to numb myself tonight.

Burn hotter, vicious girl. Let me taste your fury.

"I want to negotiate—"

"*No.*" She's always pushing, testing boundaries. Trying to *negotiate*. "No throwing knives. No bartering. No deals, Devaliant. Not tonight."

Not when I'm one wrong breath away from coming out of my skin entirely. Not when she belongs to the family responsible for every festering hurt, every memory. All the ways I'm cracked and broken until I became *this*.

Slowly, the Devaliant twists to face me. Those violet eyes flick over my gore-splattered and dusty clothes. Quick. Assessing. As if she's trying to get a read on me. Trying to find the broken bits she can press on until something fractures for her.

"This is how you come home every night, isn't it?" she asks softly. "After killing oathbreakers?"

That's where she thinks I've been. Stacking bodies. Slitting the throats of more precious Vartenans. And why wouldn't she? That's all I am to her—the killer, the monster, the nightmare they tell stories about. She has no clue what I saw tonight. Because why would it even occur to her that her people have been butchering and consuming us for centuries? That while she considers the war a distant past, some of us are still sifting through the wreckage and finding corpses to bury?

And why correct her? Why tell her the truth when the lie is so much more useful?

"That's right, Princess. Every damn night." I flash a vicious grin. "Sometimes I don't even wash the blood off before dinner. Sometimes I let it dry on my skin because I like how it feels."

I track the shallow rise and fall of her chest, the pulse in her throat. I could sink my teeth into that spot and taste her terror. Could press my fingers there until she begged me to let her breathe.

What an easy target she is tonight. Such a perfect distraction.

Tough luck, Devaliant. You're the only thing in reach, and I'm all out of mercy.

"You want to know how killing them feels?" I ask, voice low. "*Righteous*. Like I was made for it. Shaped for it. It makes me feel alive when everything else is static. And when it's over, I'm just hungry. For the next. And the next. And the next and the next. No fucking bottom. I could slaughter every last one of you and still wake up starving."

"Stop it," she whispers.

That plea only feeds the hunger. The dark, twisted part of me that wants to push until she snaps.

A cruel, mocking laugh shivers out of me. "Aw, listen to you beg just like they do. I honestly expected more from you, Princess. You're boring me. All that promise, all that potential, and you're just another disappointment, aren't you?"

Boring. The word I promised would be her death sentence. Never let it be said that I don't know exactly which of her wounds to press on. I want her to claw at me, wreck me, crack me open. Dig her nails into my skin. I'll still be here demanding *more, harder, now*. Better for her to see the butcher than someone falling apart.

The effect is instantaneous. I notice the moment it registers, the way her eyes snap up, bright with rage.

Yeah, that's it. There's the fire. Good girl. Give it to me.

"*Boring*," I say again when she doesn't rise to the bait. When all she does is pant in these shallow little gasps. "Maybe Amara's lessons didn't teach you shit after all. Did her goodwill finally bleed the fight out of you, huh? Or is this what you were like on the altar?" I ask to twist the knife that much deeper. "Lying there so fucking obediently every time they sank that dagger in? I bet you begged then, too. I bet you cried. I bet you were *pathetic*."

She explodes.

With a snarl, she slams her palms into my chest with enough force to knock the breath from my lungs. I rock back on my heels, a savage pride unfurling in me.

Finally.

"Oh, come on. I know you can do better than that," I hiss. "*Tear into me*."

She shoves me harder. "*Stop it!*"

"Why? This is the most honest you've been in weeks." I grab the dagger from my hip and force it into her hand. "Here. You want to hurt me? Do it properly. Make it count. Carve into me so deep I feel it for days."

Like that night in your rooms when you cut into me so deeply, I can still remember the ache.

Her anger feeds a darkness in me that's been starving for weeks. For years. It keeps building—this storm inside my skull, fire crackling under my skin and through my veins.

I want her *teeth*.

She hurls the knife away, and it skitters into the shadows. "Stop it," she says again, and there's something ragged in her voice, too close to concern for my liking. "Just. Stop."

"Why should I?" I grip her thighs and hoist her up, slamming her back into the door. She twists to break free, but I press my hips forward, pinning her in place. "Aren't I giving you what you expect? The monster? The villain? Well, here I am, Devaliant. The same bastard you met in Hellevig." I trail my lips along her jaw, not quite touching. "You loved it that night in your room, didn't you, vicious girl? Cutting into me. Making me bleed. I bet it's the only time in your pathetic life you've ever felt powerful. Because Alexios bled you dry, and used you up again and again and again—"

She thrashes against me like an animal caught in a snare, feral and snarling and incandescent in her fury. And she's so stunning, so beautiful, I can hardly breathe through it.

"There was this woman tonight," I lie, the words spilling out before I can stop them. Anything to keep this fire burning. Anything to make her hurt me. "Reminded me of you, actually. Similar face, same entitled way of breathing." I lean forward and brush my lips against her ear. "When I was killing her, I thought about you. I imagined it was your throat under my hands. Your voice begging me to end you. Will you beg me, Devaliant? Will you *plead*?"

Look at me, I demand silently. *Don't you dare flinch. Not now. Hurt me. Please, please, please fucking hurt me.*

And she does. Her nails score the flesh of my shoulder, leaving marks as she struggles against my hold. "Fuck you," she growls. "You disgust me. I *hate you*."

A snarl shudders out of me. "Good. Hate me more. Hate me

while you're hurting me. Hate me every moment. Make it the only thing I feel."

Images strobe through my mind in flashes—wings and sightless eyes, gore and death. All those lives lost. The stench of pyres and the rubble and the grief so crushing that there's nowhere to send it but out.

I can't breathe. She's what's keeping me together. The only person in two realms who can destroy me the way I want. She's jagged glass ready to cut me open until I spill out all this *rot*.

Her eyes snap to mine, and realization skitters across her features. There's a gradual softening in her face—a terrible, dawning understanding.

And I'm pinned. Caught. Unable to move.

Don't say it. Don't you fucking say it.

Her hand curves around my nape, the touch tender. "Something went wrong tonight. You're in pain. I can see it." When I do nothing but stare down at her, panting hard, she whispers, "What happened, Evander? Why are you trying so hard to make me hurt you?"

The sound of my real name on her tongue is like a blade to the chest.

Oh, fuck you. Fuck you for the way you're looking at me. Fuck you so much.

I slam my palm against the door beside her head just to watch her flinch. To get that horrible gentleness off her face.

"You want to know what gets me off more than the killing?" I say, voice ragged. "Playing with you. Fucking with your head. Because strip away all that practiced sweetness, and you're just as twisted as I am. Just as hungry. Just as vicious. That's why cutting me made you come alive. Because for once in your miserable life, you got to be the one holding the knife." I meet her stare, letting her see every ugly, squirming thing inside me. Daring her to look away. "We're the same, Devaliant. Both of us rotting from the inside out. The only difference is that at least I'm honest about it."

I drop her to the floor and wrench myself away from her, stalking down the corridor without a backward glance. I don't stop until I'm barricaded in my room with the door slammed shut behind me. Only then do I let my shoulders sag.

Viscera clotting stone. Piles of blood-matted plumes. BC. The Bloody Court.

Something rears up in my throat. I stagger into the washroom and collapse to my knees in front of the toilet. Then I'm retching, throwing up everything in my stomach until there's nothing left but blood and bile.

22

BRYONY

THERE'S AN OLD Vartenan tale that says everyone is born with two snakes coiled around their heart.

Both begin life with equal potential, nourished by human emotion. The dark snake feeds on fury and pain and the things we bury deep. The bright snake eats love and happiness—all the sweet things that feel good.

One snake is destined to twist more snugly around your ribs, to become part of you. Over time, it nourishes you with the emotions it fed on and gives back everything it took. The other snake is destined to starve and die.

The one that lives is the one you feed.

Every time I entered the Void, the shadow snake just kept getting fatter. When my uncle left me on the Duehavn, and I woke up with all that rage inside me, it gorged itself on the feast.

And now I don't know how to stop feeding it.

We're the same, Devaliant. Both of us rotting from the inside out. The only difference is that at least I'm honest about it.

Thorns tear at my skin as I pull weeds, but I welcome the sting. Ten little cuts, ten moments of distraction from his voice twisting my thoughts. *Rip. Sting. Bleed.* Bright, hot points of realness in the numb fog of everything else. If I hold tight to this pain, maybe I can block out all the rest for a little while. This is hurt I choose. This hurt obeys me.

Strip away all that practiced sweetness, and you're just as twisted as I am. Just as hungry. Just as vicious, the Wolf's words echo in my head.

"You're upsetting them again."

My heart slams against my ribs at his voice. I keep my stare focused on the ground, refusing to acknowledge him. Refusing to give him the satisfaction.

"The roses don't like it when you bleed on them in anger."

"They're strangled from neglect," I say through my teeth. "I'm amazed they feel anything at all."

"Devaliant. Look at me."

I'm tempted to tell him to leave me alone, but I doubt he'd listen. He *wants* to pry me open.

My chin tips up. The Wolf is backlit by the dying sun, feathers gilded in amber. He's shirtless, muscles and gleaming skin on display. So lovely it aches.

He closes the distance in a few measured strides. "Let me see."

His fingers close around my wrist, turning my palm to examine the damage. An electric current flows through my nerves at the point of contact.

"These are deep," he says, running his thumb over the worst cut. I barely stifle a pained hiss. "The roses are punishing you. It's how they talk. How they let you know when it's time to stop pushing."

I tug free of his hold. "I can handle a few scratches."

A considering tilt of his head. "Is this you punishing *yourself* for something? Or are you just taking your frustrations out on my garden because you can't take them out on me?"

"You'd know plenty about distracting yourself from your anger, wouldn't you?"

His eyes shut briefly. "What you're doing to yourself isn't about last night."

I could deflect like I always do. Hide behind fury and loathing, parrot the usual empty words that I use to keep people at arm's length. But that won't work on him. It never has, not from that moment in Hellevig when he looked at me, understood the hunger beneath my skin, and let me cut him open.

That shadow snake fed and fed and *fed*.

"Is this why they call you the Wolf?" I sneer. "Because you're like a dog with a bone? Weeds don't pull themselves."

"So your first thought was to hurl yourself into a rosebush and bleed all over it until something gave? Either the thorns or your skin?"

"You're the one letting them run wild in the first place! Maybe if you cared about something other than playing butcher to the realms and toying with me, your flowers wouldn't be devouring your damn tower!"

"*Enough*."

An emotion flickers across his features—there and gone too quickly to catch, but if I didn't know better, I'd almost call it regret.

Then he's crouching behind me, wings flaring for balance. He tugs me between his legs, my back against his chest. This close, his scent invades my senses—citrus and petrichor. It fills my lungs and my head until I'm dizzy with it.

"Like this." He reaches around me, caging me between his arms. "There's a trick to it."

I inhale sharply when he takes my hands, every part of me suddenly sparking to life at his touch. *Wanting*.

"If you want to understand a thing," he murmurs in my ear, "you have to learn its nature. What makes it *feel*." His voice drops low, intimate. Like we're sharing secrets in the dark. "These roses aren't like their mundane counterparts in Vartena. They'll sense any frustration and impatience lashing at them. Listen to them. They're trying to tell you something, but you're too busy fighting to hear it. Feel my hands."

I watch as he sets his hands under mine and works the soil. His movements are slow, almost reverent, as he shows me how to coax out the most stubborn weeds.

"When all the roses sense from you is anger, they lash back when you get close. Patience is key. You can't go in like a woman on a warpath, or you'll find yourself torn to shreds. You have to take your time."

My face flames, and my stomach swoops. I know he's talking about more than just the roses.

"Gentle, gentle," he admonishes when I move to yank out a gnarled root. "Prove you're not a threat, and it might surprise you how eagerly they open up and let you get at the things that hurt them."

"Since when are you interested in being gentle?"

A hard exhale against my nape. "Five minutes. That's all I'm asking. Five minutes of you not fighting me every single step. Let me guide you." His fingers lace with mine, pushing my hand down into the soil. "Breathe out the anger," he commands softly. "That violent urge to dominate, to make the world bend and break itself to your will—you have to let it go. All it will get you here is bled dry."

"Tell me you see the irony," I whisper.

His teeth graze my earlobe in warning. "Don't give me a reason to reconsider this little lesson," he whispers back.

Breathe out the anger. Let it go. Two snakes twisted around your heart. Which one lives?

The one you feed.

So I shut up. I let him lead, his body moving with mine as he shows me how to gentle the roses. It's a lot like a different kind of dance—the slow drag of his calluses against my knuckles, the indecent way we slot together, the rhythmic flex and glide of our fingers in the dirt. A push and pull. A give and take. He advances, I retreat. He demands, I yield. Over and over, as implacable as the ocean tide wearing away stone.

"Like that." The approval in his voice sends liquid heat pooling low in my belly. "You're a quick study."

It feels… good. To pour myself into this simple task and let everything else fall away. The solid warmth of him seeps into my skin, grounding me. Gentling me. Without conscious thought, I melt against him, my body going soft.

If he's surprised by my surrender, he doesn't show it. Just shifts his weight to better support me.

I lose myself in sense impressions. The drag of his calluses against my palms. The steady thump of his heart against my spine. There's no room for anger here. There is only this. Him. Me. The roses.

"So why *do* they call you the Wolf?" I ask him, filling the silence.

"Many gods have several names," he says, leaning around me to tug at a knot of turquoise weeds. "Ones given to us at birth. Ones we earn."

"That's not an answer."

Out of the corner of my eye, I see his wry smile. "What do you think I should be called?"

"Hawk, maybe. Because of your wings. Or another bird name."

He laughs softly, tightening one arm around my waist as he bends forward to whisper in my ear, "Do I remind you of a bird?" His teeth graze my neck. "Or do I remind you of a wolf?"

Well, he's got me there.

"Wings aren't unique in Scillari," he adds. "Earned names don't come from something we're all born with."

"Then how did you earn your name?"

He goes quiet, and then, "You ask too many questions."

I don't push. I file the secret of his name along with all the others—why he lets these roses grow wild when he clearly loves them, why he hates my family. All of these little bits of him that he keeps hidden away, stacking like stones. Because he's approachable like this. Vulnerable. The male beneath the god is someone I might like if we were anyone but who we are.

"It's almost nice," I say into the deepening twilight, "when you're not threatening to devour my heart."

A stutter in his breathing. I feel the whisper of a smile tucked into the crook of my neck.

"Why, Bryony Devaliant. Was that a compliment? Should I be worried?"

"Just enjoying the change of pace." I focus on the hypnotic flex of his fingers against mine. On the way his skin shimmers like stardust in the falling night—such a striking contrast to the opalescent sheen of my own. "Waiting for us to revert to our usual animosity."

The arms bracketing me go tense before forcibly relaxing. "Not everything has to be a battle. Sometimes a god is just a male, wanting to make you feel good after making you feel bad." He pauses, and when he speaks again, the words sound like they're being dragged out of him. "Sometimes he says and does unspeakable shit he can't take back. He fucks up and tries to make it right."

"Is that your way of apologizing?" I risk a glance at him.

"Yeah. It wasn't—" He blows out a short, frustrated exhale. Warm against my nape. "Last night wasn't about you. Not really."

There had been an emotion on his face yesterday. Past the manic gleam and the snarl and snap of his jaws at my jugular was a pain so deep that it cut like glass.

"Something hurt you," I say, choosing my words carefully.

Something broke you.

"Yes."

My heart trips and stumbles. I clear my throat. "A lot of injuries bleed beneath the skin," I say softly, thinking about my days in Hellevig. "You can't see them, but you feel them with every breath. It's worse when someone else is there to witness you break apart." My hands are trembling now, but I force myself to continue. "Especially if it's someone you hate. Like you're handing them the knife, knowing you'll end up bleeding out all over the floor. But it's easier, too, because they're already primed to hurt you. And that means you don't have to be the one to dig your fingers into your own wound. You get the agony without the guilt."

He doesn't say anything. Just rests his chin against my shoulder, and something in my chest hitches at the casual intimacy of it. At how easily we slot together when we're not fighting.

"You don't have to tell me specifics," I say. "Keep your secrets if you need them. But don't ever use my hands to hurt yourself again. Not like that."

His chest expands against my back on an inhale. "I won't," he finally says, so soft I almost don't hear him.

We stay like that for a few more minutes. Watching the sun bleed away, listening to the breeze rattle through the trees. His hand strokes mine.

Then he releases me and rises to his feet. I feel the loss of him immediately.

"Here." He unhooks the double sheath at his waist. When he presses it into my palm, the hilts are warm from his skin. "Two throwers, Turpori steel. One for tending my garden, and the second as an apology."

I run a finger over the dagger. "And the other two that Amara says I need?"

He flashes a smile. "I don't part with god-forged steel on a whim, nemesis. You'll have to earn them. Surprise me, and they're yours." He strides back toward the tower. "Try not to antagonize my roses again," he calls over his shoulder. "When you're finished here, come find me. I'll see to the damage."

And I'm left alone with nothing but the lingering sensation of his touch.

If you want to understand a thing, you have to learn its nature.

I exhale and think of Evander's hands guiding mine. Closing my eyes, I breathe in the sweet perfume of the roses and let all my emotions drain away until there's nothing left but purpose.

The one that lives is the one you feed.

The thorns part for me like water.

23

BRYONY

THE RHYTHMIC THUD of blades hitting their marks greets me when I enter the Wolf's armory.

My breath catches. He's shirtless, muscles rippling as he launches a dagger into one of the straw targets lined up on the other side of the room. The warm glow of the illumination sigils on the walls dances across his wings and sweat-dappled skin. He runs a hand through his damp hair and sights the target. Inhales. Releases.

Thunk. The weapons group so closely together that the hilts almost touch.

"Hey," I say, leaning against the door.

He glances over. Those eyes flick over my body in a slow sweep, taking in my belted silk robe, my hair still wet from the bath. "I see you managed not to shred yourself on the roses again." He lets another blade fly. "Progress."

"The roses and I came to an understanding." I cross to the weapon racks, running a finger down one of the stiletto blades. "I want to talk about the knives."

He drops into a chair, legs stretching. I can't help but let my gaze linger on the way his muscles shift with the movement, on the trail of dark hair disappearing into his waistband, and the graceful V-shaped ridges on his torso. That sweet, subtle curve emphasized by light and shadow.

"Let me work my magic on today's battle trophies first, and

let's see if you can convince me about those weapons," he says, patting his thigh.

I've lost count of how many nights we've done this. These healing sessions have become a sort of ritual, simmering with the unspoken *thing* between us. He likes it, I think. The way I lower myself onto him, letting my body sink into his, slow and steady. That I'm too stubborn to beg for the pleasure he offers each time.

It's just another game we play. But tonight, I want to throw him off-balance. I want my victory.

So I go to him. I lift the hem of my robe and straddle his lap, pressing my knees to his hips. His scent envelops me—sweat, smoke, a hint of spice. The Wolf's palm presses into my lower back, pulling me close until I'm right up against the rise and fall of his chest. His warmth seeps through my silk robe, and it takes everything in me not to grind against him to relieve the ache between my thighs.

His other hand finds my bare knee, igniting sparks as he drags his touch up, up, up along my inner thigh, and then down. Grazing. Teasing. When his power finally reaches for me, I sigh. It sinks deep and searches for today's damage—cuts, bruises, breaks, tears. And I want. Fiercely. *Uselessly.*

Every touch carries a different meaning. The grasp of his fingers is, *let me undress you.* The slow drag of his magic is, *I could make you feel so good.* And every so often, his eyes lift to mine in a silent message I hear with every panting breath: *let me have you.* He'd do it so well, too. He'd shatter me apart, then put me back together again, shiny and new.

But that's not what tonight is about. So I grit my teeth, lock my muscles, and swallow down the moans building in my throat. Bit by bit, he heals me, soothing away every ache and pain until my skin is unmarked again.

"One of these days," he whispers, "you're going to stay right here after I fix you up, and I'm going to make you forget every reason you shouldn't let me have you."

"But not today," I say.

"No," he agrees. "Not today." He sits back, his power retreating as his hands fall away. "Make your case."

"You told me to earn the daggers. I want to compete with you for them."

Those amber eyes flare with interest. "I'm listening."

Got him.

"Three shots each at the target. Whoever hits closest to the center three times in a row wins."

"You want to challenge a god to knife-throwing," he says flatly. "An Eternal who's been training for centuries. Just to be clear."

"If I beat you," I continue as if he hadn't spoken, "you give me the other two daggers. And you let me draw first blood when you come to hunt me in Vartena."

"And when you lose, what do I get out of it? A free show and a chance to gloat?"

When, not if. His arrogance would be infuriating if it weren't exactly what I was counting on.

I smile and lean back, resting my hands on his thighs. "*If* I lose our wager, you can do *anything* you want to me. Tonight only."

He goes still, gaze darkening as it drags over me, the amber irises nearly swallowed by black. The Wolf, for all his power and cruelty, is still just a male—so easy.

"Anything?" His voice is a low rasp.

Good. Let him be hungry. Let him starve.

"*Anything*. No restrictions, no safe words. Deal?"

His chest rises and falls faster, hands flexing on my hips. "This feels like you're angling to fail on purpose." His fingers glide down my stomach, slow and teasing. "Poor little nemesis, have you been lying in bed with your hand between your thighs, wondering how I would feel instead? Is that what this is about? Because you don't have to lose a contest to get me inside you—"

I seize his wrist, so close to where I'm wet and aching. "Win tonight, and you can lower this hand another inch."

The corner of his mouth twitches. "Only an inch?"

"Maybe two, if you're nice."

He tilts his head, studying me like he's trying to figure me out. "You know I could probably hit those targets blindfolded, right?"

"Then prove it. We'll blindfold you."

"Hmm." He grazes his other palm up my side. "When I win—"

"*If.*"

"*When* I win," he says, fingers digging in, "I'm going to use this body. Fuck it however many times I want. And by the time I'm done, the only name you'll remember is mine, and all the ways I can make you scream it." He leans forward, dragging his lips down my jaw, whispering, "Maybe I'll even let you come if you beg real sweet."

The promise in his voice makes my thighs clench. But I force myself to slide out of his lap and pluck a scrap of fabric from the wastebasket beside the weapon rack—some old rag he uses to clean his knives. The Wolf tracks my movements as I tie it over his eyes, careful not to catch on his hair.

"Whenever you're ready," I say, pressing a dagger into his palm.

He stands, testing the weapon's balance. Then he takes a deep breath and throws. The blade streaks through the air, hitting the center of the farthest target. I hand him another blade, another, watching that cocky smirk grow as each weapon hits its mark.

Yanking off the blindfold, he flashes me a sharp grin. "Top that. If you can."

I brush past him, letting my shoulder graze his chest. He sucks in a sharp breath and a thrill goes through me—anticipation. "You know what I love about wagers?" I peruse the weapons cabinet, fingers trailing over hilts and blades. "It's all in the details. The precise words. The parameters. In our agreement, I never specified the type of weapon we had to use. Only that it had to hit closest to the center."

I see the instant it clicks. His eyes sharpen and fix on my hand as it closes around the recurve bow mounted on the wall.

"One of the benefits of growing up in Hellevig," I continue, testing the draw, the tension, "is that all noblewomen are trained in the 'genteel' arts. Painting, pianoforte..." My smile sharpens. "Archery."

He growls as I nock the first arrow, imagining it's his heart I'm aiming at. I draw back until the fletching grazes my cheek, breathing in. Shifting my aim just slightly. *Exhale...*

And release.

The arrow hits the leftmost target. *Bullseye.*

The Wolf's hand clenches at his side, the barest tell.

"Seems those 'genteel' arts paid off," I say mildly. "One down. Let's up the stakes."

I lower the bow, reaching for my robe's sash. The silk whispers as it falls to the floor. The Wolf's eyes flare, taking in the black lace and silk nightgown. Sheer mesh clings to my breasts and hips, hiding absolutely nothing. There's naked... and then there's this. Bait dangled on a hook to tempt a monster.

"What the fuck are you doing?" His voice is a low rasp.

"What's it look like? You said to surprise you if I wanted the full set of knives." I run a hand down my side, smiling as he tracks the movement. A muscle flickers in his jaw. "So consider this a thank you for the present. You did get this for me, didn't you? It came in my clothing bundle last month."

I slide my finger over the delicate lace barely covering my nipple. A harsh breath leaves him. He says something under his breath that sounds like a curse.

"Tell me something," I say, reaching for the second arrow. "When you brought home this nightgown, what were you thinking about? Me wearing it?" I slant him a look as I nock the arrow and draw it back. "Or were you too busy imagining all the ways you'd get me out of it?"

The arrow buries itself in the target, right next to the first. Dead center.

I grin. "Two for two. Sure you don't want to just give up?"

He's so still, every muscle tense and ready to lunge. To grab. There's no concealing the hunger in his expression, as if he's thinking up all the ways he'll dominate me, claim me, make me his.

But I'm not done yet.

I spin the third arrow between my fingers. "No? Okay then, one last question. In these fantasies of yours, did you take your time undressing me, or did you just bend me over and fuck me in it?"

His chest heaves, hands flexing at his sides. I have the Wolf right where I want him, and this power is dizzying. It's depraved how much I want him on his knees for me. At *my* mercy for once.

"You really want to know?" he asks roughly.

"I really want to *win*," I reply with a slow grin.

And maybe torture him a bit. Payback for all the nights he'd left me aching after those healing sessions.

The embers in his irises glow. "I thought about having you in every way." The admission seems torn from somewhere deep. Somewhere aching. "Against every wall. Bent over every table. In every bed. I've fucked you a thousand different times in my head. Made you scream. Made you beg. Made you break."

Heat pools between my legs. I know what he's doing—he's telling me what he'll do to me if I lose. Making me imagine all the ways he'd take me. But I've been living with the Wolf leaving me wet and wanting for five weeks. Every damn night he heals me, my body reminds me how good he could fuck me. It's not going to work.

I bring the bow back up. "That's too bad. Because tonight, you'll go to bed aching and desperate. And alone."

I let the last arrow fly. It hits right in the center, not even a millimeter of space between its sisters. A perfect grouping.

Victory.

"I won," I taunt, facing him. "Say I won fair and square."

He stares at me, and he looks furious. *Ravenous.*

"Come on, Wolf. Three little words. 'You beat me.'"

Scowling, he snatches the bow from me and tosses it aside. "Fair and square? That was cheating, you arrogant creature."

I grin slowly. "Was it? Or did I outplay a stronger opponent? *Move. Countermove. Disarm. Attack*, remember? It's not my fault you walked right into it."

For a breathless moment, I can't tell if he's going to kiss me or kill me.

But then he laughs, and it's the most beautiful sound I've ever heard, resonant and deep. And dangerous.

His amusement feels like he's slitting my throat.

"Just wait," he says, leaning into the weapons cupboard to pull out a leather bundle. "When you least expect it? Payback's going to be a bitch, Devaliant."

The Wolf sets the bundle on a table and unrolls it to reveal two daggers perfectly matching the ones he gave me in the garden. They're exquisite—the steel folded and layered in the unmistakable rippling patterns of Turpori craftsmanship. These aren't just weapons. They're works of art.

"Satisfied?" he asks.

"They'll do."

"Oh, they'll *do*, will they? Entire kingdoms have been razed for steel like that. Maybe show a little appreciation."

I can't tell if he's serious or trying to get a rise out of me. It's impossible to know with him.

I reach for the blades, but he's suddenly there at my back, scent invading my senses. Making it difficult to focus on anything but him.

"Want to know a secret?" he asks, plucking a dagger from its sheath.

He sets the edge above my collarbone. Not pressing. Just resting there like a promise. Like a threat.

"The first cut is always special. These blades are ancient. They've tasted kings and warriors. Generals and thieves." His free hand slides up to grip my jaw, angling my head back. "They remember every drop of blood that's ever christened them."

My breath comes faster now. "Is that so?"

I feel his smile against my neck, hungry and sharp. "Oh, yes. They remember *everything*."

There's a sudden, bright flare of pain as he slices the blade across my chest. My lips part on a gasp. Before I can process what's happening, he ducks down and—

His tongue sweeps over the shallow cut.

A whimper slips out of me, and he answers with a groan, lapping up the trickle of blood. He ends his taste with a tender kiss.

"Been wanting to taste you for weeks," he murmurs. "Ever since you stopped talking to me. Drove me fucking crazy."

This isn't happening.

But it is. And worse—I'm leaning into it. Into him. Into this dark, twisted thing between us that feels too much like falling off a cliff. No handholds, no rescue—just him and me and the long plunge to the bottom.

When he finally pulls back, his pupils are dilated, black overtaking his golden irises. He lifts the bloodied dagger and traces his tongue along the edge. Savoring every last drop of me.

"How long do you think this'll last?" His voice is rough with want. "One more month? Two? Before I get bored?"

The more interesting you are, the longer you live.

And just like that, the moment shatters. A red haze falls over my vision. With a snarl, I wrench out of his hold and shove him back into his chair. He goes down with a grunt of surprise, those massive wings flaring wide. Then I pluck the dagger from his grip and slash it across his bare chest.

And I lick the gash before it can heal.

"Now this blade will remember how you taste," I hiss, stabbing the dagger into the chair inches from his head. "And so will I."

We're both breathing hard now, our chests touching. Hearts beating against each other. He glares up at me, but his hands slide to my ass, yanking me flush against his aroused cock.

"Fuck, *I hate you*," he growls.

I lean in close, lips brushing his ear. "Then hate me harder."

His hips jerk, rolling up to meet me in a slow, dirty grind that makes my breath catch. I match him without thinking, our bodies falling into a rhythm as natural as violence. Graceless. Artless. As inevitable as gravity. My head falls back as he thrusts up against me. The chair creaks with each movement, a counterpoint to our harsh breathing.

"I hate everything about you." His hands roam over my back, my sides, grasping. "I hate your smart fucking mouth and how it asks too many questions. I hate how you feel against me."

Liar, I think as he dips his head and flicks his tongue over my pulse. *You love it.*

I rock into him harder, chasing friction. His fingers dig into my hips hard enough to bruise, to mark me. I imagine him covering me in blue and brown and yellow shaped like his fingers. Like the imprints of his teeth. Every mark would be evidence of his unraveling control, hidden beneath my clothes like secrets.

"I hate how you touch me," he rasps, lips moving to my jaw. "Hate that I get so damn hard whenever I see you."

It's aggressive, almost violent, the way we collide. The way his hips slam into mine, his hard cock grinding against my pussy through our clothes.

But there's poetry too. In the rough noises he makes when I ride him just right. The reverence of his touch, his mouth as he kisses down my neck. His breath shaping secrets against my pulse. Like a dark liturgy. Like worship.

And maybe it's madness—this desperate urge to offer myself up to his mouth and hands, to take in all his darkness. To let his edges cut me open until we both bleed.

I don't give a fuck if you die, he said weeks ago. But I'll make damn sure he remembers me. I'm going to carve myself so deeply into his bones that when he kills me, he'll never be free of me.

I wrap my hand around his throat, squeezing until I feel his pulse spike against my palm. Hard enough to make my point.

Leaning in, I let my lips graze his ear. "This is killing you, isn't it?" I whisper. "Wanting me?"

He goes rigid beneath me.

Got you.

"*If you want to understand a thing, you have to learn its nature*, right?" I say, throwing his own words back at him. "You know what I think? You hide behind cruelty because it's easier than admitting I make you feel anything but rage."

He sneers. "Shut up. You're nothing."

"*Nothing* doesn't make you pace outside my door because I'm not talking to you. *Nothing* doesn't drive you insane." I press my nails into his chest, relishing the way his muscles jump. "I'll bet there isn't a day that goes by that you don't think about me. You hate me because I'm under your skin, and you're still trying to dig me out. You fell apart when I wasn't speaking to you because you need this, don't you? My attention, my touch, *me*." I roll my hips again, slower this time, deliberate. Relishing the way his mouth parts on a breath. "Yeah, you need this so fucking bad that you get yourself off thinking about all the ways you could have me. I'll bet you come with my name on your lips and hate yourself after." I brush my lips down his jaw and breathe, "I'll bet wanting me eats. You. Alive."

I pull back slowly, drinking in the sight of him. At my mercy and speechless for once.

"Tell me something, Wolf," I say into the charged space between our mouths. "When you dream of me now, is it with my blood on your hands? Or your tongue between my thighs?"

His fingers dig into my hips hard enough to leave marks, and for a moment, I think he might finally snap and take what we both know he wants.

But I don't give him the chance.

With a final, vicious grind, I yank my knife out of the chair and climb off him. I don't look back as I gather the blades and collect my fallen robe.

"I'm going to go enjoy my new knives. Sweet dreams," I tell him with a grin and a little wave.

24

THEODORA

NO ONE TELLS you that ruling means being a performer.

Drip.

You can be taught all the right things on your father's knee—*sit straight, think before speaking, trust your instincts*—but pretending to be whole when you're falling apart? That takes skill. That takes—

The tide rushes in and yanks you under. The more you drown, the longer it takes to die. And the longer it takes to die, the deeper you sink.

Down.

Drip.

An Anchor's body is gold. You learn the value of it in how they treat you at the altar. The Oracle always runs her fingers through my hair, her touch gentle until it isn't.

"Good girl," she coos, right before she shoves the blade into my ribs.

When I gasp back to life, there she is again. Same words. "Good girl. Such a good girl." Like I'm a pet performing a trick.

Fuck. You.

Drip.

Blood is my war paint. I don't accept the cleansing after the ceremony. This body needs a reminder. It needs to know that it's not a drowning set of lungs; it belongs to a woman, and that woman is me.

So I shove off the altar and let the blood drip through my gold temple dress. Let it paint my skin. I am going to *fuck* in all this blood.

I just need to walk out of the temple, down ten steps, and get into the carriage.

Drip.

"Your Highness?" Kas, my guard, falls into step beside me.

I don't look at him. "I want it in the carriage."

I've been called many things by many lovers. *Ice queen. Heartless. Frigid bitch.* They expect tenderness after I've let them inside me, as if I owe them that. As if they're entitled to more than I'm willing to give.

I'm not interested in feelings. I'm trying to keep this body alive, and so it needs touch.

"Whatever you want," Kas says as we exit the temple.

That's why I keep him close. He doesn't ask for what I can't give, and the blood doesn't bother him. It excites him.

Sensation crashes over me in waves—sight, sound, touch. Sun in my eyes. Too many voices. Too sharp. Too much. The trick is to focus on something small when everything feels too big: the pressure of Kas' fingers, the weight of my dress, the way my heart pounds. My breath.

In. Out. In. Out. Don't think about how you can't feel your fingers yet. In. Out.

I force my legs to keep moving.

Find solid ground. Come on, Theo.

I stumble slightly, and hands close around my arms, steadying me before my trembling knees can fold.

"I have you, Your Highness." Kas' voice, low and measured. Grounding.

I meet my bodyguard's gaze, those eyes missing nothing as they note my unsteady movements. No softness there, no tenderness, only the keen assessment of a professional for his charge.

"The crowd?" I ask.

"Worse than usual." His attention flickers to the barricades outside the temple and the throng beyond. "We'll have to move quickly."

Nothing's been right in the city since Bryony's "death". Oh, we staged a lovely public funeral a fortnight ago—an empty casket, my uncle's fake tears as he convincingly told everyone that the Wolf had come for their princess. But Lucinian practice dictates a pyre with the body on public display, and generations of Devaliants observed the custom. And all Idris had to show everyone was Bryony's blood-soaked dress. Funny how skeptical the masses become when you can't produce a corpse to burn.

The only person in Vartena who knows for sure that my sister is alive is me. I destroy every letter the Wolf brings from her after I read it. And now that she's gone—or so the people believe—the city's collective grief has transmuted into something uglier. Restless. Hungry for answers we're not providing.

"Where is Princess Bryony?"

"Why won't they burn her? Where's the body?"

The ocean waves are closing over my head, pushing me into their depths.

Chin up, eyes forward. Don't let them see.

This is the performance. The part no one teaches you. The part you learn if you want to survive in this world.

Kas' grip tightens as he half carries me down the temple steps. The instant we clear the threshold, the crowd surges, straining against the wooden barricades. My guards form a protective circle as we approach the waiting carriage, hands resting on sword hilts.

Kas nudges me into the carriage. The moment we lurch into motion and the privacy curtain falls, I'm in his lap, dragging his mouth to mine.

"Fuck me," I say, smearing my blood on his neck as I wrap my hand around his throat.

When I nip at his lip, he growls, hands finding my hips and dragging me closer. We both know what this is. What we are to each other. He's the solid thing I cling to when the tide threatens to drag me under; I'm the outlet for his violent edges.

I can still hear the crowd's screams beyond the carriage windows.

Where is she where is she whereisshe—

Kas makes a low sound in his throat. "Tell me how you want it."

"Just shut up and touch me. I want to be sore after. I don't want to think right now."

This isn't romance. It isn't even really about attraction, although I can appreciate the clean, brutal lines of him. No, this is about feeling alive. Warmth and sensation, the temporary giddiness of frantic coupling. It's about touching someone long enough to remind myself that there's still blood moving through my veins, and the parts of me that feel broken and numb can still ignite.

I need to cram this body so full of pleasure that it forgets it was ever dead.

His fingers find their way under my skirts, yanking up the fabric. Finding the ties of my undergarments—

A shout from outside pierces through my hazed mind. Then another. And another.

"Your Highness!" One of the guards pounds on the roof. "The barriers—"

The sudden surge of voices drowns out the rest of his warning. The carriage jerks to a halt as bodies press against it. Through gaps in the curtains, I catch glimpses of faces contorted with desperation, hands reaching, grasping.

"*Where is she? Where is Princess Bryony?*"

Breathe in. Breathe out. Lock it down. Don't let it touch you.

Kas hoists me off his lap and deposits me on the opposite bench, already going for his sword. All trace of the considerate lover is replaced by the battle-hardened bodyguard.

"Stay," he orders me.

Bodies slam against the vehicle from all sides, rocking it on its wheels. My guards shout.

"*Get back! I said get back, damn you!*"

But they don't. They won't. I can hear it in their voices— that edge of hysteria that makes people dangerous. The press of bodies is too thick, barely allowing us to inch forward. My guards fight to free a path, and I catch snippets of their shouts over the din.

The horses finally break through, and the carriage gives a violent lurch. We hurtle down the street in a thunder of hoofbeats. Kas remains crouched beside me, one hand still on his sword just in case.

By the time we reach the palace gates, my hands have stopped shaking. I take exactly three deep breaths. *In. Out. Box it away for later. You can fall apart in private.*

"You good?" Kas asks, voice carefully neutral.

"Report to me in an hour," I say, not answering.

The ocean in my mind pushes me down further into the black.

I throw open the door to Idris' study without knocking. The scene that greets me is exactly what I expected—and somehow still disappoints.

"Really?" I drawl, taking in the spectacle before me. "On the trade agreements from Borgund?"

Lady Maris gasps, scrambling off the desk. Papers flutter to the floor. Her skirts are rucked up around her waist, and there's a love bite blooming on her throat.

Idris doesn't even have the courtesy to look ashamed. He just leans against the desk, stuffing himself back into his trousers. Judging by his blown pupils and the way he's swaying slightly, he's riding high on more than pussy and wine.

Pathetic.

"Get out," I say to Lady Maris. I don't raise my voice. I don't need to.

"Your Highness, I swear, I didn't mean to—"

"If the next words out of your mouth aren't some variation of 'it won't happen again,' I'll make sure *you're* the one who has to explain to Lord Aren why his proposal was crumpled beneath your bottom. I'm sure he'll be thrilled to postpone his winter shipments while we draft a replacement."

Maris flushes. She drops a wobbly curtsy, mumbles something

that could charitably pass for "begging your pardon, Highness," and flees.

My uncle squints at me, trying and failing to summon the disappointment he used to level at me when I was a child swiping pastries before dinner. "A knock would have been appreciated."

"So would a sober emperor."

Idris rolls his eyes, grabbing the bottle of wine perpetually on the edge of his desk. "Have a drink, Theo." He drinks directly from the neck of the bottle, his throat working. "It might help dislodge the stick wedged permanently up your ass."

I clench my teeth. *Don't lunge over there and punch your uncle in the face. Calm. Poise. Control.*

"Our people are getting restless," I say, forcing my jaw to relax. "They tried to drag me out of my carriage after I made my tithe."

He tugs at his clothes and downs a gulp of wine. "What do you want me to do? I already ordered them to give their tithes, and they're back at the temple."

"*Some* are back at the temple. Not all of them. You need to—"

"Go out there and soothe them? Kiss their babies? What?" He makes a sharp gesture with the bottle, wine sloshing. "They'll get over it, or an Enforcer will kill them. I'm their emperor, not their nanny."

I swear to the gods, this man is useless. I'd say it's a wonder he can dress himself in the morning, but he doesn't do that, either.

"Get over it?" My voice rises. "The city is still tearing itself apart over Bryony, and your solution is to what, exactly? Drink and rut with anything that has a pulse until they lose interest?"

"I asked for a buffer around the palace, and all royal tithes will no longer go through public streets. It's dealt with. Happy?"

"*Happy?* Dealt with?" A sharp laugh tears out of me. "All you can muster is 'Let's avoid the main thoroughfare, shall we?' while your people scream for answers about what really happened to their princess?"

The bottle freezes halfway to his mouth.

There it is, I think with savage satisfaction. *Finally got your attention, didn't I?*

"Be very careful with your next words, Theodora." His voice drops low, dangerous.

"Or what?" I stalk forward, my lip curling in disgust. "You're worse than my father ever was. At least he had the decency to die before he could drag us all down with him."

The bottle shatters against the wall beside my head. I don't flinch.

"You ungrateful little bitch." Idris stalks forward. "I took the throne when your worthless father couldn't handle it anymore. I kept this kingdom from suspecting our family was falling apart. I sacrificed—"

"*Sacrificed*? You attacked your niece and left her to die on a mountain. You were the reason she was there in the first place!"

His mouth hangs open. I haven't confronted him about what the Wolf said to me a month ago. I've been waiting until the right moment, and here it is.

"I told you," he says. "The Wolf came and—"

"Do *not*," I hiss, "treat me like an idiot. An Enforcer would have left us a corpse for the pyre. Only an incompetent would bring back bloody rags and think it was enough. Those people out there expected a funeral like we've given every other Devaliant, oathbreaker or no. They loved Bryony more than they love you."

His hand shoots out, fingers wrapping around my throat. "I did what had to be done," he snarls, squeezing. "The Eternal demanded blood, and I gave it to him. You think you're so much better?" His hold tightens until black spots dance at the edges of my vision. "I could snap your neck and tell them all you fell down the stairs in your grief. It would be so easy to say you finally cracked. That losing poor Bryony was too much. Who would question it?" His thumb digs into my windpipe. "You're just another weak little cunt like the rest of them. Too soft to do what needs doing."

I shove my knee into his crotch with all the force I can muster. He makes a sound like a wounded animal and doubles over. But I'm not finished. I slap him hard across the face, watching him stagger.

"Touch me again," I snarl, shaking out my hand, "and I'll make you beg for something as merciful as a broken neck."

Idris works his jaw, his eyes blazing.

"You've been spinning stories for so long, you probably believe your own bullshit by now," I say. "Go ahead. Try to end me. Give them another martyr and see if you last when they all realize I'm the only reason you still have a throne to piss on. They tolerated you because Bryony and I were holding Hellevig together. You think you'll last a day when the truth comes out? *Do it*, Uncle. Kill me, you fucking coward."

"Get out." This time, I hear the first faint ring of uncertainty.

"You're not a ruler," I say, soft and vicious. "You're a sad, pathetic man clinging to a title you never earned."

Idris looks like he wants to lunge at me again.

"Remember this moment," I tell him. "The day you lost Luceni. And it won't be because the Eternal screwed us or Bryony died. It'll be because you're a craven, useless piece of shit who deserves every knife in your back."

I'm out the door and halfway down the corridor before I pull in a shuddering breath that feels like swallowing glass.

The mark on my wrist throbs—Alexios' Claim, binding me to his service. To the Shroud. I slide my fingers beneath my gold cuff and trace the brand, considering.

I've heard gods can hear those they Claim—any prayer sent along the conduit, our thoughts, our desperate pleas. I've spent every day since my first tithe training my mind to be a fortress. No stray thoughts escaping.

For the first time in my life, I open myself up.

Is this what you wanted when you revoked my sister's Claim? I think, pushing the thought out like arrows. *Chaos in the streets? You've left me a mess to clean up because you couldn't stand that they loved her more than they feared you.*

Silence answers. Not that I expected anything else. Gods don't lower themselves to respond to the insects they grind beneath their boots.

I shore my mental ramparts back up behind an impenetrable

psychic barrier. I have more immediate concerns. My throat aches where Idris grabbed me, but I hold my head high as I stride down the hall.

Kas falls into step beside me, matching my pace. "Your Highness—"

"I need numbers," I say, cutting him off. "Tally my loyalists in each branch of the household, down to the scullery maids. Prioritize those closest to me during the regency."

"Give me a few days," he says. He hesitates. "Your Highness, we might not have enough—"

"Yes, I'll assume everyone's heard a version of events where I'm destined to usher in Luceni's downfall because I was the first woman to rule even temporarily. I know what story my uncle crafted when he returned from his drunken haze and sat his ass back on the throne."

Idris might be checked out from actually running this kingdom, but he's always had a gift for controlling the narrative. Lying is the only thing he does with any semblance of competence.

"They don't realize how close we are to collapse," Kas says grimly. "They still think your uncle advised you when you were regent."

"Then make them understand. He's getting more unstable. We don't have the luxury of waiting."

PART THREE

MONSTERS AND MEMORY

25

BRYONY

"THE ROSES ARE happier."

I go still at the Wolf's voice. His scent envelops me, a mix of citrus, evergreen, and magic.

It's been three days. Three days of him avoiding me. He comes into my room at night, heals my injuries, and leaves. Cold, perfunctory. None of the usual lingering touches with his hands. Not since—

This is killing you, isn't it? Wanting me?

Gritting my teeth, I sit back on my heels and glare up at him—and immediately wish I hadn't.

Every day, I forget how beautiful the Wolf is, and every day, I'm slapped in the face with it again. Dark trousers ride low on his narrow hips. A tight black shirt strains across his chest, stretching over his broad shoulders and fastening beneath his wings. His dark hair is mussed, as if he's just rolled out of bed.

Or tumbled someone in it.

A sour taste fills my mouth at the thought.

In Hellevig, we have a saying: The sweetest poisons come wrapped in honey. I've never seen anything embody that warning quite like the male standing before me. Something so beautiful you forget what he really is: a predator.

I swallow hard and force my attention back to the weeds, attacking them with renewed vigor. "Maybe they're just glad someone is finally paying attention to them. Their neglectful owner has been too busy pretending I don't exist."

I'll bet wanting me eats. You. Alive.

A breeze whips through the garden, sending fallen leaves skittering over the ground. The branches of the towering silverpines creak around us.

Finally, he answers. "I just healed you yesterday, didn't I? Cracked skull, busted ribs, ruptured spleen. One would think something that traumatic would stick, but maybe you had such a good time you've forgotten already. Or do you mean the lack of speaking? Otherwise known as your favorite tactic."

A thorn bites into my wrist as I reach for another weed, and I hiss out a curse. A thin rivulet of crimson beads up. "You're the one who likes the sound of your own voice."

He smiles slowly. "Careful, nemesis. Almost sounds like you missed me."

Nemesis. That nickname shouldn't spread heat across my skin, but it does.

I glance away. "Amara will be here any second. I'm sure you have better things to do than supervise."

"She's not coming. I'm taking a murder holiday. Specifically to torment the princess who thinks she can cheat a god out of his daggers and get away with it."

"I didn't cheat. I outsmarted you. There's a difference." I roll my eyes. "If you're planning to skulk around, you might as well make yourself useful. Bond with your precious roses. Prune something before they stage a coup and strangle us both in our sleep."

When he doesn't answer, I make the mistake of looking up again. The Wolf is grinning at me, the kind of grin that makes prey animals run for their lives. The kind that promises beautiful, terrible things.

"You know what?" he says. "I have a better idea."

Before I can blink, he grabs me around the waist and launches us into the air. The ground falls away with a single powerful beat of his wings.

"*Wolf!*" I yelp when he veers sharply to the left.

I feel his chest shake with laughter. The bastard is enjoying this.

My stomach lurches as the garden grows smaller and smaller. I can barely breathe. Can't think. His arms are the only things keeping me from plummeting.

"Put me down, you lunatic!"

"Stop squirming," he says in my ear. "You don't want to slip free when we're up this high."

This absolute bastard.

He flies us higher. The tower's surroundings fade into smudges of green and gray below. The air becomes crisper and sharper in my lungs the more we climb. Scillari spreads out below us in a patchwork of colors—the starlight rivers, the teal lakes, the forests, and the multi-hued flowers that cover the mountains. Hazy spires jut through the clouds, distant glimpses of sprawling residences carved into the cliffs.

I can't even see the Wolf's property now.

"Where are you taking me?" I ask.

No answer. Just wing beats and rushing wind. We're approaching the sea now.

That's... That's not good. Nothing for miles. No way to escape, no chance of rescue. He could drop me, and I'd vanish without a trace.

"Wolf, where—"

"This is the Osbu Sea," he says, barely audible over the wind.

Oh, good, kidnapping and vague answers. That's comforting.

Craning my neck, I glare up at him. "Why are we in the middle of nowhere? What are you doing?"

"You've been secluded in that tower for too long getting your ass handed to you by Amara," he says. "I thought you could use an introduction to an ancient Scillarian tradition. You should be flattered that I'm making an exception for your fragile human constitution."

Nothing about this bodes well.

"Dare I ask what this 'tradition' is?"

"Water landings," the Wolf says conversationally. "Mastering them is a rite of passage for young demis. We start the infants out with something small—a pond or lake. Eases them into the rush while minimizing the damage to those soft little baby limbs when they inevitably botch the angle on the first few passes." I feel his smile curve against my temple. "But you know me. I've never been one to coddle. Hands-on instruction garners much more satisfying results."

"Hands-on—"

"In fact, I believe you're overdue for your first lesson. Remember that vow I made after our little wager? The one about making you pay dearly for hustling me?"

Oh fuck. Oh *fuck*.

Every cell in my body bellows a warning, animal instinct clawing to the surface. "Wolf, don't you dare—"

"The trick," he murmurs, his lips brushing the tender skin just behind my ear, "is to streamline. Aim for the horizon, keep your chin up, and hit the water at the shallowest possible angle. Oh, and do remember to scream nice and loud for me. If you're convincing enough, I might consider fishing you out before the sharks catch your scent."

What—

"*Wolf!*"

"See you soon, you little cheat."

And then the bastard *drops me*.

There's a moment of dread where I'm suspended in the wind. And then gravity seizes me, and I'm plummeting. The sea hurtles closer, closer, *closer*. I send up a prayer to the stars, to the realm, to any power bothering to listen to the pathetic human plummeting to her death.

Please please please not like this don't let it end like this please—

Arms close around my waist, arresting my fall so suddenly that all the oxygen leaves my lungs. And then we're climbing again, the water receding as we wheel through clouds back into the open sky.

"You absolute *fuck*," I choke out between shallow breaths. "You fucking fucker!"

He laughs. "One little fall and she loses her entire vocabulary."

"*Fuck you!*"

"Honestly, that was underwhelming. Where was the flailing? The tears? The frantic bargaining for your life? I'm insulted."

"I'll be sure to scream to your exacting standards next murder attempt."

"This is basic fledgling shit, nemesis. If an infant can manage a harmless little plunge, so can you. Builds character. And bone density."

"A harmless little *plunge?*" I splutter. "Those infants have *wings!*"

"Are you really conceding defeat after one tiny dive? I thought you had more teeth than that. Or was your display in the armory a fluke?"

"My only regret is not putting that arrow through your arrogant face!"

"I don't know if you should be making threats, Devaliant. My hands might… just… *slip*." He punctuates this by releasing one of his arms around my waist.

I yelp, clinging to his other arm. "*Don't you dare—*"

We're diving again before I can even catch my breath. His body curls around me as we plunge straight down, the water rushing up to meet us. I can almost taste the brine. The foam against my skin.

This is how I die. This insane, reckless god is going to be the death of me.

At the last possible second, mere feet from the waves, the Wolf's wings snap out and he flattens us out into a smooth glide.

"I hate you," I manage. "I despise you. If I had a knife right now, I'd carve out your rotten heart."

"One would think you weren't grateful that I grabbed you before you landed in the sea, nemesis."

I take it back. Fuck the knife. I'll tear his throat out with my teeth.

"You're the worst thing that's ever happened to me," I grumble.

He laughs then, the sound so startled and genuine it makes my breath catch. I wonder how many other humans have had the pleasure of hearing it. That's all it takes to unwind the tension from my muscles.

"Do you do this a lot?" I ask, once I've managed to calm my frantic pulse.

"Play with human girls by dropping them over open water? No, you'd be the first to inspire this particular torment."

"Lucky me," I grumble. "But I meant taking off and flying until you can't see land anymore. Is that something you like?"

He's quiet for a long moment, the silence punctuated with the rhythmic beat of his wings and the faraway cries of gulls. "No," he finally says, soft enough that I almost miss it. "I haven't flown for anything but duty and death in a very long time."

Something twists beneath my ribs, a tender ache blooming like a bruise. Because I can almost see it. The male he was before the world took everything soft and gentle and left only violence behind.

It's a dangerous thought. But as I stare out at the horizon, marveling at the salt spray kissing my cheeks, my defenses waver. Because this? It's the loveliest thing I've felt in longer than I can remember. There's a fierce sort of joy thrumming through me, bright and effervescent. I want to wrap myself in this feeling and cling to it with both hands.

"Show me," I say, "what it was like to fly. Before."

The Wolf goes still at my back. His hands tighten on my waist as he shifts me in his arms until we're face to face.

The way he's looking at me... It's as if I've just handed him a blade and bared my throat. As if he's never seen me before this moment. I realize this strange, unspoken desire goes both ways—I'm not alone in wanting to pretend, for one day, that we're something we're not.

"The trick," the Wolf says, "is to surrender. To embrace the fall and trust that you'll be caught."

I swallow hard around the sudden lump in my throat. "That sounds like a dangerous game for a woman with no wings."

"No more dangerous than the game we're already playing."

His head dips, his breath ghosting across my cheek, my jaw. "I'm going to let go now, Devaliant. I need you to let me."

Let me. Such incongruous words, falling from the lips of this lovely, vicious god.

"All right," I say.

Slowly, the Wolf takes my hand and flattens my trembling palm against the beat of his heart. His skin is warm through the thin fabric of his shirt. "Feel my heartbeat and match your breathing to it. Let everything else fall away."

I do as he says, focusing on the drum of his heart against my fingers, the rise and fall of his chest as I time my inhales to his. Gradually, bit by bit, my racing pulse begins to calm.

"That's it," the Wolf murmurs. "Just like that. Keep your eyes on me and your breathing steady. Can you do that for me?"

I let out a shaky exhale and nod.

"I'm going to turn you around now. And when I let go, I want you to spread your arms out wide like they're wings. Imagine you're soaring. That you're limitless and untethered. Understand?"

"Yes," I say.

The Wolf's hands are gentle as he rotates me with one arm locked around my waist, and the other a steady pressure between my shoulder blades, until there's nothing between me and the sea below. "Arms out. Eyes up. You're going to fall, and I'm going to catch you." His lips brush my ear. "I'll always catch you."

And then he lets go.

For an instant, I'm suspended. Weightless. Everything in me seizes, screaming wrong wrong wrong—

The Wolf's arms close around me, hauling me against him. "Breathe. I have you." His heart thrums against my spine. "Do you trust me?"

The word lands like a blade between the ribs. Trust is such a small, simple thing, and handing it to the god who's going to kill me is so dangerous. So stupid.

But I don't want this to end yet.

"Just for today," I say. "For this moment, I trust you."

His exhale gusts across my nape. "Then fall, Devaliant. Fall and *fly*."

And he releases me.

This time, I don't fight the plummet. I surrender myself to gravity's inexorable pull, the swoop and fall, the giddy lurch. As untethered and free as the birds wheeling above.

Strong arms snatch me out of the plunge. I slam into the Wolf's chest with a breathless whoop, my hands finding his shoulders.

He grins. "Again?"

"Again," I say, smiling back.

I lose track of the minutes. Of the dives and catches, the rushes of fear and excitement and impossible joy. All I know is his body pressed against mine, the drum of his heartbeat in my ears. I let the fear and the doubt all fall away, the hard, ugly things tangled like nettles around my heart. No past between us. No hate or splintered things. Just the wind and the sky and the sea. The two of us rising and falling, falling and rising.

I spread my arms wide and picture myself drifting, weightless. And when I tip back into the sky, it's not a plummet. It's *flying*.

The Wolf is always there to catch me.

I surrender to the rush, let the excitement sing through my veins, and when he pulls me to him after the final dive, I'm laughing, wild and breathless. I feel impossibly light.

The tower comes into view too soon. The Wolf lands in the center of the garden, his hands flexing on my hips before he sets me back on my feet.

For a long moment, we simply stare at each other, our breath slowing.

"Why?" I ask. "Why did you do this for me?"

His knuckles graze my cheek. I fight the urge to lean into it, to chase that fleeting warmth.

"It was something you needed," he says. "And maybe I needed it too."

I almost touch him back. Almost take his face in my hands and put all my words in the brush of my fingers across his skin. Because for a little while, we were both searching for the same nameless thing out there above the waves. Both wanting. Both unable to put that strange yearning into words.

But then he steps back and drops his hand. "Goodnight, Devaliant."

The words are cool. Polite. A reminder of who and what we are, all tied up in meaningless pleasantries.

26

EVANDER

THE AIR SMELLS like fear.

There's a certain mélange that humans give off when they know death is coming. Usually, I like to take my time breathing it in, savoring the quiet before my work. The sights and sounds and scents of the next doomed village.

But tonight, I'm not alone on this hunt.

"Does this little display have a point, or are we just admiring the view?"

Bastien joins me on the cliff, his white hair gleaming silver in the moonlight. My brother and I have the same build—tall, broad shoulders, built for battle. Our wings used to contrast perfectly, his starry black to my gleaming gold. Now shadows writhe where his feathers should be, a reminder of what was stolen.

For a moment, I'm centuries younger, standing with my brother in another city. Before the war. Before the torture. Before I spent three days pouring magic into him while he screamed, the shadows growing out of the scars on his back.

And I nearly killed us both.

I roll my shoulders. "Killing is like fucking. I like to draw it out before I sink in."

Before the war, that might have earned me a small smile. Maybe he would have made some comment about that demigoddess bartender we both had eyes for back in Vallenca. But Vallenca's just rubble now, like the rest of our mother's territory. Those days are as dead as the people we couldn't save.

Some villagers scurry below, gathering kindling and tinder. That's the fascinating thing about humans—all the different ways they prepare for death. Some run, others nest. I guess people will cling to whatever lie lets them sleep when the wolves are at the door.

Bastien's black eyes meet mine, irises glittering with starlight. "You know," he says, and the calm in his voice has me bracing for impact, "rumor has it you've gone soft recently. Forgot how to follow orders."

I keep my face blank. "That so?"

"Alexios mentioned Keksa."

And there it is. The real reason he's up here on this cliff with me. Not out of brotherly concern—that ended with his wings— but as an excuse to slice me open and poke at my guts. Like I'm a math problem he can solve if he digs deep enough.

"Alexios needs a hobby," I say with a dismissive flick of my fingers. "All that pent-up energy can't be healthy."

"Spare me the evasion. It's beneath you." Shadows writhe around him, coiling along his coat. "Selfishness, recklessness, the impulse control of a toddler—those are your specialties. Not cowardice."

The irony of him questioning my behavior when he's barely around to see it isn't lost on me. Some days, I think he hates me. Hates the healing magic I used to give him the mockery of the wings he lost. He's the reason I let that power atrophy until the Devaliant inspired me to use it, and if he ever found out, I think he'd dig around in my guts until I broke.

I look away. "It was a month ago, Bas. I was bored. Don't overthink it."

"I'm aware of the self-destructive behavior you turn to in boredom. That's why I'm standing here."

"Clearly. I'd never accuse you of standing here because you wanted a social visit with your brother."

His eye twitches—on Bastien, that's practically a flinch. "That's your second evasion. Do I need to take over your work?"

"No. I'm fine. I told you it was just a whim."

Lying is a skill, and lying to Bastien is an art. But what can I say? That I can't stop thinking about her? That a *Devaliant* haunts my dreams? It's obscene, the way I'm starving for her. Unacceptable. Every time I close my eyes, I see her. Feel the press of her body against mine. Her voice in my ear, mocking.

This is killing you, isn't it? Wanting me.

"Are we doing this or not?" I growl, rolling my neck. "Places to destroy, people to traumatize. I've got a busy schedule."

Before he can say another word, I launch off the cliff. Bastien follows closely behind me, those shadow wings spreading out in smoky tendrils.

I don't hesitate or let myself think. I just reach for the bow at my back, the motions as mechanical as clockwork. *Nock. Draw. Aim.*

There's something beautiful about that first moment of clarity. My mind goes quiet and my breath settles as the rage fills me like an old friend, swallowing everything—doubt, guilt, *her* face—until all that's left is the bow in my hands and bodies waiting to fall. My arrow punches through a man's neck, and I marvel at how clean it is. How easy. It's always so damn easy once you get started.

Bastien doesn't bother with the finesse of a tidy kill—he just tears through anything that moves.

"Please," a man begs. My brother doesn't even look at him as his shadows rip the man apart.

There's a bleak sort of elegance in it, the brutal way he destroys. The way he tears apart the buildings and makes every death as violent and cathartic as possible. It's his nature now, as breathing is to the living and rotting to the dead. But where Bastien is like a storm, I am precision violence. The killing calm. I place each shot where it'll do the worst damage—throats, hearts, eyes. My focus stays on the ritual motions of draw-release-kill.

I orchestrate death like a symphony. With *intention*. A woman screams as her husband falls. Someone else begs me, and I place another shot. Doesn't matter where they run or hide. There's no escaping us. We're the dark and all its teeth, and tonight, we've come to collect.

Through the haze of smoke and screams, I take in the scale of it. The magnitude of the ugly thing we've made of this place and its people. This is what we do. What *I* do.

Movement catches my eye—a woman with pale hair crouching low behind a cart. For a disorienting second, all I see is the Devaliant's face. That same defiance in the set of her jaw.

So fragile. So painfully vulnerable in a world with no use for soft things.

Just for today. For this moment, I trust you.

I stumble with the force of the memory. It's barely a blink, a tiny break in my focus, but it's a crack in the armor wide enough for all those inconvenient flashes of humanity to come bleeding through.

Fuck.

Bastien lands beside me on silent feet, snowflakes drifting between the writhing shadows of his smoky wings. The flat void of his eyes meets mine, weighing. Assessing. Hunting for weakness.

"Something you want to tell me?" he asks.

I can't look at her. Can't risk him reading the sickness carved into my face. The hunger that's eating me alive.

"Not a thing," I reply.

Silence stretches between us. Without breaking eye contact, Bastien inclines his head toward the woman.

"Then I'm sure this won't be a problem for you."

I dredge up a brittle smile as my fingers tighten around the bow. "I'd hate to deprive you of the show."

Nock. Draw. Aim.

Bastien isn't only watching me. He watches her too, savoring each ragged breath, committing her terror to memory. And I know with certainty that he'll remember this. That he'll take this hesitation and use it like a crowbar to crack me open and dig through my insides until he finds the rot.

So I choke down my regret and let the arrow fly, watching as the light drains from a face that's a breath away from being *hers*.

Whatever's left of my conscience shrivels a bit more.

But monsters don't get choices or happy endings, so I shut it out, shut it all out, until the only thing left is the mindless, mechanical repetition. Nock, draw, aim. Release. And again. And again.

It ends. Always does, eventually. The last body falls and silence creeps back in, and I'm left with the damning moment of uncertainty still infesting my thoughts.

"Want to tell me what the fuck that was about?" Bastien's voice cuts through the quiet.

I keep my eyes on my bow. "Don't know what you mean."

"You *hesitated*."

"My hand slipped."

But he reads me. He *always* reads me. Something in my posture, some minute tell.

"Getting sentimental again, Wolf?" comes a voice from above, cold and pitiless as the void between stars. "That's three times now."

Fuuuuuuuck.

Alexios lands in a swoop of red and black wings, power lashing across my skin. There's a promise of violence in his smile.

"Something under your skin again?" he asks pleasantly. "Another inconvenient flicker of humanity when you line up that killing shot after centuries of perfect service?"

I shove my feelings down and bury them deep. "Nothing I can't cut out."

"I just hate to see you making the same mistake you made in Hellevig," Alexios says, settling his wings.

"What happened in Hellevig?" Bastien asks softly.

"The Wolf decided to play games with Bryony Devaliant instead of executing her," Alexios says. His smile is a sharp reminder that he could reveal exactly what kind of game to my brother.

A betrayal.

Bastien's gaze pins me like an insect under glass. "How merciful of you, Evander. Extending courtesy to a Devaliant."

"She's dead now," I snap. "Where's the problem?"

"Dead," Alexios repeats, "but not by your hand. Now I have a city ready to tear itself apart because *you* still haven't found them a corpse to weep over. I have Theodora Devaliant sending me messages down the Claim about riots in the streets because you left the killing to some human halfwit instead of doing it properly." He stalks closer, power crackling around him. "This is how it starts, Wolf. First, you get sloppy. Then you get soft. Then you end up like our kin—strapped to tables while humans carve you up for parts."

He casts a significant look over the smoldering rubble and ravaged bodies. "But I'm sure that's not a lesson you need repeated. Is it?"

"It won't happen again," I say.

"No. It won't." Those crimson eyes cut to my brother. "Blade, you're joining the hunt. Since your brother can't complete a simple task, I need you to find what's left of the princess."

My stomach drops. *No. No, no, no.*

"If she's in pieces," he continues, "drag Severin into it. Have him use his magic to piece her rotting carcass together into something recognizable. I want a body. I want it in Hellevig. I want them to see her."

Ice solidifies in my veins. I have to physically lock my muscles against a flinch. But Bas notices anyway—that minute tell, the panicked trip of my pulse.

He always could see right through me.

"On it," he says, staring at me.

Alexios hums. "Good. Start in the forests beyond the ashlands. Lots of crows roosting out there, plenty of carrion for them to pick at." He tips his head toward the sky. "Go on, then."

Bastien's jaw clenches. I know better than to assume he'll let this go. He's going to spend his nights examining it from every angle, puzzling out why his brother would let a Devaliant live even a moment longer than necessary.

I'm sure I'll bleed for it.

Then he's gone, launching into the air with a powerful sweep of his shadowy wings.

Alexios waits until my brother disappears before stepping in close. "Tired soldiers make mistakes," he says softly. "Doubtful ones make betrayals. Be grateful I haven't shared with big brother exactly what part of you was doing the thinking when you played games with the princess. Whatever's poisoned you, dig it out, fuck it out, or carve it out. Understand?"

I nod. I hear his unspoken threat: *Or I'll do it for you.*

27

EVANDER

THE DEVALIANT HOLDS the blade as if she were born for it.

Her violet eyes narrow as she shifts her body into the correct form. The afternoon sun gilds her hair, turning silver to fire, and catches on her cheeks as she angles her head down. She's focused. Lethal. Beautiful. I could watch her like this for hours.

Release.

The knife buries itself in the target across the garden with a satisfying thunk. My chest swells—with pride, maybe. Or is it possession? Every day she stays, it's getting harder to tell the difference.

Because the truth is, I'm obsessed with her.

"Again," Amara commands. "And this time, remember to *breathe*. You're still holding too much tension in your shoulders."

The Devaliant grips another blade. She inhales, shifts her weight forward, and lets the knife fly.

Gorgeous.

I walk over, letting out a low whistle. "Look at you, making progress with the knives you swindled out of me."

Her head whips around. "Was that a compliment?"

"Treasure it—they don't come often." I glance at Amara. "Can I borrow you for a minute?"

Amara nods. "Keep practicing," she tells the Devaliant, following me.

I lead her toward the crumbling remnants of a fountain choked with climbing roses. She crosses her arms over her chest, wings snapping, and I notice flashes of purple beneath the powder dulling their vibrancy. The true shade is one of a kind—as recognizable as mine.

"What is it?" she asks.

I shove my hands in my pockets, faking a calm I haven't felt since I found those butchered bodies in Hellevig. "Does the name Rhosyn mean anything to you?"

She tilts her head, thinking it over. "No. Should it?"

"I've been hunting vermin in Vartena." I keep my tone light, but memories of the warehouse flash through my mind—the body parts piled neatly, the stacks of blood-matted feathers. "The kind that trades in black market parts."

She flinches. "Old or new?"

"New," I say grimly.

"Fuck." Her chest expands on a ragged breath. "Okay. Go on."

"The place I stumbled across in Hellevig looked like the Bloody Court's chop shops. Rhosyn's name came up, along with the initials BC. I thought you might know something, given your familiarity with their particular brand of hospitality."

At the mention of the Bloody Court, Amara freezes. Magic crackles through the air, and the ground trembles beneath my feet. It's only a matter of time before she ascends. It's getting to be a constant low-level pressure as the realm stretches itself to accommodate another Eternal; it's carving out space for her.

"Names changed a lot in the pits," she finally says. "Some we chose, others forced on us by—" She breaks off, swallowing hard. "Rhosyn's not one I recall, but there's a lot I carved out afterward. Some memories aren't worth holding on to."

I nod. Remembering is its own kind of cruelty. No matter how deep we bury the bodies, they always find ways to dig themselves back up. Haunting us in the midnight hours and *scratch scratch scratching* their way out of the silt.

"Of course," I say. "If anything comes to you—any scrap of information—"

"I'll tell you." A humorless laugh. "Nothing quite like a stroll down that blood-soaked memory lane, right? Almost as fun as your walks through Turpori's ashes."

I wince. "Amara."

"Just promise me something. If you have to bring Alexios into this, *swear* to me you won't let him find me, okay? I don't want him to know I was taken to the pits or what I did to survive it. He can't—I need him to still think—"

Something in me gentles. Behind the hard exterior, she's still that frightened girl who fought and killed and clawed her way through that nightmare, only to emerge with pieces of herself missing.

"You have my word."

"I just… I hear the realm whispering, you know? And I think that means I'm going to become—"

"An Eternal. I know. I feel it."

She plays with the ring on her finger. The only thing she's kept that belonged to her Chosen. "I don't know if I'm ready."

"We'll handle it."

It's been five centuries since my ascension. The memories have faded, leaving only impressions behind—the cold, the crushing pressure. The way magic shredded me apart before putting me back together. I had my brother with me when I crawled out of my own ashes, steadying me as the realm heaved and bucked to accommodate a new Eternal.

The price of godhood, my mother once told me, *is that you have to die first.*

"There's a place far from any demis," I tell her. "Where you can let go without collateral damage. I'll help you through the worst of it."

"Alexios and Severin are going to feel it," she points out.

I shrug. "Then I'll combust a mountain. Throw a destructive tantrum and let them think it was one of my moods."

"And if Alexios skins you alive for it?"

"Nothing I haven't endured before."

She runs a hand through her hair, visibly composing herself. Her expression flattens, the walls bricking up. "Thank you," she whispers.

"Yeah, well. Don't mention it. Seriously, not a fucking word to anyone. I've got a reputation as a heartless bastard to maintain."

Amara snorts, some of the tension easing from her shoulders. Her gaze drifts across the garden to where the Devaliant launches another blade. "She's getting good. Fast reflexes, natural talent. Who would have thought?"

Pride flutters through me. "Me. Why do you think I let her live?"

"Because you're dying to fuck her?"

"Such a filthy mouth. Why do I keep you around, again?"

Amara gives me a look. "Because I'm one of a handful of gods who can stand you, and you need as many friends as you can get. You want to tell me why you keep looking at her with those eyes?"

Fuck's sake.

"What eyes?" I ask, playing stupid.

"You know what eyes, dumbass. Something's shifting between you two."

A memory flickers of the Devaliant in my arms as I flew with her over the Osbu. Her laughter when I caught her and pulled her close.

Just for today. For this moment, I trust you.

My chest squeezes. I shake off the image, burying the sense-memory down deep. "Nothing's changing. We're playing a game. She entertains me until she doesn't."

"Right." Amara gives a short laugh. "Just entertainment."

I count to ten and try to remember that when Amara isn't being an irritating little shit, I actually enjoy her company. Strangling her would solve nothing. And it would be messy.

"Why do you care? You're the one who dumped her in my garden and said, 'She's your problem now, asshole. Have fun killing her.'"

"Things change," she says. "People, too—usually when we're too busy looking the other way to notice. Suddenly, they don't fit into the neat little boxes we've shoved them into."

"Then I break their bones until they fit."

Forgetting is not an option. Neither is forgiveness.

"Just remember," she tells me. "Some games have no winners. Only casualties."

A cold, hard knot keeps tightening in my gut. Time to shut this down before we both say shit we can't take back.

"Stop," I say flatly. "I'd hate for this to get unpleasant."

Amara lifts a brow. "Unpleasant for whom? You? Me? Her?"

I don't trust myself to answer. Jerking my chin toward the sky, I say, "Go on. I'll finish out the lesson. And don't forget to reapply the powder to your wings if you want to hide that color."

Amara's mouth thins, but she's already stepping back and angling her body to prepare for flight. The wind picks up, stirring her dark wings.

"I'm going. But Evander? If you have to destroy her, don't break her heart to do it."

Then she launches skyward with a powerful downstroke that shakes the branches around me. I watch until she disappears behind the swaying trees, her words echoing like an accusation.

When you end that girl...

My hands clench at my sides. I can still feel the press of the Devaliant's body against mine in the sky. The way she'd laughed—unguarded, just a little bit wild. The emotion in her eyes when I caught her. *Trust.* For a few hours, she'd trusted me up there in the clouds, and a part of me keeps itching to see her look at me like that again.

I'm going to have to cut that part out of me.

Some games have no winners. Only casualties.

The Devaliant doesn't turn at my approach. Her attention is fixed on the neat row of blades placed on the table before her, but I know she senses me. I see it in the subtle tensing of her shoulders, the way her head tilts just slightly—listening and tracking me. As aware of me as I always am of her.

"Is Amara done playing teacher for the day?" She trails her fingers along a dagger's edge.

"She has places to be. I'm taking over your training today."

"Lucky me." The Devaliant selects a dagger, testing its weight in her palm. "Let's resume our game, then. I wouldn't want to slack on my role as your entertainment."

Shit.

"How much of that did you hear?"

"Whatever carried on the breeze, which was enough." She flicks the blade back and forth, movements agitated. "Don't worry about breaking my heart. I'm not stupid enough to give it to you."

"And what if I took it?" I can't help but ask.

When she looks at me, her eyes are sharp. "You'd have to carve it out of me."

She's throwing up her boundaries, retreating behind her armor. And who could blame her? We both know what this is.

I force my expression to remain impassive. Bored, even. No need to let her see how deep she's burrowed beneath my skin. Wanting her doesn't have to mean anything. Maybe fucking her *would* solve the problem.

I step forward until I'm crowding into her space, close enough to feel the heat of her and see the constellation of freckles scattered across the bridge of her nose. The flecks of silver threaded through the amethyst of her eyes.

"Where did Amara leave off?"

A shiver goes through her at my nearness. "Compensating for crossbreezes when throwing."

Settling my hands on her hips, I pivot her to face the battered target. The movement brings her flush against me, and she lets out a quiet gasp that shoots straight to my cock.

"You have a bad habit," I say, ghosting my palms up her sides, "of releasing your breath too soon. Power comes from here." I splay my fingers beneath her ribs. "Your center. You need to exhale into the throw." My thumbs find the dimples at the base of her spine and press in a gentle rebuke, watching her lashes flutter. "One fluid motion from here"—I tap her sternum—"to here." I walk my fingers down her arm in a slow drag. "Understand? Center to extremity."

Her lips part, and she swallows hard, her body yielding

against mine as if she were made to fit there. Damn, I want to do terrible things to this woman.

Dangerous thought. Kill it.

I step away, giving her space. "Now draw back and sight the target. Account for distance, wind speed, and the arc of the throw. Then breathe in."

She obeys, muscles flexing as she focuses. Her chest expands on an inhale.

"Breathe out. And let go."

The Devaliant looses a controlled exhale—and then whips forward. The knife sinks into the target, this time a little closer to the center.

"Not bad." I retrieve the weapon, pressing it into her waiting palm. "But this time, don't treat it like archery. That's more about the precise mechanics of the draw and release." I curve my body around hers again. "Knife-throwing is a more intimate art."

"How so?"

"It's about learning to move your body just right. How to pivot. The angle of your arm. The timing of your breath…" I demonstrate the motion, letting her feel the roll of my hips. "Every part of you working as one. You have to learn the weapon's weight and balance, how it sits in your hand. The right amount of pressure to apply at just the right moment." My fingers trail up the inside of her arm, and she shivers like she can't help herself. "You listen to what it's telling you. How it wants to move."

"And then?" A whisper.

"Then you build the tension." Another demonstration, slower this time. "Draw back, feeling the anticipation grow. The way everything narrows down to the moment of perfect alignment. When you let the knife fly, it's not about forcing it to hit the target. It's about trusting that all that careful preparation and intimate knowledge will guide it."

Her chest rises and falls quickly. "Like dancing."

"Or seduction."

She inhales sharply. "I… What?"

"You can't just go through the motions and expect it to work. You have to pay attention. Learn how to touch them just right…" My hand slides down her side, settling on her hip. "To create the response you want."

Another small noise escapes her—some quiet, needy sound. I pray to the stars for patience, and failing that, enough indifference to settle my hardening dick.

Control yourself, you pathetic fuck.

"Try again," I tell her, stepping away. "But this time, stop thinking so much. Let your body remember what it wants to do."

A change comes over her. Her muscles relax, and her fingers trail along the blade in a caress, like she's learning it, understanding it. Her brows pinch in concentration as she draws back. The knife leaves her hand in a perfect arc, and then—

Thunk.

Dead. Fucking. Center.

"I did it!" She spins toward me, eyes bright with victory. "Did you see that? I actually—"

The words die as our eyes meet. Her eyes drop to my mouth, and I know—*know*—she'd let me kiss her. More than let me. She's looking at me like she wants to shove me against the wall and take what she wants.

Do it, the monster in me snarls. *Take her mouth. Make her yours.*

Calm. The fuck. Down, the rational part of me snaps back.

I can't stop myself from reaching out and trailing my knuckles along her cheek. "You did well."

We're standing too close. Close enough that I can feel her breath on my face, see the way her pupils have blown wide. All I'd have to do is lean down a few inches…

She blinks hard, like she's coming out of a trance, and steps back. "I think that's probably enough for today. Can we pick up again tomorrow?"

"I won't be able to do any blade work with you for a few days."

The Devaliant's brows pinch. "Why?"

I tip my head back, considering the sky and its darkening

swathes of teal and violet. The familiar tension is already gathering, my body harmonizing with the magic in the air—the call of the realm. "Have you ever heard of Aethertide?"

The furrow deepens. "No. Should I have?"

"It's a celestial event that occurs here every century or so. A realignment of polarities and energies that brings a spectacle to the skies." I slide her a look, curious how she'll take this. "It also triggers a biological imperative in Scillari's inhabitants. Especially the males."

Color floods her cheeks. "It induces rut? In *everyone*?"

"Only the unattached."

"And you're…"

"Very much unattached." I give her a quick smile. "Humans nearly wiped out the Eternal population during the war, and it destabilized the magic. Scillari has been trying to compensate ever since."

"By triggering the drive to"—she waves a hand, that blush deepening—"mate."

I nod. "Two powerful demis can create a future Eternal. It's up to the realm to decide if a demi is worthy of ascension to claim a territory. Scillari needs at least eight Eternals to remain stable. Ten is preferable."

"I suppose that makes sense." The Devaliant clears her throat, hesitating. "You mentioned the war created an imbalance in your numbers. I thought only Eternals could kill other Eternals. How did humans manage to take out enough of you that the realm's still compensating centuries later?"

Ice crystallizes in my veins.

She doesn't know. Of course, she doesn't know. They've scrubbed their history clean, painted themselves as victims while they gorged on our flesh and power, while they strung us up and carved us apart and—

I lock it down, giving her nothing but the flat stare I've perfected over centuries. "Aren't you full of questions today."

She recognizes the minefield and retreats. Smart girl. "What about Amara?"

I weigh my words. "Amara's soulbonded. She'll feel the pull of her Chosen and do whatever she can to avoid it. He was unworthy of her."

"Her *Chosen*? Who?"

"It's rude to pry into someone's romantic business, Devaliant. Hasn't anyone ever told you that?"

"Once or twice," she says with a wry twist of her lips.

"Well, if Amara wanted you to know the details of her love life, she'd tell you. In the meantime, I'll take off somewhere where I'm less likely to"—*fuck you senseless against every surface in this tower*—"be in your way."

"Ah. Well, then." The Devaliant gives a mocking half-bow. "I hope you emerge with your cock intact."

"Your concern for my cock is duly noted and appreciated."

I'm going to bite her. Mark her up—

"Wolf." The Devaliant's voice cuts through the haze of lust. "There's something else. That name you and Amara mentioned earlier—Rhosyn. I think I've seen it before."

I go still. "Where?"

"Hellevig." She gives a sharp shake of her head. "But I can't think of the context. Whenever I try, it's like wading through fog. My mind just goes—"

"To the Duehavn," I finish, knowing exactly how trauma locks memories away.

She flinches. "Right."

The mind's last defense—building walls around the worst moments, keeping them where they can't do more damage. But those walls don't discriminate. They take everything, good and bad, and bury it all.

"Do you know where Amara found me?" The question comes out carefully, like she's bracing for impact.

"Yes."

The Devaliant exhales, and it sounds like surrender. "Take me there."

No. Every instinct screams against it. Taking her back to where she almost died, where someone tried to murder her—it's asking for her to shatter. It's not worth it. Not even if it could give me answers.

"Listen to me." I catch her chin in a gentle grip, tipping her face up to mine. "You don't have to go back. Not until you're ready."

Slowly, so slowly, she lifts her eyes to mine. "I need to see it."

Damn me. When she looks at me like that, I'm powerless to refuse her.

"All right," I mutter, opening my arms. "Come here."

She steps into my embrace without hesitation. It catches me off guard—this trust, the way she fits herself against me so easily.

I spread my wings and gather her close, launching us into the sky.

28

BRYONY

THE WIND ON the Duehavn stings my cheeks as I stare out at the ridge. All around me, the serrated peaks are knitted together by tendrils of mist punctuated by sheer, dizzying drops. There's nothing green up here. No trees, no flowers or grass. Only the dramatic browns and slate grays of the crags, the interlacing colors of the Shroud shimmering across the sky.

It's breathtaking—in a brutal, merciless sort of way.

I navigate across the uneven ground, shale skittering beneath my boots. This place hasn't changed. It's the same savage, merciless landscape that swallowed my screams. That cut into my back as I struggled against Idris' hold and took its own bloodletting when the blade did.

I wonder if some part of me is still here, spilled out across the rocks. A memorial for the Anchor. The woman I was.

The memory pierces through me, sudden and violent—struggling against my uncle, the knife as he plunged it in, staring up at the sky as I died.

You're fine. You're in control. This is just a place; it can't hurt you.

One step. Two. I force myself toward the edge. The world pitches, my head spinning as I peer over the drop.

"Careful. It's a long way down."

I focus on the distant horizon, not trusting myself to look at the Wolf. "Oblivion's tempting when the inside of my mind gets too loud."

Gravel crunches as he closes the distance between us, stepping up behind me close enough to touch.

"Where are you right now?" he asks, so soft it's nearly lost to the wind. "In your head."

"Nowhere you want to be. It's not pretty."

"I'm no stranger to ugly."

A bitter laugh scrapes out of me. "Is that a request to take a nice, long look at my scars and watch me squirm?"

"If that's what you need from me." The barest shift of movement, and I feel the warm press of his chest against my back.

Hardly daring to breathe, I stand frozen as he reaches out and catches my chin, turning my face to his. Those golden eyes are soft as they flicker between mine, as if he's trying to figure me out.

"Want to talk it out, nemesis?"

It's too gentle. Too tender. I can almost convince myself he isn't the villain of my story. That there's something warmer hidden underneath—something true. Because when he calls me *nemesis*, it's like he's telling me a secret.

But I'm lying to myself.

"You want a peek inside my head?" My lips flatten, and I turn out of his grasp. "Fine. Go ahead and poke around in all the dark corners. Maybe it'll help you sleep better when you finally end me."

The Wolf lets out a slow exhale. Then he turns to a nearby boulder and sits, wings flaring out. "Come here."

I hesitate. "Why?"

"Just come here."

When I walk over, he tugs me down into his lap and wraps those large wings around us both—a golden cocoon shielding us from the world.

His breath is warm on my neck. "There's no prize for suffering," he says in a low voice. "Pain isn't a game. Stop punishing yourself with it."

Don't.

The sound that leaves me is almost a sob, but when I try to pull out of his arms, he just holds me tighter. Keeping me still.

He keeps talking. "Swallow down enough of that toxic shit, and eventually, you go numb to everything else. Until the only thing that cuts through the static is pain—inflicting it, chasing it. It's the only way anything feels real."

Stop, I want to beg him. *Stop, stop, stop.*

He doesn't get to do this. He doesn't get to reach into my chest, pry up all the ugly bits, and act as if he understands. But he's relentless, digging deeper. Picking at all my wounds.

"So you spread that pain around like a sickness," he continues, his chest rising and falling against my back, "making damn sure everyone else is as miserable and fucked up on the inside as you are. Because why should you be the only one choking on it? What's right about bleeding out alone?"

I shut my eyes tightly. "Why are you telling me this? Why do you care?"

"Because I've spent three hundred years hurting everyone around me." He strokes my cheek, fingers as soft as mothwings on my skin. "I know revenge feels good at first. It makes you feel powerful, like you're the one in control. Like you're taking back what was stolen from you and rewriting the story so you're the one holding the blade. But it's not enough. It'll never be enough. You'll tear yourself to shreds, bleed yourself dry, and that hungry void inside you will just swallow it down and howl for more."

"It's easy for you to say," I tell him, my tone sharp. "Have you ever been powerless? Ever had everything stolen from you?"

"Yes."

Something squeezes hard in my chest. A thousand questions fill the air, going unvoiced.

"Tell me what's in your head," he whispers. "It's okay. I can handle your dark."

And I—

Break.

I shove away from him and stumble to my feet. The icy wind

slaps my face as I stride back toward the cliff's edge, needing space. Needing air. I can't let him hold me while I'm falling apart, confessing all the ways I'm vulnerable to my enemy.

But why not? Why not tell someone? Why not spill my ugliness at his feet and see if he still thinks I'm worthy of being his *masterpiece*?

The rocks where my uncle stabbed me are still rust-stained, even now. I can't look away. Can't unsee it. A snarling, vicious thing writhes in my chest, desperate to sink its teeth in and tear the world apart.

"I wanted it to be you," I say, wrapping my arms around myself. "The one to end it."

The Wolf remains silent behind me. I'm already in free fall, the truths like broken glass tumbling out of me.

"What I had before… it was never really living. I bled where they told me to bleed. Died how they wanted me to die. My agency was stripped away until I hardly recognized my own reflection."

The crunch of gravel pierces through the white noise. Then the Wolf is at my back, not pressing or pulling. Just steadying.

"In the end, even my death wasn't my own," I say bitterly. "When I was in that carriage—when Idris was bringing me here—I couldn't stop thinking that if this was really it, if I wasn't going to walk away this time, I deserved to have it on my terms. The way you and I agreed. One thing that was mine, even if it was the way I went out."

A shudder rolls through me, my nails cutting into my palms. I should stop. I shouldn't give him more of me. But I can't. The words keep tumbling out, each one cutting deeper.

"I fought. Instinct, I guess. The animal part of my brain was too stupid to realize I was already past saving. I kicked and thrashed and clawed until he pinned me to the ground." Tears spill down my cheeks, and I wipe them away. "And then Idris left me there. Alone, bleeding out in the dirt. Can you even imagine what it's like, dying like that? Discarded by your own family? It's not the knife that keeps me up at night. It's knowing

I wasn't even worth staying for. Not worth making it hurt less. I was *nothing*."

Stone scraping my spine through my cloak. Gravel biting into my skin as I thrashed. Hands at my throat.

"Devaliant."

The Wolf's voice comes from far away, muted beneath the haze. I can't tell if it's concern or impatience. The whine inside my head builds to a screech, and I can't—

"*Devaliant.*"

Distantly, I register the quickness of my breath—*in and out in and out in and out*. Marking my unraveling.

"Bryony."

I'm sure I've imagined it. The shape of my name in his mouth, those three syllables given careful weight and deliberate intent.

"Bryony. Hey, breathe, okay? Eyes on me," the Wolf commands. He brackets my face in his palms, his skin warm. "*Breathe.* Feel my chest moving against yours."

I squeeze my eyes shut and try to match his breathing, expanding my ribs against his on the inhale, moving in sync. Everything else falls away—the wind and the brutal drop and the ugly stain on the rocks. And bit by bit, I claw my way back to myself.

The first drops of rain splatter against my cheeks. I turn into it, desperate for anything to ground me in my body, in the present.

And I don't let myself think.

Gripping the Wolf's shirt, I pull him down until his lips hover over mine. Until I can taste the spice of him on every exhale, feel the drum of his pulse everywhere we're pressed together. The seconds stretch. A moment punctuated by the beat of rainfall, our ragged exhales.

Then I lean up and brush my mouth against his.

It's barely a kiss at all. Just a tentative graze, a careful sharing of breath. A hesitant question and an equally hesitant answer, full of all the unspoken things simmering between us. His mouth is a revelation. Firm and soft at once, the barest scrape of stubble, the way his breath hitches slightly when I open to him. A gentle, yearning kind of hunger.

The Wolf freezes—a perfect, poised sort of surprise, like I've startled him. I brace for rejection, the ridicule sure to follow. Because of *course*, this beautiful god doesn't want—

He gentles me back with a hand on my nape. Not a refusal, but a momentary reset. There's a question in his eyes when they meet mine.

Rain falls harder now, soaking through my clothes, plastering my hair to my skin.

"Do it again," I whisper, reckless and wild and aching. "Kiss me like I'm not Bryony Devaliant. I don't want to be her right now. Kiss me like I'm someone else."

I'm shaking. He has to see it, has to know I'm hanging by a thread.

"Who do you want to be, then?" he asks, soft as a secret. Softer than he has any right to be.

Yours.

What comes out is: "How would you kiss me if I were your lover? If you could take me any way you wanted, no holding back?"

A growl rumbles through him. The hand at my nape tightens, and he hesitates, chest moving faster. "Fuck it," he says.

Then he slants his mouth over mine.

There's no room for thought or breath. Nothing exists outside this: our lips meeting, the rain on my heated skin, the way he curls his hands into my shirt to yank me closer. As if he's starving for it, ravenous. I want to sink into this feeling and never come up for air. There's no history here. No future or complications. Nothing but the drag of his fingers through my wet hair and the friction of my hips connecting with his. He kisses me as if he's been dying for a taste and wants to savor it. He kisses me like maybe he wants to keep me.

He kisses me like a liar.

"I shouldn't be doing this," he breathes.

"You're not," I pant against his mouth. "We're just pretending. None of this is real."

Some complex emotion flickers in his features. Then he pushes his lips to mine, shutting me up, shutting us both up. The Wolf's tongue slides against mine, gentler now. Exploring. Enjoying me. One of his hands cups my nape, gentle as he angles my head to kiss me deeper.

"Confess something," I rasp, shaking now. Wanting. "A secret you'd tell her, but never me."

His fingers tighten in my hair. "When you weren't talking to me, I'd pace outside your room late at night, trying to think up ways to get you to say something. I heard your soft sighs through the door one night. Trying to be quiet, muffling your sounds." He nuzzles into my neck, whispering, "You make the prettiest noises when you come."

Oh, gods.

Images flash of all those times he's healed me—left me aching and wanting. And after he'd leave, I'd lie face down on the mattress, slip my fingers into my pussy, and pretend I was riding him. I'd shout my climax into my pillow, thinking he wouldn't hear. But he did.

Heat gathers between my thighs as I picture him standing outside my door, listening to all those intimate sounds. Was he ever tempted to come in? To touch? To do all the wordless things I wanted in the dark?

"Tell me more," I say.

"When you start, your breathing gets shaky." He kisses along my jaw, his hand grabbing at my shirt and sliding underneath to graze the skin of my stomach. "A little uneven, like you're holding it in. Like you can't get in enough air. I wondered how many fingers you use. If you start with one and work your way up to two, then three, as your breathing quickens. If you grip the sheets and imagine it's me."

I almost say his name. *Evander.* But then that would make this real. Shatter the game, force us to confront the reality of who we are.

He's relentless now, tearing down barriers. "How often? How often do you fuck your fingers in my bed?"

I swallow. "After you heal me."

He groans, nuzzling my pulse point. I know he has to feel how fast it is, how unsteady. "What would you have done if I knocked? If I came in?"

An exhale shivers out of me. "I would have said yes."

His eyes flash with heat, and then his mouth is on mine again. I lick the rain off his lips. Savor the taste of him. Lightning streaks across the sky, the rumble of thunder lost beneath the roar of blood in my ears. We're connected at every burning point, and I can't think past the heat of his hands, his body caging me in, the taste of rain on his mouth.

I've never been touched like this. Rough and reverent, coaxing and commanding. This is madness. Mutually assured destruction. This must be what damnation feels like—wanting the thing that will inevitably annihilate you.

But I can't stop.

"Tell me what you would have done to me," I say. Drunk on sensation and aching to see how far I can push. "Tell me how you'd take me if I belonged to you."

He goes still and pulls back, expression suddenly clear and sober. "We're just fooling around, right?" The words land like a fatal blow. "Just playing pretend?"

Reality seeps in, dousing the flames. *What am I doing what am I doing what am I doing?* I forgot myself. I forgot what we are.

If you're worried about breaking my heart, you shouldn't be. I'm not in danger of giving it to you.

But I am. I hadn't been honest because it's so much easier to feign indifference than to let the Wolf realize he's burrowing into my vulnerable places and making me forget armor.

My expression shutters, a wall slamming down. "Of course. What else would it be?"

Something flickers across his face, there and gone too quickly to catch. "No getting attached. No catching feelings," he says firmly. "Just games."

The reminder twists like a knife. He's letting me down easy, as gently as he's capable of. I'm the fool who forgot myself.

I lock down those messy, inconvenient feelings until my voice is steady. "I already told you, I'm in no danger."

I can lie just as easily. There are no soft places between predator and prey. No kindness to be found in the space between the blade and the killing stroke.

"Take me back," I say. "Maybe something will nudge loose about Rhosyn later."

Lightning flashes across the sky, followed by a loud clap of thunder. The Wolf lifts me into his arms, but his touch is perfunctory, indifferent. The rain falls harder.

I've never felt so cold.

29

BRYONY

THE MOMENT THE tower breaks through the clouds, the Wolf's entire body goes taut, and his arms tighten around me like he's preparing for a fight.

"*Shit*." He banks hard to the left, wings slicing through the air.

"What is it?" My fingers dig into his shoulders at the sudden change in direction.

He lands on one of the terraces, his hands firm on my waist as he sets me down. "Stay inside until I come to get you, understand?"

"Why? What's wrong?"

"We have company." He scans the gardens below, jaw tight. "One of Alexios' Enforcers. Someone who won't hesitate to cut you open."

A chill snakes down my spine, but I nod. "Okay. I'll stay out of sight."

The backs of his fingers brush my cheek in a fleeting caress, and then he's gone, vaulting over the railing in a flash of golden wings.

I know I should listen and retreat inside like he ordered, but curiosity itches beneath my skin, a restless tug I can't ignore. Holding my breath, I creep to the railing and peer over the edge.

A demigoddess perches on the garden fountain with her long legs stretched out in front of her. Her dark hair glints in the fading sun, falling in a long braid down her back, tied off with a pretty red ribbon. She rises when the Wolf lands a few feet away, dusting off the loose, airy dress she's wearing. *This* is a warrior? Did she get fancied up for him?

"Hi," she says to the Wolf. Of course, her voice is pretty, too.

"Arcadia," he greets. "You look lovely."

I scowl down at my dirty training clothes and the dirt under my fingernails. Has he ever called me lovely?

She grins. "Don't I always?"

The Wolf snaps his wings closed, his lips lifting in amusement. "Don't tell me you came all this way to fish for compliments."

"Of course not." Arcadia steps closer, and I can't help but notice what a striking pair they make: her silver wings to his gold, both of them with that same glittering skin. Like they were designed to match. "I wanted to make sure you were okay after the warehouse. See if you needed anything."

Warehouse? What warehouse? My scowl deepens.

"I'm fine," he says, his voice gentling in a way that makes something twist in my chest. "You didn't have to check on me."

That ugly burning sensation stabbing through my chest is new enough to irritate me, and clear enough to be identifiable: *jealousy*. I'm jealous of her. And when she smiles at him, I have to swallow back the growl building in my throat.

Because it's a smile that says, *we've fucked.*

"Yes, well," she says, "I worry when you go quiet. An annoying habit I can't seem to kick." She takes a deep breath as if steeling herself. "But, listen… do you still want me for the centennial? I'd ask Elias, but I don't want to share, and his room's too crowded for my tastes."

The Wolf arches a brow. "There's always Gabriel."

"Sure," she says with a shrug, "but he's a decent consolation prize at best if you're not available."

He lets out a laugh, shaking his head. "You really know how to make a male feel special, Cady."

The bottom drops out of my stomach. Cady. Not Arcadia—*Cady*. The familiarity in that nickname speaks of a long history. Something I can't compete with. I shouldn't even *want* to compete with it, and yet the envy is burrowing deeper, settling alongside the yearning. That ache since he kissed me on the Duehavn. Erasing every reminder that I shouldn't want him, that he's no good for me.

"I notice you're not saying no."

"Haven't said yes either," he points out.

She closes the distance between them, and I grip the balcony railing so hard it bites into my palms. *Move*, I think desperately. *Step back. Don't let her—*

But he doesn't move. He stays exactly where he is, letting her invade his space like she belongs there.

"Oh, come on. You've spent every Aethertide fucking me in the sky, against the wall, or bent over every surface. If you want to try out someone new this cycle, just say so. I won't take it personally."

Heat floods my cheeks, my throat working around a sudden surge of nausea as her words register. She wants him for the rut—like she has every other cycle.

Every. Other. Cycle.

In the sky, against the wall—

I can't breathe through the emotions battering against my ribcage. Can't reconcile the male who held me in the rain, who kissed me like I was drowning and he was air, with someone who has *centuries* of history with another woman.

Bent over every—

Arcadia stretches up on her toes, and I wrench my gaze away before her lips find his. I don't think I could survive seeing him touch her the way he touched me.

It meant nothing. He was just pretending.

The words chase themselves around in my mind as I stumble into my bathing chamber. With numb fingers, I yank off my rain-soaked clothes and sink into water just shy of scalding. The calming scents of chamomile and lavender rise with the steam, but it does nothing to quiet my chaotic thoughts.

Nothing drives out the memory of his hands, the heat of his mouth slanting over mine. The way he cradled my face like I was something precious.

Why did I let him kiss me?

The rational part of my brain knows exactly why—because he was there when I was falling apart. Because he caught me and put me back together, and for a few minutes on that miserable mountain, he made me feel like I mattered.

We're just playing pretend. Right?

"Fuck this," I snarl, surging up from the water.

I can't stay trapped in here with my spiraling thoughts. Can't keep replaying the press of his lips, the scrape of his teeth, the way his hands—

No. I need to move.

I dry off roughly and yank on a thin shift. I'm not even sure where I'm going until I find myself at the library door. Maybe it's the hush that draws me in, or the mix of smells—old paper, leather bindings, the perfume of roses. Something to focus on. To calm.

The sunset streams through the towering windows, painting the red roses twisting up the columns in shades of orange and gold.

I wander deeper into the stacks, trailing my fingers along the spines, not focusing on any of the titles. I keep seeing Arcadia's face reaching for his. With an exhale of frustration, I jog up the spiral staircase to the gallery that overlooks the library.

A large wooden table occupies much of the space, strewn with maps and antique instruments. The far wall is covered in paintings of pastoral scenes with rolling hills, forests with crumbling ruins and castles, others of hunts and battles.

But the one in the middle steals my breath.

It's a couple locked in a tight embrace. Their wings touch, covered in spatterings of gold and purple. His head is bent into her throat, her hands twisted in his hair as she arches her neck for him. He grips her thighs hard. The details of their joining is lost to shadow, but there's no mistaking the intensity, the desperation in their hands and bodies.

This is a portrait of hunger. And all I can think is: *I want that. I want someone to burn for me like that.*

Another image flickers across my mind—the Wolf and

Arcadia, her silver wings against his gold feathers. Does he take her like this? Like he'd die if he couldn't have her? Does he yearn for her?

The crackle of power announces the Wolf before the rustle of wings. I don't turn, not when I'm this stupid with want.

"The garden's clear," he says softly.

I just nod, still staring at the painting. I don't ask about Arcadia—whether he kissed her, or if he'll go to her when the rut hits and biology makes the choice for him. I don't ask if what happened on the Duehavn was real or just another game we're playing.

I'm afraid of the answers.

"Do you like it?" His voice is hushed, as if he's unsure. "The painting?"

"It's beautiful." My fingernails curl into my palms as I hear him move closer. "Haunting. Like they're afraid to let go of each other."

"These were my mother's," he says, right behind me now. "She collected art and stories from all over the realms. Most of the books here belonged to her. She had this thing about seeing beauty in anything, no matter how broken or small. This tower was a private sanctuary away from her responsibilities. Where she could just... exist. Be all the messy, complicated parts of herself she had to hide everywhere else."

My throat tightens. "The roses?"

"Were hers." There's something raw and aching in the words. "She loved them. Babied them. Sang to them when she thought no one was around to hear her shame the songbirds."

Guilt floods me. All those times I mocked the overgrown gardens, it never occurred to me that he was preserving echoes of someone he loved—that letting the roses grow wild hurt less than pruning away her memory.

"I'm so sorry. I didn't know—"

"How could you have?" He gives a harsh laugh. "You see this tower as a monster's lair. But even monsters had mothers once."

What happened to her? Where is she? But I swallow my questions down, afraid of shattering this rare moment of vulnerability.

"This painting is called 'The Lovers'." His chest presses against my back, breath hot against the nape of my neck. "It hung in my mother's sky garden for centuries. A pair of Celestials caught on opposite sides of an ancient feud."

"Celestials?"

"Primordial gods. The original creators from the stars." His lips brush my ear like he's telling me a secret. "There used to be more realms than just Vartena and Scillari, but the ancients fought for power and tore their worlds apart. Some say their dying magic birthed the first Eternals. The gods in this painting were heirs to warring realms. No matter how often their rulers ripped them apart, they kept crashing back together. My mother was obsessed with them. She'd spend hours staring at this piece."

His palm finds the dip of my waist, fingers splaying wide. I have to remind myself to breathe as heat spreads under my skin. That ache in my chest expands, treacherous and hungry, and in that moment, it's far too easy to imagine I'm the woman in the painting—powerless against the pull of someone I shouldn't want.

"They sound like idiots," I breathe.

A low chuckle. "No doubt about that. Young, dumb, and reckless. They knew it'd end bloody." His voice drops lower, rougher. "Didn't stop them from meeting in dark corners to bite and snarl and fuck like the world was ending. Couldn't keep their hands off each other."

Like us, I almost say, but I bite back the words. Because there is no us.

"Every night, he'd go to her," the Wolf says, his hand trailing maddening circles on my hip. "Always in the dark. No lamps, no names. I suppose it let them pretend, for a time, that they weren't enemies. That it was okay to want each other."

I shut my eyes, remembering the wind lashing my hair on the Duehavn. The unrelenting rain. His body against mine.

Kiss me like I'm not Bryony Devaliant.
Then who do you want to be?

"How did he touch her?" The question slips out before I can stop it.

He looses a ragged exhale. Then I shiver at the brush of his lips on the juncture between my neck and shoulder, more breath than touch.

"Softly, at first." He continues sliding his palm over my hip, up and down, up and down, as his mouth wanders. "Cautiously. He'd drag his knuckles over her cheek and let his breath play on her skin." A graze of his lips over my pulse, lingering. "Like he couldn't believe she was letting him near. That she wasn't shoving him away."

"And then?" I whisper.

"Then he stopped pretending he could be gentle." His fingers squeeze me hard. "Stopped acting like he didn't want to wreck her. Like he hadn't been dreaming about getting his hands on her since the first day he saw her." One hand drifts lower, dragging my shift up, skimming his fingers over the skin of my inner thigh. "She wanted him to be rough with her," he says hoarsely. "To be a little mean with it. To grab and take and *claim* until she was covered in his marks, until there was no mistaking who she belonged to."

I'm panting now, my nails digging into my palms as I fight the urge to turn in his arms. Each filthy word threatens to pull me under and shatter all my defenses.

"He'd bite her here." Teeth graze my pulse point. "And *here*." A nip at the curve of my shoulder. "Anywhere he could get his mouth on her. So that even when she was alone, even when she was standing in her palace or kneeling at her Celestial ruler's feet, she'd feel the sting and ache of him and remember."

I squeeze my eyes shut, sparks dancing behind my closed lids. An image rises unbidden—the Wolf pinning me down in his bed, one hand wrapping around my throat as he thrusts into me over and over and *over* again.

His whisper drags me to the present. "He had her every way

he could—bent over her desk, pressed against the wall, spread out on the floor. He was addicted to her. Her taste. Her sounds. The way she'd sink her nails into his back when he fucked into her."

"And he—" I swallow thickly. "He wanted that? The pain?"

"Oh, he lived for it." He takes my hand, guiding it under my shift. "There's truth in pain when you mix it with pleasure. In the way we hurt each other. The sounds we make when we stop pretending to be anything but what we are."

The Wolf's fingers twine with mine, shoving them into my undergarments. A broken moan spills from me as he pushes my fingers into my pussy, the angle perfect. He starts working in and out in shallow thrusts, his other arm looping around my waist to anchor me against him.

"Wolf..." I bite my lip, the pain a sharp counterpoint to the pleasure.

He groans softly. Shoves our fingers deeper, more insistently. I lean back into him, riding our hands, pressing the heel of his palm against my clit.

"They whispered confessions in the dark that they'd deny come dawn," he rasps, his breathing harsh. "Told lies that felt like truth and truths that cut like lies. *I don't need you. I could walk away. You're not under my skin.* And then came the truths, the things their bodies couldn't deny. *More,* and *harder,* and *right there, fuck.*"

I love his voice. The low register like warm liquor, the way his lips shape the words against my skin. Heat coils low in my belly with every ragged breath, every plunge, every filthy word he breathes into my skin. I reach back to tangle my fingers in his hair, needing something to ground me. He grips my hip in a silent encouragement to keep fucking myself. Keep chasing.

"He'd keep her on the edge for hours." We're both panting now, my bitten-off moans filling the space between us. "Pleading so pretty, just how he liked it. In the dark, their hate burned just like need. And it felt so. Fucking. Good. To forget who they were supposed to be. To lose himself in that sweet"—his lips sear the curve of my nape—"*tight*"—his fingers push in *deeper, faster*—"pussy. He fucked her so good she felt it for days."

Oh gods oh gods *oh gods*—

"Come on," he growls. "Show me. Show me how good it feels when you stop fighting it. When you let yourself have what you want."

The tension snaps. With a final thrust, I climax with a sharp cry. He keeps working our fingers through the aftershocks, wringing out every bit of pleasure until I'm gasping. Until I can't feel anything beyond this moment—this surrender. The heat of him against my back. My chest burning to get in air.

His touch gentles as I come down. Lips graze my shoulder, my neck, my jaw. A nuzzle of his cheek to mine. My heart slams as I sink into him.

For a long moment, there is only the rasp of our breathing. The drum of the rain against the windows, the wind through the trees.

Slowly, carefully, he withdraws from me and straightens my shift with gentle hands. "Every touch between them," he whispers, stepping away, "was an act of betrayal."

My chest caves. I squeeze my eyes shut against the sudden sting. "They died, didn't they?" I ask, unable to turn and meet his gaze. Afraid of what I might see there. "In the end."

"Of course they did." Flat. Final. Like a blade between the ribs. "What else could happen?"

I swallow past the tightness in my throat. "Then why do it? Why risk everything?"

"Because sometimes the pain of having someone for a few hours is better than the agony of not having them at all." He inhales, then lets out a breath, slow and ragged. "Desire doesn't give a fuck about should or shouldn't. We want what we want, even when we know it'll destroy us."

The words hang between us like a death sentence. Like prophecy.

Before he leaves, I force myself to ask the question I've been dreading: "Are you going to take that demigoddess up on her offer to get you through Aethertide?" When he stays silent, I add mockingly, "In the sky, against a wall, bent over any surface?"

There. Now he knows that I watched them in the garden. That I heard everything she said. *Did you kiss her after I left? Did you make plans to meet her? Do you want her? Would you ever want me?*

I hold my breath, waiting.

"I'll be alone," he says softly.

The soft click of the door is like thunder in the silence he leaves behind.

30

BRYONY

"I haven't seen you eat shit this enthusiastically since day one," Amara says with a smirk, twirling her blade.

I'm on the ground again. Today has been an impressive test of perseverance—and by that, I mean enduring the humiliation of Amara kicking my ass for three hours. I don't think I've managed to get a single hit in.

A snarl builds behind my teeth. "Don't strain yourself with the compliments. Wouldn't want you to pull something."

She snorts, shaking her head. "Why don't you just... take a minute. Gather up the shredded bits of your pride."

I flop back into the grass, too wrung out to even think of a good retort. I let my eyes drift closed, and the Wolf's face rises to the surface of my mind like it always does when things are too quiet. I wonder where he is right now. If he's out on one last slaughter in Vartena before the rut hits, or locked away preparing for the onslaught.

I'll be alone, he'd said, and those words haven't stopped repeating in my head since he walked away and shut the door behind him.

"So. Anything you want to talk about?" Amara asks. Because, naturally, she can't let me have even a second of respite.

Desire doesn't give a fuck about should or shouldn't. We want what we want, even when we know it'll destroy us.

Something twists hard in my chest. I shove the memory down deep and chain it up where it can't cut me open.

"No idea what you're getting at," I say, playing stupid.

"Uh-huh. Well, you were making puppy eyes at tall, dark, and dickish during drills yesterday." She points her dagger at me for emphasis.

I smack the dagger away. "I did *not* make puppy eyes."

"Please. Your whole face went soft and dopey when he tossed you that little scrap of a compliment. *Classic* puppy."

Heat crawls up my cheeks. "Are we done with the interrogation portion of today's ass-kicking? Let's move on to something more productive. Like me punching you repeatedly in the face."

Amara just laughs. "Please. The way you're moving right now? You'll be in your grave before I take off tonight."

Wait. What? I push up on my elbows. "You're going somewhere?"

"Caelestis. The Aethertide Festival is the only time I get to lose myself in a crowd without Alexios sniffing me out."

Why would Alexios be looking for you? I almost ask, but then a flicker of memory fights to surface—cracked leather spines, gilt-edged pages, beautiful illustrations of a place in the clouds. Stacks of forbidden books in my father's study that I wasn't supposed to touch but pored over anyway, hungry for a glimpse of the world beyond our borders.

"Caelestis is… a city?" I ask, chasing that wisp of memory—the maddening sensation of *almost* grasping it.

"Yep. Picture one big citywide orgy, but with great wine and even better food." Amara watches me chew my lip in thought. "I can hear you thinking too hard. Spit it out, Devaliant."

"That name the Wolf mentioned yesterday," I say. "Rhosyn. It's familiar, and I think…" I shake my head, straining to call up the particulars. "I could swear I saw it in one of my father's books when I was little. Something about Rhosyn and Caelestis. If I could see it, I might be able to recognize something from the illustrations—"

"Absolutely not." She gestures at me, movements sharp. "Did the endorphins from the beating scramble your brain? One look at that opalescent skin and everyone would know you're a Devaliant. Taking you there would be like dangling a slab of meat in front of a pack of starving dogs."

I resent being compared to a slab of meat, but I concede the point. "Does the festival have masquerade protocol? Veils, costumes, that sort of thing? For people who want anonymity?"

She blows out an annoyed breath. "Sure, some demis cover their faces. But any male with a working nose will clock you as mortal if he gets within a wingspan. Won't matter how good the costume is."

"So use your scent to mask mine," I say, an idea forming. "Won't everyone be too busy looking at the sky to notice me?"

"That's so not the point." Amara drags a hand down her face.

And I *know* she's right. It's foolish to even consider leaving the Wolf's tower and putting myself in a city full of demis who would probably be all too eager to tear me apart. But I can't stop thinking about yesterday—the grim set of the Wolf's mouth, the quiet urgency in his voice.

I've been hunting vermin in Vartena. The kind that trades in black market parts.

I can't say that's one I recall, but there's a lot I carved out afterward. Some things aren't worth remembering.

I don't know what any of that means, but Amara's response had made something cold settle in my gut. They've been echoing over and over again in my thoughts—because she and the Wolf share this secret that I have no right to.

"Can I ask you something?" I say.

"Might as well." She rubs her forehead with a sigh. "While we're passing ludicrous ideas back and forth."

"The Wolf mentioned black market parts yesterday. During your conversation." She looks up, expression icing over, so I quickly add, "Is Rhosyn—whatever it means—important to you both?"

For a long moment, she just stares at me, holding her elbows in tightly as if she's warding off a memory. A breeze kicks up, sending leaves skittering across the flagstones.

Then she blinks. "Yes," she says roughly. "Very."

That answer carries old wounds that haven't healed, the kind of memories that burrow deep. Like rot. Like the Void. If there's anything I can do to help her ease even a fraction of that pain, I will. I owe her that much.

"Then let me help. I'll follow your lead. No risks, I promise."

"Ugh, fine," she says, raking a hand through her hair. "We'll go, see if anything there jogs your memory, and then leave. Immediately. I want us gone before the males are so deep in rut they'd screw a knothole."

I wrinkle my nose at the mental image. "Got it."

Amara nods sharply and spreads her wings. "I'll get us something to wear. Go make yourself semi-presentable and wait for me in your chambers."

"You can't be serious."

The gown Amara lent me is barely more than strategically placed fabric held up by wishful thinking. The soft blue silk is embroidered with gold and silver threads, with a neckline dipping well past the shadow between my breasts to expose my stomach. It leaves my back entirely bare, and the sides are slit up to my hips. One wrong move and everyone will be intimately acquainted with parts of me that have no business knowing the open air. The delicate chains crisscrossing my chest and shoulders are supposed to hold it all up, but I'm beginning to have my doubts. This thing is more jewelry than a dress.

"Dead serious." Amara doesn't glance up from where she's crouched at my feet, tracing intricate whorls and lines down my arm with a pen of metallic paint. She's been at it for nearly an hour, covering every exposed inch of my skin, which is basically *all* of it. "No Caelestis without the dress. Take it or leave it."

Twisting, I watch the markings shimmer across my skin. "What do all these symbols mean?"

"Nothing." The answer comes way too quickly. She waves a dismissive hand and clears her throat. "Just some ritual Aethertide nonsense that'll help conceal that sheen on your skin."

"That was an evasion."

"Too damn bad." She caps the paint pen and gives me an appraising look. "There. You'll do." Her own gown is a rich blue several shades deeper than her eyes. A silk hood sits low on her brow, obscuring the distinctive shade of her hair. The symbols inked on her limbs are different from mine. "In the dark, with the paint, you'd pass for a demi. Probably."

"Are we *certain* this will help me blend? I've worn underwear with more coverage."

"At a Scillarian Festival?" She snorts, spinning me. "Tits out, wits out. You'll fit right in."

"Wow. Really comforting."

I crane my neck to see whatever fresh indignity Amara's inflicting on me. Her hands move quickly, weaving something into the chains at my back.

"Are those ribbons?"

"Missing wings are a common sight at gatherings like these—lots of demis have turned to accessories like this to conceal the damage from the war." She finishes tying them off and steps around to face me. "You have to be smart tonight. If the wrong people discover what you are, they won't hesitate to make an example of you."

I start to tell her I'm not an idiot, I *know*, but she cuts me off with a sharp slash of her hand.

"This isn't a game. I'm trying to keep your insides from becoming your outsides. Here, this'll help you blend." She reaches into her bag and pulls out some shimmering fabric—a shoulder-length veil. "Between this, the paint, and my scent to cover yours, you should be good," she says, fixing it in place.

The fabric is gauzy enough that I can see, but it obscures my face and hair to lend me an added layer of anonymity.

Amara draws a slender blade from her bodice, its silver handle worked in an intricate serpentine design. "One of my favorites. Strap it to your thigh and pray you don't have to use it."

I take the knife, my throat tight. "Thank you."

Amara just rolls her eyes. "Thank me by not getting caught.

If I bring you back to the Wolf with so much as a scratch, he'll string his bow with my entrails."

We slip out into the gardens, and she offers me an upturned palm. "Let's fly."

Caelestis. The Crown of Asteria.

In Hellevig, travelers and troubadours spoke about its glittering towers and aerial gardens. I had hazy memories of seeing the painted illustrations in the books, but nothing could have prepared me for the reality.

The city spreads out before us in a string of floating islands topped with shining towers and sprawling terraces. Waterfalls pour over the edges, mist sparkling in the glow of a thousand drifting lanterns. Bridges arc over the open air between the islands. On each one, sky gardens burst with blue, violet, and green glowing blooms. Golden vines climb the columns in intricate spirals. The entire city pulses with magic.

"Is your wing all right?" I call to Amara.

"Just a twinge of pain. See anything familiar?"

Studying the city again, I notice a slender spire stabbing upward near the city's heart, its proportions familiar. That tower looks nearly identical to an illustration from one of my father's books.

I point at the spire. "There. I think I've seen a drawing of that place. What is it?"

"It's a residence now for high-ranking demis. But when humans held the city, it had a different purpose."

"Can you land in that area? I want to look around."

Amara angles her wings, sending us into a steep dive until she flares wide and pulls out of the drop. We land on an elevated stone plaza overlooking the city.

Demis fill the streets below, dancing and weaving through the crowds. Their faces and bodies are adorned with symbols in the same metallic paint Amara used to disguise my skin. Some wear elaborate headdresses fashioned from twisting horns and crystals, while others are decorated in silk and strings of gems that leave little to the imagination. Wings of every hue spread wide—from deepest midnight shot through with starlight to pale white that shimmers like opals. Their wings drip with dainty chains and jewels that shimmer and chime with every movement. Thousands of wingless demis mingle in the crowd, their backs adorned with ribbons, paint, or gemstones.

I reach up, nervously adjusting my veil.

"Stop fussing," Amara says. "Half the people here are in masks or veils."

She's right. My nerves settle slightly. With my face hidden, I'm just another body in the crowd. Anonymous.

Amara's fingers close tightly around mine. "Come on. Keep your wits sharp. We can't afford any slip-ups."

We descend from the platform into the throng below. At once, I'm submerged and overwhelmed by sensation. The aroma of incense and spice is thick in the air, chased by the perfume of foreign flowers. Wild music pounds from every direction, drums beating out a relentless, frenetic beat. A rhythm to fuck to. To fight to. There's violence in it, hunger. The kind of wildness that begs to be purged in pleasure.

I nearly stumble when a male demi drops into a bow as we pass. Not to me—to Amara. And he's not the only one.

I tug at her arm. "Do they know you?"

Her face hardens. "No."

"Then why—"

"*These.*" She gestures to the symbols she painted on her skin. "They might as well say Property of the Biggest Asshole In Both Realms. They're not bowing to me."

I look closer at the symbols painted across her skin. Where I have spirals and geometric patterns, she has runes that reach like branches down her arms. Right at the hollow of her throat is a circular design with smaller symbols.

"But we're trying to blend in." I sweep my gaze across the crowd. "Can't you just… clean them off?"

She looks at me like I'm insane. "Sure. And if some idiot in a rut haze decides to grab my ass, then my Chosen feels it. Next thing you know, he's tearing through the city, ripping off faces. These marks warn every male with functioning eyes that I'm soulbonded to someone they don't want to fuck with."

Yikes. "Good gods."

"Yeah."

We weave our way toward the market square, navigating through knots of celebrants. Tables line our path, filled with dozens of different platters—fruits dripping with nectar, glass flutes with bubbling drinks.

A breathy moan catches my attention as we duck beneath a stone arch. I glance over to see a demigoddess sprawled on a bench, wearing only strategically draped ropes of pearls. A demigod kneels in front of her with his head buried between her thighs. Her hands twist in his hair, nails raking across his scalp as she urges him on.

My face burns. I'm suddenly all too grateful for the veil.

"First time at an orgy?" Amara snickers, tugging me away.

"Shut up."

"Never seen a male go down before? The Wolf's been holding out on you. I've heard he's good with that mouth."

I flush hotter and yank my arm free. "I said shut up."

Her laughter follows me as we push deeper into the crowd. We emerge into a circular plaza dominated by a massive, roaring bonfire. The flames gutter and dance, and sparks pinwheel up into the sky.

She pulls me into the shadow of a stone portico. "Here." She snatches two flutes from a tiered fountain and presses one into my hand. "Drink this."

"Do I want to know what it is?" I lift the flute, eyeing the bubbling pink liquid.

"Solstice wine," she says, sipping her own. "The recipe's as old as the first cities. It'll put hair on your chest."

I lift my veil just enough to tip the glass to my lips. The flavor blooms on my tongue: crisp and sweet, with notes of apple, honey, and ripe berries. I can't bite back the faint sound of pleasure at the taste.

Amara grins. "Good, right? So. Anything coming back to you about Rhosyn?"

I take another measured sip, savoring the subtle spice as my gaze wanders across the teeming plaza. "In Hellevig's archives, there are records of Caelestis during Vartena's occupation." I study Amara, trying to gauge her reaction. "They mention some of these towers being used as a launching point for attacks deeper into Scillari."

Something flashes in Amara's face, there and gone too quickly to parse. "You're not wrong. The Eternal who ruled this territory before Alexios was slaughtered in the first days of the siege. His palace became a glorified barracks."

I shiver. "How did we kill Eternals and gain a foothold at all? Everything I've read suggests it should have been impossible."

"Yeah, impossible." She laughs, but there's no mirth in it. "Or through stolen magic."

My blood goes cold. "What do you mean?"

When she turns back to me, her expression is flat. Harsh, almost. "There are some things we don't tolerate being brought to light. How's that human saying go? Let sleeping gods lie?"

Amara's voice carries a clear warning. She won't be sharing anything else with me tonight.

I raise my hands. "Forget I asked."

Above us, the first star flickers and winks out.

Amara grips my arm. "It's starting. Watch."

Another goes dark, and then another. And then—

The sky shatters. Purple, yellow, red, green—a dazzling eruption of color and luminous ribbons streaking through the dark. Falling stars pour from the firmament, leaving trails of glittering dust in their wake, until the air shimmers in a luminous haze.

It's a storm. A deluge. The stars rain down in a glittering flood until the entire city shimmers and sparks with magic, a current that skates across my skin like a caress. Pleasure pools thick and languid in my veins. I've never craved touch like this before. It's almost too bright, too sharp.

The crowd erupts. Some demigods take flight, dancing through the star-streaked sky with their wings spread wide. Laughter rings out over the crowd. Everywhere I look, faces are tipped back in rapture.

"How long does it last?" I whisper.

"Three days." There's something wistful in Amara's smile when she turns to me, as if she's remembering a half-forgotten dream. "We need to go," she says apologetically.

I nod, and she takes my arm, navigating us through the crowd. We've barely taken three steps when a word rises above the din, stopping me cold.

Hellevig.

I whip around so fast that Amara stumbles. Across the courtyard, a cluster of demis gather near a bonfire, one male waving his hands as he speaks.

"—mortals and their drama. Nearly made us late to the first falling thanks to whatever's lodged up their collective ass this time around."

"Out with it already," another snaps. "Not all of us are looped in on the latest Vartenan gossip."

The first one leans in. "The Princess of the Blood fell out of favor, and her loyalists were all killed. Or so I heard."

Theo.

Ice spreads through my veins. Suddenly, I can barely breathe around the crushing pressure in my chest.

Amara is at my side in an instant. "What is it? What's wrong?"

"My sister." I can barely speak through the panic. "Theodora. I need—I have to know if she's okay."

She looks over at the demis, then back at me. "Stay here. Don't move. I'll see what I can find out."

Then she's slipping into the throng, the dark fall of her hood swallowed up between one blink and the next. I stand frozen, my pulse roaring in my ears.

Please, please let Theo be all right. If anything's happened to her—

The crowd surges without warning. Bodies jostle me from all sides, and I lose sight of Amara's blue hood in the sudden crush.

"*Amara!*"

My voice is lost in the swell of noise. I'm buffeted on all sides as I struggle to reach her last location. Elbows dig into my ribs, wings bump against my head, but I keep shoving, keep moving—

And stumble to a halt, my attention snagging on an ancient tree. I've seen it sketched in faded ink on a crumbling page in my father's study.

My feet carry me forward, the press of revelers fading to insignificance. As I draw closer, I notice something else—faint scratches in the weathered cobblestones, markings faded with time and weather. Barely more than a suggestion. A word.

Rhosyn.

Brow furrowed, I take an unconscious step nearer, ducking beneath a low-hanging arch—

And collide face-first with a demi.

Hands grab my shoulders, steadying. "Easy there. You almost—" The words cut off with a sharp intake of breath.

Slowly, I tip my head up. The demi's expression makes dread tighten in my gut. His eyes rake over me, hard and calculating, like a hawk eyeing a mouse.

My veil. It's still in place, concealing my features. *I'm fine. I just need to—*

His nostrils flare as he sniffs the air.

"Excuse me," I say. *Stay calm.* "I'm—"

"Human," he says, so softly I almost don't hear him over the blood roaring in my ears. "I can smell it on you."

31

EVANDER

I TRACK THE Devaliant's scent across the night sky.

Caelestis' spires emerge through the mist ahead, all lit up for the festival. Thousands of lanterns float on the breeze as I approach. The drumbeat of music reaches for miles, a grating, relentless beat of the festival's fertility rites. I've never bothered to attend—I prefer to take my pleasure in private—but the Devaliant is missing, and I know exactly who's responsible for dragging my human to this floating deathtrap of a city.

Amara. That reckless, insufferable—

Another punishing wave of rut-fever whites out my vision. I grit my teeth, getting my wings back under control. My cock is so damn hard it hurts. The start of Aethertide is always the worst time: everything burns too bright, too much. My skin is hot. The urge to hunt, to claim, to mark pounds through my veins as I swoop down to the largest island in the chain.

I land in a crouch on the cobblestones. My magic flexes, seeking her. Demis surround me, their power signatures grating against my heightened senses. One female across the road eyes me with interest, but I bare my teeth in a snarl.

Not what I want.

Not *who* I want.

I shut my eyes, breathing hard through my nose. Tasting the air. Sorting through the layers of sensation. I block out the spice of ichor wine, the musk of arousal, the stinging bite of magic.

There it is—a ribbon of sweetness curling through the chaos, unmistakable.

Her.

I let that tempting scent guide me through the throng, past the markets, toward the bonfires. I round the corner into a small courtyard and pull up short.

Every predatory instinct suddenly flares to life.

A demigod has the Devaliant backed against a wall. A red haze fills my vision, and suddenly, I'm picturing exactly how it would sound if I snapped his spine with my bare hands and ripped out his heart.

Then I notice the dagger in the Devaliant's hand.

Remember her training. Let her handle this.

Jaw clenched, I force myself to lean back against a nearby pillar and observe. A veil covers her face, but there's a lethal intent in every line of her body. The way she shifts her weight. The calculated stillness before she strikes.

She shoves the blade into the demigod's side.

"Fuck," I breathe.

If my cock weren't already hard, the sight of my Devaliant this dangerous would have done it. The graceful pivot of her body—movements that Amara has spent hours teaching her, honing until they've become instinct.

The demi staggers, blood staining between his fingers, but my girl's not done. She angles low to hamstring the bastard.

That's it. Make him bleed. I want to see him suffer.

I'm so caught up in watching her that I almost miss it—his hand reaching for her veil. The only thing hiding who she is.

I move in a blink, pinning the fucker to the wall by his throat.

He scrabbles at my forearm. "Wait," he wheezes. "She's a human—"

I squeeze harder. Something gives beneath my fingers. "That human," I say through my teeth, "is *mine*."

Behind that veil is her face. Her identity. The family name that would get her killed in this city. The decision makes itself, really.

I pull back and punch my hand through his chest.

The Devaliant gasps behind me. But I'm focused on the wet crunch of bone, the sudden give when I shove into his ribs, the way his beating heart constricts against my palm. A rattling whine leaves him as he fights against me. Pointless.

"You shouldn't have messed with her," I whisper.

Power floods from me into him, burning everything it touches—heart, lungs, muscles. The demi's skin splits with glowing cracks, and embers drift from his gaping mouth as he incinerates beneath the heat of my magic. No screams, no whimpers, just him strangling on my flames.

Someone in the crowd lets out a sharp cry, but no one intervenes or comes to his aid. They know what happens when someone fucks with what the Wolf of Asteria has claimed.

This is a lesson.

When I yank my hand out of the demi's chest, he collapses to ash at my feet. Not even a body. Just a pile of dust.

I pull back my power, forcing down some of the madness. Breathing hard, I turn. The Devaliant is—

Fuck. Me.

I'd been so distracted by her fighting earlier that I didn't notice the dress. Sweet merciful fuck. The Devaliant is draped in semi-transparent silk that barely qualifies as clothing, held up with nothing more than ribbons and delicate chains. The slit along her thigh is high enough to show off the curve of her ass and inform every male in the vicinity that she's not wearing anything underneath. When she lifts a hand to straighten her veil, I see her nipples pebbling through the fabric. She's every depraved fantasy pulled straight from the filthiest corners of my mind.

My control shatters, and I lunge for her like a feral animal.

Her back hits the wall. She gasps as I bury my face against her neck, dragging in her scent—jasmine, arousal, the sharp tang of fear that shouldn't excite me but does.

"You." The word comes out in a growl. "What the fuck are you doing here? Do you know how dangerous—how *stupid* it was to come here? To Caelestis of all places? I almost—"

Burned down half the city looking for you. Tore apart everyone who got in my way.

I cut myself off before the truth can slip free and try to remember how to form coherent thoughts. *Don't lose it. Not here. Not yet.*

My glare drops to her body, and that's when I notice what's painted all over her. "Why *the fuck* are you covered in fertility rite symbols?" I snarl.

I hear her sharp breath through the veil. "What?"

"This"—I rub at the paint on her arm for emphasis—"is an invitation to fuck. *To be fucked.*"

And I want to kill every male who's seen them.

She blinks. "Oh."

"*Yeah, oh.*"

Her chest rises and falls, tits straining against the fabric of her ridiculous dress. "Amara painted them on me to blend in. How was I supposed to know what they meant?"

"I'm going to strangle Amara," I mutter.

"Why do you even care? I thought you weren't getting *attached.*"

I'm not going near that. That way lies madness and stupidity and things I can't afford to examine too closely. Why is she always like this? Why can't she just—

"Don't throw my words back at me. Not when I can barely think straight enough to remember whatever bullshit I said."

"Then what am I supposed to think?" The Devaliant throws up her arms in frustration. "One day, you're telling me not to catch feelings. The next, you're burning someone alive because he touched me and losing your mind over some paint."

"You don't get it, do you? That spiral on your hip? That means you want to be taken in public. The circuit on your thigh? Means you want multiple partners. That symbol on your back says you prefer submission. The—"

She slaps my hand away. "Enough, I get it."

"Every demigod in this city is looking at you like you're wearing a sign that says 'breed me.'"

"I said I didn't know. It's not like you gave me a lecture in Scillarian fuck symbols when I found out about Aethertide just yesterday."

"*Quiet, Devaliant.*"

I ghost my knuckles down the delicate notches of her spine. Lingering in the divots above the lush curve of her ass. She shivers as I follow one of the chains down between her breasts, watching gooseflesh rise in the wake of my touch.

"*Devla svaust,*" I groan. "You have three little glyphs right between your tits that tell every male in Caelestis that you want someone to dominate you."

"Then stop looking there. My face is up here."

"Your face is behind a veil, you're barely dressed, and you're covered in symbols that are making me insane. Which part *should* I be looking at?"

She makes an annoyed sound. "Listen. The word Rhosyn—I remembered it from an old book in my father's study. It mentioned a connection to Caelestis, and—"

I can't take it anymore. I shove up the veil just enough to bare her throat and sink my teeth into her pulse point to shut her up. Because I don't care about the book right now. I don't care about rational thought. I don't care about trying to justify this absolute mess of an excursion. Not when every inch of paint on her skin is screaming at me to shove her down, take her, make her mine. Kill anyone who even sees her with these symbols boldly declaring how she wants it.

I *told* her to stop talking.

She tastes like starlight. Like oblivion. Like everything I've ever wanted to corrupt. My sanity crumbles, and all I can think about is spreading her open, and licking into her until she screams my name to the sky—

Sharp nails rake down my nape, digging in as she shudders. Her breaths are fast and shallow. In the space between each one, my control unravels a little more.

"Wolf." She pants as I nibble another mark into her skin. "You need to focus."

"Oh, I'm focused." There's a laugh somewhere in my voice, but it's a jagged, mirthless thing. "I'm so very, *very* fucking focused. So focused I can't see straight."

"That's not what I meant."

"I know what you meant. You're thinking, and it's by far your worst quality." I push my thigh between hers, biting back a groan when she rocks against me. "I'm not interested in thinking right now. Not when you smell like this. Not when you feel like this." My lips brush her ear. "The symbol on your thigh says you want to be taken from behind. Would you like that?"

Her breath catches.

I drag the veil over her lips and crush my mouth to hers, swallowing her surprised gasp. The taste of her obliterates thought, narrowing everything down to the press of her body, the addictive sweep of her tongue.

"Is this just rut?" she whispers against my lips. "Would you care if it were Arcadia painted in these symbols?"

Arcadia? I yank back. "Why the fuck would I care about Arcadia right now?"

"Because you've had her every Aethertide. That's what she said, right?"

I set my hand on the wall beside her head. "Would it get you to stop asking stupid questions if I made you come so hard that you forgot how to speak? Is that what I have to do? Should I tell you what every symbol on your body means and how many ways they're telling me to defile you?"

Her fingers curl into my shirt in response, and the sweet scent of her arousal blooms. Damn me. I take her mouth again, rougher this time, biting down until she lets out a helpless whimper. Her hips grind into mine, chasing friction.

I wrench away with a shuddering breath.

Control. Control. Just a little longer.

"We're leaving. Now." My voice comes out low and rough as I straighten her veil. "Because if we don't take off in the next few minutes, I'm going to eat that pussy in public, and I need to get you somewhere safe. Don't leave my side."

She gives a sharp nod. Smart girl.

The Devaliant presses close as we navigate through the crowd. I clutch her hand tightly, terrified of losing her in the sea of bodies. More than a few demis give her appreciative glances as we pass, and I crush her against me to mask her human scent with mine.

"Eyes front, asshole," I snarl at a leering male.

His gaze darts between my gore-streaked hand and thunderous expression before he blanches.

More irritated hisses follow us through the plaza, but no one's stupid enough to get in the Wolf's business over the woman at his side or the demi he just incinerated. Not when he's clearly in the grip of Aethertide's madness.

"Next time, just ask me to paint you instead," I mutter to the Devaliant. "At least then you'd be wearing my marks instead of the fuck-buffet menu Amara smeared all over you. You'd be covered in *touch her and die* symbols in every language."

"But you're single," she says, because she lives to irritate me at every turn. "Isn't that why Aethertide affects you like this? That's what you said yesterday."

There was peace in my life before she blundered her way into it. I slept. I functioned. I had just enough sanity to get through the day without murdering everyone who glanced at me wrong. And now look at me. I'm a barely functional wreck with a perpetual hard-on and a craving for the very last pussy in two realms that I should want.

I shoot her a glare. "If you don't stop moving that bratty mouth, I'll gag it with my dick."

Amara finds us at the edge of the square, falling into step as I haul the Devaliant toward a deserted alley. And it's only centuries of iron discipline that keep me from shaking the everloving shit out of her.

"You," I snap, jabbing a finger in Amara's direction. "When my higher brain functions crawl out of whatever rut-induced hellscape they've fucked off to? Oh, you and I are gonna have words."

"Listen," she starts, hands raised. "She said she wanted to help about Rhosyn."

I bare my teeth, a snarl building in my chest. "You painted what's mine in *sex instructions* for other gods to see."

Her eyebrows shoot up at the words *what's mine*, and if I were even slightly more sane, I'd be backtracking. I'd be making denials. I wouldn't be saying stupid things. But the fever is pounding through my head, insisting those symbols are for *me*, and everyone who's seen them needs to have their eyes removed.

"She needed to look like everyone else," Amara insists, because she clearly has a death wish. "I gave her the most common ones."

"She could have been discovered. She could have died. So shut up while I'm still letting you breathe."

Amara's jaw tightens, but she's smart enough not to push. She knows exactly how close to feral I am right now.

She turns to the Devaliant instead. "Those demis didn't know anything useful about your sister, so I'll go to Hellevig myself and find out what's happening. I'll come back the morning after Aethertide passes. I can take you to my place in the meantime until the Wolf's… situation stabilizes."

And it's exactly the wrong thing to say because it trips some primal switch in my brain. I snake an arm around the Devaliant to pull her more firmly against my side. A growl builds in my throat.

Mine. Stays with me.

"Wolf." The Devaliant's voice is soft. Breathless. "I'm staying. It's okay."

I shudder. Something cracks open in my chest at her words. A mortifying sound, close to a purr, rumbles through me as I nuzzle into her, breathing her in. Setting my mouth right over the symbol at her neck for *mine*.

"If there is a single mark on her she doesn't beg for…" Amara lets the threat dangle.

I'm already spreading my wings. "Yeah, I got it."

Then we're airborne, the city falling away until it's nothing but a blur of light far below.

I tug off the Devaliant's veil to smell her better, to drown in that addictive scent that's driving me mad. The Devaliant buries her face against my neck, and a shiver goes through her, her fingers tightening on my shoulders. So close to the most sensitive part of my wings—the erogenous covert feathers closest to the skin. No other lover has ever touched me there, and it's madness that I'm even considering commanding her to.

The night sky splinters around us, stars shattering into ribbons of color that twist and dance through the darkness. It catches in the Devaliant's silver hair and dusts her skin in shimmering opal. She's the most beautiful thing I've ever seen.

I should say something. An assurance that she isn't about to be fucked within an inch of her life by the animal wearing my skin. That somewhere beneath the rut-fever, I'm still capable of sanity.

But that would be a lie, and if nothing else, I'll give the Devaliant the dignity of honesty.

In no time at all, the tower comes into view. I aim for the garden, touching down on silent feet. Carefully—so carefully—I set the Devaliant on her feet and force myself to step back.

"Get inside." I'm amazed the words emerge as anything close to intelligible. "Now. Before I forget how to be careful with you."

She hesitates, and I think, *Yes. Fucking please. Just give me an excuse to snap. To push you down and take what I want—*

The Devaliant must see something in my face because she's moving before I can act on the impulse. I follow her through the halls, staying close enough to hear her rapid exhales. It's only when we reach her chamber that my control finally shatters.

I've got her caged between my body and the door before she can so much as gasp. The sound she makes incinerates the last scraps of rational thought. The Devaliant tips her head back, baring her throat—an offering and a surrender.

Here, it says. *You can have it. I yield.*

"*Evander.*" A ragged whisper.

Of course she'd use my name right now when I'm out of my mind with want, and that's all it takes to push me over the edge.

So I take her mouth the way I will take the rest of her—with tongue and teeth. Starving and reverent. I'll worship every inch of her until my name is etched on her bones. Until there's nothing left of me but what she chooses to keep.

She makes a sound that's half prayer, half plea. Begging me to have her. I imagine myself tangled up in her limbs, inside her. Imagine how wet she'd be, how she'd sound when I moved. Would she grasp me like now? Would she want me to take her harder?

"The symbol on your neck?" I whisper. "It's asking for someone to Claim you tonight."

She swallows hard. "And would you? If I hadn't ordered you not to?"

I can't. You aren't for me.

So I toe open the door and nudge her gently across the threshold. "I think the marks on your body are making promises you don't want to keep, and I'm not in my right mind." I step away. "Lock yourself in. Wash the paint off. Don't come out until this passes."

Please. Please just obey me for once in your contrary existence.

She studies my face, and I brace for her refusal. For the inevitable, disastrous moment she throws herself against my discipline to see how far it bends.

But then the Devaliant dips her chin in a nod.

It takes every shred of my control to slam the door shut. Panting, I slump against the surface, tip my head back, and just breathe, and breathe, and breathe. I try to claw back some semblance of sense and sanity.

We want what we want. Even when we know it'll destroy us.

32

BRYONY

I CAN'T STAY in this room for another second.

The Wolf told me to lock myself in here—what, a day ago? More? I haven't eaten since before Amara flew me to Caelestis, and I've tried every distraction I can think of. I've picked up books and tossed them aside. Tried to sleep. Watched the aetherlight dance across the ceiling.

Nothing works.

Pressing my ear to the door, I listen hard, but there's only silence on the other side. The sort of eerie quiet that settles over old places at night. For all I know, the rut-fever could have driven the Wolf to the other side of the tower, as far from me as he can get.

My stomach growls, insistent now. If he thinks I'm going to spend three days in here wasting away to nothing, he's out of his mind.

I unlock the door and ease it open. The hinges let out a groan, and I pause, pulse racing. Nothing. So I hurry down to the kitchen.

The table is a mess of half-prepared food left abandoned. Platters of cheese, bowls of apples and pears, some bread. I make quick work of the cheese and bread first, then I snatch up an oatcake, slather it with berry preserves, and devour two. I lick each finger clean, so distracted that I forget why I shouldn't be in here.

Until a soft groan shatters the quiet.

Slowly, I turn. And there, filling the doorway, is a very large, very beautiful, very naked, *very* aroused god.

The Wolf's black hair is tangled around his face. He clutches the frame, breathing hard. I can't help but drink in the sight of him—his bare, muscled chest, the lines of his abdomen, the tantalizing cut of muscle framing his hips. Those appealing V-shaped lines that guide my gaze downward.

Oh. *Oh my.*

"Eyes up, Devaliant."

Heat floods my cheeks, but I force myself to meet his stare. This isn't the Wolf I'm used to. Not the cold, calculating male with an assassin's control. *This* god is more lethal than the executioner—stripped down to his most base self, with no civility to blunt his edges. He's staring at me like a feral animal in the woods.

He looks like he wants to eat me alive.

He looks like he might enjoy it.

Somehow, I find my voice. "You're looking rough, Wolf. Trouble sleeping?"

A muscle in his jaw tics, the only sign that he's heard me. That he's even fully present. "What part of *stay in your fucking room* was unclear?" His fingers flex on the doorframe like he's fighting the urge to grab me.

"Even prisoners get fed," I argue. "I was starving."

I step back as the Wolf moves closer.

"You want to talk about hunger? *Starvation?*" He cages me against the table, palms flat on either side of my hips. "I've been in my room for the last sixteen hours with only my hand, your scent, and the most depraved fantasies for company."

I suck in a sharp breath. Images flood my mind. The Wolf, naked and glistening with sweat, working that big cock with urgent strokes. Moaning my name as he finds his release.

"You have no idea how many times I've imagined fucking you," he continues mercilessly. His palm skims up my side to the curve of my breast. "Spread out beneath me. Bent over my desk. Shackled to the wall with my cock buried deep inside you. This entire tower is saturated with your scent, and it's driving me fucking insane. I can't think about anything else except this clawing desperation to have you. *That*, Devaliant, is starvation."

His hand curves around my nape, and some long-buried instinct shrieks at me to go limp. To run. To do anything but stand here and let him put his teeth so close to all my soft parts. Because the Wolf is a weapon, and I've seen what those brutal hands can do.

I know with a blinding certainty that he wants to take and take and take until there's nothing left.

And maybe I want him to.

The Wolf's head dips, and I feel the drag of his parted lips. He nuzzles into my neck, making a low, hungry sound as he breathes me in. Scents me like the wild thing he is.

"Here's what's going to happen," he says. "You're going to walk backward. Slowly. Eyes on me, no sudden movements. Don't run, and don't ever give me your back, or the instinct to chase will be impossible to ignore."

I shiver.

"And *don't*," he murmurs, "bare this pretty throat to me again unless you want me to bite."

In the silence, there is only the rasp of our breathing. And with each shared exhale, a single truth crystallizes.

He wants me. Not in some abstract way, but with the kind of violent need that drives creatures to tear each other apart. It's written in every line of his body, in the unsteady rise and fall of his chest, the clench of his fists. In Caelestis, he'd called me *his*.

I'm the one with the power here. Me.

"And what would you do?" I ask as I reach behind me for the vessel of honey. "If I bared my throat and begged for your teeth?"

I dip my fingers into the sticky-sweet syrup. Slowly, so slowly, letting him track the movement. A low growl escapes him as I bring my hand to my lips and drag my tongue over my fingers in a long, slow lick.

Aroused gods, I've been warned, are governed entirely by their most primal desires. An inferno that consumes and incinerates anything foolish enough to stand in its path.

But I can't help but want to destroy.

"What," he grits out, "are you doing, you reckless creature?"

I savor the last of the honey, holding his gaze. "*Move. Countermove.* Isn't that our game? I'm just leaning into my role as your entertainment."

"Listen to me very carefully," he says, leaning close. "I'm not a good male. And you need to understand that, before you do something you regret. Keep pushing, and I'll pin you to the floor and ruin you."

I'm almost sure he'll do it. That he'll spread me out and *devour*. And I'd let him. I'd let him fuck me, bite me, put his hands all over me, and do whatever he wanted.

The Wolf shuts his eyes with a soft groan. "You're not wearing anything under that chemise, are you?"

My breath hitches. "How can you—"

"Rut dials everything to eleven. So whatever filthy shit you're imagining? Stop. Because I can smell exactly how wet you are, and it's making it real fucking difficult to remember all the reasons I shouldn't bend you over this table and take what you're so clearly offering."

Lift me onto the table, I want to say, *and have me.*

He steps away and drags a palm down his face. "This is a rare moment of restraint that I'm absolutely going to regret. Get your ass to your room, and I'll let you keep your skin."

The Wolf is on the verge of shattering. Barely leashed and vibrating with the need to pounce. To claim and conquer and consume.

I slip past him, careful not to brush his outstretched wing as I head for the archway. I keep my eyes on him, just like he said to, never giving him my back.

But when I reach the door, something in me seizes. Rebels. Because as I stare at this god who's straining for control, I realize I don't want careful. I don't want controlled. I'm tired of being small and silent and tiptoeing through a world that has only ever sought to destroy me.

So I bare my teeth in a smile. The Wolf's pupils flare, his control fraying another inch.

"Devaliant," he growls. "*Don't.*"

I turn and run.

One heartbeat. Two. Three. Then the thundering chorus of pursuit. The Wolf's footsteps pound behind me, the sweep of his wings churning the air.

I don't slow. Not even when his power scorches through the air and strokes along my spine in a blatant caress. No, he won't get me that easily. I leap up the stairs, taking them two at a time, and something fierce and wild sears through my veins when I hear the Wolf's growl.

The chase fills some primal need I didn't know lived inside me, one that sings and claws and spurs me on. Drawing me up through the tower's higher levels. Making him *chase*. Because I want him exactly like this—wild and feral and starved for me. His footfalls are closer now, all that power gliding along my skin like he's readying me. Getting me wet.

An arm snakes around my waist and wrenches me back into a hard body.

The Wolf lowers his face into the crook of my shoulder. "That," he murmurs, "was unwise."

"Was it?"

"Mm. You'll regret this in the morning when you remember what I am."

"You'll be the worst mistake of my life," I agree. "But right now, I don't care. Make it worth it."

"In that case—"

With a brutal yank, he rips my chemise away, leaving me naked and panting. He shoves me face down on the hall table.

"*Stay.* And grip the table." Every nerve ending sparks to life when he splays his palm over the small of my back to pin me in place. "Should've known it would come to this. All that wanting between us was destined to end messy."

I wrap my fingers around the table's edge, waiting for those questing fingers to dip lower. To part my thighs. But the Wolf only squeezes my hip, a little chiding.

"Before we play, we need to establish a ground rule. If you had to pick any word that would stop me, no matter what depraved, filthy things I was doing to this body when you said it…" His other hand drags down my thigh, raising gooseflesh in its wake. "What would it be?"

I squeeze my eyes shut, a shudder rolling through me. It takes every scrap of concentration to find my voice again. "Why?"

"Because yesterday you put yourself at risk in Caelestis." His palm presses more insistently into my hip. "Means I'm in a punishing sort of mood. Give me a word, or I'm picking for you."

I try to think of something, anything, to ground me. Prevent me from drowning in his scent, his heat, the thrumming energy of his magic skating over my bare skin.

"*Ishkah*," I manage. The Lybräian command for *cease. Halt.*

He leans over me and nips my jaw. "And if that pretty mouth is busy?"

"Two taps. Anywhere."

"Don't forget your other orders. Grip the fucking table and be still."

The smart thing would be to disengage. To flee to my room, throw every lock between us, and establish some much-needed distance. But the wild thing behind my ribs is howling for freedom. It wants to roll in his scent, lick over his sharp edges until it draws blood. I want to poke the beast until it bites. To see what lives on the other side of that ironclad discipline when it shatters.

"My trip to Caelestis seems to be working out for me," I say. "Maybe I should defy you more often if this is my rewar—"

He bites the join of my shoulder and neck. A hiss escapes me at the sudden flare of pain-pleasure. I imagine the picture I must make like this, bent over and spread out like an offering.

"Earned rewards are sweeter." His voice is a dark purr against my ear. "Remind me of your word so there's no confusion."

"*Ishkah*," I breathe.

A pleased hum resonates through his chest, vibrating along all the places we're pressed together. Then he's smoothing his palm over the curve of my ass as he flattens me more snugly against the table.

I hold my breath.

The first crack of his palm against my skin is a sweet, stinging shock. It sends me jolting forward, a choked sound tangling in my throat. Then he's delivering another. *Slap*. Another. Spanking me hard, setting my nerve endings alight, kindling a wildfire beneath my skin. The sweet-sharp blows wind me tighter and tighter, pushing me toward some precipice.

"Defying a god in the middle of rut is idiocy," he says. His other hand keeps me ruthlessly pinned, an unspoken demand to submit. *Take it and like it*. He slaps my ass again. "It deserves a lesson in obedience."

I'm panting now. "This... Isn't this my lesson?"

The Wolf leans forward, caging me more tightly between the table and his body. His erection presses against me. "Oh, nemesis," he murmurs as his fingers push between my thighs. "This is the warm-up. You shouldn't be this wet when I'm punishing you."

"Does that... that mean you aren't going to—"

"I'm going to fuck you. That was never a question." He punctuates the filthy promise by sinking a finger inside me. I gasp, my fingernails digging into the table. "First, we're going to play a little game."

I can barely think. "What kind of game?"

"Simple." He slides his lips up my jaw and whispers in my ear, "You run, I hunt."

His thumb flicks over my clit and I arch against him with a rough cry.

"*Fuck*," I breathe.

"You're going to use every trick Amara's taught you to evade me." He works me in a lazy slide, as if he has all the time in the world. "All that training? Time to put it to use."

"Rules?"

"Rule one. You stay naked."

He adds another finger, thrusting harder now. My hips follow his hand, chasing pleasure. Chasing release.

"Rule two," he continues. "If you make it too easy, you get nothing from me. No mouth. No cock. Just your own hand tonight. The longer it takes me to find you, the harder I fuck you when I do." He punctuates that filthy promise with a slow grind against me, letting me feel every hard inch of him. "Last one. When I catch you—and I *will* catch you—no begging. No mercy. It gets to be too much, you tap out. Give me your word one more time so I know we're clear."

"*Ishkah.*"

"Good. You get five minutes. Then I'm coming for you." He steps back and spanks my ass one last time. "Run, Devaliant."

33

BRYONY

I BURST OUT into the garden, my lungs burning.

Aethertide paints the sky in ribbons of indigo, emerald, and deep purple. Between the flickering hues, the stars rain down in glittering streaks that illuminate the ground as I sprint between the roses.

A branch snaps in the darkness.

Shit.

I bolt into the trees surrounding the Wolf's tower, my bare feet finding every sharp damn thing on the forest floor, but I don't slow down or falter. I've learned to shove pain down deep.

Stay low, Amara's voice thunders in my head. *Watch your footing.*

A darker voice, hungry: *Run faster. Make him work for it.*

Aetherlight paints the woods in shades of blue and green, bright enough to light my way. Nothing exists but this—my hammering heart, the chase, knowing the Wolf's out there hunting me. Wind stirs the branches overhead. Then…

Crack.

The sound comes from my left. Closer than before. Is he toying with me? Has he already caught up?

I push harder. I want him starving when he finds me, out of his mind. We've been playing this game for weeks. Pushing, pulling, taunting, teasing. All those touches when he healed me, our kisses, his fingers inside me—every day leading us toward this like kindling just waiting for the right spark. My goal is to crack him open and let the hunger take its due.

I want his mouth to taste like violence when he kisses me.

How long have I been running now? Minutes? Hours? I lose count of how many times I slip into the shadows at the rustle of wings. Evading him, denying him, tempting him.

The longer it takes me to find you, the harder I fuck you when I do.

So I make him work for it.

Every minute that passes fuels the heat inside me. It's primal. It's animal. It wants to be conquered. To finally have the Wolf in the ways I've imagined in the midnight hours with my hand between my thighs.

Through the skeletal branches, a rocky outcropping promises a hiding spot. I scramble over the boulders, loose scree biting into my abraded feet as I heave myself over the ledge—

And freeze.

Because he's here.

The Wolf crouches low. His eyes are nearly black, just a thin ring of gold around pupils blown wide. His wings arc behind him, gleaming in the aetherlight.

"Found you," he growls. He lunges for me, his fingers wrapping around my throat. "Did you enjoy making me chase you? Getting me all worked up?"

I bare my teeth. "You still haven't earned it."

"Vicious girl." His grip tightens a fraction. "I'm going to fucking wreck you."

I yank out of his hold and lunge. No thought, no hesitation, just my body colliding with his, frantic to mark him as he's marked me. To bite and claw. But before I can savor my victory, his mouth crashes down on mine.

It's annihilation in the shape of a kiss. The Wolf meets my brutality with his own, stealing breath and reason until I'm drowning in the taste of him. Nothing exists except his lips and the bruising pressure of his grip.

"Yield," he says.

No. If he wants to conquer me tonight, I'm going to make him bleed for the privilege.

I kiss him hard enough to bruise, to hurt. My teeth sink into his lower lip until he bleeds for me. A groan rumbles through him, but he doesn't stop. He just keeps kissing me, keeps taking, keeps trying to make me submit.

But that's not what I want. I want to be hungry tonight. Animal. Feral. I want to fucking *own* him.

I seize a fistful of his hair and wrench his head back, sinking my teeth into the junction of his neck and shoulder. Hard enough to break skin. Hard enough to make him feel it, to remind him that he may have caught me, but I'm not prey.

"Fuck," he breathes, reverent. "Do that again."

So I do. I bite down harder this time, savoring the copper-salt taste of his blood. The way his body strains against mine.

My triumph is short-lived. He locks an arm around my waist and spins us, pushing me against the rock wall. My hands slap against the stone. His palm flattens between my shoulder blades, pinning me down, telling me without words that it's time to yield, to surrender. And I'm trapped. Exposed. Every part of me pressed to every part of him.

"Spread your legs."

Part of me still wants to fight him. I don't move.

His fingers sink into my hair, tugging sharply. "I said *spread them*."

This time, I obey. Cold air kisses my inner thighs as I widen my stance.

The Wolf's hand slips between my legs, and he gives a soft groan when he pushes his fingers inside me. "Is this from running? Or is your pussy always this wet for me?"

I turn my head and nip at his jaw hard enough to sting. "Just shut up and fuck me."

"That's my girl," he says with a soft laugh, slipping his fingers out.

And then he lines his cock up and pushes into me, forcing the breath from my lungs. It hurts—too much, too fast. But I wanted this.

The Wolf freezes, every muscle in his body going rigid. "Devaliant…" His voice changes, softens. "Are you—"

"*Stop.*"

I don't need his pity. Don't want him to care that I've never done this. I want the feral god right now. So I shove back against him, taking him deeper, forcing him to move. My fingernails scrape against rock as I brace myself.

"You said you'd wreck me, remember?" I look over my shoulder, catching his eyes. "So wreck me."

His eyes darken. Then his hands clamp down on my hips hard enough to bruise as he withdraws until only the tip of him stretches me open.

"Palms flat on the rock," he orders.

I obey, bracing myself.

The Wolf thrusts hard into me, the force of it lifting me to my toes. There's nothing gentle about how he takes me. Nothing careful. Only the aching stretch of his cock, the sweet-sharp edge of *too-much-not-enough*. Only snarling need and the frenzied coupling of two creatures learning each other's teeth. I'm not me anymore—just *his*. Something dark and hungry lives in my skin.

His hands grip me, yanking me back to meet every brutal snap of his hips. Like he's using me, shaping me into what he needs, taking what he wants without asking. But didn't I tell him to? Doesn't that make us even? Since I'm using him too?

I think I might die if he stops.

It's a defilement. Desecration. Pleasure so sharp I can't breathe, can't think, can't focus on anything but the pleasure suffusing through my veins. Release hovers just out of reach. That coil of heat, that thing I've chased alone in my bed at night, imagining his hands instead of mine. *Almost, almost, almost—*

"*Harder*," I say.

My voice doesn't even sound like mine, but it doesn't matter. Because I need to feel this tomorrow. Need the reminder that for once, I wasn't careful. Wasn't smart. That I just took what I wanted.

His teeth find my shoulder—not gentle, not asking. His thrusts sharpen, fucking me deeper, faster, not caring if it hurts. I'll have bruises tomorrow where his fingers dig into me, but I want them there. Need them there.

I earned every single one.

He shoves in harder, his pace punishing. Stretching me, filling me. Pushing so deep. "You have no idea," he pants, breath ragged, "how many times I've thought about this. About messing up all that pretty. Seeing what you look like when I'm fucking you."

"And what do I look like?"

He breathes softly in my ear, "You look like someone I'd keep, if you were anyone but you."

I feel everything. The heat of his body against mine, the spicy scent of him, the hard slap of his hips. Stars streak across the sky, and their light catches on his skin, on mine, on the places where we're joined. He grips me so tight it hurts. Like if he loosens his hold even a little, I'll disappear.

And I give him what he wants.

I let go.

Pleasure rips through me, violent and sudden. I tip my head up to the stars and shout my release. I can't breathe, can't think. Only the solid heat of the Wolf's body keeps me from drowning, from falling. My fingernails scrape against the rock, breaking, bleeding. I don't care.

"Evander."

His fingers dig into my hips as he slams into me one last time, rhythm faltering. With a curse, he slaps his hand against the rock beside my head, splintering it under his fist. The heat of his release stings between my thighs. After a few shallow thrusts, he goes still, curling his body over mine.

For a minute, there's nothing but our breathing—mine ragged, his deep. As if we've both been drowning.

The Wolf's forehead rests between my shoulder blades, his palms gentling over my sides. I let myself savor this stillness, with the sweet ache blooming in places I didn't know could feel this good.

"Bryony," he whispers.

My name shouldn't sound like a prayer. Like a vow. But it

does, and it rattles something loose inside me—an emotion that's too immense to be contained, pressing against my lungs. It feels like vulnerability. Like terror. Like some bright, fragile thing starved for all his softness. It suddenly hurts when I breathe, that light expanding and expanding until it's as if I've swallowed a star—too much, too big, burning me up from inside.

I want to cut it out.

But that's the thing about falling—you never think about the damage until you're already halfway to the ground.

"Hey." He turns me around, those gold-ringed eyes searching my face. "You okay?"

Each brush of his fingertips is a confession, a claim. As if he doesn't already own every inch of me. As if this feeling isn't still burning in my chest.

I nod, forcing my expression to stay even, neutral. If I speak, I think I'll say something I can't take back. Something like, *keep me.*

"Cold?" he asks, rubbing my arms.

I nod again.

He works his jaw as if he's figuring something out. "Let's get you back," he murmurs, scooping me into his arms and spreading his wings.

When we land in the courtyard, I expect him to put me down. He doesn't.

"Bath first," he says. "Then my bed."

I almost argue. Almost remind him in pitiless terms that what we just shared changed nothing, that he's no more entitled to me now than he was yesterday. Getting fucked out of my mind by a savage god? An excellent decision. Willingly spending the night naked in my future executioner's bed for an encore performance? A level of insanity I'm not prepared to claim.

Still, I'm filthy and sore and exhausted. I need to get clean.

I close my eyes and let him carry me through the halls to his chamber. His bedroom is exactly as I imagined and nothing like it at all. The tall windows admit a wash of aetherlight that illuminates the enormous four-poster bed with black sheets.

Past that is a comfy-looking dark leather chair covered in stacks of books. The red roses have climbed nearly every inch of his walls and ceiling, still open and in bloom even in the darkness.

The Wolf doesn't give me time to process my surroundings. Just carries me into the adjoining bathing chamber and sets me on my feet beside a sunken tub big enough for his wings.

Steam curls from the water as he fills the bath and gathers some bottles. The warmth licks at my skin, chilled after all that time spent naked in the elements.

He eases us both in, settling me between his thighs. I tip my head back with a sigh as floral-scented steam curls around me. A shiver rolls through me as his fingers thread through my hair, untangling the snarled mess with surprising care.

"Too much?" he asks.

"No." I fidget, trying to tamp down the emotions battering around my ribcage. "Just new."

"Lean back. Let me take care of you."

So I do. He works the soap into a lather and glides his palms over my spine. He's meticulous in his attention, as if he's trying to memorize me in this rare, soft moment. Cataloging all my injuries. His power reaches for me, sliding across my skin and healing the bruises from his hands, the places where branches sliced into my skin during the run, the cuts on my palms, my injured feet. Comforting. Soothing.

He reaches for my inner thighs, and I tense, bracing. Ready to shore up the cracks broken open by his gentle hands.

"Easy. This is just…" He exhales, and it sounds oddly unsteady. "This isn't about getting you wound up again. Just cleaning you off and making sure you're all right."

Holding my breath, I let my legs fall open.

The Wolf slides his hand along my inner thighs and I bite back a moan as he gently brushes fingers along my pussy, his magic soothing the soreness before he backs off. His palms smooth over my skin in circles. So careful with me, almost reverent as he washes my breasts, my belly. There is no demand in the drag of his fingers, no seduction. No intent beyond the act of caring for me.

It's unbearable. Tenderness has no place between us. I should pull away, armor myself. Yet, as I tilt my head to study his face, the words wither. Our gazes catch and hold. The pad of his thumb finds my bottom lip, dragging until my mouth falls open on a sigh. Something complicated twists his features.

"You're too quiet," he says. He seems almost uncertain. "Did I hurt you?"

"No more than I wanted."

The Wolf's eyes flicker between mine. "Then what's happening in that head of yours? Trying to convince yourself that this was a horrible idea? That you should have said *ishkah* before I had you up against that rock?"

"I was just thinking that for someone so dangerous, you're far too good at being soft."

"Only for you." He strokes the damp hair from my brow and cups my cheek. "Temporary insanity brought on by rut-fever."

"Is that all it is?"

"What else would it be?"

I don't have an answer for that. Not one I'm willing to give.

His mouth finds mine, the kiss an unhurried glide of lips and tongue. Lush and intoxicating. So different from the way he claimed me before, all violence and desperation.

When he finally lifts his head, I'm dizzy. Drunk on the feel and taste of him.

"When you're like this," I whisper, "I have to remind myself."

"Remind yourself what?"

"That you're very dangerous for mortal women with fragile human hearts."

"Then it's a good thing *this* mortal woman is too clever to catch feelings." His head dips, lips shaping the words against my temple. "Stop thinking so hard, Devaliant. It's inconvenient."

"Is this…" I struggle to find the right words. "This gentleness. Is it just part of the biological process? Soothing your partner after breaking them?"

"Rut-fever comes in waves. I'm using the time between to give aftercare to the human I just found out was a virgin and didn't tell me."

I make a noncommittal sound but offer no real response.

He doesn't press, just resumes his reverent exploration of my body. Skimming his fingers over my ribs, up and down, stroking until I'm drowsy.

With a kiss on my temple, he reaches over and snags a small glass bottle from the collection on the rim of the bath. "Drink all of this," he says, pressing it into my hand.

I uncap it and sniff. The scent is medicinal, but not overwhelming. "What is it?"

"It's rare for gods and humans to have children, but we're biologically compatible. It prevents pregnancy."

Oh. I down the entire bottle and set it aside. "Thank you."

He returns to stroking my hair, pushing it back from my face. "Will you be mine for the rest of Aethertide? You can say no."

I was prepared to reestablish boundaries, build up my walls, and return to my room. But the way he's touching me—speaking to me—is so careful that I'm not ready to let it go. When was the last time someone took care of me like this? Let me be wild?

"Yes." I settle my hand over his. "Do you need me again?"

I feel his smile against my nape. His breathing quickens with excitement. "In a few minutes. And again after that. Until neither of us can move."

When the Wolf deems me sufficiently clean, he dries me off and settles me in his bed. The mattress dips as he slides in beside me.

He feels like safety, like shelter. And I'm too strung out and sex-stupid to question the complicated tangle of feelings I shouldn't have for the god who's going to kill me.

So when he rolls me under him, spreading my thighs with his knee, I let him.

He takes his time with me, drawing out every sigh and moan. Sucking bruises into my skin as he fucks into me, nice and deep and slow, like he's savoring me this time. I lose myself to the hazy pleasure of it. To the filthy words he breathes into my skin, to the sweet ache building between my thighs.

He maps my reactions—every hitch in my breathing, the helpless arch of my spine. And when he's wrung every drop of ecstasy from me, he hauls me into his lap and starts all over again. It's too much. It's not nearly enough.

When he finally pulls me on top of him, spent and satisfied, he says, "During Aethertide, I'm Evander."

"Just Aethertide?"

He's quiet for a long moment, his heart thudding under my ear. "Just Aethertide," he says, very softly.

A few days to have this. To pretend this is something simple. Where I'm not a Devaliant, and he's not my executioner.

You look like someone I'd keep, if you were anyone but you.

"Then I'm Bryony," I whisper back.

He shuts his eyes and gathers me closer against him. "Night, Bryony."

34

EVANDER

I wake up to cold sheets.

Of course, Bryony bailed as soon as the fever dimmed, and I managed to fall asleep. Who could blame her? I've been fucking her all night, touching her in ways I have no right to, saying too much in my half-mad delirium.

You look like someone I'd keep.

And I need her underneath me again.

Her scent pulls me to the gardens. The stars bleed light across the sky, the aetherlight casting everything in shades of teal. Thousands of stars fall like rain.

My skin is too hot now. The rut-fever is burning through my veins after the reprieve, a relentless drumbeat—*need, want, take. Need, want, take.* Drowning out everything else.

Her scent catches me halfway down the path—jasmine and dark spice, the lingering traces of sex. My magic is saturated in her skin. When rut has me in its grip, everything is primal, and last night, I wanted to mark her up all over. Claim her as mine.

I round the corner and stop.

She perches on a crumbling wall, one leg dangling over the edge, the other tucked under her. That sheer slip she's wearing is practically useless. I can see the bite marks on her throat and the bruises I sucked onto her collarbone—handiwork I couldn't bring myself to heal just yet.

I watch her. Doesn't matter how many times I see this girl, the same thing always happens: it's like a knife to the chest every time.

She shouldn't matter to me. To an Eternal, mortals are ephemeral. But Bryony Devaliant? She's shrapnel. She's nails and broken glass, and I can't dig her out of me, no matter how deep I cut. Some girls, once under your skin, can never be carved out. Not without taking pieces of you with them.

"You planning to stand there all night?" she asks, still studying the colors dancing above us.

"Depends." I walk closer, crossing my arms. "You planning to sit out here all night and expect me to keep my hands to myself?"

She gives a little huff. "I just needed air. To think."

"About?"

"Some demis in Caelestis were gossiping about trouble in Hellevig. I woke up worrying about my sister." Bryony drags a hand through her hair. "What if Theo tried to take the throne? What if she—" She stops and swallows, rubbing her hands on her thighs. "She didn't say anything in her letters."

I snort. "Well, if your sister knocked Idris off his throne, I'd call it an improvement."

"Yes," she says quietly. "He hasn't been right since losing his daughter. And Theo keeps trying to fix everything. She always does."

"Amara will get answers."

"I know. I just…" She catches her lower lip between her teeth. "I hate not knowing if she's okay. Sorry about abandoning you like that."

"Worrying about siblings?" I shrug. "I get it."

Honestly, her family dysfunction has nothing on mine. If Bas follows his pattern from the last two Aethertides, there's a village in Vartena that's about to learn what it means to be in the path of a god who's lost his humanity. My brother hasn't fucked in centuries. Now he just kills.

"The Blade is your brother, right?" she asks. "You never talk about him."

I give her a tight smile. "Nothing to talk about. We don't see each other much." Not anymore. For three hundred years, he's been a stranger. "You and I have unfinished business, and you're not going to get out of it by bringing up Bastien."

"Is that so?" she asks, plucking at her chemise.

"Don't play coy. You didn't tell me I was your first."

"It didn't seem relevant."

I swear, she's the most deliberately obtuse creature I've ever met.

"Devaliant. I was half out of my mind from rut. I could've hurt you."

"Please." She rolls her eyes. "Amara's broken practically every bone in my body daily for the last five weeks. And you've never cared about collateral damage before."

"I've never fucked a virgin sacrifice before, either." I drag a hand down my face, frustration spiking. "Forgive me for trying out this novel concept called *giving a shit*."

She lets out an incredulous laugh. "Oh, so *now* that the post-coital glow has faded, you care? How many times were you inside me last night, again?"

I'm not answering that question. I lost count. The only reason she's still able to move is because I keep healing her so I can have her again.

"If I'd confessed, would it have slowed you down?" she presses. "Altered your angle of approach? Or just inspired you to find a more convenient surface to bend me over?"

My cock twitches at the memory. I actually have to clench my hands into fists to keep from grabbing her. But this is a game, a careful balance of want and patience and conquest.

"I would've fucked you on any surface I could get. Floor, wall, tree—didn't matter as long as I got to hear you scream my name." I step closer, watching her pupils dilate and her chest move a little faster. "But yeah, maybe I wouldn't have spanked that disobedient ass the first time. The chase through the woods? That would've been later."

"I don't need soft," she says with a withering glare.

"Wasn't offering it."

"I don't want rose petals and silk sheets. I wanted—"

"To be devoured, I know. And I don't deny myself the things I crave. Especially the dangerous, chaotic ones."

"Of course not. Usually, you just gnaw on them until they stop twitching. Must have been refreshing to have something fight back for once."

Oh, I like her mouthy. I like her *mean*. This is the woman who's scratched her name into my soul with bloody fingernails. The one who cuts with her words and fucks like she's fighting.

"Careful, sweetheart. You keep up that bratty attitude, and I'll have to spank you again."

Bryony swallows hard, squirming a little, but says nothing.

"But from now on," I say, "when we play? I expect honesty. No holding back. No lies of omission. Are we clear?"

"You want honesty? Fine." She lets out a hard exhale. "Nothing in Vartena was ever mine. My body, my time, my choices—all of it belonged to other people. My virginity was just another commodity to be traded. Another thing they could take from me. So last night, for the first time in my life, I chose. I wanted you, so I took you. I won't apologize for that."

I see it with a sudden, stark clarity—a girl broken for her realm, doomed to be chewed up and spat out by a world intent on using her up. Sacrificed on a god's altar and expected to smile as she's stripped of agency. All those people with their hands on her, deciding her fate and bartering her away piece by piece.

Her uncle trying to kill her was just the final insult. The real violence was every day they told her she belonged to everyone but herself.

She shouldn't have handed me this. Shouldn't have pressed the shape of her hurts into my palm and expected me not to squeeze until the world fractures. Because now all I want is to peel the skin off every arrogant fuck who thought to collar her, starting with Alexios.

Bryony slants me a look. "Stop."

"Stop what?"

"That thing you're doing with your face. The brooding.

Men only brood for two reasons: they're planning something stupid or angsting about their feelings. So which is it? Murder or manpain?"

"I *scheme*, vicious girl. I plot and plan and sharpen my claws. I dream up new and interesting ways to make people suffer."

She arches an eyebrow. "What's the difference?"

"Brooding is for poets and lovesick fools. *Scheming* is for monsters."

"A semantic argument at best."

I grin slowly. "Want me to lay the bodies of your enemies at your feet? Stack their skulls in a monument to your glory?"

What? Destruction has always been my love language, and Bryony Devaliant is a dark and hungry god shaped like a woman. I want to worship at her altar.

A reluctant smile tugs at her lips. "That's horrifying, dramatic, and unnecessary, but sweet. I'll pass on the corpse pile, though." Bryony hops down from the wall and closes the distance between us. The aetherlight filters through her thin chemise, silhouetting the graceful curve of her hips. "You say the loveliest things for a male who claims to loathe me."

"You make me feel a lot of things. Most of them vaguely homicidal."

"And the other things?"

Everything I have no right to feel, not for anyone. Especially not for you.

"Irritated. Frustrated. Occasionally murderously possessive," I say instead. "Right now? So ravenous I can barely see straight."

I reach for her, ghosting my fingertips up her body. Skimming over her ribs, beneath the curve of her breast. Her breathing goes a little ragged.

"How much of this is Aethertide?" she asks. "Were you like this with Arcadia?"

The question is guarded. There's a subtle tension in her shoulders, as if she's bracing herself.

I move closer, until we're breathing in the same air. "Jealous, nemesis?"

"No."

"Liar." I lean in and graze my teeth up her throat. "What if I touched her exactly like this, fucked her the way I fucked you? Made her scream and beg so pretty—"

Her hand shoots out, wrapping around my throat and digging her nails in.

"Mmm." I give a laugh. "That *feels* an awful lot like jealousy."

"When we're together, you don't think about anyone else. Understand?" Her voice is almost a snarl, fingers tightening until she's digging into my pulse.

Then her mouth is on mine, greedy and artless. I sink into it with a groan. She tugs at my hair, fingernails a sweet sting against my scalp as she presses closer. Her scent fills my head—that intoxicating combination of midnight blooms and arousal, and I think, Oh. This. This *is what madness must feel like.* Wanting the woman most likely to destroy me, and not caring anyway.

I break the kiss and whisper against her mouth, "Jealousy tastes good on you."

"Shut up."

"But I like this side of Bryony Devaliant." I kiss her again. "Demanding Bryony." I grip her slip and drag it off her shoulder, following with my lips. "Possessive Bryony." I yank her clothes off the rest of the way. The aetherlight dances over her bare skin in silver-blue patterns—catching on her cheekbones, the hollow of her throat, the dip of her waist. "*Greedy* Bryony."

"I said shut up." She pushes me away. "And take off your damn pants."

That's right. So fucking greedy.

You shouldn't want her like this.

But I do. I've had more lovers than I can count, fucked my way through the centuries with males and females, humans and gods. I've seen Bryony naked, had her spread out beneath me, mapped her body, taken her over and over.

And she still leaves me breathless.

I strip out of my trousers. Power thrums beneath my skin—Aethertide making everything sharper, more intense, more *present*. A fever cured only by her.

Bryony looks my naked body up and down, slow and hungry, then drags a palm down her face. "It's actually offensive how beautiful you are."

"That's the trick." I sink to my knees in the grass. Catching her by the hips, I draw her down until we're skin to skin, heartbeat to heartbeat. "Monsters are always beautiful. The prettier we are, the easier it is to fool a clever girl into letting us devour her." I drag my nose along her jaw, biting softly at her earlobe. "Would you want me even half as much if I were nice?"

"No," she sighs, melting into me. "I really wouldn't."

My blood sings at the admission—victory and satisfaction. Because this raw, messy want? Knowing that does it for her, too? *That* is so much better.

Because I'm exactly what she needs. What she craves in the dark.

"That's right." I walk my fingers up her spine, relishing her little shiver. "You don't need gentle. You need a lover with teeth."

Tipping forward, Bryony nips at my jaw. "Put your mouth between my thighs."

I lean down and bite the inside of her thigh, soothing the sting with my tongue. Then I'm shoving her legs wider. I look my fill, admiring the sight of her.

"Such a perfect pussy," I say. "Tell me I'm the first to worship you here."

A shiver rolls through her. She nods. Shy, almost.

Fuck, yes.

I grin slowly. "Let me show you how a god prays."

Starting slowly, I taste and tease with barely-there kisses. Stroking, exploring, getting her used to it. Learning her taste. She makes these sweet little noises, fingers curling into my hair.

"More," she moans.

"Patience," I say with a light nip on her thigh.

I thrust my fingers into her. She arches off the ground with a sharp cry. I grin, running my tongue over her in a long, slow lick. Then I press my mouth to her clit and suck, light at first. A moan shudders out of her. I do it again, harder this time.

"*Oh, fuck,*" she gasps.

There it is.

Her hands grasp my hair as I eat her out. I pin her hips, holding her still for every swipe of my tongue and plunge of my fingers. I could feast on this pussy for days.

Drawing out her pleasure is the sweetest torment. I crook my fingers just right and feel the tension singing through her, begging for release. But I'm patient. I take my time, memorizing which licks make her moan. What pace makes her shudder. The way I slide my tongue inside her pussy and her hand grips my hair hard enough to sting. I work her through it, letting her savor me on my knees for her. Worshipping her just like I promised.

"That's it," I murmur. "Ride that high for me."

Her breathing is shaky. She lifts her hips, chasing my mouth, fucking herself on my tongue. I grip her thighs hard and shove them wider, ruthless now.

She climaxes with my name on her lips. Her nails dig into my nape as I give her a few more little licks, ending with one last tender kiss to her inner thigh.

"I love the sounds you make when you come," I whisper, nipping up her body.

I pause to cup her breasts, flicking her nipple with my tongue. A gentle bite before licking a path to the other. She moans, fingers scrabbling against my shoulders.

"Fetch the dagger from my trousers." I nudge my hips forward, letting the head of my cock drag against her. "Side pocket. Mind the spring-loaded hilt."

She fumbles for my discarded clothes and drags the weapon free. Before I can blink, she has the point beneath my jaw. I have to bite back a groan. She's so damn beautiful.

"Leave it there until I tell you otherwise," I say.

Bryony lifts a brow, head tilting. "Does a knife at your throat turn you on, Wolf?"

"*You* with a knife at my throat turns me on. And it's a reminder of what we are to each other. We'll always exist on either side of this blade. No catching feelings, not even when I'm inside you."

I surge forward in a rough thrust that has her head slamming back into the grass. The edge of the dagger kisses my neck as I set a relentless rhythm. She's not pressing hard enough to cut me, but enough to remind me of the cost. Of the price I'll have to have her.

"Come on," she says between panting breaths. "I know you can fuck me better than that."

My hands tighten on her hips. "You want harder?"

"As hard as you can give me. Make me feel it for days."

A distant part of me knows I should stop before I'm past all saving. I could love her, I think. I could let her crack my ribcage and curl her fingers around the misshapen lump I call a heart, hold it gently. Sift through the scar tissue until she finds something worth salvaging.

But she won't find it. Because anything worth holding got burned out of me long ago. So instead, I'll give her everything else.

I fuck her harder. *Mean*. I want to make her hurt for me. My teeth find her breasts, her ribs, her stomach. Marking her up, branding her with the shape of my need. I chase our mutual destruction until everything narrows to ecstasy and pain.

"Evander," she gasps out.

"Say it again." I punctuate the words with a dirty grind. I hitch her legs higher around my waist, hitting that spot that makes her tremble. "I want to hear it."

"*Evander.*"

"*Louder.* Scream it for me."

"Evander!" Her nails draw blood. "Fuck, right there, don't stop!"

"What would the people of Luceni think," I rasp in her ear, never easing up, "of their princess begging a god to fuck her good?"

She whimpers when I slide my hand between us. Circling her clit, pushing her higher.

"You think they'd still bow if they knew?" I pant. "If they saw the marks on your thighs? The way you came apart for me? That their perfect, pure Princess of the Blood wanted it so hard she let me bend her over, lay her down, bite her, bruise her. Let me desecrate every fucking inch of her body. That her pussy gets wet for me before I even touch her. Come on, tell me. What would they think?"

Her nails dig into my shoulders. She doesn't answer.

"Do you even care?" I press.

"No." She locks her ankles around me to pull me deeper. "They didn't treat me like I was real."

She's right. Because the woman writhing beneath me isn't the one who stood before her subjects with that empty smile. This is Bryony—wild and demanding, the one who takes what she wants.

She's the fierce creature demanding *more, harder, now.*

"Know what I think?" I find a merciless rhythm that has her gasping with each thrust. "I think they had it all wrong. You never needed to be protected. You need *this*. To be dirtied up. Fucked out. Screaming my name."

She bites her lip. She's close. I can feel it in how she tightens around me.

"You don't belong on a pedestal," I manage between breaths. "You belong right here. Getting fucked beneath the stars. In the wild. In the dark. With me."

I grab her thigh and hitch it higher, watching her mouth fall open when I hit that perfect spot inside her. The knife digs in a little deeper. Climax hovers just out of reach, my veins heating. Sparks crackle along my skin. My wings ignite, and flames lick along my feathers.

Bryony's grip on my shoulder tightens. "*Evander!*"

She comes with a strangled cry, her body arching off the ground. The blade slips, slicing burning lines into my throat, and the sting makes everything sharper. Brighter. Blood trickles down my chest, spattering onto her pale skin.

I've never seen a canvas so beautiful.

I follow her over the edge. My hands grip her tight as I spill inside her, thrusting shallowly. My magic explodes outward and slams into the earth around us. A concussive wave of flames that burns the grass beneath us.

Then there's only silence. Just our breathing, the groan of branches around us, and the crackle of fire.

I tug the blade gently from Bryony's slack fingers and toss it aside to lift her into my arms. She makes a soft, contented sound. Only then does she notice the surrounding foliage.

"You've singed your garden," she says with a laugh.

I chuckle as I survey the damage. "I spared the roses."

Her lips skim my neck, right over the thin lines where she'd marked me. Our breathing is harsh as I carry her inside.

"I can't decide," she finally says, "if I'm going to kiss you or kill you when this is through."

"As long as you're the last thing I see in this fucked-up eternity of mine, I don't really care which one you pick."

As we pass the door with the obsidian seal, I reach out and brush my fingers over the carvings in a familiar ritual—a habit as ingrained as the instinct to grab for a weapon when threatened.

"Are you ever going to tell me what's behind that door?" she asks.

My jaw clenches. "No."

"Gory trophies? Jars of viscera?" She's prodding now, looking for weak points. Gaps in my armor she can worm her fingers into and pry apart.

I don't smile, not even to maintain this delicate illusion of tenderness. That place is as sacred to me as this realm.

"That room is not up for discussion."

I brace for her to argue. To pry and dig and excavate like she always does.

But Bryony just... settles. She rests her cheek against my shoulder and winds her arms loosely around my neck, a gesture so simple and sweet that it cracks my chest wide open.

I've murdered armies without blinking. Tortured enemies, ended bloodlines, and razed kingdoms to rubble and ash. But this? *This* is annihilating. This gesture of trust. Of softness.

Two things I sure as shit don't deserve.

And this is why she can never know what's in that room, I think as I shoulder into my bedchamber. All the dead things in there are for me, and they are the real dagger between us.

She'll never look at what we are the same way again.

I gently lay her on my sheets. Bruises mottle her skin, vivid smudges blooming across her breasts, her belly, her legs. My marks.

Mine.

I trail my knuckles over a bite on her inner thigh. "I can heal these for you if you'd like."

I'd rather lick them, I don't say.

"I'll wear them a bit longer," Bryony decides with a secret smile, stretching languidly. "I've earned them."

For a moment, I imagine keeping her like this—sprawled out in my bed. Well-fucked and satisfied, with my ownership unmistakable.

"Careful," she murmurs, eyes fixed on my face. "You're doing it again."

"Doing what?"

"Scheming."

I settle in bed next to her and pull her on top of me, groaning as she settles right over my cock. Right where she belongs. The rut-fever stirs again, demanding more.

"Just enjoying you while I can." I grasp her hips and guide her down, shuddering as I slide into her. "Enjoying this pussy, too."

"I suppose you'd better make the most of it, then," she says, riding me slowly, drawing it out. "It's temporary."

"Yeah, they do have that saying about mortal girls."

"What saying?"

I curl my fingers against her skin, setting the pace, lifting her up and down my cock. "Not for a long time, just for a good time."

The bed frame creaks as she rides me faster. "Know what humans say about gods?" She bites my earlobe, and I almost come right then. "That they'll fuck you then forget you. But I won't let you forget."

"Oh really?"

"That's right. When you take someone else into your bed in fifty, or a hundred, or a thousand years from now, all you're going to see is me. My face, when you shut your eyes. My taste, when you're kissing her. My voice, when you're inside her. I'm going to wreck you for everyone else." She rocks her hips in a slow grind that has me seeing stars. "I'm going to be your favorite memory."

Something in my chest goes tight. I can't look away from this fragile mortal woman who's embedded herself beneath my skin. Because she's right—I'm going to have to accept a world in which Bryony Devaliant no longer exists.

And I'll be the one holding the blade that ends her. I have to be. Because anything else would be a betrayal.

I swallow hard. "You think so?"

"Yes." She kisses me, soft and searching. "The most fun you'll ever have."

Maybe she's my penance. My *hamartia*, as the Vartenans would say—the fatal flaw that will be my undoing. The price I pay for all my sins.

"You asked me if this was just the Aethertide," I say, rolling us so I'm on top. Caging her beneath me, my wings flared. "A product of celestial meddling and biological imperative."

"And?" Her fingers trace patterns on my chest, right over my thundering heart.

"I'd crave you in any lifetime. Across every eternity. Every version of me would want every version of you, whether I lived one day or ten thousand years," I whisper against her mouth. "And damn me, you were a good time."

I wonder if she'll feel my touch for days. If she'll ache with the memory of us. I wonder if the bruises I've put on her body will linger—a reminder of what we are. Of all the blasphemous, brutal things we've done.

I'm going to be your favorite memory.

No, I think as I kiss her. *You're going to be my cruelest one.*

# 35

ALEXIOS

A THOUSAND CLAIMED voices crash through me, screaming their feelings all at once.

Love. Hate. Need. Their whining never stops. Every breath I take pulls more of their chaos into my lungs. I breathe in, and they're there. Breathe out, and they're still there.

It's unbearable.

Meanwhile, I've been fucking courtiers for thirty-five hours straight while Aethertide burns in my blood. I'd rather swallow broken glass than father a child with any of them, but my wants don't matter.

Because the realm is screaming at me.

Three centuries since the first rut hit after the Devouring, and it's only gotten worse. Back then, Scillari whispered and gave a gentle nudge. Now? It howls and forces gods together like rabid animals every hundred years.

But it won't stay that way, not with so few demis powerful enough to ascend and replace the Eternals we lost in the war. The magical deficit leaves the realm vulnerable and unstable. If we don't have more potential Eternals soon, Aethertide will be every damn year.

I shift uncomfortably on my throne. My cock is hard, and all I want to do is bite and tear and fuck until there's nothing left of me. Maybe I should just walk to Asteria's deepest ravine. See if even this immortal body can survive that fall. Because between the rut, holding the Shroud, and the voices…

I'm not going to last.

"Your Majesty?"

I look down at where a courtier kneels at the foot of the dais, another face I won't remember tomorrow. I've seen a hundred just like her.

They blur together after a while. Pretty dolls with breakable bones, something to use up and throw away. Just vessels to pour my madness into.

"Strip," I rasp. "Wait for me. Five minutes."

I need her right now. Need to slam into her and make her cry, to bleed her until the hunger stops. But I need her to wait more. Need to know I can still tell myself no. That I haven't completely lost my shit.

Five minutes. Three hundred seconds until I can forget, for a few moments, all the lives bound to mine. The needs that aren't my own. I'll drown them out, bury myself in sex until I can't think or feel anything else but animal need.

I hear her undressing—the soft rustle of fabric, the tiny nervous breaths she tries to hide.

Wait. Sixty seconds.

Wait. One hundred seconds.

Wait—

The chamber doors burst open. Bastien stalks in, shadow wings flaring, face remote and unreadable.

"Blade," I say, sitting up straighter. "You have news?"

He inclines his head, a tightness to the set of his shoulders I don't like. "The princess' corpse is still unaccounted for. I don't sense it anywhere in Vartena."

For a disorienting second, the snarled threads of the Shroud constrict around my chest, compressing and compressing until I'm certain my ribs will buckle inward. Hellevig's deficit left a gap in the veil's magic I'm still burning myself alive to hold together—all caused by that damn princess' flock.

"How difficult can it be," I grind out, "to locate one dead human? I marked her. Felt the connection snap when she died. My power leaves traces, Bastien. You should be able to track it blindfolded." I lift a hand to my temple, trying to massage away the ache. "Was there anything else? Or did you just come to tell me you can't do your job?"

He doesn't answer. Instead, his attention slides to the far wall where the naked courtier waits, her skin flushed, hair tumbling over her shoulders. His nostrils flare. Shadows curl around his boots.

I almost smile. We might be Eternals, but we're not above the failings of biology.

"Let me off the leash," he says, cold and flat, still staring at the demigoddess.

I study his face. Those black eyes that hold galaxies. Those shadow wings that never quite settle. Bastien without constraints isn't a weapon you wield; he's a natural disaster you point in a direction and hope to survive.

"Find another way to deal with rut." I give him a thin smile. "Do it the old-fashioned way and fuck it out like the rest of us. Or use your hand if you're still too disgusted by the idea of letting anyone touch you."

Low blow. I see the hit land.

A muscle in his jaw tics. "Not an option. Seventeen hours."

I rise to my feet, lightning dancing across my fingertips. "Seventeen hours," I repeat softly. "Like the twelve you took last centennial that left the western coast of Vartena a smoking crater?" I close the distance between us. "How do I know you won't slip up again and turn on my Claimed?"

"I've done the math."

"Fuck your math. When the rut-fever takes over and the bloodlust hits, your calculations won't mean shit. Try again."

"I can track the girl's corpse at full power."

My anger pauses. Now *that* is interesting.

Bryony Devaliant's missing corpse is becoming a problem. And problems make my head ache worse than it already does. I need Hellevig compliant, but I can't have that if they keep wailing for her remains.

"*Fifteen* hours." I seize his chin between my fingers, and a stillness goes through him at my touch. I know he hates this. "I'll even throw in a village of oathbreakers you can tear apart. Consider it a gift." My grip tightens. "But don't go near my Claimed again. You remember where you ended up, don't you, Blade?"

I feel that tiny flex in his jaw. The one that tells me he'd love to have his shadows tear me apart.

"All that dirt pressing down," I whisper, my lips close to his ear. "The darkness so complete you forget what light looks like. Twelve years buried alive was a kind punishment for breaking the Accords. There's a reason gods who want to die beg to be unmade and buried beneath the realm. They want to sleep. But you didn't sleep, did you? Imagine a century with nothing but our dead for company."

His pulse quickens beneath my fingertips. The only tell.

"I've lived it before, you know. When I was much younger than you are now, and still a demigod. My bones were so fragile. My father's other punishments were too extreme for an object lesson, so when I tell you it could be worse, I mean it. I doubt I spent much of the first thousand years of my existence not disciplined for some slight, real or fictitious. Imagine the weight of rocks crushing your lungs, the soil filling your mouth when you finally broke enough to scream." I drag my thumb along his jawline. "Your fingers bloody and broken, clawing upward through rock and dirt, inch by inch. Never knowing if you'd reach air. Never knowing if he's buried you too deep this time. Do you remember what it felt like to go mad down there? Because I do."

"Yes." The answer is flat, emotionless.

"Then we understand each other." I release him, returning to my throne. "Enjoy your village. Try not to make too much of a mess."

He leaves, the door booming shut behind him.

As I settle back on my throne, the whining static gnaws at the edges of my control. So many voices battering the inside of my skull. I can't think, I can't *breathe*...

From the corner of my eye, I catch a flash of purple—a fevered illusion. A glimpse of my sister's dress from the last day I saw her alive.

I squeeze my eyes shut. "Don't," I snarl at her. "Not now."

You can't keep going like this. My sister's voice. As if she's standing beside me and not a figment of my fracturing mind. *You're breaking yourself.*

"Your Majesty?"

That gentle voice drags me back to the present.

I lift my gaze to the courtier. Her pale wings—dove gray, delicate—are tucked tight against her spine.

"Come here." I pluck open the fastenings of my trousers and wrap my hand around my cock. "If you've changed your mind, now's the time to run. I won't punish you for refusing."

She hesitates, breath quickening.

Honestly, she should be afraid. I am ancient and hungry and only half-sane.

"I won't make this offer again." My tone is sharp. I don't have the time to soothe timid courtiers. "Decide."

The sweet scent of her desire fills my lungs as she draws near, and beneath it all, the clarion call of her blood. "Take what you need," she whispers, holding my gaze as she steps between my thighs. "My body is yours."

Thank fuck.

I grasp her hips and haul her into my lap, positioning her above my straining cock. A shift, an angling of bodies as I take care not to touch her wings—because even rut-stupid and half out of my mind, I remember the sanctity of a demi's wings. Then I bury myself inside her with a brutal thrust. She arches with a sharp cry.

I rock into her with ruthless, punishing strokes. Shoving deep, deeper, until my vision blurs and yes, more, *harder.*

Her pulse flutters against my fingertips where they cup her neck. I duck my head, lips brushing her skin.

"This is going to hurt," I murmur against her throat. "Try to keep the screaming to a minimum."

She swallows and nods.

And I rip into her jugular with my teeth.

Her blood floods my mouth, a rush of heat and copper tangling together on my tongue. I drink and drink, desperate and greedy. Losing myself in the wet heat of her, the drum of her heart, the sting of her nails sinking into my shoulders.

The Shroud's threads loosen infinitesimally, the crushing pressure on my chest easing to a dull throb. Not gone, never gone—but muted. Manageable.

For a few moments, I drift. Insensate. Nothing exists beyond this—the flex of muscle under skin, the rhythmic slap of flesh, the warmth of her. Aethertide's fever easing the more I fuck up into her.

Click-click-click.

Footsteps pierce the haze. I lift my head to see Zephyr framed in the doorway, arms crossed. Watching. Those black-and-silver mismatched eyes flick over the courtier, and something tightens in her features.

See anything of interest, Whisper? I keep moving, rolling my hips nice and slow now. *Something you want? Something you like?*

Zephyr unfolds her mind to me, the familiar walls and fortifications lowering. Her cool, collected thought patterns lap against my own, the only mind I know of that doesn't feel like plunging a hand into a bucket of glass shards. But it's not easy for her anymore; I sense the effort it takes, the strain to let me in.

After I sent her to Eternal Calder's court three hundred years ago, she came back different. Still Zephyr, but… less. There are pieces missing.

I remember that night. She had stood in my chambers with blood still drying under her fingernails, and her eyes had been empty.

"He needs to be put down," she'd said simply.

She told me enough—the bare minimum to justify killing Calder—but not what he'd done to put that look in her eyes.

Still, I did what kings do and eliminated the threat. While humans raided our villages and the realm went to shit, I dropped everything to deliver that judgment.

I put an Eternal in the ground for her.

After that, Zephyr built walls around herself that no one could scale. She'd never been particularly warm, but this was different. This was ice—the kind that burns when you touch it.

But on days like today, she keeps her headspace soft for me. Sanded down, nothing serrated to slice me open when I inevitably bleed into the secret spaces of her.

I'm making sure she'll survive your attentions mostly intact, Zephyr says. *You're not blessed with an endless supply of demis willing to play donor and bedmate.*

She'll live. Report.

You have a situation.

I give her a sharp smile. *Just one? Must be a slow day.*

She glares, motioning toward the exit. *Get rid of her. I've got news out of the Dark Court and I'm not giving it while you're balls deep. Finish up.*

Finish up? Hmm. I lean back and watch Zephyr as the demigoddess bounces on my cock, letting my gaze trail over her and imagine how my spymaster's glittering, light brown skin would look against my sheets. That long black hair undone and spread across my pillow. Her long legs would fit so nicely around my hips—that's one memory I've indulged in weak moments. She and I *fit*.

I imagine her glowing like starlight when I make her come.

You're staring, she murmurs.

You're letting me, I say back.

Her mismatched eyes flare. Does she like it? Does she hate it? She's not looking away.

I grip the courtier's hips harder, driving deeper. The demigoddess moans, but I barely hear her. Suddenly she's the best fuck I've had in a while, because I'm picturing Zephyr writhing against me. Zephyr's ragged breaths in my ear. Zephyr's pretty noises.

When I come, I make damn sure she sees my face and watches me spill with her name burning in my throat.

I want her to know.

Let her chalk this unforgivable slip in control up to the fever. Let her believe it's only the mindless sex, the madness of Aethertide that pushes even kings to their knees, and not the truth that's been eating me alive since before she built those walls around her mind.

I let her believe the biggest lie I've ever told.

The courtier slumps forward against my chest. I hitch my hips up and ease her off me, ignoring her moan of protest as I set her carefully on her feet. Her pupils are blown wide. Blood still pours from the ragged wound in her neck, soaking the tops of her breasts. There's something vacant in her expression. Something I put there.

"Get yourself to a healer," I tell her. It's as close to gentle as I know how to be. "Take the rest of the day to recuperate. You've earned it."

She bobs an unsteady curtsy and mumbles words that might be *yes, my king,* or *thank you, my king.*

Once Zephyr and I are alone, I allow my shoulders to slump. The lightning that's been dancing along my skin all day fades to sparks.

"Go on, then," I say roughly. "Don't leave me in suspense. You didn't come here to watch me fuck."

Her lips tighten. For a moment, I think she might actually say something about what just happened between us.

She doesn't.

"Missing demis." Zephyr's all business now. "I have confirmed disappearances in Nyholm aside from our own here in Asteria. Wraith is trying to manage the situation."

I scrape my palm down my face. "Wonderful. So the fleshtrade is slipping through wards all along the Shroud."

"They say the king's secrets say something about the king." Zephyr folds her arms across her chest.

"Then they say I'm falling apart, don't they, Whisper?" I give her a bleak smile. "There's still time to turn this to our advantage. After I killed Calder, Severin wasn't exactly feeling charitable. He only agreed to peace with Vartena if I took on the Shroud and the Claimed alone."

"You punched him in the face, Storm."

"He touched what wasn't his to touch," I remind her. "I wasn't concerned with pleasantries. But the cracks in the veil make my position clear."

It galls me to admit to weakness, but Zephyr's seen me at my lowest. If I can't be honest with her, who's left?

Her eyes sharpen, that keen strategist's brain working. "You think this crisis will bring Wraith back to negotiate?"

"Depends on how desperate he is. Missing demis across the realm changes things. Makes for good leverage." I pause, watching her face carefully. "Especially if I told him the truth about his brother."

She yanks at her jacket collar like it's suddenly too tight. "If any part of you still values what you once had with Severin, you won't use that information. He loved his brother. It's not something you can take back."

I hate that damn uniform. The buttons up to her neck, sleeves hiding all of her skin. I remember her that night at the Court of Illusions—the green dress that clung to her curves, the bare shoulders I couldn't stop staring at. Couldn't stop touching. And she'd let me. For one night, she'd let me put my hands on her.

Now, every inch of her is hidden away. From everyone. From *me*.

It's not just a uniform; it's a wall.

"Look at me."

She does.

"I know why Calder had to die. What I don't know is what he did to you after the winter ball."

Her nostrils flare slightly. "He found out what I am."

My fingers curl into the throne's armrests. *No one* knows what Zephyr is except me. She'd never be safe. Any sick fuck who wanted power would be after her.

"Whisper." My voice goes soft, tender. Only for her. "I need to know what he did to you, sweet girl."

The endearment slips out before I can stop it. It's been three hundred years since I last called her that. Since Calder.

I hear her breath stutter. Her lips part.

Then she tugs on that jacket again and straightens. "What happened in the Court of Illusions stays buried with Calder," she says flatly. "My trauma isn't currency for your political games. Let Wraith believe whatever the fuck he wants about his brother. I won't relive it just so you can have leverage."

Every time I press, she builds her walls higher. Already, I can feel her mind pulling back, some of those sanded edges sharpening in defense. Telling me to back off.

So I do.

"All right. Then I need intelligence. Find out how severe the situation is with the demis in the Dark Court. I need to know what I'm dealing with before I make my move."

Zephyr's mouth thins, but she jerks her chin in grudging assent. "Fine. But a word of caution, if I may be so bold—"

"You may not."

"—strong-arming Wraith strikes me as unwise."

"Objection noted."

For a small eternity, she just looks at me in that unflinching way she's done for thousands of years. No doubt marking every cracked, battered piece of me. We go too far back for pretenses. She knew me before my ascension. Before death and duty broke me open and stitched me together wrong.

"Understood," she says. "In the meantime…"

She arches a pointed brow at me. At my disheveled state. My skin is heating with another wave of rut-fever, and my cock's already hardening.

I groan. "Don't start."

"You need to finish out Aethertide—*uninterrupted*—before doing any complex diplomacy. Get your head out of your ass. This is a shit time for politics."

"You're overstepping," I say mildly.

"I'm worried."

"I'm fine."

"You're not."

"You're within smiting range," I remind her.

"Please. In your current state? I'd like to see you try."

A rough chuckle claws its way out of me. "Bold words for the female who interrupted my *other* business." I stretch my wings wide and relax against the throne, letting my thighs fall open. "Unless you're volunteering to pick up where the other one left off?"

Zephyr's mouth parts, a brief tell in an otherwise flawless facade. Her stare snags on my bare skin, trailing over my tattoos to my hard cock. Aethertide might not slam into the females as viciously, but she's not immune. And as far as I know, there's no one warming her bed.

I wonder who's ever earned that particular privilege. If she's as wound tight in private. If she lets another male see what's beneath that high collar.

She shakes her head. "You already know the answer to that."

I pause, weighing my next words. Tasting their shape, their vulnerability. "It doesn't have to change anything, Whisper. Not with us."

Empires have risen and fallen in all the time I've wanted Zephyr. I waited nearly seven thousand years just to kiss her, and never again had the privilege. The first and last time was at Calder's winter ball—and then she'd retreated behind ice and distance.

For an instant, her composure slips. "I won't complicate my duties with intimacy, not even for celestial events. If you need release and a blood donor to find supplementary power to hold the Shroud, find it between a courtier's thighs. They're gagging for it."

"I'd never feed from you, Whisper." I give her a small smile. "What if I just wanted you this one centennial?"

Zephyr's expression darkens. The air goes charged with tension as she closes the distance between us on silent feet, black wings flaring. The flat of her blade kisses my neck, its edge dimpling my skin.

Her eyes hold mine. "Storm," she says, very softly, "I'm not a toy to be bent to your whims. I'm the only friend you have left who isn't afraid to tell you when you're being an idiot. That doesn't make me a convenient cunt to fuck during Aethertide."

Tipping my head back, I bare my jugular to her. The only creature alive who can press a knife to my throat and live. "Have I ever told you that you're my favorite? And not a *convenient* anything."

"Thank you. But I'd prefer compliments when you're not thinking with your dick." She pulls the dagger away and sheathes it.

"You're right," I say. "My apologies. I'm not handling this well."

Her gaze softens again. "You're a wreck."

I catch her hand in mine. "What would I do without you?"

"Crash and burn, most likely. Want me to send in another courtier?"

"Someone durable, please." I release her. "Don't stay."

I can't have her here close enough to touch. To want. Not during Aethertide.

An emotion flashes across Zephyr's face before she tamps it down and replaces it with that mask of cool professionalism. A curt nod, and then she's gone.

36

EVANDER

THE SCENT OF blood hits me before I even open my eyes.

Bastien is here.

I roll out of bed and grab my pants off the floor, almost tripping as I yank them on. The pressure of his power prickles along my skin.

Bryony's still asleep, her silvery hair spilling across my pillow. The sheet's slipped to her waist, revealing the constellation of bruises I painted across her torso.

Something twists hard in my chest, but I push whatever emotion this is down deep and lock it away. My brother will sense the weakness.

The garden air is warm as I step outside. Bastien stands among our mother's roses, blood garish in his bone-white hair, splashed across the stark angles of his face. It's dripping from his fingers onto the soil. The fading cerulean and pink aetherlight makes the red look almost black against his skin.

His eyes stop me cold—twin voids of obsidian, empty of all recognition. The eyes of something feral that's slipped its chain. Then his power flexes, vast and crushing, as if it's being shoved down my throat.

Fuck. Alexios let him off his leash for Aethertide.

"Bas." I keep my tone deliberately light, like I can't taste the violence saturating the air. Like I don't notice the madness. "I see you've been enjoying yourself."

Nothing. No reaction. Just that dead-eyed stare. "Made some

corrections." His answer is devoid of inflection. Mechanical. "Restored the balance."

Balance. The word sends a chill through me. When the rut-madness takes him deep like this, everything becomes equations. Blood debt to be paid. Red ink to be balanced in ledgers only he can see.

He turns back to the roses. "I planted these with Mother. Did you know?"

"No," I say carefully. I touch the knife at my waist, ready for anything. He's unpredictable when he's like this.

"We spent hours out here together before you were born." His voice softens, almost normal. Almost like my brother again. "She showed me how to prepare the soil, how deep to plant each bush. Which ones needed more sun. She let me name them. I called that one Vasha, for our grandmother." He crushes the rose in his fist, blood and petals mixing together. "I was only one hundred and ten when you were born. You were this tiny, screaming thing. Red-faced. Squirming. Your wings weren't even formed yet, just nubs on your back. Your little fists kept punching the air." He looks at me. "You were always so fucking loud, Evander. I hated you the moment she put you in my arms."

I abandon the knife and begin pulling my power instead. Bastien doesn't reminisce. Ever.

"Babies are loud." I keep myself calm. Controlled. "It's what they do."

"That's what Mother said. She told me I needed to look after you, because brothers protect each other. So I taught you to fly. Remember?"

My chest tightens as I recall the two of us soaring over the Osbu, his starlit feathers to my gold. He'd been my brother then, not this stranger wearing Bastien's skin. I would have done anything for him, sacrificed whatever I had to.

Like craft wings out of the shadows, even if it nearly killed me.

"Yeah," I say softly. "I remember."

"You were so small. But you were fast, and so eager to keep

up." His thumb traces over a thorn. "I got used to having you around and following me everywhere. Asking endless questions. I picked you up when you fell. I learned to love you." Some real emotion flickers in those black eyes. "As much as I'm capable of loving anything. Which is why I can't stand it when you lie to me."

I don't ask what he means or why he's here after avoiding my tower for decades. I already know.

An image of Bryony flashes without warning—her hair resting on my pillow, body marked by my fingertips and teeth, soft and sleep-warm in my bed—

I shove the memories down deep, but not quickly enough.

Bastien's head tilts. "You're leaking emotion all over the place. Arousal. Possessiveness. Frustration..."

"It's Aethertide," I snap. "I'm not a puzzle for you to solve, so keep your prying ass out of my head. I'm not in the mood for nostalgia."

I'm an idiot for dropping my guard like that. I might as well have sent Bastien an engraved invitation to carve her up.

His power unfurls, testing my defenses. Those pitiless eyes fix on me as he closes the distance between us.

This is the monster.

This is not my brother.

"While you've been rutting like an animal," he says, "I've been in Vartena looking for Bryony Devaliant's corpse. And her body is nowhere to be found."

My blood turns to ice. I know that keen focus in his voice. He's latched on to the scent of betrayal, and he won't let go until he's torn it open to see what bleeds.

Bastien steps closer, until we're breathing the same air. "So I tracked her body to Scillari. And the only trace of her I can sense"—he inhales deeply, deliberately—"is here. With you. So I'll ask once, and don't lie to me. Why is her scent all over you?"

I only have a split second to brace myself before his power slams into my psychic walls hard enough to rattle my teeth. He scrabbles through my mind, seeking a way in, a vulnerability. Greedy for all the secret moments I've stolen with her. Moments I can't let him see.

The feel of her in my arms, and the taste of her skin against my tongue. The little gasps and sighs she makes when I—

"Enough!"

Light explodes from me in a violent burst. Bastien stumbles backward as I unleash everything I have. My wings snap out, the flames licking up toward the night sky. Heat singes the air. His shadows rise to meet me, swallowing my light while my flames burn through his power. Soil cracks under our feet. The atmosphere thickens and squeezes my lungs as I call every bit of magic I can access before Alexios' invisible collar chokes me off. I'm leashed and Bastien isn't, and if he decides to slaughter Bryony in her sleep, I can't stop him.

"Remember who you're threatening," I snarl as my wings flare brighter. Hotter. The roses around us begin to wither and smoke. "Try forcing your way into my head again, and I'll tear you apart."

A vein pulses at Bastien's temple. His face is cold as ever, but his eyes—there's a banked fire there. Something ugly and wild that I haven't seen since the war.

"Is. She. Breathing? Is she in *our mother's* tower? Have you been hiding her all this time?"

His shadows stretch and grow, devouring everything until the garden disappears. Until the stars and aetherlight above us are gone, and there's nothing but endless black and the two of us standing in it.

I meet his gaze and don't flinch. "Yes, she's alive. And you know what? She's my assignment, not yours."

A blade to the belly would be kinder than this. If he saw even a glimpse of how she's crawled under my skin…

He'd destroy her. Tonight.

In our native tongue, we had a word for this feeling. *Byargski*. The gnawing dread when the thing you want most is slipping through your fingers and you're powerless to stop it. That bone-deep certainty that a reckoning is bearing down on you like an avalanche.

And right now? That reckoning is wearing my brother's face, and it's out for blood.

"Swear it," Bastien says. "Swear you haven't Claimed her. That you haven't soulbonded with her."

"I haven't." Not a lie. "She doesn't mean a damn thing."

I say it like my chest doesn't ache when she smiles, when she breathes, when she exists in the same space as me. Because none of it matters; I'm still going to end her. That hasn't changed.

But I need to be convincing.

"Fuck's sake, Bas. It's been centuries since I took my time killing a Devaliant, and this one has a mouth that's good for more than talking." I shrug. "She's a nice piece of ass to enjoy while I'm bored. It's just fun."

His expression goes colder. "*Fun.* They aren't meant for fun. Not after what they did." There's a fine tremor running through him now. "I've seen the older sister. You know why they glow like that. Why are you keeping her?"

There it is—another fracture in his control. A hitch in his breathing, there and gone too fast to track. And I see him. The *real* him, the brother I knew before the world broke him and carved out everything soft.

I wish I could serve Bryony up to him on a platter. Let him have his fill of Devaliant blood, drown himself in it, if it meant never having to see that look on his face again. That awful, empty despair. What kind of brother am I that I can't even do that?

But I can't. Because hating her turned into needing her when I wasn't looking, and now I'm lost. Every time I picture carving into her and watching the light fade from her eyes, something inside me riots.

Sentiment. In its most lethal form.

"Because it's not enough to tear a Devaliant apart," I say, lying to him. Lying to myself. "I want to break her first. Get her to trust me. The other day, she tried telling me she wasn't catching feelings, but she looks at me like what we're doing is more than just fucking. You want to know how to hurt a Devaliant? Let her think she's special. Then let her realize she's been spreading her legs for the monster who's going to slit her throat anyway. It was all a game she thought she could win."

I don't tell him how I traced her freckles last night while she slept. Don't tell him I'm counting heartbeats instead of plotting where to stick my knife.

"That had better be all this is," Bastien says. "You swore you'd never abandon me. Not for anything."

He thinks I've lost my way. That this fixation has made me weak, compromised me. And maybe he's right. Maybe Bryony has dug her claws in so deep I'll still be trying to get them out ten thousand years from now.

Doesn't make it hurt any less—the accusation, the doubt.

I square my shoulders. "I haven't forgotten."

For a moment, neither of us moves. Then Bastien steps forward. His fist cracks into my jaw hard enough to snap my head back. White-hot pain blooms, copper flooding my mouth.

"The princess gets five days," he says, his voice lethally soft. "You can shatter her precious, preconceived notions and savor the betrayal in her eyes before you end her miserable existence. Carve her up. Bathe in her blood. Fuck her corpse, for all I care."

His eyes are twin black holes. I wonder, distantly, if this is what mortals see before they die. If this is the Void that greets them, cold and eternal.

"But if you're lying to me," he breathes, "if you Claim her, or worse, soulbond with her? I'll dig my fingers into your chest and crush your traitorous heart in my fist."

I think he loves me in whatever broken way he still can.

I think he hates Devaliants more.

37

BRYONY

THE FIRST TIME I let a man fool me, he cut open my throat.

Five months after my father died, the court decided we'd mourned enough. Summer meant festival time in Luceni, and nobles from across Vartena came to dance, drink our country's wine, and meet the three princesses of marriageable age.

Percival Whitworth was from Brevig. He asked my cousin Odessa to dance first—proper protocol—but his eyes never left me. Not once.

He had this smile. One dimple, right corner. The kind that makes something low in your belly tighten. When he took my hand for a waltz, I noticed that he had a deep voice that made me blush. His hand at my waist felt different than the dance instructor's. Warmer. Intentional.

After, he'd poured wine into a goblet and handed it to me. "Show me the festival," he'd said.

We wandered between the stalls that servants had spent days setting up on palace grounds. Lanterns were lit everywhere, strung from trees and posts. The air had smelled like cinnamon and summer flowers.

I remember his laugh. The way his fingers brushed mine and his palm settled on my lower back. Now I understand—a princess who rarely left the palace made for easy prey. I heard stories on my father's knee about wrathful gods, but I was not warned about what men do to the women who anger them.

So when Percival Whitworth asked me to follow him into the woods, I went without hesitation.

His lips were soft. That surprised me. I liked kissing, the weight of someone else's mouth on mine, the warm press of a man's body. I'd only kissed two boys years before that, behind columns during dance lessons. This felt more real.

Until his hand shoved up my skirts.

I pushed against his chest. "Stop."

His grip tightened. His eyes changed as he pushed back harder and rougher.

"No." The word felt strange in my mouth. Princesses weren't supposed to say it; we were taught to nod and smile and agree. "No."

"Shut up," he hissed, all that charm vanishing like it had never existed. "You can't be all that different from your slut sister."

He pressed a blade to my neck to quiet me.

I struggled anyway. A guard on patrol heard me and intervened. Percival didn't run or cower, just stared down at me while the guard's sword pressed into his back, like I was the one who'd done something wrong. Like I'd disappointed him.

He slashed the dagger across my throat before the guard could get him off me. My scar is a reminder that a man will still smile when he plans to hurt you.

But some lessons you have to learn twice.

Evander's words to his brother echo through my thoughts as I slide beneath the sheets.

Let her think she's special. Then let her realize she's been spreading her legs for the monster who's going to slit her throat anyway.

I've always known what he is from that very first glimpse of him in the Hellevig palace woods. But hearing him talk about toying with me? It lodges like glass behind my ribs. It hurts so much I can't breathe through it.

The door clicks open, spilling light across the floor.

"Bryony?" His voice is dark and intimate. Tender. Like he gives a damn.

Like he isn't trying to soften me up to hurt me worse later.

I pretend to be asleep, like I've been here this whole time. As if I hadn't sneaked into the gardens and eavesdropped on him with his brother. The mattress dips as he climbs in beside me, his palm skimming over my waist. My jaw clenches.

Percival Whitworth's hands were soft until they weren't.

"Wake up. My rut-fever's broken," he breathes against my ear. "There's something I want to show you."

I tense. Is this it? The moment he slides a blade in?

Swallowing around the sudden tightness in my throat, I roll over to face him. "What is it?" The question comes out small.

Something complicated, almost like regret, ripples across Evander's features. There and gone in a blink—an illusion, maybe.

Then he's grabbing my chemise from the floor and pulling it over my head. "A surprise. Do you trust me?"

Four simple words that rip through me.

I want to break her first. Get her to trust me.

The cold reality of it knifes deep. This strange, fragile thing between us is nothing more than an illusion. It's the same game we've been playing since he came into my bedroom in Hellevig and pressed his dagger to my throat.

What are you doing?

Playing with my food before eating it.

I shove the hurt down, lock it up tight. "For tonight, I trust you. Just for tonight."

And never again.

His breath hitches. Then he's sliding his arms beneath me and scooping me up, carrying me out to the garden.

The roses are painted in opalescent shades by Aethertide, the usual pulsing red glow more like starlight now. The air is thick with the flowers' decadent perfume.

"Close your eyes." When I tense, he gentles me with a squeeze, ducking his head to nuzzle into my hair. "We're just flying."

Okay. He's still playing with me, then.

So I let my eyes flutter shut, surrendering to the familiar

swoop in my stomach as he launches us skyward. The wind whips through my hair. I press my face into the crook of his neck and inhale, memorizing the scent of him, the way his skin feels against mine. The pressure of his fingers as he traces idle patterns over my spine.

I want to capture this stolen moment in amber before he turns on me. I'm going to remember what a liar looks like, sounds like, smells like.

At the end, I won't beg.

His lips graze my temple. "Look, Bryony."

The sight steals the air from my lungs.

Color, so much color. Indigos and rouges, emeralds and golds all tangling together, the stars strewn through the expanse like diamonds on black velvet. Aethertide gentled, but no less lovely. The celestial storm ripples and flows, its reflection shimmering on the placid surface of the Osbu until sea and sky meld together.

And in the water, as far as I can see, are ribbons of turquoise and purple. They glow against the black like entire galaxies trapped in the depths of the sea. Each wave sends another ripple through the hues, shifting shades.

"It's beautiful," I say.

Is that what this is? A final tender moment before he kills me?

"Aethertide's light activates bioluminescent algae in the water," Evander tells me, spiraling us down to a narrow crescent of the shore. He alights on the sand, bare feet sinking in. "Would've been a shame for you to sleep through a once-in-a-century event."

He lowers me to the ground.

"I suppose I won't be around for the next one," I say, stepping away. It comes out too flat, too raw.

Evander goes still, hands flexing at his sides.

I don't wait for his reply before stripping off my chemise and tossing it aside. The night air pebbles my skin as I wade out into the shallows. Effervescent streaks of teal and lavender swirl around my calves with each step, leaving glowing contrails in my wake.

Fabric rustles behind me, followed by the soft noise of clothing hitting the sand.

"Never took you for the indecent bathing sort," Evander calls.

So we're not going to talk about it, then. We're still going to play pretend. One last game for Aethertide, while he's still Evander and not the Wolf.

One last game before I lose.

I glance over my shoulder. The aetherlight loves him, gilding the sculpted planes of his body as he strides into the surf after me. It catches in his tawny feathers as he flexes his wings. What was it he told me last night?

Monsters are always beautiful. The prettier we are, the easier it is to fool a clever girl into letting us devour her.

But I wasn't clever, was I? I was so, so stupid.

"I figured I should live a little." I flash him a brittle smile. "Enjoy the scenery before it's ripped away."

His eyes flare, lips compressing into a flat, bloodless line.

And then he's on me. His mouth is gentle against mine, the barest pressure. As if he's savoring the taste of me. I shiver as his kisses skim my cheekbone, my temple, my jaw. He's breathing me in like he's trying to pull me into his lungs and keep me there.

He's fucking with me. I know that. The thing is, he never lied about what this was, never promised me anything. But somewhere between his healing hands on my wounds and his body over mine in the dark, *I'm* the idiot who let myself believe this might be real.

That he might decide to let me live, after all.

"What would you think," he murmurs, "if I took my time tonight? Kissed every inch of your skin? Learned what you taste like under the stars?"

I hate him. I hate him so much for this.

It's so easy to sink into him, to surrender to the seductive pull and let him take me apart. To pretend, just for a little while longer, that he isn't meticulously planning my destruction even as he holds me like I'm something precious. Something worthy of worship.

It's been centuries since I took my time killing a Devaliant. And this one has a mouth that's good for more than talking.

I pull away. "How about a game first?" I ask with forced lightness.

His head tilts. "What sort of game?"

The kind where I dig my fingers into all his soft, hidden places, and pry up his secrets. Discover why he and his brother hate my family.

I deserve that much.

"Answer a handful of questions honestly. Think you can manage that?"

His expression sharpens. "Only if you agree to the same."

"I suppose that's only fair. We each get three chances to refuse before forfeiting victory to your opponent. The winner chooses the penalty, and the loser endures."

"And the prize?"

I lift my gaze to his. "Complete surrender."

She's a nice piece of ass to enjoy while I'm bored.

Evander's hand finds my wrist beneath the water, his thumb sweeping over my pulse in a deliberate caress. Teasing. "I accept your terms. Ask your question."

I don't even pause to think. "Before you were Alexios' Wolf, who were you?"

Something dark passes through his features. For a moment, I think he'll refuse to answer.

"A prince," he says flatly.

A startled sound leaves me. "An actual prince? With a crown and everything? Of where?"

I try to picture him in court finery, but it's impossible to reconcile with the savage god before me.

Evander smirks. "You're up to four questions, greedy girl. But I'll indulge you. My brother and I were princes of Turpori."

"The Court of Radiance?" I can't hide my surprise.

Our history books barely survived the war, but I'd read what little remained. Turpori was a territory of light and metal, ruled by Astraea, who was ancient even among the Eternals. She'd been one of the last to fall before the Accords were struck. I could never figure out how humans had managed to kill a goddess that old and powerful.

Evander nods. "When my mother—" His voice catches, and my heart squeezes painfully. "When she died, her territory was divided between Alexios and Severin. That's our way. Land always returns to surviving Eternals."

I want to reach for him and smooth my fingers over the stark lines of his face until that grief eases. Until I remember—

She looks at me like what we're doing is more than just fucking.

So I say nothing.

He gives his head a sharp shake as if to dislodge the memories. "I've answered you honestly. Now it's my turn." His eyes rake over me in a slow, deliberate sweep of my body. "Have I lived up to all those sordid stories your people tell about me?"

Under any other circumstances, I'd assume he was fishing for compliments. But right now, I recognize it for what it is: armor. He's trying to reestablish our usual push and pull. Our familiar roles.

I'll allow it. Just this once.

"I suppose you've shown a flash of legend from time to time," I say.

His mouth lifts in genuine amusement. "Well, now I'm intrigued. Elaborate for me? Unless you'd like to use one of those vetoes."

"The bards had plenty to say about you. I think it started with all the girls who got wet just looking at your face in the temple murals. But they left out some details. I never heard a single story about how the Wolf likes to fuck the women he's planning to butcher."

Something in his face shuts down like a door slamming closed. "No," he says. "You wouldn't have. Since you're the first."

It's hard to think past the sudden roaring static in my head. The reckless, destructive need sharpening its claws in my chest, as if I'm standing at the edge of a precipice and counting down to the fall.

You want to know how to hurt a Devaliant? Let her think she's special.

Evander shifts. The aetherlight dances over his wings, catching the top gold feathers. A drop of water glides down his cheek as he stares at me. "What are those five scars on your inner arm for?" he asks quietly.

"I'll trade you my scar stories if you tell me what's behind the door with the obsidian seal."

His hands curl into fists beneath the water. "No."

"Then my answer is the same. Ask me something else."

The water laps against my skin in the silence. A few seconds pass in silence.

"What we do together in my bed," he says finally, his thigh brushing mine in the water. "These games we play. Do you enjoy it? Does it make you feel good?"

As if he needs verbal confirmation of what he can undoubtedly scent on my skin—arousal, the lingering musk of sex, all of it betraying me more than any confession. And with it, all the complicated emotions.

Inhale. Exhale. Shove the truth down deep and bury it.

"I like everything you do to me," I whisper.

And right now, I hate him for it.

A pleased smile tugs at his mouth. "Good."

I need to hit back hard before he crawls any deeper under my skin.

"Why are you and your brother bound to Alexios?" I ask.

His body goes rigid. Something dangerous flashes across his face. *Don't*, that expression tells me. *Don't even fucking think about it.*

But I don't stop. Can't stop. "I thought Eternals were all equal. So, how did that happen? Why don't you rule territory if it's Scillarian practice for demesnes to pass to the remaining Eternals after one dies?"

Sparks dance across his wings. His beautiful face hardens into something ancient and terrible. "That," he says, his voice dangerously soft, "was a whole fucking inquisition crammed into a transparent attempt to knock me off-balance."

"Feeling overwhelmed?" I smirk. "Fine. I'll be nice. Pick one to answer and I'll save the rest for later."

"Non-negotiable. To all of them."

Dark satisfaction rises. First blood to me. I've found a chink in his armor, and the ruin-hungry creature pacing in me thirsts for more—more chaos, more destruction.

More truth.

I close my fingers around Evander's wrist. "What happened to your mother?"

"Non-negotiable." A warning snarl.

A smarter person would retreat, but he's going to kill me anyway. Might as well burn everything down first.

"Why do you hate my family?"

His hand tightens on my wrist. "*Non-fucking-negotiable.*"

Power lashes from him in blistering waves, and a sudden pressure compresses my lungs. The sea churns and hisses. But I don't so much as flinch. We were always heading here—every touch, every night together, every damn day, was just the path leading to this inevitable cliff.

"Why does my skin glow like this?" My voice rises, almost shouting now. "You want to know all my secrets? Want to pull me apart? Then give me something back."

I've seen the older sister. You know why they glow like that.

"Non-negotiable! Fucking *stop*."

I laugh bitterly. "That's really rich. You get to poke around in all my broken places, drag out every ugly thing inside me. But the second I touch yours, it's non-negotiable?"

He shoves me against the sea rocks, irises blazing with inner fire. "Shut your mouth. Or I swear to you, this ends with my teeth in your throat."

But it's too late. I've already hurled myself off the cliff. My rage burns higher, hotter, consuming any shred of sense. And now there's nothing left but the freefall and the promise of impact.

"You know what? Let's change our negotiation. We both know how this ends, so just do it already. Kill me." Angry tears burn my eyes, but I blink them back. "You've had your fun, right?

Fucked the stupid Devaliant princess until she forgot what you are? Was I a good piece of ass, do you think? Worth the effort?"

Evander's eyes widen just a fraction. His lips part. No sound comes out.

Now he gets it. Now he knows I heard him talking to his brother about using me up and throwing me away when he's done.

"Say something," I whisper, hating how unsteady I sound.

Nothing. Just the sound of waves between us.

"Right." I let out a bitter laugh. "You wanted to know the stories they tell about you in Vartena? They love warning us about the Wolf's cruelty. How you make your victims scream and beg before you finish them. But they leave out the real artistry, don't they? The part you love most?"

He doesn't react beyond the slow clench of his jaw.

"Those stories never mention how much you get off on mindfucking the women you screw." I slam my palm hard into his chest. "Telling me that you're trying out giving a shit? You really know how to lay it on thick, don't you? All those perfect words. Those calculated touches. The way you look at me when we're alone. But I'm nothing to you, right? Just a disposable fuck-toy to pass the time! A nice piece of ass dumb enough to bend over for her executioner!"

His chest rises and falls too fast for someone trying to look calm.

"You think I don't see it?" I step closer until my chest touches his. "Give the Devaliant bitch a knife, and let her think she matters. Let her think she has control." I grab his arm when he tries to turn away. "No. *You look at me.*"

His golden eyes meet mine, unreadable.

"Because what else would a woman who's only known blood and death want more than a taste of power? That's the real trick, isn't it? Convince her she's special before you gut her. Make her death so much worse than anything she's known on that altar. I have to hand it to you, Wolf. Breaking someone before you kill them? That's skill."

Evander's face is cold, but I catch the nearly imperceptible flinch, there and gone.

Good, I think savagely. *Bleed for me. Feel it. Hurt.*

"I was so wrong," I say. "When I said you were just like Alexios? Turns out, you're actually worse."

I push him away and wade to the beach, where I yank my chemise over my head.

"We're done here. Take me back to the tower," I tell him. "Now."

We touch down in the gardens, and Evander sets me on my feet. He turns away. Done with me.

But I'm not done with him.

"Your room," I call out, and he freezes mid-step. "You failed the game on the beach. I want what I won."

His shoulders rise with a deep breath, and I can almost hear him counting to ten in his head. When he pivots halfway, the look he gives me could skin a person alive. Like he's calculating how small the pieces should be when he's finished with me.

But he doesn't say a word. Just turns and stalks toward the tower.

Fine.

I follow. He reaches his room first, shedding his trousers. Flawless skin and muscle and golden feathers gleam in the aetherlight slanting through the window.

"Well?" He spreads his arms. "Get on with it. I assume you didn't drag me here to gawk."

"On the bed." I remove my chemise, baring myself completely. "On your back, arms above your head. Spread your wings."

For a moment, I'm sure he'll refuse. That he'll lunge and tear me apart for the audacity.

But then he goes to the bed and settles against the sheets. His wings fan out wide until the tips brush the floor, and I forget how to breathe. He's a decadent expanse of golden skin, his glowing eyes tracking my every move. Laid out like a sacrifice.

Only there's nothing submissive in the way he watches me.

Come unravel me, that sinful sprawl sneers. *Conquer me if you think you can weather the cost.*

Slow and deliberate, I set one knee on the mattress. His fingers flex, digging into the sheets, and a breath hisses through his teeth. As if it's taking everything in him not to lunge up and drag me under him.

I've never felt control like this. Towering over a god, bending him to my whims. It's a rush I never want to come down from.

I crawl up his body in a slow slide of skin against skin. He shudders, his throat working around a swallow. I take my time touching him, tracing my fingers over his chest, brushing my lips over his stomach. I want to memorize this. Hoard it like an ill-gotten treasure before he rips it away.

This is power—the flutter of his pulse beneath my palms, the strain of his muscles as he fights to remain motionless, compliant. The way his breath hitches when I finally settle on top of him.

This god is mine. Mine to ruin. Mine to defile.

He's a liar, but there's no truth more honest than his heartbeat, and it just sped up for me.

"So what'll it be, nemesis?" Evander sneers. "How will you make me sorry?"

I slap a palm over his mouth and settle my weight more firmly across his hips. "Shut the fuck up and be still. It's my turn to use *you*. And the only words I want to hear out of that filthy mouth are my name and *please*." I breathe the last word into the infinitesimal space between us. "*Please* is the only prayer I'll accept from you, Wolf. It's the price you pay to touch me again."

I grind my pussy along the rigid length of his cock. Evander makes a choked sound, almost pained.

Then I reach between us, position him, and sink down. The stretch burns, but I don't stop until I've taken all of him. Evander's eyes slam shut as a low groan claws out of his throat. His hands grip the headboard, muscles straining as he fights to keep still, to let me set the pace.

"Eyes open," I say, scratching my nails down his stomach. "Watch who's fucking you."

Those gold eyes snap to mine, and there's fury there. Hunger. Something else I don't want to name. I roll my hips, testing, taking him deeper.

"That's it," I gasp, working myself on the thick glide of his cock. "No more games, no more pretending. Tonight, I want you fully present. I want this burned into your memory. So when you finally put that blade in me, you'll remember that once—just once—you were mine."

Something crosses his face that I've never seen before, like I've shoved a knife between his ribs and twisted.

Good. I hope it hurts. I hope he carries this for eternity.

"Who's fucking you?" I whisper.

"Bryony," he gasps.

Good, I think. *Shatter for me.*

He meets me with hitches of his hips—half-thrusts quickly leashed, as if he can't stop himself. As if he's physically holding himself back from seizing me, from flipping me over and pounding into me until I scream.

"Say my name again."

"*Bryony.*" It's raw. Reverent and furious.

I rise on my knees before slamming back down, palms braced on his chest for leverage. His hands tighten on the headboard. The scent of scorched wood fills the room as his magic lashes out.

"Now say the word I want to hear," I whisper. "One word, and I'm all yours."

Darkness pools in Evander's eyes, drowning amber in depthless black. Still, he doesn't reach for me.

I lean down until I can feel the uneven gusts of his breathing. Until we share the same air, the same agonized heartbeat. "You want me under you again? Screaming your name until my voice gives out? Fucking *say it*."

And he does. His undoing, shaped into a single word.

"*Please.*"

A snarl. The Wolf snapping his jaws and admitting defeat.

I cradle his face between my palms and press a chaste, almost tender kiss to his lips. "Don't you ever forget this. Don't forget that I'm the only one who's ever made you beg."

With a growl, Evander surges up and flips us over, slamming me back into the mattress.

His weight settles over me—and then he's on me, in me, *fucking* me. His mouth crashes over mine, swallowing my gasp as he notches my legs high around his waist and thrusts hard. He's seizing control. Laying his claim just as thoroughly as I laid mine.

"Do you still hate me?" I pant, the words hitching on a brutal thrust.

"With every fucking breath," he says.

Snarling, I reach up and sink my fingers into his hair. Wrench his head back until the cords of his neck strain. "Then fuck me like you hate me."

He bares his teeth, and then his fingers wrap around my neck, squeezing. My pulse flutters against his palm, my lungs straining.

"Now it's your turn to beg." He slams hard into me. "Beg me for mercy. Go on, beg me real pretty."

Dark spots dance at the edges of my vision, the air turning thin. I stare up at him through the asphyxiating haze—at the savage twist of his mouth. The depthless hunger in his eyes.

"Are you going to tap out?" he breathes into my ear.

No. Break me.

"I could make you pray to me." He punctuates the filthy promise with a hard thrust, until I feel the stretch and burn with every breath. "I could make you pray every fucking night you have left."

"I don't pray," I gasp. Constellations burst across my darkening vision.

Not to gods or kings or monsters.

The hand at my throat tightens. The air thins further, my head swimming, heat licking through my veins. Bright and cold and utterly ruthless.

Evander draws me into a brutal kiss, forcing my head back into the pillows. His teeth sink into my bottom lip.

"By the time I'm done with you, the only prayers you'll remember will be the ones you scream for me."

And I believe him.

I believe this beautiful, vicious creature will tear me apart and reshape me in his image, shatter me into a million pieces, and make me beg him to put me back together. And he'll do it again and again, until nothing is left between us but worship and teeth, tongue and claws, ashes and blood and stardust.

There's something severely wrong with me. Because the pressure around my throat and the brutal thrust of him inside me, stretching me past what I think I can take, is sending me careening toward a precipice I'm suddenly desperate to fling myself over.

I meet Evander's feral, ravenous gaze through the smoldering black, and I am infinite. Incandescent.

I take everything he gives. All the hurt and hunger pouring out of us. Fucking like we'll destroy each other. Like we already have. If he plans to be my end, then I'll burrow into the darkest parts of him, scatter myself through his veins like broken glass. So that every time he draws breath after I'm gone, he'll bleed. He will hurt.

Pleasure all but blacks my vision, violent and seemingly endless—the racking shudders of orgasm, the bliss. The wings at his back flare wide as he slams into me one final time, grinding against my center as he finds his release.

As the fog of climax recedes, awareness returns by degrees. I feel him everywhere—the drum of his heart, his warm skin against mine as he removes his hand from my throat and checks me over, his touch gentle as he uses his power to heal the bruises.

I should dislodge him. Roll him off me and stagger away to lick my wounds in private. Reestablish distance and lines of demarcation. But this moment, with sweat drying on our skin and his scent in my lungs, is a reprieve. I'm not ready to relinquish it yet.

So, I just breathe. And for a time, Evander allows it. His fingers card through my hair, soothing me like I'm precious. Something cherished.

But I'm not.

It was all a game she thought she could win.

I compose myself and push him off, not looking at him as I get out of bed. "If you need it again tonight, use your hand. I'm done being your toy."

38

BRYONY

THE SKY IS the color of a fresh bruise as I step out into the garden.

I hug my arms tight around myself. It's not just from the cold. Every brush of the breeze feels like Evander's touch skimming along my skin—teasing, maddening, inescapable.

I hate that every little sensation reminds me of him. Every touch, every kiss, every whispered word of praise was just another weapon in his arsenal, designed to hurt me. And I let him. When I started trusting him, I might as well have given him the dagger and bared my throat.

I suppose I should be grateful. At least now, I know where I stand. The Blade drew a line in the sand, and it was a brutal reminder of my fate.

Four days now. Four measly sunrises until the hourglass runs out, and the Void comes calling. No more lies, no more pretending.

No more negotiation.

The familiar thrum of magic prickles along my nape a moment before wingbeats shatter the pre-dawn hush. Amara touches down in a flutter of dark feathers, her wings folding against her back.

She cocks her head, pale eyes studying me. Looking for blood, probably. Bruises. Bite marks. Any evidence that the Wolf used me too roughly. But he'd healed them all after that brutal fuck hours ago.

"Well," she drawls, "you're in one piece. That's fortunate. Did he treat you well? Do I need to launch his eyeballs into the Osbu?"

Heat floods my cheeks as a wave of sense-memories bombard me. The exquisite stretch and ache of him inside me, hitting that spot that made stars burst behind my eyes. The weight of him between my thighs, pressing me down. The slick glide of his sweat-damp skin against mine. His nose buried in my hair as we panted our completion.

I could make you pray to me. I could make you pray every fucking night you have left.

No. Stop.

I shove the images down. Box them up with all the other treacherous things I can't afford to want.

"I'm fine. Wasn't anything I didn't beg for." I fold my arms over my chest. "But I don't want to waste time talking about the Wolf. Tell me about Theo. Did you see her?"

Amara sighs. "I spied through the windows. The palace is crawling with Idris' loyalists, and he's keeping her confined to her chambers. Since he can't exactly kill Alexios' only other Anchor..."

Dread turns my blood to ice as I imagine my sister at my uncle's mercy. Idris has been itching to put Theo in her place for years.

"Did they hurt her? When you found her, was she—"

"Nothing that won't heal," Amara says. "Some nasty bruising. Defensive wounds on her knuckles where she went scrapping. Looks like she gave as good as she got. Laid out one of Idris' bootlickers cold, from what I heard."

I squeeze my eyes shut, trying to breathe around the vice clamped over my lungs. My nails cut into my palms, and I relish the bright flare of pain. It gives me something to focus on.

"You couldn't get her out?"

Amara scrubs a hand over her face. "Tried to. Almost fucked it all sideways, too. I remembered the bastards guarding her have Alexios' Claim, and he'd feel it the second I made a move.

Since I'm not an Eternal yet, I couldn't survive the punishment. Having him splatter my brains across the palace corridor from a thousand miles away would defeat the purpose of a rescue."

Still, letting Theodora stay locked up while I'm here with the Wolf is unthinkable. If I have four more days, I intend to make them count.

I exhale shakily. "I'm going to Hellevig."

Amara's eyebrows shoot up. "You want to run that by me again?"

"Theo needs me. So I'm going to get her."

"Not alone, you aren't. What exactly is the plan here? Storm the gates and fight your way to her royal chambers?"

I roll my eyes. "Please. I'm reckless, not suicidal." I turn to pace along the garden path, restless energy buzzing beneath my skin. "There's a network of old war tunnels under the palace—escape routes in case the enemy breached the walls. Theo had them cleared and fortified after she took the regency. No one will even know I'm there. You can fly her to my family's old hunting cabin in the south. It's isolated."

She hums her approval. "Not a terrible plan. But I notice you're not tripping over yourself to get the Wolf in on this mission."

"That's because I'm not."

"What, afraid he'll swoop in and steal your shot at playing valiant rescuer?"

"He made it clear I'm free to go whenever I please. I negotiated the terms when I agreed to stay here." I run a hand through my hair. "The Blade knows I'm alive. He gave the Wolf five days to end me before he finishes the job himself."

Amara's mouth falls open. "You're shitting me."

"Afraid not," I say with a bitter laugh.

Something complicated moves across her face. "He could always Claim you, you know." She says it gently. Like she's trying to brace for impact.

And oh, there it is—that laughable suggestion. As if Evander would ever lower himself to Claim me. The only time he ever brings it up is when he's trying to manipulate me.

If you're lying to me, the Blade's words to Evander whisper in my memories, *if you Claim her, or worse, soulbond with her, I'll dig my fingers into your chest and crush your traitorous heart in my fist.*

"I'm disposable, remember? His entertainment." Something squeezes in my chest. "The Wolf won't Claim me. And I don't want him to."

I'm amazed my voice emerges steady. Level. Because even now, with fury simmering in my veins and his betrayal still fresh, some pathetic scrap of me hurts at the rejection—at how easily he played me.

"An Eternal's Claim is ironclad," Amara presses. "Not even Alexios can touch you if the Wolf lays one on you. It's the oldest, most sacred law."

I shake my head, throat closing up. "No. He doesn't give a damn about me."

I'm just having a bit of fun. It's not like I'm keeping her.

"That's not true. I've seen the way he looks at you—"

"Like he wants to fuck me," I snap. I let out a shaky breath. "I've made my peace with it." *Liar*, a small, treacherous voice whispers. "I'm not binding myself to another god."

Especially not him, I don't say. If he Claimed me, he'd sense how close sentiment has burrowed into me. I couldn't tolerate the excruciating intimacy of his ownership.

"Wait here for me," I tell Amara. "I'm going to go pack a few things, and we'll go."

She nods, her gaze searching mine. "Okay."

I stride back into the tower. As I wind through corridors, my mind refuses to settle.

I'm done being used. I'm through with his secrets and games and manipulations. After everything, he deserves to have me pry his armor wide open.

I stop at the familiar door with the obsidian seal.

His secret. The one line I'm not meant to cross. My heart

kicks behind my ribs as I stare at the mark carved into the center of the door. It's pulsing red, like a fresh wound.

It's fitting, in a vicious sort of way, that he'll wake up and find his precious door open. One final "fuck you" to the god who unmade me.

So I twist the handle. Power crackles along my skin as I step over the threshold.

39

EVANDER

THE SUNLIGHT SLANTING across the sheets wakes me—or maybe it's the silence where Bryony's heartbeat should be.

I was so wrong. When I said you were just like Alexios? Turns out, you're actually worse.

I'm proud of her, honestly. I could have given excuses about lying to my brother. That I was only trying to sell him on my typical depravity, my well-documented history of impulsivity and immortal boredom. Dressed it up in pretty words and reassurances like I wasn't still planning to shove the knife into her.

But I am, and she deserved the opportunity to scream at me and remind me what a greedy fuck I am. And when she made me beg for it, I deserved that, too. That pointed reminder that I might be the god, but she holds the real power here.

I stare up at the roses stretching along the ceiling, studying the pulsing, vibrant color of their blooms. The roses have been whispering about her all week. Their thorns stretch toward her whenever she passes, like they're trying to snare her, keep her. She babies them like my mother did, and now the realm is showing me how pleased it is.

Go to her, you idiot.

I shove into a pair of loose trousers, not bothering with a shirt. Her scent pulls me down the corridor like an invisible chain, but it doesn't lead me to her room. Not where I expect her to be.

The door at the end of the hall is open, and the obsidian seal is pulsing red against the dark wood.

She didn't. She *wouldn't.*
But she did.

I shoulder into the chamber, incandescent with fury. With old hurts wrenched viciously into the light.

She stands beneath the twisting canopy of the chamber's ancient tree. The black branches rise thirty feet toward the domed skylight, covered with leaves the color of dried blood. The thick trunk is carved with the deep gouges of my dagger.

And wrapped around the tree are roses. Winding up the trunk and every branch, crawling along the walls. I stopped coming in here when they began to overtake the tree, a pointed message from the realm to its chosen king.

This grief is making you waste away. You're squandering your power.

Bryony turns. The stained glass above paints her in shades of violet and cobalt, catching on her opalescent skin and silver-white hair. Her expression shifts—an apology and something softer. Something that hooks into my withered excuse for a heart and twists until I'm carved open, and the only word between my teeth is *please.*

"You had no right," I snarl. "I made one rule—*one* damn rule in this tower."

She flinches, but she doesn't retreat. Running would be too easy, too simple for a woman who seems determined to court destruction.

"I know. I'm sorry, I shouldn't have..." She swallows hard. "But why hide this? It's... beautiful. I thought I'd find—"

"What?" I snap, stalking closer. My bare feet sink into the packed earth I'd gathered from Turpori's wreckage. "Preserved corpses? Trophy rooms filled with the remains of my enemies? Some sick collection to confirm what a monster I am?" A laugh scrapes out of me. "Sorry to shatter your illusions, Princess, but even I'm not that predictable."

"That's not what I—"

"Save it." Power crackles beneath my skin. She has to feel

it—the static charge, the sting of barely leashed magic—but she doesn't back down. "You wanted to see the darkest parts of me? Fine. Let me give you the grand tour."

I drag my knuckles down the pitted trunk. "This is a griefwood. They're grown in Scillarian households as an extension of the mourning process. Watered by the tears and blood of the bereaved, fed by the corpses tangled in its roots. They're living headstones. This one once sat in the courtyard of my mother's palace. I carved every mark myself in the days after her court fell. Each one symbolizes someone I lost."

And each gouge is a wound that will never heal.

"There are so many." A broken whisper.

A tightness spreads through my chest. "What did you expect? You're standing on a mass grave."

I watch the knowledge settle in her expression—the parting of her lips, the clench of her fingers.

"You asked me once how humans managed to kill so many gods," I say. "Well, Devaliant, here are the mechanics of deicide. Pay attention because I'm only going to say this once."

I crook my finger beneath her chin, tilting her face to meet my stare. She shivers but doesn't flinch. Doesn't look away as the air thickens with the rising swell of my power, the electric thrum of it.

"First," I say softly, "you take a very special blade. A godkiller forged by an Eternal gifted with the power of metallurgy and imbued with their magic. Then, you set it right between our wings, where the skin is soft. Where we're weak."

Her breathing goes ragged and her pulse flutters against my fingertips, but she holds my gaze as I lean in and breathe my next words into the charged space between our mouths.

"And then you start *sawing*."

She makes a noise like I've struck her.

"Shh, don't flinch now. You wanted this, remember?" My lips brush the shell of her ear. "Let me tell you what your sick fucking family did to my brother. His wings were kissed by starlight once. Our mother used to say that the realm had taken its time crafting them. And your ancestors pinned him to a table and laughed while they carved him up."

I swallow past the lump in my throat. Force myself to keep going. "Wings are the one thing even an Eternal can't regenerate. Did you know that? It nearly killed me to craft him a replacement out of shadows. There's a deadland a hundred miles wide in the Duehavn from the power it took to make my brother whole again. But do you want to know the real reason your family mutilated him?"

I pull back just far enough to search her stricken face. To watch the awful knowledge bleed into her expression. "Consumption, sweetheart," I say. "When humans ingest our flesh, they steal our magic for a little while. They take what we have because they want it for themselves."

Her hands cover her mouth. Bryony makes a wounded sound, fresh tears spilling over.

"When Bas and I made it back to Turpori, it was just smoking rubble and rotting bodies. Your family and their legion used Bas' power to put down our people like animals. We found what was left of our mother scattered through the throne room." I choke out a broken laugh. "I'm sure Vartena spun it real nice in the history books. *The Godkiller Crusades*, right? That's what they call it? But here in Scillari, it's the Devouring. And that's what it was. Our bodies consumed until the dead outnumbered the living."

I'm breathing hard, panting. The words spill faster, harsher. Tumbling over each other. "That kind of loss destroys you," I rasp. "It fills you up with poison until all you know how to do is spread it." I drag in a shuddering breath, and it hurts. *Fuck*, it hurts. "Bas and I almost destroyed half of Scillari in our grief. Alexios had to bind our power—but he promised us justice. At that point, I didn't care who handed me the knife, as long as it wound up in a Devaliant's ribs."

The memories rise in a hungry tide. I take her hand, marveling at the contrast between our skin. At the glitter of mine against her pale luminance. "You wanted to know why you shine like this. The real reason you Devaliants are so damned pretty." I graze my fingers over her cheek, whispering, "There's no demi in your lineage. None of you is *special*. It's tainted blood, vicious girl. Your ancestors devoured so much immortal flesh that it changed them. Polluted your bloodline. And they passed it down to you."

My hand slides to the nape of her neck, twisting into her hair. A few rough tugs, and her head tips back, baring her throat. "All this exquisite skin I love marking up? It's born from atrocity. Every time I look at you, it reminds me of the dead."

A small sound escapes her. A tear trails down her cheek, and I watch its progress in mute fascination. I want to chase it with my tongue, lick into her mouth, and swallow down the broken sounds she makes until she understands that this is how it's always going to end.

"Can you even imagine the violence it took to make me this monstrous?" I ask her. "And I'm monstrous down to my fucking soul, Devaliant. Your family made me this way. I want you to know that when I rip out your heart, it won't be personal. Just prophecy. There's an old saying in Scillari, *Drevikt, vahn nevikt.* In vengeance, rebirth."

I bring her closer, until my lips brush her jaw on every word. "We'll always rise from the ashes. And when we do, we'll drag our enemies into the dark. We all pay for the sins of our ancestors in the end. You'll just pay in blood instead of gold. And there's a vicious sort of symmetry in that, isn't there? The daughter of a house built on dead gods and devoured magic, destined to die and die and die again. Atoning for the crimes of history with the only coin we monsters trade in: suffering."

I nip at her earlobe, swiping my tongue over the slight sting. Gratified when she shivers against me, hands coming up to clutch at my shoulders.

"If there's any mercy to be found in this ugly world, it's that mortal lives are so fleeting. Not like us, cursed to carry our hurts through the ages. It lingers and festers and eats us alive."

I gentle my grip on her wrists. "Listen very carefully," I say, cold and clipped. "You do not step over this threshold again, or I'll strip the flesh from your body and use it to bind the histories of everything your bloodline has taken from me. You Devaliants and your wars and your bottomless *fucking* entitlement. Say you understand."

I wonder if she can feel the animal snarl building in me, rabid and aching to fight. Because she just detonated a bomb in the no-man's-land between us, and now I've been left to bleed out.

She only stares at me, her face full of an emotion I can't name.

"*Say something*," I snarl.

But she doesn't. She just leans forward and slowly presses her cheek into the crook of my shoulder.

Stop. Stop. Fucking stop.

I don't want this from her. I don't want her to show me all the broken parts of her and remind me that, in another life, I could have loved her so damn much I bled with it.

Tough shit, Wolf. We don't always get what we want.

I dig my fingers into her nape. "Say you hate me."

Her lips are unbearably soft as they graze my jaw. She remains silent, just touching me. Getting up close, where I can still smell myself on her.

"I could make it happen," I tell her. "I could make you hate me so much you'll claw out your own heart just to be free of me." I'm breathing hard, fighting for control. Losing. "Say it. Remind me what we are to each other."

Her knuckles brush over my cheek. Her lips part on a gasp, and I'm lost. I slant my mouth over hers, swallowing down the startled moan. She opens for me, desperate. She tastes like rain and destruction. Like the end of worlds.

"Nothing's changed." I'm shaking, I realize. Trembling against her. "We're just fucking each other. That's all this is. Understand? It means nothing."

She wraps her arms around me, and my chest heaves as she holds me close. "It's okay," she whispers. "Evander. It's okay."

I can't breathe. I can't think. I let her hug me like she's trying to hold all my splintered pieces together.

"Let me have you," I say, grasping at her clothes. *What am I doing? What am I doing?* "Forget everything I said before. Just let me have you again."

"*Ishkah*," she whispers against my lips.

I go still at the word, tempted to pretend I didn't hear it. That's her line written in the sand, but she's already scuffed mine out, and why should I listen? She wants me; I can smell it on her. I can make her yield. Make her mindless.

But then she speaks again, and it's barely louder than an exhale. But I feel it like a knife to my heart.

"I'm leaving."

The words drop like a stone into water, rippling out and out. Because contained in them are so many things left unspoken.

"Amara's waiting for me," she continues, like she's not gutting me alive. "After I left you last night, I wrote down everything I remembered in Caelestis about Rhosyn and left it on my desk. It… It's an anagram. *Onrhys* is the word for 'serpent' in Lybräian. It's a symbol of House Devaliant." She wipes a tear away. "You mentioned black market parts to Amara, so it's probably another reason for you to hate my family. But you deserve to know."

My chest constricts. "Bryony," I breathe.

"Let me say this. I owe you a truth before I go. My only non-negotiable."

She reaches for my hand. Takes it between her own, and slowly, slowly, she pushes up her sleeve to reveal the neat row of scars along her inner arm.

"You asked about these. I want you to understand what they mean." She guides my finger to the topmost mark, a jagged line of silver. "I once told you that after the Void, nothing feels real. Everything is fog and static. So I have a ritual."

I frown, uncomprehending. Her smile is terribly gentle. Sad in a way I can't bear.

"One," she says softly. "Breathe. It's always the first thing when I wake up on that altar. I force the air in and out of my lungs until I remember how they work."

My throat closes up as understanding dawns. As the pieces slot into place, ugly and aching.

"Two. Feel." Another scar, a second rung on the ladder. "Sensation, texture. The grit of stone, the chill of the altar." She looks up at me through her lashes, and it's like a punch to the sternum. "The brush of your hands on my skin."

She traces the third mark, and I can't look away. Can't speak.

"Three. Name," she continues. "They can take everything else, but they can't have this. I am Bryony. I am my own, no matter how many times I die."

The next scar is larger. Angrier. "Four. Present. When and where, even if I'm not sure I want to be there. The temple, the palace." Her breath hitches. "This room. Your bed. With you so deep in me, I can't tell where I end and you begin."

I want to wrench my hand away. I want to lace our fingers together and never let her go.

"Five." The last one. "Real. This moment, right here. You and me and the blood in our veins. Your heart against mine." She laughs a little, but it sounds like a sob. "Us. This. It's the realest thing I know, even if…"

Even if it has to end.

I squeeze my eyes shut. Try to breathe around the fist in my chest, the crush of it. Because this shouldn't hurt so much.

"I'm so sorry for what they did to you." Her voice is low. "And that's not enough. I know it isn't."

There's only the cadence of our breathing in the silence, the splintered pieces of us. She brings my palm to her cheek. Nuzzles into the contact, and I feel the wet slide of tears against my skin. The delicate flutter of her lashes.

"So this is what's going to happen," she continues. "You'll let me leave here because that's the bargain we struck. And then you'll hunt me in Vartena, and when you catch me… it'll be my death that settles the score. One insignificant mortal to balance the scales. It's only fair, isn't it? A tithe long overdue. So, kill me however you want. Do whatever makes the pain less for you."

There's a word for what I'm feeling. This gnawing ache

burrowing into all my soft places. A word I can't tell her, or I'll never let her go.

I can only watch as she leans up to brush her lips over mine. The contact is feather-light and devastating, a goodbye and an apology. A feedback loop of hunger ricocheting between us.

I taste salt. Smoke. Sorrow. The drum of a shared heartbeat, frantic and stuttering. It feels like flying and plummeting. Like losing solid ground. She presses her forehead to mine, our noses brushing—fighting for air, for equilibrium.

"You told me once that you would crave me in any lifetime, across every eternity. And I wanted to tell you… I'd find you in all of them. At the end of everything, when the stars winked out one by one. In the dark and the cold and the nothing. So I'll wait for you, in some other forever. Where there's no blade between us. When we can mean more than nothing."

Then she turns away, and every instinct howls at me to lunge and pin her down. But I don't. I lock my muscles and clench my jaw until my teeth ache.

"Three days," I tell her, and there's no gentleness left. No softness or sweetness. "I'll give you three days to settle your debts. And then I'm coming for you."

Bryony pauses at the threshold. "I'll be waiting."

PART FOUR

LOVE IS THE THING WITH TEETH

40

BRYONY

AMARA LANDS US in the woods outside of Hellevig. The familiar spires and red roofs of the palace pierce the sky in the distance, and the walled forest where I first met Evander is visible even from here.

The memory of his touch lingers on my skin—the press of his mouth, the honey-rough rasp of his voice. Everything I can't have. Everything I don't get to keep.

All this exquisite skin I love marking up? It's born from atrocity.

When he kissed me under the griefwood, I felt the echoes of wounds that will never heal, losses that fester and rot. All the dark places inside him my family helped create.

Can you even imagine the violence it took to make me this monstrous?

My chest clenches around the memory of his words. He's spent centuries with that loss lodged behind his ribs like a blade. Centuries with nothing to bleed out the poison.

"You good?" Amara asks, tucking her wings close.

I swallow past the lump in my throat. "Yes," I say. "Tunnels are this way." I jerk my chin toward a crumbling stone archway nearly swallowed by vines. "Help me with the door?"

The rusted grate shrieks as we heave it open. Amara conjures a wisp of light, its blue glow casting shadows on the decrepit entrance.

She arches a brow at me. "Charming. You really know how to show a girl a good time."

"Would you prefer I waltz up to the palace gates and announce myself?"

"Point taken."

We descend into the tunnels, each step kicking up decades of dust and debris. These passages haven't been used since the god-human war, when my ancestors needed escape routes in case the gods breached palace defenses. The decay is clear in the scent of mold, the drip of water in the distance, the cracks along the walls.

After a while, we reach the hatch that will spit us out in the palace kitchens.

"Wait here," Amara murmurs. "I'll scout the patrol patterns."

She scales the ladder and disappears up into the kitchens.

Hurry, I urge her in my head. *Hurry, hurry, hurry.*

After a few minutes, a soft scuff signals her return. "East wing guards just cycled through," she whispers as she descends the ladder. "Servants have been asleep for an hour at least. We've got maybe ten minutes before the next patrol."

I set down my pack, already mapping the route in my head. "I'll get Theo myself. If any guards need dealing with, better not risk Alexios sensing your involvement."

Her mouth thins, but she doesn't argue. "Watch yourself, then. There's a guard posted at her door you'll need to handle quietly."

"Got it." I check my daggers in their sheaths, their weight already warm and familiar. "Be ready to fly her to safety once we clear the tunnels."

"And you?"

"I'll deal with my uncle and hide out until you circle back." I swallow hard. "Thank you. For everything."

"Thank me by not getting caught. Now get up there."

I haul myself up. The kitchen is eerily silent at this hour, massive brick ovens cold and dark. I stick to the walls, muscle memory making my footsteps soundless as I move past shelves laden with preserved goods.

My heart hammers against my ribs. I take off down the corridor, skirting pools of shadow, keeping low. The thick runner muffles my steps as I head for the antechamber and up the stairs to the family wing of the palace.

Hurry, hurry. Get Theodora and get out.

I'm passing the second-floor landing when a jaunty whistle splinters the hush. Heavy footsteps echo up the stairwell, growing louder.

Guard on patrol.

I press myself into the deepest shadows, lungs burning as I hold my breath and track the guard's progress—the steady tromp of boots drawing closer, then beginning to fade as he continues his rounds.

My heart thunders. I count my breaths. In for seven. Hold. Out for eleven. Repeat. Just like Amara taught me.

When I ease out of hiding, the final stretch of the corridor unfolds before me. At the far end, a guard slouches against my sister's door, his head nodding toward his chest.

I creep forward on silent feet. Closer. *Closer.* Just a few more steps separate me from my target. The guard's breathing remains deep and even.

Until suddenly, it isn't.

He jerks awake. His brow creases in confusion when he sees me—*recognizes me*—and he opens his mouth to speak. But I'm already moving. My palm clamps over his lips, and I slide my knife free, driving the blade deep into his throat. Hot blood wets my fingers as I twist the weapon loose.

He collapses to the carpet. Crimson spreads around his body, pooling beneath my boots. I stare at him for a long moment, something cold and ugly twisting behind my ribs—a snarled knot of feeling too tangled to parse.

Focus. No time for guilt.

I slip into Theodora's chambers. Moonlight spills across the floor, painting everything in shades of silver. And there, sprawled in the center of the bed, is my sister.

"Theo, wake up."

"Bry?" Her voice is thick with sleep as she stirs and sits up. "What are you *doing* here?"

"Rescuing you, obviously."

She gapes at me for a heartbeat, chest heaving, and then she launches herself at me in a fierce embrace. "Gods, I've missed you, you reckless idiot."

"You didn't tell me anything in your letters." I hug her back just as hard. "Overthrowing Uncle? I had to find out through demi gossip."

Releasing me, she fumbles for the bedside lamp. "I hadn't played my hand yet. The bastard struck preemptively and moved to corral my supporters. I'm almost impressed, truthfully. It's the most initiative he's shown in ages."

The light flares, throwing her face into sudden, horrifying relief. Bile claws up my throat. One eye is blackened and swollen shut, and her lip is split down the center. Bruises bloom across her delicate features.

"I'll fucking kill him," I breathe.

"And I'll gladly help you hide what's left of the corpse. But later."

Theo begins pulling clothes from her armoire. She strips out of her nightgown, donning plain trousers and a shirt.

"What about your loyalists?" I ask, helping her lace up a pair of boots. "The ones who tried to help you?"

"Dungeons, most likely. Along with anyone else who didn't fall over themselves to bend the knee when Idris started cracking skulls."

"We'll figure out how to free them once you're safe. How many?"

"A few dozen guards. Some staff. Idris' men killed Kas." The last words are quiet. Theodora was fond of her guard, not just as a lover. She clears her throat and composes herself. "What's the escape route?"

"The old war tunnels," I say. "I have a friend waiting to fly you somewhere safe."

Her head snaps up. "And where will you be during all this?"

"Staying behind to deal with Idris."

"Absolutely not." She grabs a coat, yanking it on with agitated movements. "Either we leave together, or not at all."

"Amara can only fly one of us, and someone has to keep Uncle occupied. He and I have unfinished business. Now stop arguing. Let's go."

I crack the door and peek out into the hall, listening hard. The guard's body lies where I left it, his blood a sticky dark pool soaking into the carpet. I edge into the corridor with Theodora silent at my back.

She glances at the corpse but says nothing. Always practical, my sister.

I lead the way, sticking to the shadows. Two guards round the corner, deep in conversation. Their laughter rings out. I dart a frantic glance over my shoulder, but it's too late to backtrack, and the only cover is—

There.

I seize Theodora by the arm and haul her into a cramped alcove. Her panicked breaths match mine.

Please walk by. For once in your miserable lives, just keep walking. Please.

But of course, they don't.

One of them spots the body sprawled in front of my sister's door and swears, drawing his sword. The other follows suit, shifting into a defensive position as they advance down the corridor.

"When I say run, you run," I whisper to Theodora. "Understand?"

She nods.

I explode from the alcove. My first strike slices through the nearest guard's extended sword arm. He shrieks and staggers back, his weapon clattering to the floor. I strike again, getting him right in the throat.

The second guard's sword strikes in a dark blur. I duck under the swing, coming up inside his guard to bury my dagger in his armpit. Blood gushes over my knuckles as I wrench the knife free. He crumples to the floor.

I motion for Theo to run.

She flies past me toward the stairs. We're halfway down when I hear shouts from above, the pounding of booted feet, and then the clanging peal of a bell.

The alarm.

Fear detonates in my chest. I seize Theodora's elbow and haul her onward, but we're not fast enough. A trio of guards spills around the corner ahead.

I shove my sister behind me. "Don't wait for me. Get to the tunnels *now*."

Then I launch myself at the guards.

Amara's lessons take over, guiding my steps. My movements are economical and precise. Every strike aims to kill. I duck and spin, my knives flashing, darting to open throats and sever arteries. What I lack in raw strength, I make up for in speed and viciousness. Nothing exists outside the hammer of my pulse and the burn of my muscles. There is only the dance, the deadly poetry of motion.

One guard goes down. A second staggers back, hand clamped to the wound in his side. The third manages to backpedal out of range.

Behind me, Theodora cries out. I whirl to see Idris with a knife at her throat.

His eyes flicker over me. "Well," he says. "If it isn't my niece, back from the dead." He jerks his head at me. "Drop the knife or I'll bleed her."

I clench my jaw and study the hold he has on the weapon. If I'm fast—

Idris digs the blade in harder, opening a shallow cut. Theodora goes rigid.

"*Drop it, Bryony.*"

My weapon clatters to the ground.

"Good. The ones up your sleeves, too."

Teeth gritted, I shed blade after blade. All the daggers I earned from Evander during our game. The remaining guard surges forward to wrench my arms behind my back, and reinforcements flood the corridor. More swords than I can count are leveled my way.

"Orders, Your Majesty?" the guard at my back asks.

"Take them back to Theodora's chambers. I want every man on the doors until I give the word. And ready the funeral wood," Idris says. His gaze flickers to my sister. "You should be glad, Theo. We've finally got a body to put on the pyre."

41

EVANDER

THE ROSES ARE dead.

Not in the process of dying. Not wilting.

Dead.

Every last one of them withered in less than a day, their once vibrant petals now brittle and black.

It's almost poetic. Bryony breathed life into these blooms, nurtured them when I couldn't be bothered. Showed them more tenderness in a handful of days than I've managed in centuries.

And now they're gone, just like her.

"*Fuck!*" I whirl, slamming my fist into the nearest wall.

Stone crumbles. Flames erupt across my wings as I turn and pace the garden.

Scillari's always been a bitch with its messages, but it used to be more subtle. For hundreds of years, it let me wallow in my own shit, let me hide away in this tower. The roses that grew wild and untamed were just little reminders. *Hey, asshole, remember you have power you're wasting.* I could ignore those.

But this? This is deliberate.

The garden didn't just die. It was executed. The realm's own personal "fuck you" for making Bryony walk away and letting the only person who made me feel something real in three centuries slip through my fingers.

I fucked her like I could purge her from my system. Like I could steal enough of her to fill the void in my chest that grief left behind. I want her etched into my bones, tattooed beneath my skin. I want to paint her throat purple with the press of my teeth and leave a map of fingerprint-shaped guides to all her weak spots.

Here is where she shivers. Here is where she sings. Press here to make her curse. Bite here to hear her beg.

Claim her. Keep her. Ruin her for any other touch but yours.

But if I did that, I'd be an even more selfish piece of shit than I already am. What I did to her can't be described as anything but a defilement. Demanding pieces of her—all of her—until she's carved down to nothing but the shape of my wanting wasn't a kindness. It was a theft.

Those stories never mention how much you get off on mindfucking the women you screw.

Yeah, she took one look at the jagged, ugly sprawl of my obsession and recognized it for the monstrosity that it is.

Well done, Devaliant. Full marks for perception there, sweetheart.

That's the way of gods and monsters, isn't it? We don't love—we devour. We conquer and hoard until there's nothing left. We can't gentle our teeth or blunt our claws.

Give me your devotion. Your submission. Every breath and broken scream. Give me give me give me...

I am a creature of infinite need, bent and breaking on the altar of one mortal woman. And that's the cosmic joke, isn't it? That when a thing hungers the way I hunger, it has precious little to offer in return. Just takes and takes and takes until it splits you open and leaves you gutted. I want to die with my teeth in her throat and her claws in my chest, ripping me open until she looks at me and sees someone worth keeping instead of putting down.

Here are all the wretched caverns, Devaliant. Here are all the screaming hollow places that no amount of touching, tasting, taking, fucking, *will ever fill.*

Do you still want your Wolf?

Alexios once told me that desire is the most selfish of all impulses. That it drives the infected to incinerate worlds. I'd laughed it off, too young and stupid to heed the warning. Monsters like me don't *want*. But now that she's gone, all my ugly wanting is pouring out, and I finally understand.

I could lose myself in it, I think. In the contemplation of ruin... of the mess she's made of me. And maybe some part of me is grateful she left before I could infect her with this crude emptiness that gnaws and gnaws and—

A sudden burst of power tears me from my thoughts.

Amara hits the garden square in an explosion of leaves, gasping for breath. Sparks of power flare and gutter around her. She's on the verge of a magical flameout, and her weaker wing must be in a lot of pain.

I'm at her side in an instant, grasping her arm. "Breathe, damn you."

I help her onto the garden bench. Amara's eyes slip shut as she drags in a lungful of air.

"What happened?"

"Flew through the Shroud as fast as I could. I tried... Idris, he..." She coughs. "Bryony's sister was in trouble, so she went to help, and he... he has her. They're readying wood for the pyre."

I go still. Cold purpose settles in my bones.

I knew Bryony planned to settle things with Idris. I should trust that she'll solve her own problems, mete out her retribution. But the feral thing wearing my skin doesn't give a shit about *shoulds*. It wants to raze Hellevig to the ground and paint the whole damn realm red to keep her safe.

Idris Devaliant has debts to pay, and I intend to be his most devoted collector.

"Give your wing some rest and then make yourself scarce," I tell Amara. "I have an overdue reminder to deliver to Hellevig about its place, and Alexios will feel it. Stay out of the blast radius until the dust settles."

Amara studies me. "Can you... do anything to the Claimed with Alexios' leash on?"

I grin slowly. "I'm nearly as strong as Alexios, and I've had a long, *long* time to learn how to slip my collar. He can't keep his grip on the Shroud and me at the same time." My power flares again, and I let it fill my veins until I'm blazing with it. "And Bryony Devaliant is *mine*."

Because here's the truth—the secret I've been trying to outrun. It's pointless and trite and hopelessly mortal.

I love her. I love her, and it's the most idiotic, suicidal thing I've ever done in the entire thousand years of my existence.

And I would rather let the world burn than lose her.

I slice through the night sky toward Hellevig Palace. The speed, the chill, the burning strain in my shoulders—it all fades beneath the relentless drumbeat of a single imperative.

Find her and destroy anyone who touched her.

I reach for the tether that shackles me to Alexios, that suffocating collar cinched tight around my power—and I *pull*. The response is an instantaneous cold so searing it scorches my skin.

What the fuck do you think you're doing? His voice slams through my head.

Disobeying.

Another lance of agony. My wings falter, nearly dumping me out of the sky. I wrench myself upright with a curse.

I'm not in the mood for your shit, Wolf.

I grin. *One day, if the realm blesses you with someone who owns your heart the way she owns mine, you'll get it. You'll understand what it feels like to raze worlds for her.*

Then I sever the connection and brace for the backlash.

It's like swallowing an exploding star—like Alexios carved a path into my ribcage and cracked my bones open one by one. But I'd cut out my heart and eat it raw if it meant getting to Bryony. I'd let the god-king tear the wings from my back if those were the terms.

Because monsters like me—we don't just love. We obsess. We fixate. We annihilate anything that threatens what's ours.

Hellevig sprawls beneath me, the red spires jutting up across the landscape. The palace emerges into view. The sun is just rising over the compound, casting long shadows across the ground. It looks almost peaceful.

Shame I have to kill everyone.

I angle my wings and dive, the wind screaming past my ears. My boots hit the courtyard with a crack that splits the stone. Guards stumble back when I straighten to my full height.

"Alarm!" someone shouts. "*Sound the fucking alarm!*"

The idiots fumble for their swords, and I let out a chuckle. "Really?" I ask them, tilting my head.

One's eyes go wide. More guards swarm in, weapons raised—twenty, maybe thirty of them, circling like they think numbers will save them.

I smile. "All right, then. Go ahead, everyone."

They strike all at once, and I let loose the beast inside my skin. Let it shake off the rust and stretch its claws.

And I let it *sing*.

Bones crunch and splinter in wet, tearing sounds muffled by the roaring in my skull. Someone's screaming. Might be me. Might be the hysterical din of the palace sentries pissing themselves.

I don't know. I don't *care*.

I'll reduce this palace to rubble and leave it a monument to my wrath so they understand the shape retribution takes when someone puts their hands on what's mine.

Through the frenzy, Alexios rakes my mind. Talons sink into my brain as he tries to yank me back under his control. I stagger under the onslaught. He's beneath my skin, a thousand hooks ripping me open.

Obey, he snarls, *or bleed*.

In answer, I send him a mental image of myself creating a spear of light and punching it through a guard's chest. It burst out the other side in a spray of gore.

Option three, I say. *Immolation*.

Fire magic surges in my veins and builds in a wave of rippling heat. Guards scream as armor melts, sloughing from their bodies along with charred skin and muscle. The stench saturates the air.

I could compose arias to the dulcet tones of men boiling alive in their own skin. It never gets old. It's the simple things, you know?

Alexios slams into the barricades of my mind. *Listen to me very carefully. If any more of my Claimed die, if you so much as look at either of my remaining Anchors wrong, I'll melt the gray matter in your skull and make you lick it off the floor.*

The world flickers at the edges, and blood trickles over my lip. Instinct shrieks at me to submit, to fall to my knees, but no force in this realm can bring me to heel except for *her*.

I seize the nearest soldier. "*Where. Is. She.*"

A garbled keen is his only response.

Wrong answer, you trembling little cunt.

I snap his neck and drop the corpse, stepping over a dozen bodies as I stalk toward the palace stairs. A beautiful massacre, just for her.

My Devaliant has always deserved nice things.

"*Enough.*"

My head snaps up. Idris Devaliant stands at the top of the steps wearing his imperial red robes, lip curled as he takes me in—the disdain of a ruler looking down on an insect. But it's the figure on her knees before him that stops the breath in my lungs.

Bryony.

Her hands are tied behind her back, and Idris' knife is at her throat. There's blood on her face, in her hair, saturating the tattered fabric of her shirt. She must have put up a damn good fight.

That's my girl.

There is no pain I would not endure for her. No horror I would not rain down on her enemies until the bards sing of the Wolf and his Chosen for a thousand years.

Idris drags my Devaliant close as he descends. "I should have known she'd slither from the grave and get one of the god-king's dogs to join her cause."

I grin. "What can I say? Your niece has excellent taste in monsters. Give her to me."

His grip tightens, and the blade makes a shallow cut along her throat. He'll be paying for that. I'm the only one who gets to make her bleed.

"The Eternal wants her for the pyre," he says. "When Alexios rescinded his Claim, she became nothing. Worthless."

"Is that what you think?"

Movement snags my periphery—one of the few remaining guards, too stupid to play dead and taking advantage of my distraction to slip in close. I flick my wrist, halting him mid-step with an invisible tether.

"She's not worthless to me," I say softly. "And now you've gone and cut her. That's my privilege."

I close my fist.

The guard's scream fills the courtyard, rising into something almost musical before it cuts off. In seconds, there's nothing left of him but ash spiraling in the air.

Another guard turns to run, but I extend my power and squeeze. The sound of his ribs splintering is like kindling being snapped in half. His body crumples to the ground.

"Interesting thing about anatomy," I say, returning my attention to Idris. "Doesn't matter if it's a god or a human, if you squeeze at a thirty-five-degree angle, you can pulp the lungs inside the chest cavity. Learned that one from the last asshole stupid enough to put hands on my woman like she was *nothing*. And you know, there was this great moment right at the end—a singular squeal. He actually tried to suck his own liquefied organs back down his windpipe when I tore out his heart." I step over the body. "It was almost disappointing how quickly he died. But when it comes to *my* woman, I don't have my usual restraint."

Idris blanches. "Fuck, you actually want her, don't you?"

"Yeah, I want her." I flick a glance at where he's holding her. "And I'll slaughter every bastard who's ever put hands on her."

His face has gone ashen and slick with a sheen of sweat. Good. Let him feel the gravity of his mistake, the weight of my undivided focus—a thousand years of ruthless violence and unholy appetites sharpened to a ferocious point.

"You can't hurt me." He swallows hard. "I'm an Anchor."

I shake my head, clicking my tongue. "You've still got your hands on what's mine."

The emperor makes a panicked noise and immediately releases her. "Take her, then. Claim her. I don't care."

"I care," I say, still grinning. "And *my* claim isn't the one that matters here. *Hers* is."

My power lashes out, yanking the blade from Idris' grasp and wrapping around his throat. The weapon clatters to the ground. He gags, fingers scrabbling uselessly at the phantom noose cinched tight around him.

I look at Bryony, and I hope she sees everything I feel for her—love and the kind of devotion that would annihilate realms.

Another tendril of my power snaps the cuffs binding her wrists. "Have at him, vicious girl. Let's find out how prettily you can make him scream for us."

The smile she gives me nearly brings me to my knees.

Then Bryony slams an elbow into Idris' stomach. She snatches up the blade, drives it to the hilt in her uncle's thigh, and rips it free.

Idris screams. It's high and keening—the scream of a coward. A nice, beautiful aria just for her. I settle in to watch her destroy him.

"*That*," Bryony says, "is for the Duehavn." She plunges the knife into his stomach. "That's for making my death last as long as possible."

She yanks the blade out and stabs it into Idris' chest next, falling on the ground with him. His whimper is almost precious. Damn me, I could watch her do this all day.

"*This?*" Another brutal stab. "This is for leaving me there to die alone like I was nothing."

I'd always known that if I ever took a Chosen, she'd have to be someone savage. My mother used to tell me no one else would match me. This woman? This fierce, glorious creature splattered in blood and taking her vengeance? She's it for me. If she were a religion, I'd pray to her.

Bryony wrenches Idris' head back. I want to compose music to the sound of his airless keening.

"Look at me." Her voice is a dark rasp as she notches the dagger beneath his chin. "I want my face to be the last thing you see before the Void takes you. And I want you to remember that this is a better death than the one you gave me."

Then she shoves the blade into his jugular.

Idris' hands scrabble weakly at his throat. The sound of him choking on the blade fills the courtyard. Bryony keeps her eyes on him, never looking away, just watching as he gives a last rattling exhale.

Then she gets to her feet, head thrown back, her chest heaving. She's a portrait of vengeance—of survival. And in the entire span of my existence, I've never seen anything so heart-stoppingly gorgeous.

I hold out a hand, power still crackling over my skin. "Hey, nemesis."

Her grip tightens on the dagger's hilt, and fuck me if it doesn't make me want to lay myself at her feet and beg her to cut me to pieces. *Feed me my own heart, Devaliant.* Why not? She already owns it.

"You're early," she says lowly.

"Amara came to me."

Her eyes snap to mine, and for a devastating moment, I drown in the accusation, the raw betrayal there. "I would've been fine. We agreed on three days—"

"I know. I know, just…" I swallow. "Let me hold you. Be mine right now."

Something in her uncoils at that, a subtle release of tension in her shoulders. She drops the knife and lets me pull her close.

"Evander," she says, so soft it's barely more than an exhale against my chest.

I love the way my name sounds in her mouth. She shapes it like a prayer. I want to hear her say it every way there is—gasped into my skin, when the sun rises in the morning, moaned in climax. I want to hear her say it every damn day of my eternity, if she's willing to take my battered and broken soul and let me tie it to hers.

I want to keep her.

We stay like that for a moment, just breathing. Existing. My fingers clench in her hair as I drag the scent of her deep into my lungs. I'd hold her forever if I could.

"Bry?"

Bryony yanks away from me. I turn to see Theodora Devaliant staggering down the palace steps and through the slaughter. She's battered, her face covered in bruises, and one eye is swollen shut. To her credit, her expression remains neutral even surrounded by carnage. Seems the elder Devaliant sister has seen plenty of death before.

"Theo," Bryony says. "The guards?"

"The ones on me either fled or died." She glances at me with a stern expression. "Wolf. I'll credit you with impeccable timing."

And absolutely nothing else, asshole, that look says.

I don't usually stick around after delivering Bryony's letters to her sister, but over the last five weeks, I've come to appreciate Theodora Devaliant's unwavering ability to stare at me like she's about to give me a prize for mediocrity.

Bryony smacks me lightly on the arm. "Go heal my sister."

"I'd tell you to ask nicely, but I see you're in a commanding mood." I approach Theodora and lift my hand. "May I?"

She nods curtly.

Settling my hand on her cheek, I extend my power to mend all her cuts and scratches. The bruising on her ribs, the scrapes on her knuckles, the swollen eye.

"I see you haven't lost your flair for dramatic entrances," she tells me.

"Apologies for the mess, but your uncle had an unfortunate accident. Fell on a blade. Repeatedly. After threatening what's mine."

Theodora cuts a glance over the courtyard. "An improvement to the masonry, I'm sure."

I keep my power as brusque as a healer, with none of the lingering tendrils of heat I use to tease Byrony and make her chase my touch.

When Theodora is all healed up, I return to my Devaliant's side and pull her into me.

"Thank you," Theodora says. I notice the considering tilt to her head as she takes in my possessive grip on her sister. Her attention returns to Bryony. "Well?"

Bryony tenses. "Well what?"

"Is it true?" Theodora presses softly. Gently. "What he said. Are you his?"

I brace for her response. Because I fucked up at the griefwood and I said things I can't take back. I've manipulated her, cut her open, hurt her. And I'm undeserving.

But she just says, very quietly, "I'm his."

And that…

Fuck.

I think I could live and die and resurrect in the space between those words. I think I could make religions out of the way her mouth shapes them.

Theodora only nods. "While I appreciate the help, Wolf, this presents a new set of political headaches—"

A spike of agony lances through my skull. I hiss through my teeth—I can't hold Alexios off much longer.

The princess' expression sharpens. "Go," she says. "I'll handle things here. If my sister gets so much as a scratch from you, I'll rip my way into your realm and tear you apart myself. We clear?"

I nod. "I protect what's mine. You have my word."

Then, because I'm nothing if not a gracious guest, I stretch my power through the courtyard, seeking the dead. Magic shimmers down my outstretched hand, and every body littering the courtyard—except Idris—bursts into white-gold flame, immolating down to the bone in a matter of moments until only ash remains.

"A parting favor," I tell Theodora. "To minimize the mess. Left you the asshole for the pyre."

The flat look she serves me could strip paint. "This is still a mess. One I'll have to clean up while you fly off into the sunset." She pinches the bridge of her nose. "Just go, Wolf. Keep her safe."

42

BRYONY

EVANDER ANGLES US into a slow, circling descent about an hour outside of Hellevig. The ground rushes up, resolving into a small clearing nestled in the forest. He lands hard, the impact jarring through me.

"A little gentler on the landing next time?" I mutter as I extricate myself from his grip. "Before you rattle my bones right out of my—"

The words wither as I turn to face him. Blood streaks his face, leaking from his eyes, nose, and ears.

"You're bleeding," I breathe, reaching for him.

Evander captures my wrist. "It looks worse than it is."

He's lying. It takes severe damage to make an Eternal bleed like this.

"Are you dying? Be honest with me."

A mirthless chuckle barks out of him. "No. I'm receiving a lesson in obedience."

My brows squeeze together. "Alexios isn't taking kindly to your rebellion, is he?"

"Oh, he's delighted. My organs are currently liquefying themselves in celebration." With a wince, Evander sinks down onto a nearby rock, his wings settling around him. "Now then." He pats his thigh. "You're hurt, and I'd like to put my favorite mortal back together again while I'm still coherent."

His *favorite* mortal. I almost sneer at him, remembering his words to his brother. *She's a nice piece of ass to enjoy while I'm bored.*

Right. I'm sure I've been the most entertaining plaything he's had in ages. Definitely the only one who's never put up with his shit.

I level him with a flat stare. "I don't want you healing me. Not when you're like this."

"I've had a few centuries to get good at compartmentalizing the pain when Alexios yanks the leash. Get your ass over here."

My nails bite into my palms. It's a physical ache, this need to crawl into his lap and bury my face in the warm crook of his neck. To breathe him in until he's the only thing in my head.

But he's just a god mending his favorite fuck-toy.

"Quick and impersonal," I force out.

And just like that, the warmth that had crept into his features disappears, replaced by the cold, unreadable mask of the Wolf. "Fine."

I lower myself onto his thighs and brace for the onslaught.

His magic sinks into me, seeking out all the contusions with unerring precision. But it's brisk, perfunctory—a dispassionate mending stripped of gentleness. In and out and done.

The space between our bodies becomes an ocean of distance. An expanse where fragile, impossible things curl in on themselves and quietly wither.

But then, I always knew how this story ended: in blood and destruction. I thought I was so careful. That I'd shored up the crumbling walls of my stupid, stubborn heart. Sealed all the stress fractures and boarded up the rotting doors. That I wouldn't let the Wolf tunnel through my armor and take up residence in the rubble.

I miscalculated. Let him past my guard to burrow where soft girls keep their dreams and tender hopes.

Because I caught *feelings* for the beautiful knife destined for my back.

It was all a game she thought she could win.

I flinch at the memory of Evander's words. Because I forgave him at the griefwood, but it still stings. I wonder if this is what lunacy feels like. Wanting something so desperately even as you understand, intimately, the shape of its ending.

And stupidly wanting it anyway.

When Evander's power finishes knitting me together and withdraws, I lunge off his lap. "Thank you for playing along in Hellevig. For holding me and making it convincing. I know it was to placate Theodora, but I-I'm enforcing your end of our bargain. You promised me a head start, and I intend to use it."

To wallow and prepare myself for heartbreak.

I turn on my heel, gravel crunching beneath my boots. Already seeking the winding deer trail out of this copse. I don't know where I'm going, and I don't care. Just away.

But Evander's voice yanks me up short. "I wasn't playing along."

The world goes still like the charged hush before a storm. My heart slams against my ribs.

"Nothing I said or did in Hellevig was for your sister's benefit." His voice is quieter now, almost... hesitant. As if he's tasting the shape of his confession. "I held you because I needed to touch you. Because I was losing my mind after you left." An uneven exhale leaves him. "My mother's roses are dead. Just up and withered. Because the realm knows what I've been too craven to admit."

No.

He doesn't get to do this after shattering me into so many pieces. He doesn't get to demolish what's left. Fuck him.

"I heard you the other night," I say, keeping my tone even, "with your brother. You were *very* clear about what I am to you." I glance over my shoulder at him, my fingers flexing. *Control, Bryony.* "So you can save the mind games. I won't fight you in the end. I'll let you take your vengeance as neatly as possible, but I'm asking you not to make it hurt more. If I've made you feel even an ounce of compassion, give me that much."

I've never seen so much quiet devastation in his face before. "Alexios lets Bastien off the leash for a few hours each centennial," he says quietly. "With him at full power, there wasn't a damn thing I could have done to stop him from killing you. So, I had to be what my brother needed to see. I had to—" His jaw flexes. "I had to lie to us both."

The ache in my chest gives a vicious squeeze. "Why are you doing this? Is this another game? One final twist of the knife?"

He closes the distance between us, caging me against the trunk of a tree. "If this is another game, then I'm admitting defeat. I'm telling you that you've won." His head dips, lips grazing my cheek. "Nemesis. I'm telling you that I've fallen wretchedly, stupidly in love with—"

"*Stop*. Please, don't." I can't breathe around the pressure in my throat. I squeeze my eyes shut, fighting for balance.

But Evander grazes my jaw, his touch unbearably tender. As if I'm precious. Cherished. "Look at me."

"*Ishkah*. I *can't*." Hot tears streak down my cheeks.

Please stop.

I scrabble for composure, but I'm unraveling, splitting at the seams, and if I don't get away from him—

"Just this once, I'm not obeying that word," Evander says, wiping away my tears. "Because when Alexios comes for me—and he *will* come—I need you to be untouchable. To belong to me so completely that not even another Eternal can contest it." He tenses like he's bracing himself. "I'm impulsive. Cruel. Selfish down to the fucking marrow. But I love you, you chaotic, reckless girl. I love you, and losing you would break me. So let me Claim you."

And there it is—the killing blow. Like he's cracked my ribs open and seized my heart in his fist.

Because this is *so much worse* than him despising me.

"A Claim isn't love." I push at his chest. "It's *ownership*."

Something complicated moves across Evander's face. All the raw, wretched *wanting* laid bare. "Listen to me very carefully, you impossible creature. I would never demand your submission or your surrender—"

I snort, arching a brow.

"Outside of mutually enjoyable naked scenarios," he amends.

"But I'm not asking for that. I'm offering all of me. Every fucked-up, unworthy piece. It's all yours."

He backs up to unfasten his shirt from between his wings, shrugging the garment off. His skin glows in the light, muscles shifting.

And then, in a move that steals the air from my lungs, he sinks to his knees.

My heart rate picks up. "What are you doing?"

"Proving a point. Do you have any idea what it means for a god to kneel? To prostrate himself? To let *anyone* touch his wings?"

Slowly, he takes my hand and guides it to his wing. My chest tightens as I glide my fingers along the soft arch, marveling at the way the feathers resettle. So many emotions expand through my chest, too big for my body to hold them all.

Evander's lashes flutter closed as a shiver rolls through him. A faint groan rises in his throat, and the sound tugs at something low in my belly.

"This is the most profound gesture of surrender we can offer," he says hoarsely as I stroke his feathers. "Exposing our wings is like baring our throats. Giving up everything we are to the one person in the realms we deem worthy. No one's ever touched my wings before, Devaliant. Just you."

A small, secret part of me fractures. The part that still harbors impossible yearnings. It fills my veins with light, with the reckless urge to take what he's offering.

So I do. I keep nudging my fingers through his covert feathers. Evander tips his head back with a moan, wings going loose and pliant as I explore.

"This is a privilege reserved only for Chosen." His words are raw. "Those we invite to share a soulbond. A *reciprocal*, permanent Claim. One a human hasn't shared with a god in my lifetime."

Slowly, so slowly, Evander withdraws a blade from his boot and presses the hilt into my palm. The metal is warm from his skin, the cross guard inlaid with an engraving of a wolf with its teeth bared in a snarl, wreathed in flame. His insignia.

"You deserve a choice." He places his hand over mine and gently curls my fingers around his dagger. "There are two paths ahead of you, and I'm asking you to pick. Carve your mark into my skin. Reclaim every shred of agency stolen from you and take me in trade. Be my equal and walk at my side for eternity." He looses a breath, composing himself. "Or cut me loose right here, right now, and I swear to you I'll never again burden you with my inconvenient feelings. One word is all it'll take, and this will be the last you ever see of me."

I stare down at him, at this god kneeling in supplication for me. Offering up his wings to my touch after everything he told me at the griefwood. Offering me forever.

His eyes meet mine, and he whispers, "Can I be yours?"

It's too much. My thoughts tangle in a maelstrom of *want* and *shouldn't* and *please, please let me have this. Let me keep him.*

I'd always thought of gods as marble. Unchanging and impervious, their hearts closed to anything but conquest and the subjugation of the small, soft things. But Evander doesn't demand I gentle myself into some digestible shape, all my awkward pieces sanded down to fit. He meets the feral thing behind my ribs with bared teeth of his own and calls it lovely. Calls it right.

"You're thinking very loudly." Evander's voice is filled with a quiet sort of longing. "Talk to me, nemesis."

Slowly, I lower myself to the ground. Until we're kneeling face to face, close enough to trade breath.

"Tell me what's going on in that head of yours," he says, quieter this time. Almost tentative, like he's bracing for a blow. Steeling himself against rejection.

"I'm thinking you must be out of your damned mind." My hand tightens on his blade's hilt. "Because I need you to be absolutely sure that you want me bound to you for eternity."

Something flashes across his features—impatience and hunger and desperation. "Bryony..."

"Let me finish. Please." I force myself to hold his gaze. Let him see all the longing. The hurt. "I have to give you an out. Because there's no coming back from this, and I don't think I'd survive it if I felt your regret through a soulbond. Knowing I was the worst mistake you ever made. I don't know anything about soulbonding with gods, but I'm not like you. I'm just—"

"A human. I know. I don't care."

"I'll never be able to fly with you, Wolf."

"Then fall with me." His expression softens. "I don't know anything about this kind of bond either, but if it's anything like two gods, you'll share my lifespan. That's enough for me."

I blink hard against the sudden sting in my eyes. "Please be sure."

A low sound leaves him. Then his mouth is on mine, soft and searing all at once. His kiss is like a whispered confession. A vow sighed against my skin as he tips his forehead to rest against my own.

"I've never been more sure of anything in my very long existence." His thumbs stroke over my cheekbones, catching the tears that escape. "There's no part of me that doesn't crave you, no part of me that isn't already hopelessly, stupidly yours. The thought of touching anyone who isn't you makes me want to tear the world apart. You're it for me, nemesis. It's only ever been you."

I swallow against the sudden thickness in my throat. "But I don't have a godmark. I'm not—"

"Then give me whichever mark you choose. Cut it into my flesh, carve it into my bones, I don't give a fuck. Just make me yours the same way I want to make you mine."

My heart feels like it's going to slam right out of my chest. With shaking fingers, I press the edge of the dagger to Evander's chest above his pectoral. Flesh splits beneath the steel, and I form the jagged lines that spell out my Claiming.

The eight-pointed star symbolizing the first that lit the sky at my birth.

I lower the blade. "What comes next?"

"I taste your blood, and I'll open my power up to you. Decide where you want my mouth."

Where don't I?

I shrug out of my coat and pull off my shirt. Cool air meets my naked torso, but I barely feel the chill. Snatching up the dagger again, I choose a spot just below my collarbone and score a shallow line before I can second-guess myself.

Evander makes a low sound. Then he's surging forward, hands grabbing my hips as his mouth seals over the cut. Pleasure lances through me at the sting. The slick drag of his tongue. I twist a hand in his hair, and he keeps going, groaning against my skin. His power thrums through my veins as the Claiming begins to take hold.

"Your turn," he says.

He brings my wrist to his lips and brushes a feather-light kiss to the frantic thrum of my pulse as more of his power rushes into me. It gathers beneath my skin until a new mark takes shape over where Alexios' used to be. Luminous gold limning my flesh in delicate filigree.

Eight lovely points form on my wrist in gilded ink—a more elaborate twin to the sigil I carved into him.

"Now bite me," Evander commands, baring his throat. "Don't be gentle."

My teeth sink into the corded muscle of his neck, and I bite down until he shudders against me. Until the copper tang of him spills hot and sweet across my tongue.

Nothing has ever tasted so holy. So profane.

He plunges his hands into my hair and tips my head, pressing his mouth to mine and kissing me deeply. Chasing the taste of himself. Of us.

I'm lost to it, to him. There's no up or down, no air, no gravity. Nothing exists except sensation. The torrent of memory and feeling roars through the place where our souls collide.

The fundamental parts of me rearrange to accommodate the shape of him. It's separate and symbiotic all at once. Two sets of heaving lungs, straining for oxygen. That's his heartbeat pounding beside mine. His soul flooding me with *mine* and *always* and *let me keep you*.

His love is more natural disaster than emotion. It does not

bend. It does not yield. There are no words in any language to capture the depthless intensity, how completely it consumes him. I'm on fire and I'm drowning, and I'm certain this will shatter me. Because it isn't gentle, it isn't sweet. It isn't something I can cup in my palms like glass or hold tenderly to my chest.

It's a storm. A war cry.

Evander's hands are everywhere, now. Unlacing my boots. Stripping me with ruthless efficiency. Hot palms and clever fingers skate over every part of me.

"Fucking exquisite," he rasps. His trousers and boots meet mine on the forest floor. "You're so damn perfect."

His mouth follows the path forged by his fingers. He pushes me against the tree, holding me up as his mouth nudges between my thighs. Each reverent swipe of his tongue against my pussy, each press of his lips, feels like an act of worship.

He whispers words in a language I don't understand, but somehow, I know it means *forever*. Means *always*. The translation bleeds through our bond in fits and starts—in vows of vengeance and fidelity. In oaths to raze entire kingdoms to ash for me.

His hands tighten, digging into my hips hard enough to bruise. When he opens his eyes and looks up at me, the breath leaves me in a rush. It's awe and adoration, worship and want.

My Chosen, I hear him think as he licks into me. *Mine*.

Then he rises and kisses me again, and I taste myself on him— my blood, my pleasure. I'm lost. I drown myself in the slide of his tongue against mine as he delves deeper, hotter, tasting and taking and devouring.

Evander's hands slip beneath my ass, gripping me tight. I wrap my legs around his waist as he pins me up against the trunk. The rough bark scrapes my shoulders, but I barely register the sting. Not when he's notching his hips between my thighs, his cock a blunt pressure against me.

"Look at me," he says. "Don't take your eyes off me."

Our stares lock as he slowly pushes forward. Then he begins to move. Hips rolling in a slow, deliberate rhythm. Pulling out only to surge back in, again and again, settling into a pattern that has me digging my heels into his ass. Clutching him closer. Deeper.

This isn't like Aethertide. This is slower, tender, and more raw than I knew sex could be. A declaration of intent. All the while, his eyes remain on my face, tracking the flutter of my lashes, my breaths, the helpless part of my lips as sensation winds tighter.

"I tried so hard not to love you," Evander tells me with a thrust that has me seeing stars. "But then you left, and I didn't know how to be in a world that didn't have you in it."

I dig my nails into his shoulders, urging him on. "Couldn't even keep the roses alive for a day?"

A breathless huff of laughter stirs my hair. He slides his palm down to press against the small of my back, shifting his stance, hitting deeper. "That's right. Never stood a chance." He presses a kiss to my jaw. "I don't know that I'll ever deserve you. I'm not a good male. I'll never be easy."

"If I wanted easy, I wouldn't have fallen in love with a god."

He laughs. Then he readjusts his grip on my thighs until he can push them wider, sinking deeper. He fucks me a little harder. A little more focused. His cock drags over a spot inside me that sets my veins alight. He shifts his weight, wedging a hand between us to skim down, down, and then his fingers press to my clit.

My head thumps back against the trunk. "Right there."

He rubs in tight circles, timing it with each thrust. My back bows, and my muscles clench down as pleasure builds and builds.

"That's it," he breathes. "Come apart for me. Let me feel you."

He leans down to lick my pulse before setting his teeth to the delicate skin—a bright burst of pleasure-pain that sends me hurtling over the edge. I splinter with a fractured cry. There is only the clench of my body around his, him inside me as he buries his face in my hair and groans his completion against my neck. The ragged symphony of our breathing and the thundering of our hearts as they gradually slow.

Evander nuzzles me, his chest expanding with a deep inhale like he's trying to memorize my scent. To carry it with him always.

Carefully, he peels us away from the tree and lowers us to the grass, cushioning me on a wing. He props himself up on his elbow and trails reverent fingers over my face. "Hey, Chosen." There's an entire liturgy of longing distilled down into those two words. "How are we feeling?"

I turn my attention inward to the glittering tapestry of him in my head. He's everywhere—threaded through my every breath, bleeding into all the hollow spaces I didn't even know were empty until he filled them up and made them his.

"Yours," I tell him. And it encompasses everything. "I feel like I'm yours."

Evander's eyes flare. "Again."

"Yours."

Something eases in his expression. "I like the way that sounds."

A comfortable silence settles between us. I lift a hand, idly brushing the symbol carved into his chest. The cuts have already healed over into thin, silvery scars.

"Will these stay?"

Evander covers my fingers with his own, pressing my palm flat over the steady thud of his heart. "Chosen marks always stay."

"And you want that?"

"I want everything with you." After a lingering press of his lips to mine, Evander sits up. "I hate to cut this short, but I need to take you back to the tower."

With a groan, I tug on my discarded garments. By the time I finish lacing my boots, Evander is dressed.

I give his wings an indulgent stroke. "And after you take me back?"

Evander opens his mouth to answer, but then his head snaps up. He narrows his eyes at the treeline. "Go," he snarls without taking his attention off the trees. His tone brooks no argument. "Run, Devaliant."

So I do.

43

EVANDER

"BASTIEN," I SAY, my voice steady despite the unease slithering down my spine.

Those obsidian eyes fix on me as he emerges from the trees. "You've been busy. I saw you made quite a mess in Hellevig."

There's a dangerous calm to the words, a dispassionate sort of observation, but I'm not fooled. His power is gathering, the pressure building in the air. Shadows writhe across the ground.

He tilts his head as he scents the air. "You're struggling. Ruptured organs?"

"Kidneys, twenty minutes ago. But my power's sorted it. Probably."

I spare a moment to cast my awareness down the tether that connects my soul to Bryony, sending a pulse of reassurance. *Keep moving, vicious girl. Run until I tell you to stop.*

Her reply drifts back. *Is it Alexios?*

My brother. Move your ass, Devaliant.

Then I slam down my mental walls, halting the flow of sensation between us. No need for her to feel every hit I'm about to take as Bastien extracts his pound of flesh.

My brother takes another long inhale, scenting again. "You soulbonded. I can smell her Claim all over you."

There's no use pretending. No way to sidestep or spin the truth into something more palatable. So I don't bother.

"Yes."

Something flashes across Bastien's features—a fleeting crack in that impassive mask. It's there in the tightening around his eyes, the almost imperceptible tic in his jaw.

If Bastien had actual expressions instead of microsecond blips in an otherwise flawless veneer of control, I'd call it incandescent rage.

"You looked me in the eye," he says with that eerie calm that's a thousand times worse than yelling, "and swore you'd end her. You lied to me again."

I dig my nails into my palms until it stings, using the small pain as a focal point—an anchor. Because I deserve whatever's coming. We both know it. I made a promise to my brother, and pissed all over it the second I fell stupid in love with the one woman I was never supposed to touch.

"I'm protecting what's mine."

We want what we want. Even when we know it'll destroy us.

"Yours," he says. "The mortal with the blood of our enemies in her veins. That's what you're willing to trade your honor for?"

"Don't—"

But before I can choke out another word—before I manage to throw up my mental shields—a wave of shadow slams into me and lashes through my mind. Frantically, I try to shore up the crumbling bulwarks, but I'm weakened and sluggish. My power is drained after the shit I pulled in Hellevig.

"Do you remember," he murmurs, "the vows you swore to me after you pulled me out of the Bloody Court?"

Vertigo crashes through me. The sickening swoop in the pit of my stomach. And then the world is pitching around me, Bastien's shadows rising to blot out the sky as he drags me under.

Down, down, down—into the rawest depths of recall.

The dank stone of the Court's killing floor flashes through my head in flickers and starts. The stench of sweat and spilled viscera. And there, chained at the center of it all…

My brother.

His wings gone. They'd carved him up like a slab of meat, stole pieces of him that could never be replaced or regrown, even with an Eternal's power.

And after, when I finally fought my way to him? When I cut him down and dragged his broken body back to Scillari? I swore to him I would make it right.

"They held me down and used me, Evander," Bastien says, still in that remote tone. "Violated me. Mutilated me until I was unrecognizable. And I never begged, not even when they took my wings." He straightens, flicking a leaf from his coat. "There's a very specific sound it makes when they hack through a limb that size. The tendons pop and snap. Bones splinter. And it feels like the worst nightmare imaginable. You get dizzy. Detached. Like you've slipped out of your skin, and you're watching it happen to someone else. You know what carried me through? What kept me fighting?" His eyes meet mine. "Knowing you would come. That you'd rip me out of that place and keep your promise to avenge us. Or have you forgotten that, too?"

I grit my teeth, reaching for composure. But all I see is Bryony, bright and burning in my mind. The glittering mark of my shiny new Claim glowing on her wrist.

You told me once that you would crave me in any lifetime, across every eternity. And I wanted to tell you... I'd find you in all of them.

Bastien's expression darkens. "Yeah. That's what I thought."

And then he's on me.

His fist cracks into my jaw in an explosion of agony. I feel the bone pulverize and taste the hot, copper gush of blood flooding my mouth. He hits me again—a brutal impact to the ribs that sends me sprawling.

"Fight back," he snarls.

Another ruthless blow to the solar plexus.

I hit the dirt. Fire screams along my side. "I'm sorry. I'm so damned sorry."

He looms over me. "*Get up.* Get up so I can put you back down."

Slowly, I force myself to my feet—and I finally understand what this is. What he needs.

He needs to hurt something. Needs to make it bleed and bleed and fucking bleed, the way he's done for centuries. I'm the only thing that can weather the hit. The only one who'll let him bruise his knuckles on me and not hit back.

So when Bastien slams me into the dirt, I don't resist. He tears into me. He cracks me open and pulls me under the thrashing surface of his rage, and I let it fill my lungs. I drown in the cold of his anguish.

There are certain things we do for the people we love. Hurts we willingly hold close and secret, because it's the only way we remember how to be real. How to feel anything at all. Bas and I, we've got no language for kindness, not after everything. The war hollowed those soft places out until all that's left is scar tissue. This is how we speak without words now. This is our ugly, broken love—the savagery we carve into each other just to feel something.

So I let my brother take his retribution. I let him break my bones and split my skin and rupture my organs. Because I earned this brutality. This is my penance, the only absolution he'll allow me.

I lie here and take it because I promised him vengeance. Swore that one day, we'd paint the realms red with the blood of everyone who stole from us, who profaned our mother's corpse for power. Who took his wings. Who made us into what we are.

Instead, I went and fell for a girl guaranteed to rip us apart.

"You selfish, backstabbing fuck." Bastien punctuates each word with a ruthless blow to my face. "You knew"—*Crack*—"what she was." *Crunch*. "What she meant." A brutal punch to my nose, cartilage snapping beneath his fist. "But you let her under your skin, anyway."

I spit out a mouthful of blood. "I love her. More than anything."

It feels like sacrilege to say the words out loud. Like speaking them here is its own sort of betrayal. As if I'm casting all those vows I swore into the pyre and letting them burn alongside the family we once were.

Bastien goes still above me. Something shifts in his gaze—and for an instant, I glimpse the male I used to know. My steadfast older brother, with a wry slant to his mouth and laughter glinting in his obsidian eyes.

"Then you're going to lose her," he tells me, almost gently. "And it'll rip you to shreds." Then he pulls his fist back and punches right through my ribcage to wrap his fingers around my heart. "I told you what I'd do if you bonded with her. Warned you what it would mean."

I cough wetly. "I know."

I want to tell him to keep going. To pry me open and dig his fingers in. Tear out all the messy, mangled bits. No half measures. No careful handling.

But then a new voice cracks through the haze. "That's enough."

The Eternal of Asteria lands in a rustle of red and black feathers, his wings kicking up eddies of fallen leaves.

Alexios' face is a beautiful mask, betraying nothing as he takes me in. "Get your hand out of his ribcage, Blade. He'll need at least half an hour to regrow that heart if you crush it, and I want him lucid."

Bastien wrenches his hand out of my chest. I suck in a gasping breath, swallowing down bile.

Alexios' power fills the clearing, thick enough to choke on. I snarl weakly as it presses down on me, sinks claws into my mind, and commands me to be still. He crooks a finger, and my spine arches as his magic forces me upright. Fire sparks over my skin. My own power strains against its bonds, begging for release, but there will be no battle here. No contest of wills.

I can only kneel.

He studies me before cutting his attention to Bastien. "Do you need a minute?"

My brother rolls his shoulders. "I'm good."

Alexios radiates the kind of stillness that has heralded the deaths of entire armies. "Where is she, Wolf?"

I bare my teeth. "Dunno. Had some real important appointments to keep. You know how it is."

"You're dangerously close to outliving your usefulness."

I spit a glob of blood at his feet. "Must've struck a nerve with you, huh? This one mortal girl. She really got under your skin. Can't blame you, honestly." I laugh. "She's under mine, too."

In a blink, he lunges. Seizes a fistful of my hair and wrenches my head back, forcing me to meet the glow of his eyes. And there he is—the despot, the subjugator. The god-king who has razed empires and salted the earth where they once stood.

"This girl," Alexios says, soft and dangerous, "nearly killed me when her followers abandoned their tithes. It tore holes in my Shroud that the fleshtrade has used to hunt our people like animals. Or did you forget that detail while you were falling dick-first into betrayal?"

His grip squeezes harder. The leash tightens another merciless notch. "So, for my education, tell me why you think I should spare your precious Bryony instead of snapping her neck. You've defied the Accords. Slaughtered my Claimed. Idris is dead by her hand, and I'm down to my last Anchor. It's only a matter of time before the Shroud fails entirely. So convince me, Wolf. Give me a single reason to let your Devaliant walk."

"Because I made her my Chosen."

Silence.

His eyes snap to Bastien, demanding confirmation. My brother dips his chin.

Alexios' expression flattens. "You never did know when to stop *pushing*. It may go against our oldest laws for me to kill her outright, but there are so many ways to make a thing hurt without it dying." He jerks his chin at the trees where Bryony disappeared. "Blade, fetch her for me."

44

BRYONY

MY BOOTS SLAP against the ground as I race through the woods.

Evander's voice echoes through my head. *Keep moving, vicious girl. Run until I tell you to stop.*

Is it Alexios? I ask.

My brother. Now move your ass, Devaliant.

A tremor racks through me, but I shove it down and lock it away. I can't fall apart now.

So I don't slow, even though my muscles are burning. I grit my teeth and push myself harder, pumping my arms at my sides. Amara trained me to flee just in case.

Stop. Evander's command is sharp. *Make yourself small and hide. Don't make a sound. Don't even breathe.*

I stagger to a halt, chest heaving as I scan for cover. *There*—a tangle of massive roots in a hollow beneath a tree. I wedge into the narrow space, trying to control my breathing and draw air into my burning lungs as shallowly as possible. I listen hard to the distant shrieks of birds and the susurrus of wind through the branches. Every tiny noise seems magnified.

A twig snaps. Dead foliage crunches under a heavy boot.

And then a figure materializes out of the mist.

The Blade's face resembles Evander's—the severe slant of those dark brows, the sharp cut of his cheekbones, and a strong, square jaw. But that's where the similarities end. Because where Evander is all tawny skin and gilt feathers, his brother is monochrome. Stark. His hair is white, skin pale. He's like a sculpture given breath.

But it's his eyes that make my stomach drop. They're black—*true* black, like the unending abyss between stars, fathomless and cold. Primordial instinct gibbers at me to *run run run* as that stare sweeps the clearing.

The Blade steps forward, and the shadows bend and cling to him like a living shroud. His power saturates the air, seeking.

Looking for me.

Don't think. Don't feel. Don't exist.

I reach for Evander—only to slam into an impenetrable psychic wall. Panic claws at my chest as I press my incorporeal fingers against it anyway.

And white-hot agony spears through my skull.

The wall is there for a reason. His tone is gentle but brooks no argument as he nudges me back. *Alexios' collar is cinching tight. Leave it be and stay hidden. Please.*

That *please* destroys something in me. In that brief connection, I felt what Alexios is doing to him. That magical collar is crushing his throat, choking him, hurting him.

Because of me.

Fuck hiding. Fuck playing it safe.

I won't leave him to handle this alone while I cower in the dirt like a frightened child.

Taking a deep breath, I step out to face the Blade. "Take me to Alexios."

He turns his head slowly. The weight of that obsidian stare flays me open, and it takes every scrap of control not to look away. His eyes catch on the mark shimmering at my wrist.

Nothing. Not a word. Just those eyes boring into me. Then—

A ripple in the air, a sudden crushing pressure.

And he's in my head.

I scream as his power tears through me. There's no gentleness, no care as he rips into my mind, peeling me open, layer after layer. My thoughts are all exposed for his relentless perusal.

He finds where I keep my memories of Evander—every touch, every kiss, every moment we've shared in the dark.

Evander's hands on my body.

His mouth on my skin.

His voice in my ear.

All my stupid, desperate, hopeless *wanting*.

My knees hit the dirt hard, but I barely feel it. Fracture lines spiderweb through my psyche. My temples pound with the overwhelming press of his magic spilling over me in wave after wave, threatening to tear me apart.

"*Stop*," I gasp out. "Please!"

And miraculously, he withdraws, leaving me trembling. I slump forward, trying to remember how my lungs work. How I'm put together.

Why are you in pain? Evander's voice. So focused on me, even as an Eternal's collar strangles him.

The wall is there for a reason, remember?

The Blade looms over me with a gloved hand outstretched. There's no warmth in that beautiful face, just the unspoken threat of what happens if I refuse.

Bile coats the back of my tongue, but I grasp his hand and let him wrench me upright. He sweeps me against his chest like I weigh nothing. The shadows around us writhe and stretch, forming those wings that aren't really wings at all—just darkness given form—and then we're airborne.

We touch down in the clearing minutes later.

A harsh gasp leaves me when I see Evander. He's on his knees in the center of the glade, drenched in so much blood I can barely see skin. His flesh is knitting the remnants of serious injuries back together.

His head whips up. *Bryony.*

There's so much agony packed into my name, but I lock my walls down until all I can hear is the roar of my pulse as I force myself to look at *him*.

Alexios. God of Storms.

Back in Vartena, I had grown up under the looming presence

of his stone effigy every time I offered my blood on its altar. But that icon is a child's fumbling rendition compared to the god standing before me.

He's like a force of gravity threatening to subsume everything in its path. His wings are resplendent in black and red, and his eyes are an intense, glowing scarlet. A metal clasp holds his shoulder-length black hair back from his face. I look for some flaw in those elegant features, in that warrior's physique that's every bit as strong as Evander's, but I find nothing. He's beautiful. Breathtaking, even.

"Don't," Evander snarls. "Whatever heroic bullshit you're about to try—"

Alexios doesn't even look his way. Just flicks his fingers like he's brushing away a fly, and Evander's words die in a wet gurgle. Fresh blood pours over his lips.

I dig my nails into my palms. "*Stop*."

The Eternal of Asteria turns those burning eyes on me. "I have to admire your nerve, if nothing else." He crosses his arms. The sleeves of his shirt are rolled up to reveal dark tattoos in a flowing script on his forearms. "It's almost impressive how thoroughly you've managed to fuck up the natural order of things."

My hands tremble. "You mean how you upended my life? Tore away my protection on a whim?"

"When your little zealots abandoned my temple for your gates, they damaged the Shroud near past mending." His red eyes narrow, as if he's imagining all the inventive ways he could make me hurt. "And now you've turned my Enforcer into your lapdog."

"They weren't my *anything*," I snap. "Maybe if you weren't an absent god, and if my uncle did his job as a ruler, they wouldn't have been so desperate for someone who gave a shit about them."

Something dark flashes across his face. I've hit a nerve. "Then we'll focus on what you did do, girl. You killed an Anchor under my protection. Even in your realm, that has consequences." He circles me, those massive wings flexing. The tattoos on his arms pulse red. "Let's make something clear. Being the Wolf's

Chosen might save your life, but it won't save his. That wall he's built to shield you from his pain? I'll tear it down until you feel everything I do to him. A human might reconsider her choices after she feels her mate being flayed alive."

It's suddenly hard to breathe around the knife in my chest as images flood my mind of Evander being tortured. Skinned. Bled. *For me.*

I force my emotions down. "What do you want from me?"

One dark brow arches. "Want?" A low, cruel laugh. "Oh, Princess. This isn't about *wants*. The Wolf slaughtered my Claimed in Hellevig, and an Anchor's been murdered against my wishes. The Accords demand payment in blood. The only question is whose—yours or his."

The kind of damage an Eternal could take is unthinkable. Intolerable. Evander could endure centuries of pain if Alexios wanted.

"He did it for me," I say. "I'll take his punishment. All of it."

Evander thrashes against his invisible bonds. *"Don't—"*

Alexios flicks his fingers again as the invisible lash of his power wraps around Evander's throat. Fresh blood spills from his nose and trickles down his lips. Despite the pain, his eyes never leave mine, pleading mixed with that familiar fury.

You reckless creature. His snarl slams into the walls I've built in my mind.

I refuse to let him in. Not now. If I feel what he's feeling, I'll unravel.

"Name your price."

Alexios studies me, as inscrutable as the statues in his grand temple. "What would you sacrifice for him, Princess? Where's your breaking point? A little pain? A lot of it?" He leans close enough that I can feel his breath on my cheek. "Are you willing to die for this?"

The silence stretches. I feel Bastien's cold stare on me, assessing. Waiting for me to crack.

"I'd do anything," I say firmly. "Everything."

"Hmm. Your family has a reputation for saying one thing

and doing another. So, when Amalthea Devaliant crawled to me begging for clemency mid-war, I had her demonstrate her sincerity. I'll do you the same courtesy. Three tests to prove your conviction. Complete them, and I'll consider the Wolf's slate wiped clean."

Bargain for Evander's leash, a voice whispers in my head.

I glance at Bastien, but his expression gives nothing away. *What?*

His leash, Bastien repeats, his mental voice cold and flat. *You're his Chosen. You can demand that his full power be restored.*

Why are you helping me?

Nothing. He's gone from my mind as quickly as he entered.

I swallow, hoping I'm not falling into a trap. "That's not enough."

Alexios' eyebrows shoot up, as if no one has ever dared to counteroffer.

"If I survive your tests," I continue, "then his power should be unbound completely. That's my right as his Chosen."

"Bold little human," Alexios murmurs, eyes narrowing.

"You can't kill me directly, so I'm guessing this is your loophole. So I'll take my chances."

Some calculation clicks behind that burning stare. "I'll accept that bargain."

Insist on fair terms, Bastien's silent voice instructs. *Parameters within human tolerances, or there's a distinct possibility this agreement will be worth less than the air you waste making it.*

"It has to be something I can conceivably do," I press, following Bastien's advice. "The tests. I have to be able to succeed. I can't win if it's rigged."

Alexios dips his head in acknowledgment. "Fine. Possible, but not easy. I'll suppress the magical feedback you share with Evander as his Chosen. He stays in power-suppressing cuffs until you earn his release."

A low growl of protest comes from Evander before he breaks off with a hiss of pain.

And that solidifies my resolve. The Wolf of Asteria doesn't

show weakness, not unless he's in the kind of agony I can't conceive of.

"Let's seal it," I say.

Alexios stretches out his hand. I hesitate, but out of the corner of my eye, Bastien gives me an imperceptible nod.

Slowly, I place my palm in Alexios'. He plucks a small blade from the sheath at his wrist, slices open my skin in a shallow cut, and repeats the motion on himself. He presses our wounds together.

Power pours into me, the formation of a new tether. A shining golden cuff forms around my wrist—the physical mark of our deal.

Alexios wrenches me forward until bare inches separate us. "Sealed in blood and magic, Bryony Devaliant. For the duration of this game, you're mine."

Then he releases me with a shove, turning back to Evander. "Get your Chosen to my palace, Wolf. And Blade, keep our boy on his best behavior. Her first test starts tomorrow."

45

BRYONY

THE PALACE MATERIALIZES out of the mist as Evander dips into a tight spiral. Towers of opalescent stone cut through the clouds, their surfaces catching the sunset and breaking it into red and gold shards. The compound spreads across the mountainside as if someone had carved it directly from the peaks.

This is Alexios' palace? I ask Evander.

Silence. Like a psychic door slamming in my face.

Still sulking, I see. Lovely.

Evander dives, sending my stomach plummeting. Details resolve as we plunge closer—gold and silver tiles on the roofs, copper accents glinting along the crenelated battlements and turrets. The entire place gleams red and gold in the waning sunset.

Everything rests on a precipice of rugged rocks. Teal runes flare on the walls, humming with power—the magical equivalent of a raised portcullis.

We soar over the manicured gardens dotted with pale winter blooms. Frost rimes the topiaries and fountains, the spitting streams frozen into glittering crystal arcs. Courtiers wander down the paths in silk dresses, dripping in glowing gems with trapped flames.

The flagstones rush up to meet us—until Evander snaps his wings out, bringing us to a jarring halt. I fight down a surge of nausea as he sets me on my feet.

Alexios lands beside us in a flurry of feathers. Bastien touches down a beat after that, his wings a shifting shroud of shadow.

"Blade," Alexios says coolly, "escort Evander to the cells. Princess, you're with me. I'll show you to your room."

I brush my hair out of my face. "No thanks. I'll stay with Evander."

Evander makes a furious sound from behind me. "Go with him."

I whirl. "Oh, *now* you've decided to acknowledge that I exist? How big of you."

He just glowers at me.

Alexios' burning gaze flicks between us. "Spare me the lovers' quarrel. If the girl wants to wallow in a cold dungeon all night, that's her prerogative. Blade, take her to the Wolf's cell, but don't let her inside. If he gives you any trouble, remind him what it feels like to be in the pit."

"Understood," Bastien says. He turns his void-dark stare on me and Evander. "Come with me."

We fall into step behind him as he stalks off down the path. The breeze carries snippets of hushed conversation from the courtiers, and I feel their stares as I follow Bastien through the looming doors into the palace.

The atrium unfolds before me in a dizzying sprawl of polished marble. Columns wrapped in gold vines rise on both sides, supporting arches adorned with delicate metalwork. Chandeliers scatter light across the glossy floors. To my left is a fountain shaped like a serpent with water burbling from its open jaws.

Courtiers linger through the halls in a sea of multicolored wings—vibrant purples and emerald greens, deep indigos and ambers. Their cold stares sweep over me, some openly repulsed, others unreadable. No one offers a reassuring smile as we pass.

Every conversation dies the deeper we walk through the halls. My skin prickles with the electric hum of their power, as if they're braced for a threat.

Their stares keep dropping to my wrist—to the glowing eight-pointed star that marks me as the Wolf's Chosen—but there's no awe in the staring. All I see is disgust. *Contempt*. As if I've stolen something that was never meant for me.

It takes a moment for it to fully sink in—I'm not just a human; I'm a Devaliant. Some of these demis probably watched my ancestors butcher their families. I'm sure they'd rip me apart without Evander's mark protecting me.

"You good?" Evander's deep rumble snaps me out of my spiraling thoughts.

I swallow hard and nod. Evander's brow furrows like he wants to say something else, but—

"*Wolf.*"

We both turn as a familiar demigoddess with dark hair and silver wings stalks toward us. Arcadia. The demigoddess who'd touched Evander in the garden that day like she'd done it a thousand times before. Who'd grabbed him for a kiss like she owned him.

She doesn't slow down or hesitate, just storms up to Evander and slaps him across the face. He staggers back a step, a red print already blooming on his cheek.

"You soulbonded with a *Devaliant?*" Arcadia hisses, wings flaring. "Have you lost your fucking mind? Did someone knock the last shred of sense out of your skull when I wasn't looking? Or did you just decide to spit on everything we lost?"

A ripple goes through the assembled court. Shame scalds my cheeks. The back of my neck prickles as the weight of a hundred judgmental gazes settles on me.

"Lovely to see you too, Cady." Evander rubs at his face. "Been practicing that slap? Got some real power behind it."

Cady again. I know it's stupid to be jealous. He's lived for centuries before me. But the possessive part of me—the part I didn't even know existed until Evander—wants to claw her eyes out.

"You think this is a joke?" The hardness in Arcadia's voice cracks, revealing something raw beneath. Something that makes me want to look away. "Why *her?* Of all people, why would you Choose—" She swallows thickly and glances away.

I suddenly feel like I'm intruding on something private. Something I have no right to witness.

"Arcadia." Bastien's voice is oddly gentle. Like he knows exactly what she's feeling. "That's enough."

She sends him a venomous look before whirling on me. Those mercury eyes dissect me from head to toe like I'm something she found rotting on the bottom of her boot. "You think you belong here?" she sneers. "You'll never be one of us. The Wolf might have Chosen you, but you're just a pet he'll get bored with. You're not a queen."

She storms off. I stare after her, my blood roaring in my ears. *Pet.* The word burrows beneath my skin like a splinter. I'd been so focused on saving my sister and not dying that I hadn't let myself consider the rest—that if I win Evander's freedom, I won't just be bound to a male.

I'll rule beside an Eternal.

Bastien's eyes meet mine, and I read the unspoken accusation: my presence is salt in old wounds, a living reminder of everything they lost.

Evander's hand grazes the small of my back, steadying. "Eyes front. Don't let them see you flinch."

I nod, grateful for the grounding touch.

We leave the main hall, following Bastien down a labyrinth of corridors. With each turn we take, the press of bodies thins out until it's just the three of us, our footfalls unnaturally loud.

Before long, we arrive at a spiral staircase delving deep into the crags of the mountain. More runes flare, bathing the walls in red as we descend, the air growing colder with every step. The lights from above fade until there's nothing but the weak illumination of the sigils lighting our way.

At the bottom, cells line the narrow hallway. The torchlight catches on dark stains covering the floor. I've spent enough time in Hellevig's temple to recognize dried blood when I see it.

"In," Bastien orders his brother, swinging open the nearest cell.

Evander steps inside without argument. The cell is barely big enough for him to stretch his wings. He stands motionless, not even flinching as Bastien secures a set of thick cuffs around his wrists and ankles. The metal ignites, flaring with pale light as the restraints seal into place, and the stink of seared flesh fills the air. My gorge rises as I realize what I'm seeing.

Turpori steel. The only thing in the realm capable of suppressing an Eternal's power.

"What happens if he fights?" I ask. My voice emerges steadier than I feel. "Alexios said something about a pit."

"Where Evander was headed before your bargain." Bastien winds a set of chains around Evander's torso, immobilizing his wings. "Complete sensory deprivation. Magic-suppressant cuffs. A long climb through miles of dirt to reach the surface, depth depending on the king's mood."

A shudder runs through me. "You've experienced it?"

His hands pause as he tests the final cuff. A minute tell, his composure fracturing for the span of a blink. "Twelve years. It's unpleasant."

And then he's striding from the cell and slamming the barred door behind him.

I sink to the floor and arrange myself against the wall, as close as I can get to the male on the other side.

Bastien looks at me, unreadable. As if he's trying to puzzle out the shape of me. To slot me into predetermined boxes with neat, tidy labels.

"I'd advise selecting proper quarters," he says. "A bed, a bath, a door that locks from the inside."

I almost laugh. "Thanks, but I'm good here."

His eyes narrow, and I know I've surprised him. Stepped outside whatever narrative he's constructed for me. "Don't say I didn't warn you."

He starts away, but I scramble to my feet and hurry after him. "Wait."

Bastien turns back, the broad line of his shoulders rigid.

"Why did you help me earlier?" The words tumble from me in a rush. "With Alexios. You didn't have to talk me through that negotiation, but you did. Why?"

A pause. I watch the restless movements of his shadow wings. "Your mind was a smoldering wreck when I looked through it earlier. It offended me."

"Oh," I say faintly. "I can see how that would be unpleasant, but I'm not sure what it has to do with—"

"Buried in all that pathetic mess, I found what someone more sentimental might call love. For my brother." His gaze flicks to Evander, then back to me. "He let me beat him half to death without fighting back. For you. When you're involved, he clearly operates on a policy of idiocy, so keeping you alive seems like the most efficient option."

"So you helped me for him?"

He glances back at Evander again. Something complicated moves across his face. "He loves you, and he's survived enough loss to last ten lifetimes. But let me make one thing clear—if you're the instrument of his destruction, I will personally make sure you spend whatever remains of your miserable life begging for death, and I won't grant it. Ever."

I nod, fighting back a cringe. "Has anyone ever mentioned you have all the social grace of a battering ram?"

"Lies are a waste of time."

"Well. In the spirit of that honesty, I don't suppose you'd help me again?" At his flat stare, I press on. "My uncle took daggers from me in Hellevig. Turpori steel—a gift from Evander. I think I may need them for my tests."

Something cold and furious enters his features. For a moment, I wonder if I've miscalculated, if he'll snap my neck. "Girl," he says, very softly, "if you'd like to keep breathing, never mention my brother handing out my weapons again."

Yikes. Okay. Well, I'm having doubts about whether I'll survive this conversation intact.

"You know what?" I step back, hands up. "Forget I said anything. Great talk! Really productive!"

His eyes narrow. Then he turns away and strides off down the corridor. Such a charming male. Like talking to a rock, only less pleasant.

I sigh and return to my place beside Evander's cell, easing onto the ground.

"Nemesis," Evander says from the other side of the bars. "What in the name of fuck did you say to my brother? His face nearly arranged itself into an actual expression. It was like watching a statue contemplate murder."

"You could have warned me that *he* was the one who forged my daggers. I would have gone to the grave never mentioning them."

Evander winces. "Ah."

"Your brother is… a lot. Did you know he flayed my thoughts wide open earlier?"

I decide not to mention the way Bastien laid bare all the messy, tangled snarls of feeling squirming in my chest where Evander is concerned. All that desperate wanting.

"Of course he did. Invasive prick." He sighs. "I don't know what I did to offend the stars that they cursed me with a lunatic of a Chosen. A madwoman intent on courting her own destruction."

I just flash him a smile. "You're *welcome*."

"Don't you dare sit there looking all innocent." He gives his chains a pointed rattle for emphasis. "You haven't done a single sane thing—"

"Which instance of insanity are we talking about? The one where I'm voluntarily sleeping in a dungeon, or the deal with Alexios? I'm doing my best to keep you on your toes."

"Every single idiotic choice you've made since you ended up in my keeping, starting with me. I'm the worst idea you've ever had."

"But you're my favorite bad idea." I reach through the bars, wiggling my fingers in invitation. "Hold my hand. I need comfort."

"No. If I weren't chained up, I'd bite you for being such an insufferable pain in my ass."

"Why did I tie myself to you again? Refresh my memory."

"Temporary insanity?" A shrug. "Good dick?"

I angle myself to better see his face. "I love you. I suppose that's the reason."

He goes still, not even breathing—as if I've reached into his chest and squeezed his heart in my fist. "Loving me doesn't mean throwing yourself on a blade for me, you impossible creature."

"But that's what happens when you tie your soul to someone else's." My fingers find his. "You get all of it. The ugly parts. The broken pieces. The stupid, reckless need to put yourself between them and pain. My methods are questionable, but my heart is sure."

And that's the crux of it, isn't it? Love isn't pretty words and tender touches. It means standing in front of a blade meant for the one who holds your heart and bleeding so they don't have to.

It means hurting to spare them from pain.

"You have no idea what's coming," he says, fingers tightening around mine. "The shit Alexios will put you through. He doesn't play fair, and he doesn't lose."

"I've been playing games with men who want to hurt me my entire life, Wolf."

I watch as the firelight from the wall sconces limns the angles of him gold, casting the rest in stark shadow. There's a terrible beauty in those contrasts—the light and void, the dualities comprising this god I've bound myself to.

"Just tell me why," he says softly. "Why make that bargain?"

"Because I can't watch you suffer. Because you let me touch your wings after everything you said at the griefwood." I stroke my thumb over his, slow and tender. "No one's ever belonged to me before. That means I don't run when things get too hard. I'm staying and fighting even if your people despise the queen you Chose."

The bond shudders between us. I feel him, the fiery star-bright heart of him, even muted by the Turpori steel cuffs. If he didn't have those on, I know I'd experience a swell of emotion like back in the clearing, as if his love for me was a blaze devouring us both.

"I don't remember when I stopped hating you," he murmurs.

"I lied when I said I did. You were so bright, it hurt to look at you, and I hated what that did to me." A ragged inhale, like every word is being dragged out of him. "I'd rotted in my own pain for centuries. Then you swept in—a living reminder of my grief—and suddenly I couldn't breathe through how badly I needed you. It's hard to let go of hurt. But they'll adore you. Because I did. I do."

My smile goes soft. "I think that makes you a good male."

"Only for you, vicious girl. And you don't have permission to die on me. Come back to me every night. Swear it."

"I swear."

"Good. Because if you don't, I'll rip apart the Void between this world and whatever comes after. And I'll never let you out of my sight again."

"Is that supposed to be a threat or a promise?"

"Both." He brings our joined hands to his lips, kissing my knuckles. "Always both with us."

46

BRYONY

I BARELY MANAGE an hour of sleep all night. The dungeon's damp seeps through my clothes, settling in until I can't remember what warmth feels like.

"Get up. I can hear your teeth chattering all the way over here."

I peel my lids open to find Evander watching me from his cell, his amber eyes glowing in the shadows. His chains clink together as he shifts closer to the bars separating us.

"There's a big comfortable bed upstairs with my name on it," he says. "Use it before you freeze to death."

I tip my head against the wall behind me. "What kind of Chosen would I be if I abandoned my post?"

He lets out an irritated huff. "A live one."

Before he can lecture me further, footsteps echo down the corridor. A servant rounds the corner, pale green wings tucked tight to his back like he can't bear the thought of this place sullying them.

"The king summons you to the dining hall, Princess."

"Be careful, Chosen," Evander says.

I offer him a wry smile as I push to my feet. "Aren't I always?"

"No. That's what worries me."

The servant doesn't wait. He turns sharply on his heel, expecting me to follow. I head after him through the winding corridors to the upper levels, where the chill of the dungeon gradually gives way to warmth. I shake feeling back into my numb fingers as we head through the corridors.

The palace shines even more in the daylight. Tall, arched windows line the hallway, offering views of the snowy mountains beyond, with the deep vermilion hues of mid-morning light catching on the iridescent blue veins in the marble.

A few courtiers linger in the halls. They go quiet, sending me hostile looks as I pass, and I try not to fidget under the intensity of their stares. Arcadia's words echo through my memory.

You'll only ever be his pet. Not his queen.

We come to an imposing set of double doors. The servant pushes them open, spilling warm light into the hallway.

The dining hall takes my breath away. White marble columns rise up to support an arched glass ceiling. Above, the sky is a perfect crystalline blue. Chandeliers hang in midair, suspended by nothing I can see, slowly turning to cast rainbow patterns across the glossy floor.

At the center of the chamber sits a table laden with food. Meat glistens with honey and herbs, fruits overflow in golden bowls, and bottles of wine stand ready to pour. The mingled scents of cinnamon, clove, and anise permeate the air, making my stomach twist with hunger.

Alexios lounges at the head of the table in an imposing throne-like chair, his prodigious wings draped around his shoulders. Tiny sections of his hair are braided at his temples, pulling the black strands away from his face. He wears a leather jerkin that's worn in places—a warrior's clothes rather than a king's, revealing the tattoos covering his arms. The script along his forearms leads into constellations on his biceps.

When his burning crimson eyes meet mine, I see the calculation kindling in their depths. Like he's imagining how my organs would look arranged across his fancy table.

"You look half frozen." He tips his head, still studying me. "Though I suppose that's what happens when you insist on staying in the dungeons."

I cross my arms. "I'm sure my comfort is low on your list of priorities. Just above watching paint dry."

His lips twitch in what might generously be called a smile,

then his gaze drops to the chair at his right. "Sit. Even half-frozen Devaliants need to eat."

Not with a knife aimed at their bellies, I nearly snap.

But I clamp my teeth around the words and sit.

"Eat," Alexios orders.

Everything in me rails against obeying, but I have to be smart about this and choose my battles.

So I fill my plate with whatever is in front of me, spear a morsel of meat, and slip it between my lips. It's almost offensive how good it tastes. I force down a moan and eat. Chew, swallow. Chew, swallow. By the time my plate is clean, I feel marginally more human. I set down my cutlery and lace my fingers in my lap, staring at him with all the poise expected of a princess.

"There," he says, satisfied. "A simple lesson in obedience. You can be taught."

"I was hungry. If you expect a trained pet, you're going to be disappointed."

He studies me like I'm an interesting insect he's considering crushing. "You're nothing like her. Amalthea. When she came begging during the war, she called me her salvation while her kingdom burned. The war had gone on for decades, and she was half mad with grief. But then, so was I. It's funny how pride crumbles when you're choking on ashes."

I don't let my attention waver from his. I spent too damn long on that altar to be afraid of him now. "Amalthea Devaliant drowned herself in the bathtub ten years after the Accords. Did you know that?"

Nothing. Not a flicker of regret or empathy in that beautiful, cruel face. "I'd heard something to that effect. And I can feel it when my Claimed die, little sacrifice."

"Then I assume you can *feel* the fact that Devaliants don't make it past fifty because sacrificing ourselves for your precious Shroud drives us all to madness. Or do you not care about that little detail?"

There it is. The change in the air. A building pressure against my skin. "You don't want to ask me what I think your family deserves. You won't like my answer. You ought to be grateful I let any of you live at all."

I let him see all my hatred. The anger that's been festering with every death, since my uncle took me to the Duehavn and sacrificed me to this god like I was nothing. "I died over and over while you lounged in your palace, and then you yanked away my protection on a whim, so excuse me if I'm not feeling *grateful*."

The temperature plummets. Pressure builds against my eardrums like I'm sinking to the bottom of a lake. I can't move. Storm clouds gather past the glass dome of the ceiling.

"Is that what you think I've been doing?" He'd seem calm were it not for the sudden rumble of thunder outside and the sudden pulsing glow of those blood-red eyes. "*Lounging?*"

The chandelier above us trembles, and lightning skitters across his skin. I can't breathe—the air has turned solid in my lungs.

Then he blinks.

The clouds vanish like they never existed. The pressure releases. I gasp, sucking in air like I've been drowning, my fingers clutching the table's edge.

"Yes, I suppose it must have seemed that way to you," he says, almost gentle now.

I've struck a nerve. The realization should be a victory, but all I feel is the certainty that I'm about to pay for my mistake.

Alexios' eyes flick to a servant. "The Blade. Is he still here?"

"Yes, my king."

"Get him."

The servant hurries off.

Alexios settles back in his chair, just watching me.

"Another threat?" I ask.

He smiles. "No. I'm feeling indulgent."

Footsteps approach, and Bastien strides through the doorway, his shadow wings rippling behind. White hair falls carelessly across his forehead, softening the sharp angles of his face. Snowflakes are dusted along the shoulders of his long coat.

Evander's brother looks like a creature of winter, of ice, and dark, cold evenings.

He clasps his gloved hands behind his back. "You called?"

"The Wolf's human seems confused about my duties." Alexios' voice holds dark amusement. "You're uniquely qualified to deliver a lesson."

"Which aspects?"

Alexios props his chin on his fist, studying me. "Yes, I suppose she's used to incompetent rulers, isn't she? The kind who drink themselves stupid while their kingdoms crumble. Don't bother with court sessions and territory maintenance. Focus on my additional obligations."

Bastien's void-dark gaze cuts to me. "You want me to quantify the Shroud's metaphysical burden?"

"In terms blunt enough that a dense child could grasp them, yes."

Bastien nods and steps toward me. I flinch back instinctively. His power rises, a dark wave threatening to crash over me—

"Wait." Alexios crooks a finger at me. "Here, Princess. I want you close for this. Skin to skin."

So, this is to be an intimate dissection.

My heart slams as I peel myself out of the chair. Alexios grips my wrist and tugs me down into his lap, sliding an arm around my waist. I can feel every inch where we touch—the heat of him through my clothes, his chest against my back expanding with each breath. He smells of woodsmoke and thunderstorms.

His thumb brushes Evander's Claim on my wrist, the touch almost contemplative as he traces the points of the star. "There we go. Much better." He turns his attention to Bastien. "Link our minds but keep the barriers solid. I'd rather not have the Wolf battering down my door because I'm touching what's his."

Bastien's gloved hand finds my nape. His grip tightens past the point of comfort as he splays his other palm over Alexios' brow.

"Breathe," Bastien instructs. Then, "Open."

And seven thousand years of consciousness slams into me without mercy.

Alexios' thoughts slice through mine like broken glass, leaving bleeding cuts behind. I try to fight, to push back, to find some corner of my mind that still belongs to me, but there's no escaping him. I can't breathe. Can't think. Can't do anything but drown in him.

"Shh, easy." His fingers slide into my hair, smoothing it back. "Struggling will only make it worse, trust me."

And then the voices start.

At first, they're just whispers. Distant conversations I can almost understand—but they multiply, growing louder, more desperate, seeping through the cracks of my consciousness like water through broken stone.

The whispers become murmurs.

The murmurs become words.

The words become screams.

Thousands of them. *Millions*. All crying out at once—prayers and pleas and curses and secrets, pouring into me until there's no room left for anything else. My skull is too small to contain them all.

A sound escapes me—half sob, half whimper—and Alexios' arms tighten around me in response. He's not holding me to hurt me now; he's holding me together.

"Do you hear them?" he asks in my ear. "That's the smallest fraction of what crawls through my mind every second. Every prayer. Every fear. Every pathetic little whimper from everyone carrying my Claim."

I try to answer but only manage a strangled whine. His hand slides up from my stomach, fingers encircling my throat in a hold that's not quite a threat but far from gentle.

"I want you to imagine me going about my duties with this. Tending to the Shroud's maintenance, spreading tithes through the foundations. Receiving the petitions from my people and making sure their needs are met. Visiting the memorials of the war's fallen to honor our dead with all this *fucking* noise. And there you were," he whispers, "thinking I was just sitting on my ass while you bled."

His mental presence expands, sinking into my psyche and *wrenching*. Stars explode behind my eyes as pressure builds in my skull. I can't contain him. I'm too fragile. Too human.

A raw animal scream claws its way out of my throat.

"Alexios," Bastien says from somewhere far away, his usual monotone sharper. "Her limits—"

"Are not your concern." Alexios' fingers tighten on my throat, not enough to choke, just enough to remind me who's in control. All of him pressed against all of me. "Our princess wanted to understand what I carry. I'm being generous enough to show her. Aren't I, little sacrifice? I'm being indulgent, right?"

I'm coming undone. Splintering apart in his arms while he watches. My eyes roll back as his power surges again, and he just hums. Croons. Like he's soothing a frightened animal.

"Let me show you the Shroud next. My favorite burden. Your ribs will feel it first, I think. Right… here." His palm flattens against my sternum, fingers splayed wide. "Don't worry. I won't let them actually break. This is just… education."

My chest constricts, invisible bands tightening. I strain for breath. Darkness smothers my periphery, and I'm sure my bones will crack. I dig my nails into his forearms, but he doesn't flinch. Doesn't loosen his grip. His chest rises and falls against my back in that same calm rhythm while I'm suffocating in his power.

"The Shroud spans the breadth of the Duehavn mountains and plunges to the depths of the Rionese," Alexios continues. "And every competent engineer knows the cost of skimping on the underpinnings. That pain in your chest? It's a taste of the rot caused by Hellevig's deficit when all those citizens decided your gates were preferable to the fingerprick I require. You created quite the fucking mess."

Agony flares through me, and I finally try to speak. "P-Please."

"So many selfish little leeches," Alexios says, ignoring me, "gorging themselves on the fruits of my mercy while doing *fuck all* to shoulder the load."

"The lesson is done," comes Bastien's voice. "Unless you want her brain leaking out her ears before your trials begin."

For a terrifying moment, I think Alexios might rip me apart just to prove he can. His breath comes faster against my neck.

Then suddenly, blessedly, he withdraws.

The silence crashes over me. I scramble off his lap, the marble floor tilting beneath me. Then my stomach heaves. I double over and retch until my throat burns.

The stench of vomit clogs my nostrils. I stare down at my own sick, watching it blur and swim before my eyes.

"That," Alexios says from behind me, "is a fraction of what I endure. Every single day, without rest or reprieve." A rustle of fabric as he rises. "You think I *lounge* because you can't fathom what goes into keeping this realm and yours at peace. The sacrifices I make. The cost." He reaches my shoulder and leans down. "So consider very carefully," he whispers in my ear, "how much longer my patience will last if you continue pushing me. And act accordingly."

Then he's stalking toward the arched doors. "Blade," he calls without looking back, "get her to the nearest toilet. She'll be vomiting again in roughly three minutes."

"Fuck," Bastien mutters, hauling me up. "He chose to stop. I failed to account for mental trauma in your negotiations. Remember that."

Alexios was only off by thirty seconds.

An hour later, I step onto one of the palace balconies, wincing as sunlight reflects off the snow.

My head still pounds, but my stomach has settled. Bastien grudgingly brought me bread and tea after I cleaned up and changed. I'm wearing a pair of loose trousers and a plain shirt brought to me by the palace servants—too thin to keep me warm. Freezing to death would be a convenient end for me, I suppose.

The mountains loom in the distance, their jagged peaks obscured by wispy clouds. Far below, a half-frozen river snakes along the passes, glimmering like molten silver.

Alexios stands motionless at the railing as he stares out over his territory, his red and black feathers ruffling in the chilly breeze. I can't help but study him, knowing that he's enduring the clamor of human thoughts and the crushing force of the Shroud. The Eternal of Asteria hides his pain like a secret.

I step up beside him. "How much did you bleed for it? How much of yourself did you carve out to keep the realms from killing each other?"

His eyes slide to mine as he considers me. I hold his stare, refusing to fidget beneath that ancient, unsettling regard.

"Everything I was," he says. "And a good portion of what I might have been." He turns back to the view. "I can't take a Chosen, for example."

I blink. "You can't?"

"No." A muscle flickers in his jaw. "Soulbonds don't allow for both. It's either one Chosen or thousands of Claimed, so I chose."

"Your people over yourself."

"Over everything." His laugh is bitter. "You want the truth? I'm the oldest living Eternal, and I'm still young by our standards." Something dark passes over his face. Something raw. "There should be elders waiting for me to mature before passing on their knowledge and choosing to be unmade. Instead, they're all dead, and I'm left with their territories and their people and every fucking problem they left behind. Not to mention two young Eternals who've spent centuries more interested in slaughter than rulership that I'm responsible for. So, yes. I choose everyone else over what I want because that's the burden I inherited when your people butchered mine."

I flinch before I can stop myself. Wind tears at my hair, sending strands whipping across my face. I reach up and tuck them behind my ear with hands that aren't quite steady.

"And if things were different?" I venture, careful. Tentative. "Would you want a Chosen?"

His fingers clench on the railing. "Speculating on impossibilities is a waste of time. I knew exactly what I was sacrificing when I signed the Accords with Amalthea." His smile holds no warmth as he straightens and looks at me. "Another hour to collect yourself, or can we begin?"

"Let's get this over with."

Alexios raises his hands, power crackling around him. The scent of ozone fills the air as lightning skitters over his fingertips.

Then the ground trembles.

I gasp as branches erupt from the frozen landscape—thorns and twisted briars spreading across the ground in a violent surge. Consuming the landscape in blackened branches with silver leaves sharp enough to slice flesh. The branches twist and reach and knit together, forming walls that stretch to the horizon.

A maze. Alexios is forming a maze. The turns are barely visible through the dense thicket, but the entrance is visible just beyond the garden below the balcony.

As abruptly as it began, the ground finally stills.

"The key to Evander's cell," Alexios says, lowering his arms, "is at the center."

I drag my stare from the maze to him. "That's it, then? I just have to reach the middle?"

"That's it. The key is yours, if you can claim it."

I don't care for that mocking curl of his lips.

"How long?"

"Nightfall. When the stars come out, the labyrinth changes. And even your Wolf's mark won't save you then."

I look at the sun, doing mental math. Seven hours if I'm lucky. Maybe less.

"And when I find it?" I ask, not bothering with "if."

"Call for me. I'll be listening." He studies me, head tilted. "I hope he's worth it, your Wolf. It would be a shame for you to break for anything less than love."

47

BRYONY

ALEXIOS' MAZE REMINDS me of the Void. The depth, the darkness, the way it pulls you in. There's clarity at first as every sense sharpens. Then, when you're yanked deeper, it seems eternal. Endless.

The Void never wanted to give me back when I died. I would float in the dark spaces, wondering if it would keep me. I'd spin and spin with no sense of time.

Like in a labyrinth.

The twisted branches loom overhead, forming a canopy so dense that daylight barely filters through. As the hours pass, the silver-veined leaves seem to shift and elongate. But maybe that's just in my mind.

Focus. Don't let it get to you.

But it's already there. Like the Void, the maze deliberately misleads me deeper. The path ahead of me splits, then converges. Then splits again in a pattern I swear wasn't there ten seconds ago.

How long have I been walking? Hours? I can't tell anymore. The sun's position isn't clear through the branches, but the shadows keep growing longer. Nothing makes sense in this place. A corridor I passed through minutes ago now leads somewhere else entirely. I endlessly loop and loop, never knowing if I'm closer to the center or right back where I started.

"Just go to the center," I mutter, pressing my palm against a trunk for balance.

The bark shifts under my touch. Before I can pull away, something slices across my cheek. I reel back with a yelp, my hand flying to my face. My fingers come away wet and red.

What the—?

The thorn jutting from the branch glistens with my blood, and I watch as a drop slides down the barb and falls to the ground.

Then the soil *ripples* like something beneath it just tasted me.

When the stars come out, the labyrinth changes. And even your Wolf's mark won't save you then.

Oh gods. It's alive. And it's woken up hungry.

Fuck. Oh fuck fuck fuck.

I stumble back. The thorns now look like teeth—or claws. The branches extend and reach for me.

My heart slams against my ribs as I break into a run.

The paths narrow. Branches bend inward and grasp at my clothes. I duck under one, leap over another. The air thickens. Sweat trickles down my spine.

Something wraps around my ankle, and I hit the ground hard. More tendrils snake around my calves, my thighs, my waist.

"No—"

They start to pull.

The vines constrict, each thorn pushing deep into my skin. I scream and struggle against it. My blood soaks into the soil, and that only makes the vines dig harder. I thrash and kick. The tendrils constrict around my chest.

Think. Think think think. There has to be a way out—

The vines wrap more snugly around my middle and squeeze. A sudden, sickening *snap* echoes through my body as my rib gives way. I try to scream again, but there's barely any air left in my lungs.

I can't move. Can't *breathe*. Can't think through the pain. My whimpers sound like they're coming from someone else—some pathetic, broken thing I don't recognize.

I'm jerked sideways. My nails scrape against the dirt as I claw for purchase, for anything to hold on to.

The thorns drag me deeper.

So this is how it ends. After all the deaths I've endured, I thought I knew the particular cadence of this unmaking, the way a body fails by degrees. But this? This is different. This death crawls. It savors. The ceremonial knife back home seems almost kind now. What a luxury it was to be broken quickly—

The Claim on my wrist flares.

A heartbeat that's not my own thunders through me. The ghost of breath across my lips, comforting and achingly familiar.

I latch on to Evander's pulse, the only solid thing in the shifting dark. Warm. Kind. I pour myself into the unsteady connection, into the scent of him, something to wrap my fists around and haul myself to the surface. To air.

To *him*.

Because I understand now—love is the thing with teeth. It will take a bite out of you and dare you to bleed. To carve yourself open and cut a vital piece of who you are. When it's right, the pain becomes something else, something necessary. Like breaking a bone to set it properly.

But it's worth it. Every bite, every scar, every lesson that got me here.

The memory floods through me—the heat of his skin, the low rumble of his voice. Evander and I crouched among the roses at his tower.

If you want to understand a thing, you have to learn its nature. What makes it feel.

My next exhale shudders out, and I grasp the memory, letting it wash through me and over me.

Breathe out the anger. All it will get you here is bled dry.

I can almost feel the way his body had bracketed mine, the heat and solidity of him. Those hands caging my own.

Prove you're not a threat, and it might surprise you how eagerly they open up.

The vines contract again, but instead of fighting, I let my muscles go slack and surrender.

Not because I've given up.

Because I've finally understood.

I focus on the give of the soil beneath my hands. The vines still squirm, slicing into my flesh with every little shift, but I hold myself pliant and passive. Yielding.

I don't know how long I drift like that. Like I'm in the Void, just waiting to be pulled out. The dark pressing in. Time *tick-tick-ticking* past as I surrender.

Then something changes. The thorns that punctured my skin begin to ease, then gentle, as if they can sense the fight draining out of me, giving way to something calmer. More centered. Each small breath is a little easier than the last.

"I'm not your enemy," I murmur. "I don't want to hurt you."

For a moment, the vines go still as if they're listening—and maybe they are. Evander said he spoke to his roses.

"I'm just trying to reach him." My voice breaks, but I force the words out anyway. "I know you probably don't give a shit about my tragic little love story, but he's my—"

The confession lodges behind my teeth. Too small, too feeble a word for this immensity clawing beneath my ribs.

"*Everything*," I manage. "He's everything. And if I have to let you take pieces out of me to get to him, that's what I'll do. That's the bargain." A shaky inhale. Exhale. *Breathe, Bryony.* "So do it. Use me up until there's nothing left. I won't fight you."

Nothing happens, just the slow drip of my blood into the hungry soil. I'm sure the maze will swallow me down after all, digest me slowly. But then...

One tendril loosens around my ankle. Another uncoils from my wrist. The sharp points withdraw from my flesh—first my legs, then my arms. The thorns that dug deepest come last, sliding free with reluctance, like they'll miss the taste of me.

I blink up at the lattice of desiccated branches, sucking in air.

"Thank you," I whisper.

I manage to lever myself to my hands and knees. Some functioning part of my brain notes the way my arms shake, threatening to give out at any moment. Shock, probably. Blood loss. I don't have time to catalog the extent of the damage or assess what hurts.

Instead, I claw my way forward because *fuck* letting Alexios win. I'm so close to the end. Evander is waiting for me in his cell.

I promised I would come back.

You didn't survive all that to give up now, I snarl at myself. *Just a little further. Crawl if you have to.*

I've *earned* this.

Ten steps. Twenty. Each inch feels like a mile. My blood leaves a dark trail behind me—proof I was here, proof I didn't give up. The edges of my vision flicker, but I grit my teeth and shove it back because—

Something glows ahead. It's such an incongruous sight that I stumble, certain that I'm hallucinating. But no, a wooden box sits nestled among the roots with pale sigils pulsing along its edges.

I all but fall on it. It takes me three tries to flip the latch, my fingers shaking too badly to grip it properly. But finally, finally, the lid creaks open. And there, nestled in a bed of velvet, is a heavy iron key.

I curl my fist around it and shut my eyes in exhaustion.

"Alexios. It's done."

For a long moment, there is only the creak of branches and the rustling of the leaves.

Then, a whisper of feathers. A familiar thrum of ancient power.

When I force my eyes open, Alexios towers over me, his wings spread wide and blocking out what little light filters through the skeletal canopy. That burning stare fixes on me.

"Up," he tells me. Quiet, inexorable.

And gods help me, I obey. I lock my knees and shove to my feet because he commanded it. Because the alternative is the Void.

I choke down the bile at the back of my throat. When the gray recedes and my vision clears, Alexios is still standing there watching me.

"You look like something even the crows wouldn't pick over. Like a carcass left to bloat in a ditch."

I spit a mouthful of blood onto the ground. "I hate you. With everything... in me."

"Good." He smiles. "That hatred will keep your heart beating when your body wants to quit."

Alexios scoops me into his arms. The movement jars my injured ribs, and I bite my tongue against a scream. His massive crimson and black wings unfurl with a snap.

The flight passes in a blur of agony and half-consciousness. When we land in the gardens, he sets me down on the palace steps, but keeps one hand on my arm to steady me.

"You're not done," he says.

Something in his voice makes me go cold. I struggle to focus on his face. "What... do you mean?"

"You thought finding that key was your test?" His laugh is cruel. "Oh no. That was the prelude. This is the real trial."

Dread pools in my gut. "What—"

"I want you to walk through my palace, past every single courtier tortured by your family. Every demi whose parents, children, family, and lovers were slaughtered."

My stomach lurches. "You want everyone to see me broken."

He grabs my chin, forcing me to meet that burning gaze. "I want them to have a good, long look at what it takes to earn the Wolf."

"You're sick."

"I'm practical." His thumb traces my jawline. "You're a Devaliant who tied your soul to a future god-king of Scillari. Everything has a price, Princess. Time to pay up."

I try to pull away, but his grip is implacable. "Is that all? Or do you want to kick me while I'm down, too?"

"Oh, I want countless things from you, Bryony Devaliant. But right now, I'll settle for watching you drag yourself through a palace full of gods who would gladly wear your skin as a trophy. They can't touch you—this Claim forbids it." He brushes his thumb over Evander's glowing mark. "But if you fall, you'll stay down. If you crawl, they'll watch. And if you're strong enough to reach the dungeons and turn that key, maybe the Wolf will piece what's left of you back together if your heart doesn't give out first."

He releases me, head cocked. Waiting.

Asshole.

I swallow down every foul insult I'm thinking and jerk my chin in a nod.

"Remember," he says, "you chose this. *Begged* for it, even. So don't you dare waste my time by collapsing in the front hall. Make every step count."

Then he's gone in a whisper of dark feathers, leaving me alone and bleeding on his doorstep.

Go. Finish it.

The first step nearly kills me. My legs buckle, and my vision blurs from the pain. The second isn't much better. But I force my ravaged body forward because I refuse to lose.

The runes on the massive door flare and it swings open on silent hinges. And I'm pathetically grateful I'm spared the indignity of trying to work the handles with my mangled hands.

The entry hall stretches before me, packed with courtiers. Every head turns. They focus on me with varying degrees of disgust and fascination.

I let them look. Let them drink in every laceration, every broken bone. All the fractured parts of me laid bare for their entertainment. Because I've made a study of unmaking and contorting myself into whatever grotesque shape is required of me. To be broken on the altar of someone else's need.

What's one more flaying, after all this?

Drip. Drip.

My blood makes perfect circles on the white marble. I count steps and breaths. The thud of my heart, the distance to the dungeon stairs. I shut out the whispers, the laughter, the delicate gags, the snide comments. All of it.

Because this is a thing I've learned. Sometimes, the only way through a moment is to put your head down and endure it. No one's coming to help you.

Sometimes, all you can do is keep moving.

"*Filthy Devaliant bitch,*" someone hisses from my right.

Not *Vartenan*. Not *human*. They hate my family name more than anything.

A wet glob of spit lands on my cheek. Then another. And another. Flecking my hair, my shoulders. I keep my eyes forward, jaw clenched, and I keep moving.

The whispers grow to a roar. More spit. More taunts.

"Ten gold pieces says she doesn't make it to the dungeons," someone calls out.

No one can touch you, Alexios had said.

Another glob of saliva lands on my neck.

I don't look. Don't flinch. I won't give them the satisfaction of seeing me crack. My vision narrows to the floor in front of me, the next doorway, the next hall, down another corridor. Past more and more eyes burning with hatred.

My legs give out at the top of the spiral staircase leading down to the dungeons. A guard watches me, leaning against the wall, his face bored.

"He won't want what's left of you," he calls after me as I descend.

Fuck. You.

Because I promised. I promised I'd come back.

I collapse and crawl. My hands leave bloody prints on each step. Halfway down, I manage to stand again, and I keep going because the alternative isn't an option. When I finally reach the bottom, the corridor stretches ahead. Just a few more steps. I can see the door to his cell now.

Ten steps. Five. Three more. One—

"Devaliant."

I crumple just outside the cell.

"*Devaliant*."

Through my unsteady vision, I see his golden wings straining against chains, those amber eyes burning with fury and desperation.

"Bryony. Open it. Open it *now*."

Yes. The key. Have to... Have to unlock it.

My fingers shake so badly that it takes three tries to find the keyhole. Metal shrieks as the bolt slides free, and I use the last of my strength to push the door open and crawl inside.

All I hear is the rattle of his chains as consciousness slips away.

48

EVANDER

THE SHACKLES SEAR my wrists, but I barely register the pain. Bryony's collapsed just inside my cell—close enough for me to count each shallow rise of her chest.

I catalog her injuries. The damage reads like a battle map: skin shredded, bones crushed, bruises everywhere.

I've seen worse on countless battlefields. The Devouring was a brutal education, and I got real familiar with all the ways to pick a person apart. But to see such wounds on *her*—

"*Devaliant*. Wake up, sweetheart. Open those pretty eyes for me."

I track every breath and flutter of her lashes, relieved when she begins to stir. Then her eyes open. For a moment, she stares right through me. Empty.

Recognition flares, and the bond thrums.

"There you are." I croon the words, low and coaxing. "Come here."

She crawls toward me, nails scrabbling against the stone floor. A cry wrenches from her as something inside her gives with an audible snap—a rib, maybe more than one. The barest echo of agony ripples through the bond, quickly choked by the power in the shackles. It twists like a knife in my gut.

She collapses into my lap. Her skin is cold. Clammy. The scent of copper is overwhelming, and beneath it—

Demis. I smell other demis all over her, dozens of unique scents. Saliva? *What the fuck*. I don't know what test she went through, but I'll rip Alexios apart with my bare hands for this.

But I shove down the violence because my anger won't help her right now. My girl needs her Chosen, not her monster.

"Good girl," I murmur. "Don't move, okay? Stay still while I fix you up."

I brace for the backlash as I force power through the siphoning shackles. Searing feedback scorches my veins as the cuffs throttle my magic to a trickle.

Bryony shivers as the feeble pulse flows through her. "Something's different with your power," she mumbles. "It's not as hot."

"The shackles are strangling it."

It's not enough. If I can't get her stabilized, she's going to die tonight.

I cast out with my mind, seeking Alexios through the chain that binds us, but the shackles devour the connection.

So I try my brother. His natural sensitivity should compensate for the suppression.

Bastien's consciousness surges to meet me. *What is it?*

The words are curt. No curiosity, no urgency.

Take my cuffs off. I have to heal my Chosen before she bleeds out in my lap.

The link freezes over. Hardens.

No. You know the bargain's terms. The cuffs stay until she completes the trials.

Bryony shudders against me, each shallow inhale rattling. I'm ready to tear this palace apart.

Listen to me very carefully, you heartless asshole. My rage bleeds into the connection. *She's barely breathing. So either Alexios lets me put her insides back where they belong, or I'll tear out his intestines and make him fucking gargle them.*

A beat.

Graphic, Bastien says mildly. *The shackles stay, but I'll uncuff you from the wall. You can play nurse in your room where it's warm. Take it or leave it.*

I exhale harshly through my nose. Every instinct is screaming to keep pushing, to shove at Bastien's frozen apathy until it cracks. But I don't have time to wrangle him when Bryony's lips are turning blue.

Fine, I snarl down the link. *Get down here.*

"Just keep breathing for me a little longer." I kiss Bryony's temple. "Can you do that for me?"

A thin thread of assent drifts through the bond, more sensation than articulation, but I'll take it.

I count the seconds. *Twenty-eight. Twenty-nine. Thirty—*

Bastien's steps ring out, and then he fills the cell doorway, obsidian eyes flicking dispassionately over Bryony. I can practically hear the clicking of that razor-edged mind as he turns her chances over like an abacus.

"Her surviving the night is slim," he says. Cold, unaffected. "Ten percent at best."

I love my brother. Really, I do. But sometimes I fucking hate him.

"Then move your ass," I say sharply.

He enters the cell, and his hands close over the chains tethering me to the wall. Turquoise sparks dance over the metal, the ancient wards straining against his command. With a grating shriek, they finally snap, and the restraints fall away.

I push to my feet, gathering Bryony to my chest. Her ragged gasp frays another few threads of my unraveling control. Has she always been this small? This breakable?

Bastien leads us out of the dungeons. I shut out everything—the opulence of the palace, the courtiers glancing curiously at us, the reminder of their scents all over my Chosen. I shield Bryony from prying eyes with my wings as we ascend to the upper levels.

By the time we reach my rooms, my grip on our bond is the only thing standing between her and the Void. I'm pouring magic into the link and fighting the shackles with every damned step.

Bastien wrenches open the chamber doors, moving aside for me to stride through. I head straight for the massive bed and settle against the headboard, careful not to jostle Bryony too much as I cradle her against my chest.

An agonized keen escapes her.

"Shhh. I know. I know it hurts." I rock us both, sending pulse after pulse of power into her, knitting up the worst of the internal bleeding. "I've got you. Just breathe through it for me."

I glance at Bastien. He's leaning against the threshold, bored and blank as a marble statue.

With a pulse of power, he produces a new length of chain. "Don't fight me." His shadows twine through the links, forging the magic that will contain me. "I'd hate to have to gag you, but I will."

I meet that void-dark stare and nod.

He winds the chains around my upper arms and secures them to the headboard. The metal bites into my skin, thrumming with his magic, but I just shove down the pained hiss. Bryony makes a quiet, wounded sound, and it's suddenly the easiest thing in the realms to sublimate my discomfort. To relegate it to some distant corner of my mind.

"You gave her my daggers," Bastien says. I hear the accusation—a ripple in that frozen sea of apathy. "She had the audacity to ask me to retrieve them."

I push another healing pulse into my Chosen's body before responding. "She won them fair and square. Well, most of them. One was a gift."

The air thickens, shadows swelling at the room's edges like gathering smoke. The pressure of my brother's power crawls across my skin and burrows—deep and dark and devouring.

I ride out the wave. Centuries of exposure build up a tolerance to Bastien's unique brand of brutality.

"Next time you're inclined to barter away our history for a piece of ass," he says, so soft it would be easy to mistake for gentleness if I couldn't see the rage simmering in his black stare, "leave my weapons out of it."

Then he yanks on the chains in a sharp jerk, and the links snap taut. My arms are wrenched above my head, my back slamming into the headboard. I give a pained hiss.

On anyone else, it might be a tantrum. On my brother, it's as close to a sulk as he ever comes.

My Chosen stirs. I soothe her with another careful stream of power, grinding my teeth against the siphoning cuffs cinching tight around my reserves.

It leaves me light-headed. A gray haze settles at the edges of my vision.

"She nearly died for me today," I point out once the static clears. "I'd say that earns her a few blades."

I stare down at Bryony, counting her labored breaths. Allowing myself three heartbeats of incandescent fury, three heartbeats to imagine crushing Alexios' skull between my hands.

Then I lock it away. Recenter myself in the weight of my Chosen, broken but breathing in my lap.

"If I get the Devaliant's weapons," Bastien says, "it doesn't mean I approve of her and you."

A laugh escapes me. "Damn me, but I can't wait until someone comes along and cracks open that frozen wasteland you call a heart. I'll enjoy every second of watching you lose your shit."

Bastien doesn't so much as blink, but the temperature plummets another ten degrees. "Unlikely. But given an infinite timeline, I suppose anything is possible." He turns toward the door. "Try not to choke on your arrogance before she finishes martyring herself for you."

"She needs new clothes," I call after him. "Let the servants know."

"Enjoy being chained to the bed."

"Love you too."

The door snicks shut.

In the silence, there's only the rasp of Bryony's breathing, the drum of her heart against my chest. Pain brackets her mouth. I measure each shift against me, each half-muffled whimper, and feed her the dregs of my magic in careful, measured pulses. Knitting together the splintered places, soothing the hurts.

Healing is delicate work. I'd barely had time to master it as an Eternal before the war started, but I always struggled with the complexity of it. The balance of using power to mend and soothe rather than rend and burn. It feels clumsy, this language of tenderness. The syllables are strange after so many centuries of knowing only carnage.

But I learned it for her.

When Bryony's lashes finally flutter open, I slump against the headboard in relief. "There you are. Thought I'd lost you for a minute."

"You know I'm too stubborn to die." Her voice sounds raw, so I push a little power into her vocal cords to soothe the ache.

"One of your best qualities," I tell her.

She's quiet for a long moment. "Evander?"

"Hmm?"

"Can you... Can you use the deeper healing for the rest? The kind that feels good. I want it the way it's meant to be."

There's an unbearable vulnerability in the request. The trust of laying down her armor when she's weakest. How many ways can you unravel a god, I wonder? Rip out all the rotting viscera, scoop out the fetid snarls of him, and fill the void with softness and grace.

What a dangerous thing, to hand a wolf the knife and trust he won't cut. That he'll mend instead of mangle.

"Okay," I tell her. "Settle against me since I can't put my hands on you. I'm going to need you to help me out of my shirt first, all right? The more skin contact we have, the easier this will go."

Bryony shifts in my lap, reaching for the fastenings between my wings, making quick work of them. Her hands map the skin she's uncovering. Tracing over my abs, my pecs, with a deliberate sort of slowness that borders on reverent.

Absolute menace, this girl.

"Enough teasing. Lean against me and let me work."

She nuzzles her head against my shoulder.

I rest my cheek against her hair and just... breathe. Calm and steady. It's harder to reach for my power. The shackles have choked it down to guttering embers, but I still feel the spark. It takes more concentration to stoke it higher, hotter, to turn it into something I can use.

Fire sears me with the first surge I push into Bryony. I clench my teeth through the wave and shove the pain down deep. That's a hurt to deal with when she's not counting on me.

Because what's one more lashing for my Chosen?

So I flood every corner of myself with light and heat, with the intent to heal, to soothe, to pleasure—

My girl relaxes as I work, giving herself over to it completely. Letting me in. Slow and measured, feeding power into her veins. Her lungs. The secret shadowed places carved out by hurt. I trail heat and honey-gold light over her hurts in a reverent touch. Sealing split skin. Soothing the contusions, learning the shape and texture of each as I coax it to fade. Easing the aches.

I drag more power up from that bottomless well inside me and let it sink through layers of dermis and hypodermis, encouraging sluggish blood to reroute. Coaxing splintered bone to fuse, ligaments and cartilage to stitch back together. The internal bleeding takes more concentrated effort.

My magic floods the bond. Stroking, igniting, leaving shuddering ecstasy in its wake. Her breath catches as pleasure winds her up. Each rock and grind of her hips against my cock stoking the fire building low in my gut.

There's a fierce sort of pride in pushing her to this point. A savage triumph in the knowledge that every shudder and moan is because of me. I did that. I made her feel that.

Bryony throws her head back as she shatters. A choked cry escapes her lips.

"That's it." I brush the words against her temple. "Ride it out for me."

Seeing her lost to bliss, to the wildfire of my magic moving inside her, is nearly enough to undo me. The most exquisite torture.

I could lose myself in this. In watching her and knowing I'm the only one who's given her this pleasure. I'm the only one who's seen the expression on Bryony Devaliant's face when she lets go.

Minutes go by as she shudders through the aftershocks. Her now healed skin sheened in sweat, gilded by the dying firelight.

"I can't believe you." Her words slur together. "You were holding out on me."

I grin. "The offer was always on the table. Not my fault you never took me up on it."

A soft huff of laughter. "So, how much of your power does Alexios' leash usually let you access?"

"Usually? About half my full strength. But with these?" The chains clink as I rattle them. "Ten percent, if I'm being generous."

Her brows shoot up, eyes wide. "Wait. Are you telling me that mind-melting orgasm was you at *ten percent*?"

"Mmhm. You have no idea the things I'm going to do to you when I have access to all of me."

Desire floods the bond, hot and hungry. "When these chains come off," she says, "you won't leave our bed for a week. I have plans."

Our bed.

Two words said so simply. As if it's already an inevitability, the pair of us tangled up in each other long after the dust of this ordeal settles. An unthinking promise of a shared *after*.

Something squeezes in my chest, too big to be contained even in the body of a god. I need her. I need to be inside her.

"Go." I jerk my chin toward the bathing chamber. "Get yourself cleaned up. Then you're going to come back to this bed and let me fuck you until we break it."

A little shiver goes through her. She slides off my lap and pads into the adjoining room, leaving the door open—because of course she does. My Chosen delights in tormenting me.

She's barely over the threshold before she's shucking off her torn clothes. My breath catches at the sight of her. The elegant taper of her waist, her gorgeous tits, those long legs. She turns the tap for the tub, and steaming water pours forth, and she gives me a view of that luscious ass, and it's…

It's the kind of sight that could bring a god to his knees.

Suddenly, I understand the appeal of worship. The base, primitive urge to prostrate myself at her feet and serve her pleasure until she forgets everything but me. My cock. My touch. My mouth.

The metal edges of the shackles dig into my wrists as I flex my hands, nearly driven out of my mind with the visceral need to feel all that wet, warm skin and lay my claim a thousand different ways. I want to map her body. Learn every scar and blemish and perfect imperfection until I can trace them from memory.

In the bath, Bryony tips her head back with a sigh, rubbing soap into a lather on a washcloth and washing herself with economical motions. Somehow, that makes it worse—the complete lack of artifice, the unselfconscious way she touches herself. How she erases the remnants of the night's brutality, like she hadn't bled out a piece of her soul for me during that test.

It is, bar none, the loveliest sight in both realms.

Bryony's eyes stay closed as she runs the washcloth lower, dipping between her legs to clean in firm circles. "You watching?"

"I'm appreciating," I correct.

"Is there a difference?"

"Watching implies a certain distance." I shift against the headboard, chains clinking. "What I'm feeling for you right now borders on the religious, except less holy."

Her violet gaze finds mine across the steam-hazed distance. "Less holy. That's interesting, coming from a god."

"Even gods can be brought to their knees by the right kind of temptation."

"Is that so?" She bites her lip. "What does it take to tempt a god?"

You, I want to say. *Just you, existing in the same room as me.*

But the words that emerge are different, darker: "Right now? The sight of you touching yourself while I can't."

A delicate shiver rolls through her, but she just drops the washcloth and starts rubbing her cunt in firmer circles. "I'm enjoying you like this. All chained up and desperate for it. Maybe I won't let you touch me at all."

I lean forward, pulling against my chains. "Do it harder. Pinch your nipple with your other hand."

A shuddering inhale, and then she's obeying, cupping her breast and rolling her nipple between her fingers.

"Good. Now get those fingers nice and deep in your pussy.

Show me how you fuck yourself when I'm not there to do it for you."

Her eyes stay on mine as she plunges two fingers in, head thrown back as she works herself.

I let out a sigh. "You're so pretty when you do that."

It's the biggest tease, being forced to sit here and watch her take her pleasure while I'm chained up. She rides her hand in a slow, sinuous roll of her hips. I feel the echoes of her building release through the bond, each spark of heat. Feel her climbing higher, chasing relief—

"Come," I tell her, lacing my voice with the dregs of my power and shoving it at her. "*Now*."

"Oh, *gods*," she gasps.

I soak in her expression: the half-parted lips, the delicate furrow between her brows as she bucks against her palm. Her lashes flutter shut as she climaxes. A fierce, savage pride detonates in my chest because that's all for me. She's all mine.

Her chest heaves as she comes down. Her eyes are soft and hazy when they find mine again.

"Get over here," I say. "After what Alexios put you through, you deserve to be worshipped properly. Don't bother drying off."

Water sluices over her curves as she rises from the bath. She steps out and walks toward me with all that glistening skin on display, pristine and wet and prettily flushed, nearly vibrating with pent-up need.

"Crawl up here and let me taste that pussy," I murmur.

She braces a hand on the headboard as she climbs up to settle her knees on either side of my face. Close enough for me to feel the heat of her, smell the sweet scent of her arousal.

Bryony jolts with a sharp gasp as I kiss her pussy. The first taste of her bursts across my tongue, sweet and filthy. I'm greedy for her. For every moan and shudder. I flatten my tongue and drag it over her clit in a slow circle, again and again, varying the pressure.

She grinds down. Her fingers twist in my hair, holding me right where she needs me. I commit to memory all the places that make her sigh, that have her squirming, nails sinking into my scalp as she rides my face. And it's a devastation—a kind of unmaking I've never known to be used like this.

This is what worship should be, I think, drunk on the taste of her. *Not blood on altars. Not fear and genuflection. This.*

By the time she's shuddering apart on my tongue, I'm so hard I ache with it.

"I need you," I pant. "If I'm not inside you in the next thirty seconds, I'm going to lose my mind."

Bryony doesn't hesitate. Just shimmies down my body until she can get my trousers unbuttoned, shoving them down to free my cock. I exhale sharply at the first tentative stroke of her hand. My hips buck into the contact. She lowers herself onto me, both of us groaning at the slick glide. The weight of her on top of me is hot and perfect, and I can't do anything but lie there and let her use me.

She sets a slow pace. Hips rising and falling, each downstroke forcing me deeper. I am drunk on it. Drunk on her. Reduced to base instinct, to the animal roar of *mine mine mine.*

Her head tips back on a moan as she finds a more urgent rhythm. She rides me in uneven grinds, dragging a little on the downstroke, close and deep and absolutely devastating. So warm and tight and wet for me. She's something I never knew I wanted, but always craved. I spent centuries in my grief feeling like I needed to bite and claw and fuck and ruin, but this—*she*—is everything I ever wanted.

The shackles bite into my wrists as my hands fist with the need to grab and *claim*—

"Keep using me," I say. "That's it. Ride me hard. Take everything you need."

Her nails are a sweet, stinging pressure where they sink into the muscles of my chest for leverage. When she reaches my wings, I groan helplessly as she trails her fingertips along the bottom edge.

"Which part of these is most sensitive?"

"Coverts," I manage between panting breaths. "Closest to my shoulder blades. Dig your nails in."

The instant she curls her fingers into the short feathers there, everything whites out. Rapture screams through every nerve ending. My spine arches. My hips surge up to meet hers, chasing that blinding sensation.

"*Fuck*. Like that. Just like that, Chosen."

"I love you," she says roughly. Riding me harder, taking me so deep. "I love you so much."

It only takes a handful of sharp, desperate thrusts before I'm falling over the edge. I shudder through it, still arching into her. She shatters moments after with a fractured cry. I watch her shake apart on my cock, committing every detail to memory. The spill of damp hair over her shoulders, the heaving swells of her tits, her lips parted.

Our breathing is loud in the hush as we come down.

"That's three," I say when I can speak again. "Let's see if I can wring another four out of you before dawn."

The stench of other demis clings to her skin, and it's driving me out of my mind. Even after she's bathed and fucked me, I can detect traces.

Bryony's curled against my chest, finally peaceful after all that pain. I won't disturb that. Not when she fought so hard just to make it back to me. Still, I have to know.

"You don't have to tell me everything," I murmur into her hair, hating how the chains keep me from properly holding her. From wrapping her in my wings. "But at least tell me how many there were."

She goes rigid. I track the sudden spike of her pulse, the shallow draw of air. The bond between us pulses with echoes of remembered humiliation.

"I don't know what you're talking about." Her voice is too steady, too controlled.

My Chosen has many talents, but lying to me sure as fuck isn't one of them.

"Yeah, you do. The scents of other demis were all over you when you showed up in the cell. It's still there."

She flinches. "They didn't hurt me." She pulls away and sits up, hugging her knees. "They just..."

"Just *what*?" The words come out as a growl.

Bryony swallows hard. "Spat at me," she says quietly. "Called me names."

I count to ten in every dead language I know. Then I do it again, forcing myself to breathe and bank the inferno raging beneath my skin.

"Let me get this straight," I manage. "Alexios made you march past dozens of hostile demis while you were barely conscious?"

Right. Alexios just earned himself top billing on my murder list.

"No one touched me. I handled it."

So then why does she look so small? So fragile?

"You shouldn't have had to," I snap.

"They wanted to make sure I understood my place. That being your Chosen doesn't erase what my family did during the war." A bitter laugh. "And you know what? They're not wrong. It doesn't."

"Don't care," I say. "Here's what's going to happen. You're going to give me any identifying details you remember. Then I'm going hunting. Someone fucks with what's mine, they answer to me."

"You'd only make it worse." She drags a hand through her hair, frustration bleeding into the bond. "You can't just threaten people into accepting me."

"The fuck I can't. That mark on your wrist means you're under my protection. *Choosing you* means you're mine. An Eternal not doing anything to defend his mate shows weakness—"

"And it shows weakness in *me* to let you," she says sharply. "Do you have any idea how I'd look to them if I did that? I'm not a demi Chosen who already earned their respect by virtue of being born with wings. I don't get to skip the part where I earn my place here. What I need is for you to give me room to figure this out on my own and let me choose my own battles. Your love can't be another cage that denies me the right to fight for myself, Wolf."

I swallow around the sudden thickness in my throat. "I just want to spare you pain. Because no one in your life ever bothered to."

Bryony's expression gentles. "I know. But you can't. Pain is part of living. You think I don't know that by now?"

Her finger absently traces the scar on her throat—that silvery line that makes me want to burn the realms to ash every time I see it. Every time I remember how close I came to losing her before I ever had her.

"I never told you," she says, soft like a secret, "how much I wanted to die after this happened."

The words are a knife to the gut. I go still, barely breathing.

"My guards carried me everywhere when I was recovering. Not because I couldn't walk, but because they were protecting me. And I was so fucked up that I didn't even care. I was just a body to them, anyway. Why not let them treat me like one? But one day, Theo snapped. She commanded the guards to put me down and told me to *walk*. It had been weeks, and I was so frail that I collapsed over and over. I was just... I was so angry. But that anger made me want..."

She trails off, dragging in a deep, uneven breath.

"Want what?" I breathe.

When she meets my stare again, her eyes are blazing. Defiant. Beautiful. "It made me want the world to bleed at my feet. I can't tell you how many times people in my life have expected me to just... endure. The Oracles, my people, Alexios—I wasn't a *person* to them. Being an Anchor was like being buried alive in my own skin. When you came to my room in Hellevig and let me cut into you, I felt like an animal chewing off its leg to escape a trap. Anger was something I could hold on to, something that made me feel like I could be *more*."

Slowly, she reaches out and settles her hands on my chest, right over my heart. "You can't deprive me of my anger, Wolf," she tells me, calm and implacable. "So you're going to let me fall, and then you're going to let me get back up and do it again. Today, tomorrow, a century from now." Her fingers flex against my skin. "I'm going to be pregnant with our child one day, and you'll have to keep your promises. You'll have to watch me hurt and scream, even if some of it ends up being directed at you, because I'll be scared out of my fucking mind. I'll say awful, unfair things to you that I don't mean because *this*"—a rueful twist of her lips—"is a process. Us being together is going to be messy and ugly and so damn *hard* sometimes. Because humans and gods are enemies, and everyone will want to see us fail and tear each other apart." She wipes away a tear from her cheek. "We're both fucked up, and we've got more jagged edges than smooth, but anything worth fighting for is like that. You have to mix the bad in with the good."

Her hands flatten more firmly against my chest, and I feel her certainty down the shimmering tether of our bond. "I can't hide behind your wings forever," she tells me. "You can't shield me from every hurt. That's not who I am. It's not who *we* are."

I love her. I love her so damn much I can't breathe around it.

"Then be angry," I tell her, voice rough with emotion. "Scream. Rage. Break shit. Fall and claw your way back up as many times as it takes." I lift my head, catching her lips in a gentle kiss. "Have my babies. Burn this place to the ground. Just promise you'll leave room for me to offer a hand when you need it."

A wondering sort of smile touches her mouth. "I promise."

"Good." I kiss her again. "You belong with me, Bryony Devaliant."

"I belong with you," she breathes.

"*Shout it*, nemesis. My queen doesn't need anyone's permission to take up space. She owns it. She takes what's hers."

Bryony inhales sharply. "*I belong with you!*"

A fierce sort of pride explodes in my chest. "That's my Chosen. Never let *anyone* make you feel small and shut you up. Not those courtiers. Not Alexios. And sure as fuck not me."

49

BASTIEN

Mist clings to the spires of Hellevig tonight. I suppose some might call this city beautiful, if they were inclined to ignore the fact that every new building erected since the war was built on the bones of slaughtered gods. One day, I'm going to raze this whole festering shithole to the ground.

But not tonight.

My mind breaks down each variable as I near the palace—velocity, trajectory, altitude. The immutable mathematics of motion, as fixed and unchanging as the stars.

There's a certain purity to it. A peace in the way everything reduces down to its component parts, neatly labeled and filed away. Logical. Orderly. Untainted by emotions that turn people erratic and unpredictable.

I land on the balcony. A flick of my fingers, and the latch for the door crumples.

The bedchamber reeks of perfume. Gilt and ornamentation crowd every surface, garish to the point of vulgarity. But I'm only here for one thing: my knives. My blood sings in every molecule of Turpori steel, and every second they're here makes me want to raze this entire realm.

I slip into the darkened halls, each footfall soundless. The palace slumbers around me, and—

A scream rips through the hush.

I pause. *Not my problem. Not my business. Godkillers first, and everything else in this shithole can burn for all I care.*

But against my better judgment, I turn down the corridor, casting out my senses, and—

Collide with a wall. Not stone or steel, but a diamond-hard blockade of pure will, as implacable as the woman it belongs to. It shoves against my mind with brutal force.

I know that psychic signature. I've tasted it before, in a blood-soaked village heaped with Vartenan dead.

Theodora Devaliant.

When I reach the door, I don't bother with the handle. I just slam my boot into the wood and send it crashing inward.

She's pinned between two males. One is locking down her arms, and the other is forcing something around her neck—a collar. Theodora claws at the metal as a flush crawls up her face.

Intervention just slid from "optional" to "non-negotiable."

My shadows burst free and yank Theodora out of their grasp. She hits the floor. Her assailants don't even manage a word before I slide my knife from its sheath and bury it in the side of the first male's neck.

The second one tries to run. *Mistake.* My shadows catch him before he makes it two steps, the inky tendrils wrapping around his limbs, his torso, his throat, and *wrenching*. Every bone in his body snaps simultaneously—*crack-crack-crack*—spattering blood across the walls. The tendrils drop him to the carpet with a wet thump.

Killing them both takes fourteen point seven seconds, start to finish. Inefficient.

Boots pound in the hallway. I look up as three guards burst into the room, pulling up short at the sight of me standing among the carnage, splashed in gore and coldly furious. Their faces pale as recognition sets in—they know exactly who I am.

"Walk away," I tell them softly.

Their hands flex on their sword hilts as if they're actually entertaining the foolish notion of pulling steel on me.

My shadows twist around me. "You have three seconds."

They look at each other in the universal language of "fuck this, I'm not dying tonight", then back out of the room. Wise of them.

A desperate animal sound drags my attention back to Theodora. She's on her knees, hunched over, and scrabbling at the collar. Blood wells under her nails where they scratch at the metal.

"Stop that," I tell her flatly. "You'll tear out your throat."

Those green eyes snap to mine, and there it is—that spark I saw in Aldgate. That core of steel running through her. For a moment, I'm drowning in sense-memory, standing among the corpses in the village and watching this woman curl her lip in contempt as she surveyed my handiwork. A spike of pain stabs behind my right eye at the memory.

She'd shoved me out of her mind then like a psychic slap.

A shudder rolls through her, the muscles of her neck straining against the metal. "Get it off." The words scrape out of her. "Please."

Please. Such a soft, broken word from lips better suited to commands. I should savor this—Theodora Devaliant brought low, forced to beg the monster she despises. Sentiment is a destructive thing. Sticky fingers in all your tender places, scooping out handfuls until you're just a raw nerve. I should let her sit in the consequences of it, stew in the impotence for a bit.

But I'm not here to indulge petty whims, and the Shroud's more important than perverse pleasures.

So I drop into an easy crouch and reach for her. "Be still, and I'll remove it."

I'm not wearing gloves. I'm going to have to touch her bare skin.

"I bet you're getting off on this," she says. "After Aldgate."

Not an accusation. She states it plainly, almost curiously, like she's genuinely wondering what makes a monster tick.

I don't dignify it with a response. Just skate my fingers under the collar's edge to grope for a latch, a hinge, a join—anything I can persuade to pop open so I can be done with this. I'll never go anywhere without my gloves again.

The backs of my knuckles brush her skin—burning hot, pulse jumping erratically—and every muscle in my body locks up, rejecting the contact. Touching other people makes me want to flay myself raw. It brings up too much I'd rather stayed buried—the slap of flesh on flesh, all those tugging hands a prelude to a different kind of dying.

Rough palms sliding over my skin. The bite of restraints. The way they laughed as they—

No. Focus on the present. On the task. Break it down into parts: find the mechanism, disable the lock, remove the collar. Simple. Clinical. Safe.

"You're shaking," Theodora says quietly.

"Shut up."

My shadows seep into the mechanism, and the lock crumbles. The collar hits the floor with a dull clank.

I snatch my hands back the instant it's done, resisting the urge to scrub them against my pants. Later, there will be scalding water and soap. For now, I settle for flexing my fingers until the sensation of touch fades.

"An asset dying would be inconvenient," I say. "Don't let it happen again."

Theodora rubs at the marks on her throat. "I'm not your asset."

"You're the last Anchor holding the Shroud together. That makes you one." I reach for the collar and examine it.

It's Turpori steel with magic embedded in the metal.

I swallow back my low curse. Even now, my stolen feathers put my realm at risk. Whenever a human consumes those parts of me, they temporarily have the ability to create my steel. Three hundred years ago, that gave humans a flood of new weapons to use against us. And now, here it is again. Still plaguing me.

"What is it?" she asks, watching me. "Do you recognize it?"

Too observant, this one.

"No." Technically true. I don't know the meaning behind this particular configuration of runes and wards. But I will soon. I shove the remains of the collar into my coat. "Their names?"

"I skipped introductions while they were putting me in the collar." She staggers upright. Her copper hair is loose, curling around her delicate features. "What do you care?"

Her hand keeps rubbing at her abused throat. I track the movement with a predatory focus, staring at the map of veins close to the surface, starkly visible under bruise-mottled skin. Her nightgown is torn, and her shoulder is bare—easy access. I could put my mouth there, I think. Drag my tongue over that fluttering pulse, sink my teeth in, and *bite*—

I eviscerate the thought before it can fully form, and shove it into whatever septic mental sewer it crawled out of, where it can rot with the rest of my unwanted urges. I can acknowledge attraction, lust, baser impulses. Catalog the symptoms. File them away as quantifiable variables in an equation I'll never actually solve. Immaterial, in the grand scheme.

Theodora Devaliant is beautiful in the way natural disasters are beautiful—all that eye-catching destruction a trap for the unwary or the arrogant. But a Devaliant's loveliness is just a trick of the light. A misdirect drawing attention away from where the knife is about to slide in.

I pull my dagger from the stiffening corpse at my feet and clean the blade on my coat. "Alexios will want details about your incompetent security. Their response time was three minutes and twenty seconds after you screamed." I glance at her. "Unacceptable."

Her eyes narrow. "Your lunatic brother gutted every half-competent guard when he went on his murder spree through my palace. So apologies if my current security detail doesn't meet the exacting standards of Alexios' favorite butcher."

Fucking Evander. There are times I'm convinced the stars wove idiocy into the fabric of his soul. My brother's self-control has the structural integrity of wet paper. Leaving the empress unprotected because he couldn't keep his dick in his pants around her sister? Even for him, that's impressively stupid.

Tension gathers behind my eyes. I'm going to develop an aneurysm at this rate. Several of them.

"Hire new guards." I sheath my weapons. "More of them, better trained. Or Alexios will exploit an Accord loophole to assign someone to nanny you."

Theodora glares at me. "Alexios doesn't need to exploit anything. The Accords state he can't meddle in my life or rule through force, so I'll *allow* his guards until I replace mine. Now"—her hand drops from her throat—"tell me why you're creeping around my palace in the middle of the night."

"Reclaiming my property. Your sister had my knives, and I want them back."

The color drains from her face. "Tell me she's okay."

I don't bother to confirm or deny. Bryony Devaliant's fate depends entirely on the whims of a half-mad god-king and a brother whose self-control has always been more decorative than functional. The girl did not look well when I last saw her. Assurances would be premature at best.

"Irrelevant," I say. "I want my weapons."

A muscle in her jaw jumps. For a moment, I'm convinced she'll launch herself at me in a doomed blaze of defiance. I almost want her to.

"That's it? You broke in for some knives?" Her voice climbs with each word. "Who cares which realm they're in?"

I'm tempted to reach into the lockbox of her mind and squeeze until something ruptures. In one hundred and ten thousand years, I've never met a human who could keep me out. The fact that *she* can is starting to piss me off. I'm not above challenging anything that defies me by digging my teeth in until it stops squirming.

"Watch yourself," I say. "I don't play games, and you're wearing my patience thin. Any blade forged from Turpori steel is mine by right."

Understanding clicks in her expression. "I see."

How much does she know? What else is she hiding behind those walls?

I press against her mental barriers, searching for cracks. Places I can slip through and take what I want.

"Get out of my head, Blade." Her voice is soft, but her mind rises to meet me, repelling my intrusion with a hard slap. "Before I make you regret it."

I blink. "How are you doing that?"

You shouldn't be able to do that. No one can do that.
Breaking into minds is what I do.

"Your mind feels wrong." She meets my stare without flinching. A lesser creature would have crumbled by now. "It doesn't play nice with mine. What happened to it?"

An itch starts up beneath my skin. Her scent fills my head, the inescapable musk of *human*. It blankets my tongue until I'm choking on it, until my gorge rises and my fingers twitch with the need to dig into flesh and tear—

"The knives," I say sharply.

The itching is spreading. And I have the sudden, horrifying certainty that she *sees* me. Down to the rotted core, the empty space where my heart should be, all the filthy memories I keep locked away.

And she does not look away.

"Come with me," she says, cool and clipped.

I fall into step a precisely calculated distance behind her, close enough to intervene should she stumble, far enough to avoid even the suggestion of considerate hovering. As we walk, I analyze variables—the positioning of guards (inadequate), potential ambush points (numerous), structural weaknesses (laughable). And Theodora. The newly crowned empress and the sole surviving Anchor, leaving two realms vulnerable to anyone who might want to see the veil collapse and a new war sparked.

It's a disaster waiting to happen.

The armory, when we reach it, is at least marginally better defended. Iron-reinforced doors, competent locks, some attempt at organization.

Theodora leads me to a cabinet in the corner. "I moved them in there."

I trail my fingertips over the wood. My shadows shimmer down my arm, seeking the hidden tumblers like the teeth of a key. The lock crumbles, and the doors groan open.

The knives rest on a bed of black velvet, singing with the resonance of my power. The metal knows me, remembers when my hands and energy shaped it, and it croons a welcome as I lift them free.

"You need to hear something," I tell her as I push the blades into the belt along my ribs. "You won't like it."

She sighs. "Gods, what now?"

"Get pregnant. Immediately."

A startled laugh escapes her. "Excuse me?"

"The Shroud needs your bloodline to continue. Right now, your body is the most valuable thing in two realms, and tonight proved how vulnerable you are. Any halfway competent assassin could slit your throat and bring down the veil."

Her shoulders stiffen as understanding sinks in: this woman is chained to Hellevig and unable to leave without the veil collapsing. This city is now her prison.

"Are you offering to fuck a baby into me, Blade?" The words are steady. Inflectionless. "How selfless."

There's the bitch I met at Aldgate.

I curl my lip in disgust. "Don't flatter yourself, Empress."

Just the thought makes me want to heave up knives.

I turn to leave, but at the door, I look back at her standing in a pool of moonlight. "Try not to die. It's annoying enough dealing with you alive."

I knock on Evander's chamber door. Rustling fabric and a muffled curse filter through the barrier, followed by the telltale creak of a mattress. Of course. My brother's proclivities are as predictable as they are tedious.

"Yeah?" Evander calls, voice rough with sleep and other things I'd rather not dwell on.

The smell of sex hits me when I enter. Evander remains chained to the bed where I left him, and the princess is nestled under the blankets at his side. They're covered in each other's scents—that unique aroma of Chosen like an imprint beneath their skin.

She stirs as I approach, violet eyes fluttering open. I study the rosy flush of her cheeks, the way her flesh has knitted back together without even a scar to show for all her suffering. The perks of fucking a healer, I suppose.

Evander watches me with a smirk. "You're looking almost dapper, Bas. Who did you have to disembowel to manage that at this hour?"

What a useless question. As if I'd ever allow my appearance to become so dissolute.

I level him with a flat stare. "Your attempts at humor remain as pathetic as your self-control."

"Jealous? Don't worry. I'm sure we could find someone willing to hate-fuck even your cold ass if you asked real sweet."

"When I want to act like a mindless animal, I'll seek your expert advice."

I withdraw a velvet-wrapped bundle from my coat and toss it at the girl.

She unknots the bindings to find her five knives. "You got them back."

"Your sister was cooperative. Even useful despite the corpses."

A sharp inhale. "*Corpses?* Is Theo—"

"She's fine. No thanks to the idiot guards she surrounds herself with."

"And you made sure she stayed that way." Her smile is lovely enough that I almost understand Evander's obsession. Almost. If I ignored literally everything else. "It was kind of you."

Ah. She thinks she's stumbled on tenderness beneath the ice, some sentimental insanity that forced my hand tonight. How *precious*.

"Tell me something. Do you know what used to be the rarest thing in existence?" I ask her. She regards me mutely, startled at the non sequitur. "Shadowmeld orebium, colloquially known as Turpori steel. It's impossible to replicate because I'm the only being capable of conjuring and manipulating it. At least until humans got hold of my power and abused it in ways I'm still dealing with. Do you know what's now the *most* coveted commodity?"

Silence. Her brows dig together in confusion.

"Devaliants," I say impatiently. "More specifically, *viable* Anchors. And now that you've murdered your uncle and become functionally worthless, your sister is our only safeguard against the Shroud's collapse. Keeping her breathing isn't kindness. It's necessity."

Let her chew on that. She bound her soul to a god and left two realms teetering on a knife's edge. The least she can do is choke on the consequences.

I leave the room and shut the door behind me.

Alexios leans against the far wall in the corridor, arms crossed over his chest. His eyes cut to my brother's door, then back to me. "Getting soft, Blade?"

His attention intensifies, his mind shoving against mine. I allow it for a span of three slow heartbeats. Four. Then I slam my mental ramparts closed.

He just smiles.

"The girl wanted a room tonight, so I chained Evander up," I reply. Time to shift his focus elsewhere. "I was in Hellevig earlier, assessing our remaining Anchor's security. The empress had some uninvited guests."

Alexios' expression sharpens. "Kidnapping or wet work?"

"Unclear. I was more concerned with removing a collar from her neck before her windpipe collapsed." I dig the broken remains out of my coat and pass them over. "Recognize those symbols?"

He turns the pieces over in his hands. "No. This is your metal?"

I nod. "But I can't verify when the collar was made or how many of my feathers are still in circulation. I had one like that put on me in the Bloody Court to keep me contained. This one is likely to compel obedience or conceal the empress' death from you through the Claim."

A muscle tics in his jaw. His eyes slip closed, and I feel the swell of his power again—a searing, seeking wildfire roaring through the aether.

"Those fucking mental walls of hers," he mutters. "They were fascinating when we had spare Anchors. Now, they're just a liability. She only lowers them to berate me about her sister."

"The empress' mental architecture is unusual. Strong natural defenses."

Orderly, I don't say. *Elegant. Beautifully constructed.* I've never craved a challenge more.

A treacherous flicker of long-dead heat kindles at the memory of those adamantine walls. The secret, shadowed spaces behind them I want to chart—

I crush the thought ruthlessly. Salt the earth so nothing so soft can take root.

Cool disinterest. Distant respect. That's all.

"Send Elias to guard her," I suggest, wrenching my focus back to tactics. To logic and necessity. "His background will make him less hostile to the idea of protecting a Devaliant. The empress' security is weak, and she's given permission for us to keep her safe with no risk to the Accords."

"That solves nothing long-term. I need her monitored." His burning gaze meets mine, and I know with sinking dread what he'll say next. "Your psychic skill exceeds my own. Will a bond give you full access to her mind if I transfer my Claim to you?"

No.

No.

No.

My shadow wings flare wide. "No."

One dark brow lifts. "Are you refusing an order? Or admitting you can't handle it?"

"I destroy things," I remind him flatly. "I don't protect them. I'm not a bodyguard."

Power lashes against me as lightning skitters across his skin. "You do whatever the fuck I need you to do. Evander is chained to a bed, we have a confirmed fleshtrade operating in Hellevig using a codeword with possible Devaliant ties, and *your* metal just ended up around the empress' neck. Desperate times, desperate measures. I want you to *watch* her. If she has ties to the fleshtrade, I want to know. If someone is making an attempt on my Anchor, I want to fucking know."

I very carefully don't react to the revelation that there are demigod poachers in Hellevig. That he neglected to lead with that critical piece of intelligence. It's so like him to safeguard information until it suits his purposes and he can use it to back me into a corner with no recourse but obedience.

"A Claim doesn't guarantee compliance," I say. "Her mind could stay her own."

"A risk," he allows. "But a necessary one. Form a full sensory bond. You need to be able to locate her anywhere and reach her at any time. See into her thoughts for information, taste her fear, feel the shape of her wanting." His head tilts. "Can you still handle that kind of intimacy? Or have you forgotten how?"

I swallow hard. This forced link will be unbearable. I'll have to take rusted shears to the cancer of it behind my ribs. Dig it out. Trade soap and boiling water and the bright pain of flensing for the creeping rot of something far worse.

"I have the theoretical knowledge," I say through my teeth.

And aren't those the most damning words. The admittance that whatever atrophied scrap of selfhood I buried hasn't rotted to nothing after all. That some instinctual relic recognizes the animal snarl of possession. The biting need to crawl inside her skin and curl up between the notches of her spine until she can't breathe without choking on me.

Focus. Control. Breathe in and hold, lungs turned to stone.

"She might refuse," I add.

"She won't. Not if she values her life." He turns to leave in a whisper of wings. "Five days, Blade. Settle your affairs and get your shit together. I'll send Elias to mind the girl for now. And Bastien?"

I halt the growl building in my throat and shackle it down. "What?"

"Make sure she survives long enough to birth an heir. Even Evander can't put her back together if she ends up splattered across her courtyard."

Then he's gone, leaving me alone in the corridor with nothing but the thundering of my pulse and the acid taste of bile in my throat.

I wrangle the tide of threatening emotion with ruthless precision.

Breathe in and hold.

Lungs turned to stone.

This Claim will be a necessity. A component in an overarching schematic, its purpose to reinforce the Shroud's structural integrity and load-bearing capacity.

Nothing more, nothing less. The rest is altered brain chemistry. Misfiring synapses, chemicals flooding receptors. More to the point, my *cock* still works.

Lights flare as I enter my bedroom and strip out of my clothes. Every garment will have to be sterilized of the lingering scent of *her*.

I turn the tap on for the bath. Scalding water gushes forth, steam billowing to fill the space. I step beneath the spray and reach for a bar of astringent soap, dragging punishing hands over my skin again and again, abrading the flesh until it's red and stinging. Still, I don't stop. I have to cut away this filthy patina of humanity, scour the weakness from me like infection from a wound.

There is no room for gentleness here—only water and the sluicing of my blood down the drain.

50

ALEXIOS

It's the perfect weather for breaking someone.

The salt spray lashes my face as the princess and I pick our way across the shore. We're at the base of the Tokle Mountains, on the border between Asteria and Nyholm. I used to frequent this shore often centuries ago. Severin liked to fuck me against the rocks in the water, liked to listen to the rasp of our breaths while the waves lapped on the waterfront.

I breathe deep, filling my lungs with the familiar tang of brine—the smell of memories and betrayal and dead friendships.

The Devaliant princess' footsteps sound beside me. I can practically taste her burning curiosity over her next test—her dread, too. I glance at her. She's practically glowing with the remnants of Evander's power, her pale, gleaming skin catching in the light. Not even a scratch unmended. I'd nearly forgotten how powerful his healing ability was, it's been so long since I've seen it.

"You're looking remarkably whole after my labyrinth," I say. "The Wolf's power should be locked up nice and tight in those cuffs, yet here you are without a scratch. Fascinating how that worked out."

Her breath snags. I catch it, track it, and file it away with all the other fractures spreading through that composure she desperately tries to maintain.

I'm not truly surprised to find her this whole. Even bound, an Eternal is a force of nature. And one seeing his Chosen bleeding out and dying in his arms? He'd have moved mountains and slaughtered realms to save her.

But Bryony Devaliant is mine until the end of our deal, and so I want to see those cracks spread. I want her off-balance. It makes things more interesting.

"What's wrong?" I stop and face her. "No clever comeback? Or did the Wolf manage to fuck the sass right out of your mouth last night?"

A flush crawls up her throat, staining those high cheekbones. "What happens between me and Evander isn't your business."

"See, that's where you're wrong. The second my Enforcer starts straining at his leash and slaughtering humans under my protection, it becomes my business. In fact, it's the only business that matters."

My hand shoots out, grasping her chin. She flinches. Smart girl. Fear is the only appropriate response when you're a mortal stupid enough to play with gods.

"Do you know why he wears a collar, Princess? Why I keep his leash good and tight?"

Her pulse flutters beneath my grip. "He... He told me what my family did to Turpori. That the grief made him and Bastien lose control of their power."

"Lose control." A bitter laugh escapes me. "That's a pretty turn of phrase. I found a pair of young Eternals howling in the ashes of their dead kingdom, and my choice was simple: bind part of their power and aim their rage where I needed it until they were emotionally stable, or put them both in the ground. No other options. An Eternal in agony is a walking extinction event."

Three thousand years ago, one of our strongest succumbed to madness, and it took five of us to put him down after he shattered continents and boiled seas. We barely contained the damage. In the end, we had to unmake him completely.

Two Eternals in that kind of pain would have wiped out half the realm.

My grip tightens, fingertips pressing into her throat until I feel her swallow against the pressure. They're so small, these mortals. So fragile. It never ceases to confound me, the trouble they cause.

"The funny thing about immortality," I murmur, "is that it just gives us more time to go mad. With infinite years, you run out of new experiences. That's why we can't leave you humans alone. You burn so bright. You remind us what it's like to want and hunger. And in the end, that made us all into fools courting our own destruction." I stroke my thumb across her skin. "I have to admit, I'm curious about your soulbond. Does it hurt? Having your soul tied up with his?"

Bryony is silent for a moment, inscrutable as she searches my face. "Does it hurt," she returns at last, soft as a sigh, "to have all those voices in your head, and still be so alone?"

A sharp, startled laugh leaves me. Oh, but this one was wasted in her role of sacrifice. She has *teeth*. I could almost admire Evander's taste if not for the enormity of the mess it's made.

My eyes cut briefly to the shoreline past her shoulder, the narrow causeway stretching into the mist. The silhouette of the Onyx Keep juts from the glassy water, still a striking sight even in its ruins, with fog swirling lazily across its surface.

It's been three centuries since I've stepped foot across the bay. Back then, that building was grand, a neutral territory where all the Eternals met to debate and intimidate and settle our shit. Now it's gathering dust.

But Severin likes to keep an eye on it. It's the closest point of entry into Nyholm, one humans tried taking ruthless advantage of once. It's the perfect test for an arrogant little human who thinks she's worthy of an Eternal.

"Alone, am I?" I say in a low voice, a plan taking shape. "Interesting choice of words, all things considered. How would you like to spend your next trial finding out what that feels like?"

Her eyes flare wide. "What?"

Ah, there it is. The dawning realization that she is well and truly fucked. It's too perfect. I didn't think I had any appreciation left for the poetry of small cruelties, but it appears I was mistaken. I should do this more often.

I flash her a grin and reach for my power, letting it pour out of me until the air thickens and lightning skitters across my skin. My magic snakes through the metaphysical weave of her soulbond and sinks into the strands that tether the Devaliant to her Wolf. And all I have to do is—

Snap.

The girl screams and staggers away from me. I watch as Evander's mark on her wrist blinks out of existence, leaving nothing behind but smooth skin. Empty.

"There," I say brightly. "Isn't that better? No god's power keeping you safe. No mate to come charging to the rescue. Just you, Princess. Soft and fragile and completely alone."

She rips her knife free of its sheath and shoves the weapon against my jugular. "*What did you do?*"

"Put the knife away, Princess. It's temporary. Not even I can break a soulbond permanently."

"Fix it. *Now.*"

My expression goes dead. "The knife, little girl. Before you do something stupid and make me fucking show you just how bad your life can get."

But she keeps it in place, chest heaving, eyes wild with the kind of desperation that makes mortals so dangerous.

I sigh and flex my power, sending the dagger clattering over the rocks. "Now that we're done with the dramatics, listen carefully, because I hate repeating myself." I gesture across the bay. "See that fortress? That's the Onyx Keep. It's abandoned now, but it means something to the Dark King. It's also where we keep every treaty between Eternals. Your test is to slip in there without Evander's mark protecting you, find a small chest in the atrium without Severin skinning you alive, and I might be convinced to reinstate your Claim." I spread my hands. "Simple enough?"

She jerks as if slapped. "That's a death sentence."

"Probably. But you're resourceful, aren't you?" I pause, considering her. "You know, there's a singular truth between the lines of every fable. If you want something of value, *earn* it.

With blood, with pain, whatever it takes. Nothing worth having comes cheap or easy."

She glares at me. "What's in the chest?"

"You'll find out when I'm ready to show you. It'll be on a table with some old scrolls. You won't miss it. Unless you die first, of course." I start back up the beach, gravel crunching beneath my boots. "Take the boat," I say, pointing at the rickety thing at the end of the pier up ahead. I'd optimistically call it seaworthy. "My power will hide you until you reach the shore. After that, you're on your own. I'd wish you luck, but. Well." I shrug. "Try not to die, et cetera and so forth."

I keep walking, the wind snatching at my wings. After a few moments of weighing her options, the girl growls in frustration, walks to the pier, and climbs into the boat.

With a thought, I cast it away from the shore, watching until the mist devours her and I can no longer discern the glint of her hair from the silver of the water.

A familiar presence tugs behind my eyes, then.

Bastien.

Whatever you just did, Evander is ready to tear this place apart, his mental voice informs me.

Temporarily severed the soulbond for her test, I answer shortly. *He'll get over it. Or not. I don't particularly care.*

Next time, try giving me some warning. Even with the chains on, it's taking three of us to hold him down.

Put him in the cell before he rampages through the palace and ruins my day even more, please. Tell him he'll have plenty of opportunities to destroy things when he faces his challengers tonight.

I can practically feel the Blade sorting through a dozen scathing retorts, but he settles on, *As you say.*

He withdraws, and I'm left alone with the gravity of what I've just done. Because now there's a Devaliant loose in Nyholm, a feral Eternal straining at my leash, and an inevitable confrontation with Severin. Which would mean seeing him after three hundred years and not breaking every bone in his body for his betrayal.

This had all better be worth the effort, because it's giving me a damn headache.

I don't turn at the rustle of wings. I'd know Zephyr's presence anywhere—the cadence of her breath, the way the air changes and sharpens when she's near. The way my skin prickles with awareness even after all these years.

"If you're here to scold me, Whisper, save your breath."

"You could have asked me to get the chest." Her voice carries that edge I know too well—the one that says she sees right through my bullshit. "You could have had Wraith bring it."

I give her a look. "I'm not interested in dealing with Severin until I have no other choice."

"That doesn't mean you should toss the girl at his feet. Wraith's territory is in uproar over his missing demis. If he catches her—"

"Oh, I'm counting on it," I say. "And she'll either talk her way out of it, or we'll be scraping what's left of her off the walls. If she wants what's in that box badly enough, she'll get creative. This is about more than just retrieving an object."

"Storm." Something in my chest clenches at the sound of my nickname on her lips. "Do you want her to fail?"

I could feed her a line and spin the narrative—I've made an art out of it. But I don't lie to my Whisper.

I can't help but stare at her, studying the stark lines of her features, the blade-slash of her cheekbones as she stares resolutely across the water. Wind catches in her hair, sending black strands dancing. Part of me wonders what she'd do if I reached for her. If I dragged my knuckles along her collarbone and buried my fingers in her wings. If I leaned close enough to steal the breath from her lungs.

But Zephyr is a fortress right now—all smooth, impenetrable walls and ramparts bristling with spikes. And I suspect I've already filled my quota of reckless idiocy for the day.

"I'm sure you remember what happened the last time an Eternal soulbonded with a human," I say. "If that girl wants her Chosen, she needs to prove to me and every god in this realm that she's worthy of him. That includes Severin. Let her see what it costs for a human to reach for power in Scillari."

"That doesn't answer my question. Do you want her to fail?"

Always pushing me, undaunted.

"She has to die," I say. "Scillari won't let the Wolf take his throne with a human by his side. I want him to see the girl give her life to let him rule." I give her a wry smile. "Sacrifice is an act of love, isn't it, Whisper?"

Her mouth flattens. She steps back, withdrawing into that wall of duty and careful distance. "Will there be anything else, my king?"

Like a door slamming shut. The same tired lines, wearing grooves into the space between us. I lost the right to her softness when she needed me and I left her with Calder, and now I'm always being split open by the blade of her indifference.

"Go to the palace," I tell her, gaze fixed on a distant point beyond her shoulder. Letting the short distance between us expand and expand. I showed enough weakness during Aethertide. "Make sure the Wolf gets ready for the arena. I'd prefer not to have to kill another Eternal."

She nods once, and then she's gone in a whisper of wings.

I settle in to wait. Let's see if the princess has what it takes to survive what's coming.

Because that's the thing about power—it always makes you bleed for it first.

51

BRYONY

THE BOAT ROCKS as if it's trying to fling me into the sea.

Every wave that slaps against the hull sends another burst of icy water into my face. My hands are numb from gripping the sides of the boat. The wood is rotting and salt-stained—exactly the kind of vessel you'd expect from someone hoping you'll drown before reaching shore.

Ahead, the walls of the Onyx Keep emerge from the fog. The building is hidden behind the high barrier, but the stonework is imposing. It *looms*. Back in Vartena, mothers used to frighten their children with tales of Nyholm and the Dark King's wrath. How he decorates those walls with the bones of trespassers.

I never thought I'd be stupid enough to test those stories.

Another wave sends the boat lurching. I pull my coat tighter around my shoulders, but the cold suffusing my limbs has nothing to do with the frigid water.

No, this is the chill of primal terror. And I'd be lying if I said some part of me wasn't tempted to spin this rickety death trap around to Asteria.

After a few more minutes, the boat hits the shallows, and I vault onto land. It takes every ounce of strength to drag the vessel onto the narrow strip of beach. By the time I wrestle it under a gnarled tree, my arms are trembling. It's not the best hiding spot, but it'll have to do. I can't afford to waste more time.

I study the wall stretching up before me. The barrier juts out of the rocks in columns of quartz and basalt fitted together. Sea spray and dark lichen coat the stones, but where the dying light hits just right, the wall shimmers with an inner luminescence, as if someone bottled starlight and poured it into the rock.

That's when I hear it—a flap of wings. Power rolls across the beach in a crackling tide of electricity.

I jerk my head up to see a demigod soldier emerging from the mist, wearing gleaming silver armor. His gray feathers spread wide as he veers sharply toward the keep. The air warps around him, sparking with his magic, the charged scent growing stronger.

"*Shit, shit, shit.*" I press deeper into the shadows under the branches.

They hung the bodies from the walls and let the birds pick them clean.

That's what my governess told me about what the Dark King did to the last Devaliants who breached his borders.

My heart pounds so hard I'm sure the sound will give me away. But then the demigod vanishes behind a crumbling parapet.

I let out a relieved exhale. Right, then. Guard presence, unknown numbers, and clearly on edge.

This is fine. Everything's fine.

I eye the seawall again. It looks no less daunting on the second inspection—smooth as polished glass, without so much as a dead vine to offer purchase. But there's an uneven ribbon of stairs hewn directly into the cliffside that might offer a better vantage.

Better than nothing.

Keeping low, I sprint across the beach, sticking to the deepest shadows at the base of the bluffs. My boots slip on wet rocks as I navigate the terrain. The path switches back and forth, the incline steep enough to make my already sore muscles scream in protest. But I grit my teeth and focus. One wrong step, one loose stone, and I might as well ring a dinner bell for the guards.

The distant crash and drag of the waves fade to a muted roar, replaced by the wind whipping itself into a gale—

A prickle dances across my nape. Then I hear the unmistakable crunch of boots over scree.

I don't hesitate. I lunge for the shadowy cleft in the stones to my right, folding my body into the tight recess and wedging myself as far back as I can go. Trying to make myself small. Invisible.

A ball of light pierces the fog, the edges of the nimbus nearly licking the toes of my boots. A figure materializes from the mist with broad shoulders, soot-dark wings, and armor.

Another demigod sentry.

Fuck. I'm a hairsbreadth from discovery, and there's nowhere left to run. My lungs turn to stone in my chest. *Don't breathe. Don't blink. Don't so much as twitch, or it's all over.*

The guard's head cocks as he scents the air. An endless moment passes while I hold my breath.

Go. Please fly away. Please don't scent anything mortal.

The wind shifts. A sudden gust drags in the noxious scent of rotted fish from the sea. The guard wrinkles his nose and scowls, then he launches himself into the air with a powerful flap of his wings, disappearing into the mists.

I sag against the stone. If that breeze hadn't covered the scent of my mortality—

Move. Get inside before they double back.

I scan the seawall above for anywhere I might slip through, and... *there*—a fissure in the stone latticework, barely wider than my shoulders. The edges are crumbled and broken, and it's a tight fit, but if I angle my body just so—

Power lashes across my senses a split second before the heavy thump of wingbeats sounds once more.

No. Not again.

I scramble up the sheer rock face, my fingers hooking into grooves and fissures. With a silent prayer to the stars, I heave my body into the narrow gap and wiggle through. For a breathless moment, I'm certain I'll get stuck. Easy prey for Nyholm's gods. But then I leverage myself with a grip on the rocks and fall on the other side.

I hit the ground hard. All the air rushes out of my lungs, and for a second, I can't do anything but lie there, bracing for the inevitable shout of soldiers.

But there's nothing. No shouts, no footsteps. Just wind rattling through dead things and waves hitting rocks below.

Pushing up on my elbows, I take stock of my surroundings. I've landed in what must have once been a grand garden. Skeletal trees claw at the mist-choked sky, their leaves blackened and curled in on themselves like burnt paper. Statues dot the garden, depicting gods with limbs shattered and heads gone. One has a woman pressed against a male's chest, her face turned up like she's begging. Another of a goddess with her wings snapped off at the shoulder blades, reaching for a companion who's broken beyond recognition. Dark ivy wraps through eye sockets, between fingers, like it's trying to drag them all down into the earth. Because this? This is a graveyard.

And beyond it all looms the keep.

There's something eerily beautiful about this place in all its faded grandeur. The stonework is crystalline, like solidified starlight, with spires toppled and broken. Former bridges of sparkling pale rock lead nowhere now. It looks like a palace of jagged glass. The walls have battle scars—places where the masonry is more crumbled than others.

"Just go," I whisper to myself. "Finish this."

I push to my feet and pick my way between the statues, trying not to look at their faces. Trying not to think about the lovers frozen in stone and the broken limbs. Was this from the war? Or did someone… do this on purpose?

Stop it. Staying still means thinking, and thinking means remembering that being here is insane.

The windows throw back my reflection as I pass, but I ignore my warped image and spot a gap where a window shutter dangles on rusted hinges.

There we go. That's my way in.

I press my fingers into the small opening. The weakened wood protests, then yields with a soft crack that might as well be a thunderbolt in the preternatural quiet. I wait, but there's only silence.

My hands tremble as I work the opening wide enough to fit

through. The chamber beyond is dark and empty, but I swear I *feel* eyes watching me. Waiting.

But it's too late to turn back now.

In, out. Get what I came for, and get gone.

I lower myself into the room. The air presses close, thick with the scent of mold and decay. My stomach turns. I breathe through my mouth and wait for my eyes to adjust. There's not much here—a shelf clinging to one mildewed wall with old books spilled onto the floor, some trinkets collecting dust on a few tables, a telescope at the window. But that proof of someone previously here sends a frisson of unease through my gut. They watched the stars. They read these books and walked the bridges in this keep, and probably never imagined it would all crumble like this.

The desk draws me forward.

A scattering of maps peeks through the grime, hundreds of years out of date, but I'd know those borders anywhere—the spine of the Duehavn Ridge as it cleaves the realms. Two sides of a coin.

My breath catches when I spot the sigil marking Hellevig, carved so deep it nearly pierces the parchment. I can almost see the Dark King hunched over these maps, plotting my family's destruction.

The sensation of a gaze boring into my back sharpens.

I whirl, reaching for my knife, but there's only darkness. Shadows twisting in on themselves. The curtains move, but it's only the wind through the broken window.

Go, Bryony. Now.

I ease open the door. The space between my shoulder blades prickles again.

Find the atrium. Get it done.

My fingers trail along the wall as I move deeper into the keep, hurrying past dozens of shadowed doors. It reminds me of the crypt beneath Hellevig's temple—that same weight that makes you want to hold your breath. Makes you feel like you're trespassing. The air feels hungry here, too sharp, like a monster's maw waiting to devour me.

I count doors as I pass. *Seven. Eight. Nine.* My fingernails dig into my palms, and my shirt sticks to my back with sweat.

Stop thinking. Move.

I round the corner, and—

My breath catches at the vast chamber with soaring columns and a vaulted glass oculus. Even choked in dust, devoid of light, I can see the bones of what this room once was. How it would have dazzled before the war made it a ruin. Every inch of the pale stonework is carved with elaborate filigree, and there are more statues of goddesses standing regally with their wings spread, carved out of dark rock. Ivy creeps up the walls and around the staircase.

My gaze sweeps the abandoned chamber, falling to the table against the far wall with crumbling scrolls and ancient ledgers. Sitting right there is a small chest just as Alexios described.

I stumble toward it. Some last thread of survival instinct screams a warning: *Too easy too easy this is too fucking easy.* But hope is a cruel master. It drowns out the doubt as I grab the small chest and cradle it.

Then a hand clamps around my wrist, rings glinting. A voice scrapes against my ear, cold as the grave: "I don't like mortals in my territory."

52

BRYONY

I'M YANKED AROUND, and I forget how to breathe.

I'd recognize the Dark King anywhere. He may not be painted on temple murals like Evander, but the stories were clear enough that this god was as devastatingly beautiful as the rest.

He's gorgeous in that lethal way that screams *danger*. Indigo hair frames his striking features: storm-gray eyes rimmed in molten gold, high cheekbones, straight nose, square jaw. When he tilts his head, light catches on the delicate silver piercings climbing up his ear. His body is as muscular as the other Eternals, but with the lean lines of a dancer rather than a warrior. His massive wings spread wide, the dark blue feathers scattered with flecks of gold, like starlight against a deepening twilight sky.

"A Devaliant. I'd recognize that fucking skin anywhere." A slow, wicked smile curves his mouth. "I'm dying to know what made you think trespassing into my territory was a solid choice. Most people prefer to keep their internal organs, you know, *internal*."

"I'm here for the chest." I force myself to meet his gaze. "Nothing else."

"The chest?" His attention drops to the box clutched in my grip, and recognition sparks. "Please tell me Alexios didn't punt your fragile human ass into my lands for that. Though I suppose dangling an expendable mortal in front of the death god would be his brand of fuckery. Classic Storm move."

"I need it," I say, fighting the urge to step back. "For my Chosen."

A low, contemplative hum. Then he leans in, crowding into my space. I nearly yelp when he drags his nose along my skin and scents me.

"Here's the thing about that," he murmurs against my thundering pulse. "When someone starts throwing around words like 'Chosen,' there's usually a magical signature announcing to the world which pitiful bastard's soul you've tangled yourself up with." Another deep inhale. "But you? You're blank. Empty. No mark. No Claim."

I flinch at the reminder of what Alexios took from me. The place where the bond used to be aches, like pressing on a bruise that won't heal.

"So now you're going to tell me what a Princess of the Blood is doing in my territory." His voice drops, soft and deadly. "Because my demis have been going missing for months, and when a Devaliant shows up uninvited, that's what we call suspicious timing."

Of course, I've been dropped in the middle of a diplomatic crisis on top of everything else. That explains the patrols outside and the heightened security. He thinks I'm connected to his missing people. And Alexios knew exactly what he was throwing me into, that manipulative bastard.

"I have nothing to do with your missing people," I say, raising my arms. "I'm just here for the chest."

"Try again." He smacks my prize out of my grasp, and it clatters to the floor as he locks his fingers around my forearm. "I need more convincing."

His power crackles through the air, and the sleeve of my coat disintegrates beneath his grip. A ragged gasp leaves me as rot spreads from his fingers across my exposed skin.

"Going once. That's the death touch setting in. Hurts, doesn't it?"

"Stop stop *stop*. *Wait*." I try to yank away, but he just holds me more firmly. The tips of my fingers shrivel and twist, consumed by the creeping decay.

Oh gods, oh gods, oh gods—

"Going twice. Necrosis is such a fascinating process, really. First, the blood flow stops. Then the tissue starts to die. Then—"

"*Okay.*" A hitching sob hiccups out of me. "Okay, just..."

"Princess, I suggest you find better words than that, or I'll let the rot spread somewhere vital."

Fuck this.

My free hand closes around the hilt of the dagger at my waist. I rip the blade free and slash at his hand. Surprise flickers across his face, and his hold loosens a fraction—just enough.

I drive my knee up, aiming for his groin, but he shifts at the last second. The instant his hold breaks, I bolt, scooping up the chest and sprinting toward the exit. Behind me, I hear his laugh of delight.

"Now *that's* more like it!"

Run run run—

But I slam face-first into what feels like a brick wall. Magic yanks me back.

The Dark King stalks toward me, and there's something almost approving in the way his eyes glitter. "Solid effort. Most mortals just piss themselves and beg."

I don't waste my breath on words. Just pivot and slash the dagger at his chest.

He releases me with a grunt, glancing down at his torn shirt. "Changed my mind. I'll let you live a little longer—call it payment for the sheer fucking audacity. This box must be worth its weight in solid gold to you if you're fighting tooth and nail to keep it. So fuck it, I'm feeling generous. Fight for it and make it good for me."

The Dark King's power detonates. His magic sends me stumbling back, and I drop the box, gagging as the taste of grave dirt floods my mouth. The stones where I'd just been standing crack open in a deafening *BOOM—*

And skeletal hands burst through the crumbling stone.

What the fuck.

Those dead fingers grasp and claw, pulling themselves out of some crypt beneath my feet. More stones shatter as they climb out—*crack crack crack*—one after another after another, clawing up from whatever mass grave they've been rotting in. The stench hits me in a reek of putrefaction.

The first corpse finally drags itself out of the ruined stonework.

Rotten clothes and armor crusted with filth cling to its desiccated flesh. That's when I notice its breastplate is emblazoned with a crest I know intimately: the serpent eating its own heart.

The sigil of House Devaliant—and of the Lucinian legion.

My stomach drops. These are the bodies of the Vartenan soldiers who tried to invade Nyholm three hundred years ago.

"Let's play a game!" the Dark King calls. "It's called 'how many corpses does it take to make a Devaliant scream?' First to stab her gets to be alive again for a night."

What an asshole.

The corpse nearest to me turns its head, and those empty eye sockets fix on my face. Its jaw unhinges in a silent scream—and then it lunges.

I stumble back. "Shit!"

More claw their way up from the crypt beneath the shattered flagstones, each in varying stages of decay—some skeletal, some with flesh still hanging off their bones. Soon, the atrium is choked with bodies and the stink of decay.

Make space. Amara's lessons flood back. *Don't let them box you in.*

So I try to keep my distance. A corpse pounces from my left, fingers catching my sleeve, and the fabric rips as I jerk away. I bring my blade down on its legs, but it keeps crawling toward me.

"I'm upping the stakes!" The Dark King's voice echoes through the melee. "Winner gets to do whatever they want with her!"

My vision goes red. "You sick piece of shit!"

A rotting hand closes around my leg. I stomp down hard, and bones give way under my boot. Another corpse grabs for my hair, and I duck and slash, taking the thing's head clean off.

Keep moving. I can almost feel Amara correcting my stance. *They can't stab what they can't catch.*

There are too many of them. They're everywhere now, climbing over each other to get to me in an endless tide of dead. Severed arms and legs twitch and grab at my ankles. If I fall, I'm finished. I leap over the ruined stonework and the dark, gaping hole of the underground chamber where the dead are spilling from.

How many damn corpses is this asshole keeping under this place? Did he just collect every person who ever pissed him off?

Through it all, the Dark King watches from his perch on the staircase, wings spread lazily across the steps. "Having fun yet? I can add more if this isn't challenging enough." He stretches, getting more comfortable. "You know what builds character? Near-death experiences. Also actual death, but it's less useful for the learning process."

"Go"—I duck under grasping hands—"fuck yourself!"

I'm really starting to hate him.

Sweat stings my eyes. Black spots dance at the edges of my vision, and I can barely get air into my lungs. My good hand is starting to cramp around the knife handle, and I'm trembling with the effort to keep moving, keep fighting, but they're relentless. Determined. Fingers hook into my calf, and I kick free only to have another hand clamp around my elbow, threatening to drag me down—

"Hold!" The Dark King's command freezes the horde mid-motion. "Bravo, everyone. Stellar performance." He slow-claps, pushing to his feet. "Haven't had this much entertainment since... actually, no, this might be a new record. But since none of you managed to properly maim her"—he flicks his fingers and the corpses crumble into piles of bones and ash all around me—"back in the dirt you go."

"I hate you and Alexios both," I rasp, brushing the ash off my coat. "I can't decide which of you is the bigger asshole."

"Hate's such an intimate emotion. Almost as good as fear,

and definitely better than love. At least hate's honest." He walks toward me, studying me with those storm-gray and gold eyes. "Want to tell me why you're really here stealing that box, or should I call back the horde for another round? I bet we could fit a thousand in here if we get creative with the spacing. Really test that stamina of yours."

I glare at him. "Alexios sent me for the box. That's it. Let me leave, and you'll never see me again."

"Is that so? See, there's something you should know. Storm could have asked for this box at any time. We may hate each other, but we still have to play nice for politics." He stops in front of me and crosses his arms. "He sent you here because he knew I'd be interested in watching a Devaliant fight for this thing. So what do I get out of giving it to you?"

I blink, baffled. "I don't—what?"

"The box, honey. Keep up. You want it, I have it. I know exactly what's inside it." He spreads his hands. "When two parties hit a wall, they negotiate. Usually with less attempted murder."

"What do you want?"

The Dark King grins again, circling me in a slow, predatory stalk. "So many options. I could see how many organs I can remove before you stop breathing. The record is seven, in case you were wondering. Or maybe I'll keep you. Wind you up like a pretty doll and make you dance for my court. The irony of a Devaliant serving drinks to the people her family tried to slaughter? *Perfection*." He pauses, considering. "Really, it's an embarrassment of riches. Which would you prefer? I'm feeling charitable enough to let you pick."

"Before you start contemplating body parts, you should know the Wolf's my Chosen. I need the box for him. Alexios covered his Claim so you'd kill first and ask questions never."

He gives a little laugh. "Oh, right. I did hear whispers about the Wolf losing his mind over some human pussy. Hard to believe Evander's standards dropped that low."

"The laws protect Chosen—"

"The laws protect *legitimate* Claims. But all I see is a Devaliant with no proof except her word, and that means less than shit to me."

That's it, that's the last straw on this terrible day. I'm tired of everyone's shit. No more playing nice.

Screaming through my teeth, I lunge at him and slam the Dark King into the nearest pillar, burying my dagger into his shoulder. It's a clumsy strike, wild and artless. A final blaze of glory since he's probably going to kill me anyway.

He just smiles, and it's the most beautiful, terrifying thing I've ever seen. "Oh, fuck yes." He yanks the knife free, twirling it between his fingers as the wound knits shut. "I knew you'd be—" He freezes, studying the blade with sudden intensity. Then he asks with deadly softness, "Where did you get this knife?"

I step back, my heel catching on an uneven flagstone as I hurry to put space between me and the intense emotion radiating from him.

Trap trap trap, something in me gibbers. *Caught caught caught.*

"I-It's mine. Not that it's any of your—"

"Did you steal it? Buy it from a fleshtrader?"

"Of course not! I—"

The Dark King seizes my throat and slams me into a pillar hard enough to make my teeth rattle. "Then let's try this again." His fingers tighten. "Tell me where you got the knife, or I'll ask your corpse."

Stars burst across my vision. "Gift—during Aethertide. A-Ama—" I claw at his grip as pressure builds. "Amara. Her name was—"

He wrenches his hand away. I collapse to my knees, gulping desperate lungfuls of air. The roaring in my ears drowns out his next clipped words.

"—trained you how to use it, too. Didn't she?"

I squint up at him. "Sorry. Hard to hear over the sound of you trying to crush my windpipe."

"You move like her," he says with an impatient gesture. "Those turns, those strikes—that's her style all over."

I nod. Anything to keep his hands away from my throat.

He stares at me for a long moment, something raw and complicated moving in his expression. Then he sighs, shuts his eyes, and mutters, "*Fuck*." He offers the knife and jerks his head toward the door. "Take your knife and your fucking box and go."

I stare at him as I accept the blade, not understanding the sudden rigid line of his shoulders, the set of his jaw. None of this makes sense. The Eternal that parents invoke to terrify unruly children into obedience is just... letting me go with my organs where they belong? After all this? Because I mentioned Amara?

"Why?"

He exhales sharply. "Because if Amara gave you this, she'd be pissed with me if I made your corpse dance. And I try not to disappoint her, even if I'm shit at it."

I force myself upright on shaking legs and grab my prize before he changes his mind.

"Wait." He jerks his chin at my withered arm. "I can't heal your other injuries, but I can repair the necrosis."

He crooks his fingers before I can cringe away, and a pulse of his magic sparks beneath my skin. Not the same consuming arousal as Evander's, just... warmth. Like liquid sunshine in my veins. I watch as healthy flesh flows over the rotted black, whole and unblemished once more.

"There." The Dark King meets my stunned gaze, his face giving away nothing. "Good as new. Don't mention this to my Chosen, and we'll call it even."

Understanding slams into me. The reason for his mercy, the softness limning his words.

"*You*." My mouth opens and closes. "*You're* Amara's Chosen? The one who she—"

Regrets.

So that's why all those demis bowed to her in Caelestis during Aethertide. She's bonded to an Eternal. Not just any Eternal—a scary as shit death god. No wonder she had all that paint warning everyone off.

At my words, the Dark King's expression frosts over, as remote and pitiless as the void between stars. "Get out."

He turns away in a whisper of shadow and indigo feathers, his wings stretching.

I'm halfway across the atrium when his voice rings out again, softer this time. Almost hesitant.

"Was she... okay? When you saw her last? Did she look well?"

With his guard momentarily lowered—when he sounds like that, as if he's been yearning for years—I see what Amara must have seen. What made her Choose him despite everything.

I hesitate, choosing my words carefully. "She seemed happy. Strong. Still lights up any room she walks into."

"Good." There's a slight bend to his shoulders, as if hearing that answer pains him. "That's good. Glad to hear it."

"Would you..." I bite my lip. "Would you like me to say something to her? As thanks for letting me live?"

He blinks. "No."

Hard. Final. Whatever vulnerability I saw is gone, replaced by the ruthless Eternal of Nyholm, head of the Dark Court.

"Okay." I clear my throat. "I'll just be going, then. Alexios has Evander, and I'm here because I negotiated to unbind his powers. This was one of my tests."

"Well, who am I to judge someone's suicidal devotion to their Chosen?" He gestures to the door. "Get out of here before I change my mind. And Princess? Next time Alexios wants to use you as bait? Tell him to go fuck himself."

53

BRYONY

I DRAG MYSELF from the boat, the hard-won box pressed against my ribs, and every breath tastes of salt. The Asterian shore stretches before me—pale sand that glows faintly beneath the stars.

"Alexios, I'm ready."

The shriek of gulls and the crash of waves fill the silence. Then ancient magic crackles over my skin as the Eternal of Asteria lands in a rustle of crimson and black feathers. Those burning eyes catalog every bruise, every tear in my leathers, every place the Dark King's corpses grabbed and clawed and tried to drag me under. I probably look like something fished out of the harbor after a week.

"I see you found my little box," he says. "I'm almost impressed."

"Shove the box up your ass," I snap. "You knew what you were throwing me into. The security, the missing demis, the fact that the Dark King would be there to fuck with me. You set me up to fail."

A dark laugh rumbles from him. "Dangling you in front of Severin without protection was an opportunity too perfect to waste. I'll admit, the odds weren't exactly in your favor. The Blade gave you a nine percent chance of making it out alive."

Nine? Guess Bastien really hates me.

"Give me back my Claim," I say.

"Not yet. Another day without Evander's mark should help you appreciate what you're fighting for." He crooks a finger, beckoning. "You have an audience waiting."

I curl my fingers into my palm to keep from punching him in the face. "I'm not limping through another mob of demis out for my blood. I barely kept Evander from tearing half your court apart after yesterday."

He chuckles. "Where would be the fun in a repeat performance? Come here, Bryony."

Remember why you're doing this, I tell myself. *And who you're doing it for.*

Hating myself, I clutch the box to my chest tighter and allow Alexios to fold me into his arms, steeling myself as his wings spread wide.

He flies like a god with galaxies to burn and realms to raze. The landscape of Asteria blurs beneath us as he heads up the mountains to his palace, landing on the balcony of Evander's palace bedroom.

"You"—I grab the nearest pillar to keep from falling—"are a maniac."

"So I've been told. By people of more note." He holds out one hand, imperious. "The box, little sacrifice."

I hold out my prize. Some distant part of me marvels that the Dark King allowed me to have it. That he let me go because of Amara.

Alexios' red eyes gleam as he accepts it and turns it in his hands.

"I bled for that," I say. "Got throttled and tossed around by an actual god of death. I think I deserve to know what's inside."

The look he levels at me could melt the skin off my bones. "You *deserve*? Let me explain something to you, girl. You're entitled to what I decide you've earned. Nothing more, nothing less. Until the end of my trials, you're entertainment who just happens to be fucking my Enforcer."

I clench my jaw so hard my back teeth grind together. I glance through the balcony's open doors to the bed, but my Chosen is nowhere to be found. "Where's Evander? Because I want a night with him. No chains, no magic cuffs. Just us."

"I want many things in this dismal simulacrum of existence," he replies conversationally, tucking the chest under his arm. "Peace in my realms. The luxury of not having to listen to mortals whine. Funny how rarely I lower myself to begging for any of it. You seem to be under the impression that this is a negotiation. It isn't. You'll see your Chosen soon." He jerks his chin toward the bathing chamber. "Now go use the bath before I drown you in it."

I'm about to argue, but something in his eyes stops me cold. The kind of flat, reptilian stillness that says he's imagining all the creative ways he could end me.

So I shut up and obey.

Someone's already prepared the bath for me. Steam rises off the water, and the surface is scattered with pale flower petals. The fragrance of citrus and roses permeates the air.

Well. At least this is one luxury I can appreciate.

I strip, trying not to look too closely at what my destroyed clothes reveal, but it's impossible to ignore the purple bruises everywhere the Dark King's corpses got their hands on me. At least he healed the necrosis, or I wouldn't have a working left hand. Small mercies.

Sinking into the scalding water forces a hiss from between my teeth. I scrub myself raw and pink, washing away blood and grime and the lingering stench of decay.

When I finally step out, there's a gown hanging from the door made of shining fabric that resembles liquid sunlight. I scowl as I hold it up.

"Is there another dress to choose from?" I call out to Alexios.

"No." Curt. Final.

Asshole.

I step into it and begin tying up the little fastenings. The dramatic slits along both legs are held together by golden chains, and the plunging neckline and back meet at a choker-style collar that covers the Dark King's bruises. If it weren't for the shining filigree,

I'd say it were something a pet would wear, which is probably the point. The translucent fabric is stitched with strategically placed jewels to hide the parts of me for Evander's eyes only. Still, if I breathe wrong, someone is going to see my nipples.

I hate everything.

Alexios is standing on the balcony as I emerge. He turns, gaze drifting down my body, and I fight the urge to fidget beneath that intense red stare.

"Acceptable. I'm glad it fits."

"It fits like you want everyone to see my ass when I walk, so I'll go with 'barely tolerable.'" I tug at the thin fabric where it dips too low between my breasts. "Is the collar a style choice or a punishment?"

He gives a mocking tilt of his head. "You know better than anyone that when I aim to send a message, I'm hardly subtle about it."

"Yes, well"—I tug again—"I'm practically naked."

"Would you prefer I send you out wearing nothing at all?"

I glare at him instead of answering. "How long until you give Evander's mark back?"

"When we finish my tests." His eyes drop to my wrist where his own Claim used to glow, and something dark passes across his face. "I heard you, you know. Every time you climbed onto that altar and cursed me in your thoughts. You were an irritating little shit."

Ice floods my veins. "I wasn't aware you could hear me through your Claim."

"Not everything. Listening to every pathetic thought from thousands of Claimed would finish the job of driving me insane." His wings shift restlessly. "But when they started worshipping you instead of coming to my temple, I listened. And when I found out the woman I thought I executed soulbonded with an Eternal willing to raze realms for her? I wondered just how far your ambitions went." His voice drops lower, crueler. "Humans always have been grasping, greedy things, and the Wolf wouldn't be the first god destroyed by a pretty face and a tight cunt."

Fury detonates in my chest, and I get right up in his space. "I soulbonded with Evander because I love him. Because after you, the thought of another god's mark on me made me want to claw my skin off. I died hundreds of times for your precious Shroud, and what did I get for my trouble? Abandonment and punishment because an emperor couldn't control his people. I hated you then. I hate you now. And I'll hate you until they put me in the ground."

For a moment, I think he might kill me. The air between us hums with power, the smell of lightning growing stronger.

Then he laughs—a genuine sound that startles me more than his rage.

"I know." His fingers brush against my cheek. I jerk away. "I tasted that hatred every time the knife opened you up. I could drink it." Then he holds out his arm like we're attending some grand ball. "Audience awaits, little sacrifice."

I don't move.

His eyes narrow. "Take my arm and walk with me, or I'll grab you by that collar and make you crawl."

I believe him. I've seen what he does to those who defy him.

So I take his arm and let him lead me through the corridors. "Just because I'm wearing this doesn't make me a pet on a leash."

"No," he agrees, not looking at me. "Pets are easier to control."

The palace stretches in a labyrinth of soaring archways, windows, and columns engraved with delicate filigree. I don't know how he doesn't get lost here, but I suppose you memorize things after seven thousand years.

Finally, Alexios stops before a pair of doors made from gleaming basalt. Gold embellishments twine across their surface like vines, nearly covering the pulsing glow of runes. The doors shudder open with an echoing groan.

The wave of noise hits first—a deafening crush of shouts and screams.

It's an arena.

The circular structure stretches out before us. Marble columns rise hundreds of feet, their surfaces carved with scenes from ancient battles of gods locked in combat. Tiers of seats filled with hundreds of demis climb toward the open-air oculus, interspersed with platforms that float around the arena, suspended by nothing but magic.

"What is this place?" I ask Alexios.

"The Colosseum Eternal." He gives me a wry smile. "Even gods need somewhere to settle their scores."

The demis in the stands shout at our arrival, the wings forming a mosaic of colors against the stark architecture: ruby and gold, midnight blue and forest green, pure white and deepest black. The air crackles with their combined power, and their voices blend into a roar that bounces off the walls.

My attention turns to the arena's fighting pit. Obstacles are set up throughout—columns and rocks that offer cover for attacks, some blackened and shattered from previous battles. At first glance, there's nothing remarkable about the sand, but ancient runes flare beneath the surface in irregular patterns.

"Those runes down there," I say, glancing at Alexios. "What do they do?"

"Contain the violence. Without them, every fight would level the palace." Alexios gestures at the circular opening above us. "The barriers channel excess power upward, into the sky."

My eyes catch on deep gouges in the pit wall. Scorch marks score the stone, the walls partially melted in some places to form black glass.

"The last time two Eternals fought here," Alexios continues, "they cracked the foundations so badly we had to rebuild half the western section. This is where gods come to die, girl."

He steers me toward a balcony jutting over the arena floor, where a pair of obsidian thrones dominate the dais. The larger is a jagged, spiked monstrosity that appears carved from living shadow. The other lacks its companion's ornamentation but is no less imposing.

Alexios sprawls in the bigger chair. "Sit."

I eye the empty throne. "It's the same height as yours."

"An Eternal's Chosen takes a position of equal standing,

even if I'd prefer you at my feet." His expression frosts over. "Sit down, Bryony."

I can think of about a hundred things I'd rather do than perch at his side, but I sink onto the throne all the same.

A screech of metal rends the air, and everyone turns toward the far end of the arena where a rusted gate shudders upward. A hush goes through the crowd.

And I know who I'm going to see stride out onto those killing sands. Because, *of course*, it would be him.

Evander walks into the pit, bare from the waist up, with magic-suppressing manacles glinting around his wrists. Straps of weapons cross his torso, framing gleaming skin and rippling muscle. His wings flare, stretching wide and catching the torchlight until the golden feathers seem to burn. All that coiled strength and beauty is honed to a lethal edge.

I can't breathe past the panic clawing up my throat. "You said I'd pay his penance," I snarl at Alexios. "We had a deal."

"That was our agreement for Hellevig. This is about Scillari." He cuts me a sidelong glance. "You know our realm is alive, don't you? Aware?"

I give him a sharp nod, not trusting my voice.

"Then you need to understand that the Wolf's been stable enough to have his leash off for years. But that means being a king, not a pretty killer who fucks and fights because it's easier than ruling." A low laugh. "Scillari picks its monarchs. And it doesn't appreciate when a chosen king leaves its gifts to rot unused. He needs to show a pissed-off realm why he's more worthy than any demi itching to wear his crown."

I stare at the sands below. Armored demis are pouring into the arena with magic crackling in the air, ready to kill.

They circle Evander, over fifty against one. Sizing him up. Looking for vulnerable spots to drive the knife in deep and twist. But he just bares his teeth in a feral grin, amber eyes glowing.

"Tonight, those cuffs make it a fair fight for his challengers to prove themselves," Alexios continues. "Those demis think he's weak. They believe loving you has made him soft."

My mouth dries up. "And you're letting them think that?"

"I'm letting him prove them wrong."

"If he loses?" I ask, afraid of the answer.

Alexios watches me, his expression cold. As if he blames me for this. "Then Severin, the Blade, and I will put him down. It'll take all three of us at his power level."

"You'll kill him?" I ask, my stomach lurching.

"The realm would demand it. Weakness can't rule."

"But he—" My voice catches. "He can't use his power. There are too many down there. He can't—"

"He can." Alexios pins me with that ruthless, red stare. "And he will. For you."

Then he raises his hand—

And the demis attack.

One swings a massive war hammer, the head leaving traceries of lightning in its wake. Evander ducks beneath the crackling arc and comes up swinging. His dagger flashes once. Twice. His opponent crumples to the sand with a slit throat.

Evander doesn't pause to savor his victory. He's already moving, surging to meet the next wave of attackers. A demigoddess with obsidian wings sends shadows swelling from the ground to grasp for his legs, but he lets the darkness catch him, using the momentum to launch himself into a backflip that brings him down behind another opponent. His blade finds the sweet spot between armor plates before they can turn.

The air around the third demi shimmers like a heat haze before coalescing into a barrage of glass shards that hurtle toward him. Evander throws up his wings, and the projectiles ping off his feathers before tinkling to the arena floor. Then he sweeps low and takes out his attacker's knees.

It only gets bloodier from there.

Evander is feral grace. His knives sing as he paints the sands red. But for every demi he cuts down, another takes their place. The blows are taking their toll, his movements losing fluidity as exhaustion sets in, no doubt sped up by the damn cuffs.

My pulse is too fast. I can barely concentrate on the fighting below. Meanwhile, Alexios lounges beside me, just… observing. Emotionless.

"Did he ever tell you why we call him the Wolf?" Alexios' voice filters through the static. Soft. Gentle, almost. I wonder if he's trying to distract me.

I swallow before replying. "He said he earned the name."

"Oh, undoubtedly. Before the war, he was a good prince. A scholar. He had his mother's love of books and art. But that was before humans taught my kind that a crown makes fine kindling and a god's heart is a delicacy to be devoured."

A wet, meaty thunk wrenches my focus to the pit below. The crowd cheers as Evander takes down five more demis in quick succession. He's brutal. Blood coats his armor, his skin. This is a god of battle at work.

"Is there a point to the history lesson?" I ask flatly. "Or is this just another excuse to hear yourself talk?"

"I was there when the Wolf earned his name. At the battle of Sul'achan."

My blood turns to ice.

Every child in Vartena knows Sul'achan. How Luceni's legion stood against the Scillari host in the Riverlands. The bards never could agree on the finer details, but they all ended the same way—with the River Wartos running red and bodies piled so high, they blotted out the sun.

Alexios tilts his head, considering. "Five thousand human soldiers, and Evander didn't even reach for a weapon. He waded into those killing fields and ripped them apart with his bare hands and teeth like an animal. But that's war, isn't it? Strip away the civilization, and we're all just beasts in too-small skin. The only thing standing between you and the Void is how loudly you can howl, how deep you can dig, and how viciously you can bite."

I can't look away from the arena.

A demi wielding twin swords forces Evander toward the wall. But instead of retreating, he runs three steps up the vertical surface before launching himself over his opponent's head, wings snapping out. His primary feathers slice clean through his enemy's neck.

The sands are red now. There are so many corpses that he has to step on them.

"After the battle," Alexios says, "I found him crouched over a gutted soldier, gnawing at the poor bastard's throat. He was called Blaze once, did he tell you? A strong name for a strong prince who could manipulate heat and bend light to his will. But that was a different time. A kinder one."

As if to punctuate his point, Evander spins and buries his sword in a demi's gut.

I see his guard drop a fraction of a second too late—the way his opponent pivots, leading Evander to bare his flank. The wet *shunk* as the dagger hits its mark.

I shove to my feet. But before I can take a step, Alexios hauls me against his chest.

"*Watch*," he hisses in my ear. "Watch him fight for you, *bleed* for you. The depravities he'll commit in your name. This is what's left when you peel back a god's civility, little sacrifice. We kill for our Chosen. We butcher for what's ours."

Evander whirls and shoves his blade through the last demi's throat.

Silence falls over the Colosseum. The crowd seems to hold its collective breath—then the demis are bowing, acknowledging their better.

Their *king*.

My Chosen stands alone in the center of the carnage, his chest heaving, blood painting his skin and dripping from his wings to stain the sand at his feet. He raises his head, his eyes seeking mine across the distance.

I wrench free from Alexios' grasp and run down the balcony steps, vaulting over the low wall that separates the stands from the arena floor. I try not to focus on the bloody sand as my feet hit the ground.

Evander meets me halfway and crushes me against him. The metallic tang of gore fills my nose, but I hold him tightly anyway, my fingers pressing into the matted feathers of his wings. He groans softly.

Alexios' voice sounds from behind me. "Nice show, Wolf."

Flames flash in Evander's eyes as he angles his body between me and the god-king. Then he sags against me, his face finding the crook of my neck as he drags my scent into his lungs like he's starving for it.

His teeth find my pulse and dig deep enough to sting. I gasp as I clutch him closer. He bites down again, a firmer pressure.

When his hand circles my wrist where his Claim should be, I understand. The severed bond is an open wound that needs tending.

Alexios watches with a smirk. "An Eternal fresh off a victory needs to mark his mate," he tells me. "It's as necessary as air. He just killed and bled for the right to keep you. Let him bite. Let him know you're his."

"He knows I'm his," I say. "That I'll always be his."

"But do *they*?" He jerks his chin at the silent crowd. "They're not bowing for you, girl."

I freeze.

He makes a thoughtful noise. "You're a human asking to be his queen. How do you think that plays out if the demis don't see you both earn each other?" He doesn't wait for my reply before he's striding forward to pry Evander off me. "No biting," he says sharply when Evander's lips peel back from his teeth in a snarl. "She's coming with us. And you?" His nose wrinkles. "You're getting washed down before you step one foot in my palace."

54

BRYONY

"Where are we going?" I ask Alexios.

The god-king doesn't turn as he leads us down the dark tunnel below the arena. There's no ornamentation along the walls, just glittering black stone and the rush of water in the distance.

"There's a spring under the palace. The magic will heal the Wolf while those shackles keep his power locked down."

The passageway opens into a cavern. Crystals cover the walls, refracting the luminous turquoise of the waters as if we're standing inside a geode. Steam rises in lazy tendrils from the surface, carrying the scent of salt and minerals. And in the center of it all is a pool, perfectly round and glowing from within. So clear, I can see straight to the bottom.

Evander leans into my side with a pained grunt. His breaths are harsh and labored. Fresh blood oozes from the vicious slashes and punctures littering his skin.

"Is he okay?" I ask Alexios. "He's not speaking."

"He goes nonverbal when he's like this." His gaze drops to where Evander's fingers dig into my hip. "Strip down, Princess. Your soulbond's blocked, and he just slaughtered fifty demis for you. He needs skin contact to ground himself." When I hesitate, he sighs impatiently. "There's only one female in this realm whose body interests me, and it's not you. Just do it."

I grit my teeth and reach for my dress' collar to undo the buckle. The gown falls to my feet, and cool air kisses my skin. My nipples pebble in the chill.

When I look up, Evander's pupils have blown wide, only a thin ring of molten amber visible around the edges. The weight of that burning gaze rakes over me. His hands flex at his sides, as if barely leashing the urge to grab me.

"Now him," Alexios tells me.

I step closer to Evander. The bond may be shuttered between us, but I swear I can *feel* him—the dissonant thrum of hunger vibrating through him. The need.

Holding his fevered stare, I ghost my touch over his chest and follow the valley of his sternum down until I snag on the fastener securing his weapons low on his hips. I hesitate when a growl rumbles out of him.

He seizes my wrist and squeezes in warning, the pressure just shy of pain.

I'm not in control, that movement says. *Don't let me hurt you.*

"Damn," Alexios mutters. "Of course you don't know what you're doing."

"Then why don't you show me?"

"Fine." He moves behind me. "There's an art to dealing with a feral god. Follow my lead."

He pries Evander's fingers loose. I inhale sharply as his chest presses to my back. He reaches around me to slide his hands over mine, guiding me to the complicated clasps.

"First thing to remember," he breathes in my ear. "Showing fear makes us want to chase. Without the bond, he's running on instinct, and right now, you smell like prey."

I hold still, letting Alexios guide my hands. He's quick, almost forceful as he shoves a sheath off Evander's shoulders.

"Any hesitation makes us think you're weak." Alexios forces my hands lower, to the fastening of Evander's trousers. "Weak things get eaten."

Evander's eyes track every movement, muscles coiled tight. Lethal and utterly beautiful.

Alexios' breath is warm against my nape. "See the way he's looking at you? If I hadn't cut your bond, he would have fucked you in all that blood," he whispers. "That's what we do."

A shiver goes through me. "Trying to scare me off?"

"Just preparing you for reality." A pause as we push Evander's trousers down his hips. "You're doing good."

Heat crawls up my cheeks, but I say nothing.

Together, we divest him of blood-splattered leathers and weapons until he stands bare. My mouth goes dry at the sight of him. Even naked and covered in blood, he's beautiful. His cock is hard, and he's staring with the sort of desire that says he wants to consume me.

Alexios gives Evander a light shove toward the pool. "Get in the water while I teach your princess how to handle you." He glances at me. "You too. Keep eye contact with him."

The water is warm as I ease into it, like sliding into a bath. Evander's wings drag along the surface as he moves closer, his stare holding mine, ravenous. I back up until my spine hits the pool's edge, trapped between stone and six-plus feet of barely controlled god.

"Stop running." Alexios settles on the pool's edge, rolling up his sleeves. "He needs to know you won't fall apart right now."

"I'm not—"

Evander's hands slam against the stone on either side of my head, caging me in. This close, I can see the thin ring of gold still fighting against the black of his pupils.

"Hi," I whisper, reaching up to touch his face.

He turns into my palm, dragging his teeth across my skin. Not quite a bite, but close enough to make me shiver.

"Wash him," Alexios tells me, sounding bored. "The water will heal the injuries."

I cup my hands and sluice some liquid over him, soothing the hurts as best I can, cleaning his skin and wings with careful strokes. Some of the minor wounds begin to close under my ministrations.

Alexios reaches down to card his fingers through Evander's wet hair. A shudder rolls through my Chosen at the touch, his eyes squeezing shut like it's almost too much. The god-king's grip tightens in silent reprimand when Evander tries to twist away.

Alexios' molten gaze cuts to me, pinning me in place. "An Eternal fresh from slaughter needs someone strong enough to bring him back. Show me you know how to kiss your Chosen."

I hesitate as I stare at Evander's upturned face. At the need radiating from him. Even during Aethertide, he wasn't this raw, this savage. Gliding my fingers into his hair, I cup his face in my palms and press my mouth to his in a slow, exploring caress.

Evander surges against me with a snarl to crush me closer, and I freeze, my hands resting uncertainly on his shoulders.

The god-king makes a chiding sound behind us. "That's not the kind of kiss he needs from you right now, Princess." Alexios grips Evander's hair and wrenches him back from me, leaning down to graze his lips over his cheek. "I'm going to show her how it's done," he whispers. "Get her all nice and ready for you."

Then Alexios is claiming Evander's mouth with the kind of searing intensity that makes the breath catch in my lungs. It's filthy and merciless. Brutal and deep. Possessing and owning him so completely, there's no space left for anything else.

Evander arches in Alexios' bruising hold. A harsh growl builds in his chest, and the sound vibrates through me, an answering heat spiking low in my core. But the god-king only grips him tighter, one hand twisting in his hair while the other digs into his jaw. Alexios angles Evander just the way he wants and keeps kissing him. Biting his lower lip and soothing the sting with his tongue.

When the god-king finally pulls back, Evander's pupils are blown wide, his chest heaving.

"That's how you kiss a god who just killed for you," Alexios says, voice rough. He kisses Evander again and breathes, "Like you'll die if you don't. Like you'll destroy anyone who tries to take him from you."

Like you'll die if you don't.

And I know what he's telling me. What Evander needs from me. *Take what's yours.*

So I yank Evander toward me and surge up to claim his lips,

savoring the unique taste that's purely him. He groans softly as his hands map my curves, fingers digging in hard enough to bruise. He's trying to relearn me by touch, by taste, making up for the severed bond the only way he can right now.

"Less gentle," Alexios hisses. "*Bite* him, Bryony. Make him bleed for you."

Obedience has never come naturally to me, but this? This is as easy as breathing. I sink my teeth into Evander's bottom lip, and the copper-bright taste of his blood floods my mouth. His palms skim my sides to rest on the dip of my waist, yanking me close.

Alexios leans in, whispering, "He fought for you, Princess. He killed for a chance to keep you. So get on your knees and show him he's your god."

Yes.

I rake my nails down Evander's chest, loving the way he arches into the sting, starving for it. I shove him backward, and he goes easily, letting me press him against the smooth rock ledge.

"Up," I command. "Sit on the edge."

Hunger flares in his expression, but he complies, leveraging himself out of the pool to settle beside Alexios.

I move until I'm poised between his legs. With my eyes locked on his, I go to my knees in the shallows, the water lapping gently at the small of my back. I glide my fingers up his thighs. When I wrap my hand around his cock, his breath hisses through clenched teeth, and the sound shoots straight between my legs.

Those burning eyes never leave mine as I bend to drag the flat of my tongue over his cock, licking the salty tang of his arousal. Savoring the taste of him.

His hands cup my head, urging me down. Not gentle. Not asking. He's past the point of permission, and honestly, so am I. So I let him take what he needs. I hollow my cheeks and *suck*, reveling in each desperate thrust as he grips my hair and fucks into my mouth. I relax my jaw and throat, letting him hit the back on every glide.

This is a Claiming in its own way. An act of worship. Of absolution. I inscribe my devotion into his skin with lips and tongue and careful scrapes of teeth. Over and over until I'm lost to the slick heat of him in my mouth.

A dark satisfaction settles into Alexios' features as my eyes meet his. As he watches me take and give in equal measure.

"He'll remember this," Alexios says. "The way you submitted for him. The way you took him so deep when he needed to claim you."

The water sloshes around us. I dig my nails into Evander's thighs, offering myself up as the altar for his need. Breaking him just to build him back up. Sending messages without words. *Use me.* My hand slides down his cock, stroking. *Let me have it.* I go down, taking him all the way to the back of my throat. *I can take it.*

Alexios bends forward and breathes in my ear, "Pleasure is another form of prayer. Tell me, little sacrifice. How holy do you feel right now?"

Lost in this moment, in the slick push-pull of mine-yours-ours, I feel *powerful*. Like if I reached up to trace constellations, the stars would bend to accommodate my whims. Like I'm as eternal as the two males watching me. This is a kind of revelation—a god coming undone by my lips, my touch. There's a certain brutal grace in his abandon. In the little hitches in his breath, his hips lifting to thrust his cock deeper, his hand tightening in my hair when I get the right suction and movement. He's rough and reverent, controlled and fierce, all that *need* spilling out between us.

And I want it. I want to unravel him. To dig my fingers into all the dark and desperate places and put them back together again.

I want him to fucking *own* me.

My nails bite into Evander's tensed thighs as I urge him deep. His grip turns brutal in my hair. His thrusts go erratic, control slipping. I take it all, welcome the slight burn, the fullness. I suck harder, swirling my tongue, scraping my teeth lightly along the sensitive skin. His breathing turns ragged.

A low growl tears from him. Then he's coming in hot pulses against my tongue. I swallow everything he gives me, watching his head tip back, tendons straining. There's nothing more beautiful than Evander lost to bliss and ecstasy. I soothe him through the aftershocks with little licks and sucks, and his grip on my hair gentles.

Then I sit back on my heels and raise my eyes to Alexios. I can only imagine what I must look like, naked and savage in my victory.

The god-king just smiles. "Well done, Princess."

Evander slips into the water, his body loose and pliant now. Immediately, I gather him against me, cradling his head on my shoulder and burying my fingers in his feathers. A sigh shudders out of him as he rests his face in the crook of my neck, nuzzling close, scenting me. Then he shuts his eyes.

After a few moments, he relaxes and his breathing evens, then slows.

"Is he asleep?" I ask Alexios, stroking Evander's tucked wings.

The god-king studies Evander. "Something like that. The magic works best when he's not fighting it. He'll be out for a bit." Those red eyes cut to me. "Think you can handle him from here?"

I nod, fingers still mapping idle patterns along Evander's back.

The god-king rises with a soft rustle of feathers and turns to go. But something has been bothering me since the Colosseum that I can't ignore.

"They're never going to accept me, are they?" I ask him. "The demis. No matter what I do or how hard I work, I'll always be a Devaliant first."

He pauses, glancing at me over his shoulder. "Truth?"

I hold my breath and nod.

"When they look at you, they see a descendant of the people who brutally murdered their families for power. Wounds that deep don't heal pretty. Earning their respect will never be bloodless work, and even then, there are no guarantees."

I swallow around the sudden tightness in my throat. A strange calm settles over me—I know what I have to do. "Then I'll fight."

His brows lift. "Fight?"

"I'll waive my protection as Evander's Chosen and fight in the arena like he did. Put me against any demi who challenges my place at his side. Let everyone see I can be a queen in more than just name."

He studies me as if I've surprised him. "Then they get to use their full magic. If you have something to prove, don't do it by half. Prepare to bleed for it."

And die for it, he doesn't say. But the message is clear, all the same.

I nod. "If I win, we're done. You unbind Evander's powers, forgive him for Hellevig, and give him his territory."

"Deal. Tomorrow night, little sacrifice."

55

BRYONY

"PRINCESS?" A MUFFLED voice filters through the door of Evander's bedroom the next evening. "I'm here to dress you for the final test."

Evander's arm tightens around my waist, dragging me against his chest. "Tell Alexios to fuck off, Zephyr."

I should answer, but I'm not ready to leave yet. After he woke up from the healing pool last night, I didn't tell him about my deal with Alexios. But we returned to his room, and I've been saying wordless goodbyes with my body ever since. I fucked him slowly in the morning. Kissed him as if it was the first time—soft and searching, relearning the taste of him, the pressure of his lips.

For right now, this is mine. This quiet vulnerability. I want to freeze this moment.

This might be the last time.

My throat closes up. I focus on my Chosen: his heartbeat, his breath in my hair, the press of his fingers. I burn each sensation into memory just in case. Just in case I won't have him in my arms again.

Just in case.

His teeth graze my pulse point, and I bite back a whimper.

A snort sounds from the other side of the door. "Wolf. Some of us have actual work to finish today."

I twist in Evander's hold until we face each other, my fingers trailing over his jaw. He kills me when he's like this—rumpled and warm, his sharp edges gentled. Those amber eyes, still soft with sleep, are dark and hungry as he stares at my mouth.

The deal I made sits heavy on my chest. He'd lose his shit if he knew—probably chain me to this bed before letting me anywhere near that arena.

I can't hide behind your wings forever. You can't shield me from every hurt. That's not who I am. It's not who we are.

"You know I have to go," I whisper.

His fingers flex on my hips, digging in deep enough to leave marks. "Bryony." Then softer: "Don't. Don't think I haven't noticed how you've been behaving all morning."

My throat closes. "You have to let me fall, remember?"

Please don't hate me for what I'm about to do.

I force myself out of his hold. Shivering, I pull on the borrowed clothes a servant brought last night and crack open the door. The first thing I notice about the demigoddess on the other side is her eyes—one silver, one black. She's got dark hair and a face that's all sharp angles and cold beauty. A hint of a tattoo peeks out where her coat collar doesn't quite cover her neck.

"This way," the demigoddess says—*Zephyr*, Evander called her.

She leads me down the corridor and into a massive chamber with tall windows. Chandeliers and orbs of light drift aimlessly overhead, illuminating the multi-hued fabric spilled across the tables. Unfinished garments float by themselves, held up by nothing I can see. Dresses, armor, and training clothes are all suspended in the air in various stages of completion.

Two other demigoddesses are sprawled lazily against the workbenches. I recognize Arcadia—it's impossible to miss those silver wings. The other one is petite with dark gray wings.

The dark-winged female's face scrunches with disgust when she sees me. "She's so small. Why is she so small? I thought the Wolf liked something he could sink his teeth into."

Arcadia's lip curls. "Hardly seems worth the trouble, does she, Vespera?"

"Maybe I should find out why he's keeping her around. Ten seconds is all I'd need."

"Five." Arcadia rakes me with a glare. "If that."

"Stop, both of you," Zephyr cuts in. "The Wolf would rip you to shreds, and I'm not cleaning up the mess because you're feeling territorial. Take your usual fuckery elsewhere."

Arcadia's stare doesn't leave me. "I won't challenge her, Z. But I'll enjoy watching them tear her apart in the arena. You should stay for the show."

"*Out*," Zephyr snaps.

The two demigoddesses exchange looks but comply. The door closes behind them.

I let out a relieved breath. "Thanks," I say to Zephyr.

"This is why I keep my real workshop away from this cesspit," Zephyr mutters. "Strip. I need to fit you for armor properly this time."

I peel off my clothes, trying not to fidget as she studies my body as if she's able to calculate my measurements by sight alone. Maybe she actually is. "This time?"

"Yes, this time. But he was thorough." She says the second part to herself. "Got your sizes to the quarter inch when he asked for your wardrobe, though he wouldn't say who it was for."

I gape at her. "Wait—you made my clothes?"

"The nightgown was one of my better pieces. Did he enjoy it?"

Heat crawls up my neck. Gods, the way he'd looked at me in the armory when that robe hit the floor... Then both of us grinding against each other like we were starving for it.

"I—ah—put it to good use," I say, clearing my throat.

Her mouth twitches. "Yeah, I'll bet."

She settles onto a stool and extends her hands. Power fills the room as shadows twist from her palms and spill onto the floor in a wave of black tendrils. A pool forms, spreading around her feet and glittering with starlight.

A loom rises from the darkness with silver veins and old symbols pulsing along the frame. Zephyr caresses the instrument, and I watch as threads of light spill from her fingers, twisting into intricate knots and shapes in the center of the loom. My mouth falls open—she's forming *armor* right in front of me.

The leather pieces float upward one by one. Shoulder guards engraved with markings, vambraces, chest plate, all perfectly sized for me. The set shimmers like she bottled the night sky and worked it into metal.

"It's beautiful," I breathe, reaching out. The leather is smooth and warm to the touch.

"It's *functional*," she corrects, collecting the bits of gauzy underthings that materialized along with the armor. "This is what you'll wear beneath."

The underwear is comfortable against my skin as I slide it on. Then comes the leather armor. Zephyr tightens the buckles and straps as if she's done this a thousand times. There's a brisk professionalism to her movements that sets me at ease.

"The underlying layer is imbued with defensive magics," she explains as she works. "It will function as a second skin and distribute impact to shield you from injury. The main pieces are as light as I can make them while providing protection, but don't let any of those demis land a direct hit. Even the best armor only goes so far." One finger taps thoughtfully against her chin. "How much combat experience do you have?"

"Enough to know every bone in an arm makes a different sound when it snaps."

"It won't be enough," she says simply.

I don't think her words are meant to hurt—it's only the truth. The sky is blue, water is wet, and I volunteered for a violent end.

She sighs. "Look, I know what you're doing this for. And I get it, I do. But you're human. Squishy. Breakable. This"—a rap of knuckles against the leather breastplate—"will reinforce your skeleton, but it won't magically put you on par with a demi. There's only so much I can do to keep you from getting splattered." Her hands smooth over the armor, making minute adjustments. "Use your size to your advantage. You're small. Dodge fast, and they'll start taking each other out. Friendly fire's killed more fighters than you'd think when the target is quick enough. They won't play fair, and neither should you."

"Speaking from experience?"

"I'm older than Alexios," she says with a shrug. "I've seen some shit."

My breath catches when she cinches the final strap. "Why help me at all?"

She gives me a small smile. "Because I've known the Wolf since he was a demi baby on his mother's knee. He's an idiot, a pain in my ass, and about as subtle as an avalanche. But this? He doesn't do this. Doesn't let anyone close enough to matter. But he Chose you. Claimed you." Her expression sharpens. "So don't fuck it up."

The crowd's roar crashes over me as I step into the arena.

Ancient runes in the sands flare and glow blue beneath my boots. Magic burns my lungs with each inhale, an electric thrum that skates across my skin. Torches flicker along the walls of the fighting pit, illuminating the obstacles in the dirt—pillars, boulders, seared rocks. Places I'll need to take cover and rest if I'm going to survive this.

Shouts draw my attention to the hundreds of demis packing the tiered balconies and floating platforms. Wings of every color blur together—green, blue, red, gold, black. Some are shoving each other to get a better look, others are chanting loud enough to make my ears ring.

"*FUCK HER UP! FUCK HER UP!*"

"Charming," I mutter.

Fine. They can scream until their throats bleed for all I care.

My attention moves to the raised platform where Alexios lounges on his black throne with his red and black wings spread. He's got his chin propped in his hand, watching me intently. Does he want me to win or lose?

"*FUCK HER UP!*"

Alexios grins slowly, and my lip curls in a snarl. Right, it probably doesn't matter to the sick bastard. It's all entertainment to him. I can't believe I let him watch me suck Evander off. Bastard.

The chants are so loud that I almost miss a male voice shouting my name.

Evander.

He's at the arena's edge, yanking against chains bolted into the pit's thick stone wall. And he's beyond furious. His lips move in what I'm pretty sure is every curse in at least a dozen dead languages. Now he knows about my bargain with Alexios. The price I'll probably pay.

"When this is over," he mouths, "I'll kill you myself."

My lips curve into a smile. *When* this is over.

I can't hide behind your wings forever.

A metal screech echoes through the arena. The portcullis rises at the far end of the pit, revealing nine demis stepping into flickering torchlight. Skin bared, no armor in sight. To them, I'm no threat at all. Just one more fragile human to slaughter.

Good, Amara's voice whispers through my memories. *Let them underestimate you. Use that arrogance against them.*

The demis fan out in a loose semicircle. A mix of males and females, all crackling with magic that warps the surrounding air. A female with electricity jumping between her fingers. A male with fire in his hands.

"Ten gold the human pisses herself before I even touch her."

"Twenty says she's begging for mercy inside a minute."

I drop into a fighting stance—Amara's drills beaten into me after all those brutal sessions. Muscles coiled and ready to move. Ready to kill.

Amara's words hammer through me: *Get dirty. Get mean. Kill them before they kill you.*

Alexios lifts a hand. The crowd goes silent, the sudden absence of sound almost as deafening as the roar had been.

The demis attack.

The lightning demigoddess strikes first, electricity leaping from her splayed fingers. I hit the ground and roll. *CRACK!* The air at my back explodes, and the sharp stink of ozone burns my nose.

"*BREAK THAT BITCH!*" the crowd chants.

No time to think. I sense the second assault coming—the crushing pressure of gathering power that makes my ears pop. Instinct has me scrambling behind a large, red-winged warrior.

The blast hits him. The impact reverberates through my bones as his body goes flying. He crashes into the sand twenty yards away, wings crumpled and neck twisted.

One down. Eight to go.

"Thanks for that," I call out.

"Lucky dodge, little girl," the demigoddess snarls.

Another female hurls jagged spears of ice longer than my forearm. I throw myself to the side, but I'm not fast enough. Pain radiates through my shoulder, but Zephyr's armor absorbs the blow.

I shake it off and keep moving.

Keep. Fucking. Moving.

I make my legs pump faster, ducking and weaving between their attacks. Lightning cracks inches from my face. I leap as the ground beneath me explodes—too close. The sand's cratered with smoking holes, patches melted into glass by the lightning demi's onslaught. Two more demis fall in the crossfire.

"MAKE HER BLEED!"

My lungs burn. My vision blurs, and my knives are slick in my hands, but stopping means dying. I don't have the power to meet these demis head-on, so my only chance is to be quicker. Smarter.

Make the bastards kill each other.

Searing cold slams into my hip, and my entire left side goes numb. I stumble, barely managing to roll behind a partially melted pillar.

"Hiding already?" someone shouts. "Get out here, bitch!"

I use the moment of cover to gulp down air. My legs shake as I push myself to my feet.

Create openings. Make them react to you. Amara's lessons blare in my head.

I glance around the column. Four are still standing, the rest were blasted to pieces by their own side's attacks.

One male is shooting flames while another female's hands

glow with dark energy that makes shadows burst from the sand in inky vines. The ice demi is hanging back to wait for a clear shot. And the last bastard? He's sucking in power—I can feel the bite of it against my skin. A massive surge between his upraised palms, glowing blue as pure force magic forms.

I have maybe three seconds before he unleashes it.

I'm moving before I know what the hell I'm doing—just sprinting straight at him, sand flying everywhere. His jaw drops, because what kind of idiot charges to her death? This idiot, apparently.

"What the—"

Right before he lets loose his power, I dive for the ground and slide between his legs. The force wave hurtles over my head...

And slams directly into the ice demi behind me.

Her shriek cuts off as the concussive blast literally turns her inside out.

Lurching upright, I plunge my blade into the force-wielder's back and wrench it hard. Once, twice more, taking ruthless advantage of his distraction. He tries to shove me off, but I've got my second knife ready. I jam it under his chin and let his corpse fall.

Two left.

The remaining demis regroup, trading looks. Reassessing the threat level of one small human who's managed to survive this long.

"END IT! END IT!"

I bare my teeth in a feral grin. The left side of my body is still partially numb from that previous attack, but I can't stop. Not now.

The shadow controller strikes first this time. Inky vines explode from the sand to ensnare me, one wrapping around my ankle to yank my feet out from under me. The impact knocks the wind out of me.

More black vines snare my arms and legs, pinning me down.

The demi grins. "Let's see how pretty you are when we're done with you."

The flame-wielder laughs, conjuring fire between his palms. "I say we make the Wolf watch his pet human burn."

They're getting cocky. Overconfident.

Use it.

Teeth gritted, I strain against the shadows, scrabbling desperately for another dagger. Darkness digs into my skin, tightening, tightening. *There*—my fingertips brush metal.

For a heartbeat, Evander is with me. His hand on mine, steadying. *When you let the knife fly, it's not about forcing it to hit the target. It's about trusting that all that careful preparation and intimate knowledge will guide it.*

The flame demi raises his hands, magic building to an inferno—

I throw.

The blade buries itself to the hilt in his neck. His eyes go wide with shock as the flame dies, and he falls to his knees in the sand, choking around the blade.

The shadow controller's concentration wavers for a fraction of a second, and the dark tendrils loosen their grip. I wrench myself loose just as the last demi's energy gathers in her hands.

"FINISH HER!"

She unleashes a wave of shadow. I dive behind the flame-wielder where he's still scrabbling for my dagger lodged in his throat, using his body as a shield. Ice crystals form on my eyelashes. My breath comes out in white puffs.

But the fire demigod takes the brunt of the impact, flesh cracking under the onslaught of icy shadows.

Only the demigoddess is left now.

She's gathering another blast—*fuck that*. I launch myself over the frozen corpse and drive my knife up and into her gut.

For a moment, our eyes lock. Her mouth opens and closes as blood spills over my hand.

"Should've worn armor," I snarl as I twist the knife, yank it out, and plunge it right back in. And again, just to watch the light fade from her eyes.

When her corpse drops, I hunch over, breathing hard. Barely

able to catch my breath without pain radiating through my ribs. The crowd's angry roar barely penetrates the ringing in my ears.

I look up at Alexios on his dais.

"I won," I shout up at him over the din. "I want Evander out of the cuffs. *Now*."

He rises from his throne. Those red and black wings spread wide as he descends the steps to the arena floor. A hush falls over the crowd as they all watch their king step into the pit.

"You still have one final challenger," he says, smiling slowly. "Me."

56

BRYONY

"DID YOU REALLY think," Alexios says, voice soft, "that I'd let you walk without testing you myself?"

Of course not. This was his plan all along, wasn't it? I'd waived my protection in Scillari as the Wolf's Chosen and agreed to face *any* challenger. Might as well have trussed myself up with a pretty bow and laid my head on the chopping block for him.

The crowd roars. Hundreds of voices howling for blood—*my* blood. They know I'm not walking away from a challenge with an Eternal. They're going to watch me die, and they're going to savor every second of it.

Evander hurls against his chains. Metal screeches. His wings spread wide, and power flares around him before the magic-suppressing shackles choke it down, again and again.

"Stop," Alexios commands him. "You're only hurting yourself."

"Let her go." Evander's voice is ragged. "You agreed the trials had to be possible for a human to win."

"I agreed *my* trials had to be possible to win. She asked for this one. Came up with it all on her own, in fact. I exploit loopholes, and your Chosen practically drew me a perfect map right to this moment."

A calm settles over me as I catalog the damage from my previous skirmishes—the cuts and bruises, the exhaustion dragging at my limbs. Even if I could fight, it's pointless against Alexios.

But I don't care if I lose. I'm done kneeling. Done letting males with crowns carve me into shapes that suit them. When Idris gutted me on the Duehavn, that was the last time I'd ever die on my back.

So I raise my head and meet Alexios' stare. "I accept."

"Bryony, *don't*—"

Evander's shout is cut off with a flick of Alexios' fingers. The god-king's attention doesn't waver from mine, and some dark and hungry emotion flickers in those crimson depths as he watches me.

"Then let's go over a few lessons first."

The air thickens. Pressure builds in my skull. With another casual movement of his fingers, power coils around my neck, squeezing until I gasp. Black spots dance in front of my eyes.

"Lesson one," the god-king says. "Human bodies are fragile. The Wolf's soulbond gives you his lifespan, but it doesn't make you a god. You're still breakable."

Just before darkness can drag me under, he releases me, and I fall to my knees in the dirt, heaving air into my burning lungs. The reprieve lasts exactly three heartbeats.

Then his boot slams into my ribs.

Zephyr's armor buckles beneath the impact. The pain eclipses every thought until I'm left with only animal instinct—*curl into a ball, knees to chest, shrink down, make yourself small. Maybe then he'll lose interest.*

But he's holding back. He could have pulverized my bones with that kick if he'd wanted. This is restraint for a creature like him.

He kneels beside me. "You know what I love about knives?" He trails the knife down my neck, shoving away bits of broken armor. "They're intimate in a way powers can never be. Personal." The steel bites into my skin. "Almost like foreplay. Wouldn't you agree?"

I don't react. I refuse to give him the satisfaction.

"To kill with steel, you have to get up close and dirty." He begins to carve into me. I choke down a cry, blinking back bursts of light. "You understand that intimately, don't you? It's how you killed your uncle. How he tried to kill you. When you shove a blade into someone and watch the light leave their eyes, you learn something about them. And about yourself. Like you're both peering into each other's souls. The way a person bleeds shows you who they really are." He drags the tip of the weapon lower, leaving a burning trail in its wake.

I'll never forget this moment. This lesson. Even if I lived a thousand years, I'd remember the shape of this powerlessness.

"Fuck you," I manage through gritted teeth.

He laughs. "Ah, there it is. There are the sweet words I used to hear through my Claim." The blade sinks deeper. "I've been dying to make you pay for every time I heard them."

Darkness dances at the edges of my vision, begging me to slip under. Some distant part of me hears Evander's shout.

And still, the god-king carves his lessons into my skin. He doesn't hit bone or pierce anything vital. Because this is a message, isn't it? This is a reminder for the human who foolishly believed she could win a game with the God of Storms.

"Lesson two." His voice stays conversational. "When a stupid little girl dreams of ruling beside a god, that fantasy comes with a price."

Think of something else. Think of Evander's hands on your skin, his wings wrapped around you, the heat of his mouth when he kisses you. The way he looks at you like you're cherished.

As if Alexios senses my mind going elsewhere, he grips my hair hard. "You want to wear a crown in this realm and rule by an Eternal's side for the rest of eternity?" There's a stinging pain at my shoulder blade as he cuts away the decimated parts of the armor there. Making room for more marks. "Then you'll have to bleed for it. Break for it. Beg for it."

Agony whites out coherence, and *I can't I can't I can't—*

"*Look.*" Alexios uses his grip on my hair to wrench my head around. "Look at him." Evander thrashes, muscles straining as he tries to tear the bolts to his shackles out of the rock. "Look how desperate he is. How hard he's fighting for his human. How far do you think he'll go to keep you breathing? What piece of his soul will he trade?"

The blade stops and withdraws.

Then Alexios is hauling me up, dragging me across the sands to Evander.

"Heal her, Wolf," he says, tossing me at my Chosen's feet.

Alexios releases the shackles. The instant they fall away, Evander holds me against his chest. His power rushes into me in a wave of light and heat, seeking out every wound, stitching me together from the inside out.

His hands roam as he checks for any injury he might have missed. Erasing the evidence of Alexios' brutality.

"I've got you," he whispers against my hair. "You're okay. I'm so sorry. I'm so—"

But before he can finish, the cuffs snap closed on Evander's wrists again. Alexios' power seizes me around my waist and reels me in until we're pressed chest to chest.

"*You sick fuck*," Evander snarls, lunging against the chains.

"Do you see now, Princess?" Alexios tips my chin up, forcing me to meet his gaze. "This is what happens when a human bonds with a god. He'll put you back together, and I'll rip you apart. And we'll do it over and over and over because he'd rather watch me shatter every bone in your body than lose you. Tell me something. Is that love?"

I look up at him. "You don't know anything about love."

His smile is cruel, mirthless. "Oh, I know all about sacrifices for love, Princess. More than you, I think." He wraps his fingers around my wrist. "Lesson three. When gods play with mortals, we do it because we're bored. Because we like the sounds you make when we hurt you."

He wrenches my arm and snaps the bone. A scream slips out of me before I can stop it, my vision blurring as bile scalds my throat.

"There it is." Satisfaction thrums through his voice. "Scream for me. Beg if you want to make it interesting."

He shoves me away, and it's only stubborn will that keeps me standing. I grit my teeth against the pain.

"This game only ends when I lose interest," he continues, circling me slowly. "Or when you decide the Wolf isn't worth it. How long would you last if we gave you the choice? If I broke you, and he fixed you, how many times do you think it would take before you begged him to end it? A hundred? A thousand?" He snags my chin between his fingers and whispers, "When every kiss comes with a fist, how long would your love last? Would you start to resent him and count all the ways he's complicit in your suffering?"

Something snaps inside me—the last thread of restraint.

I draw my last dagger from its sheath at my hip with my uninjured hand, and I let him see every dark, howling thing inside me. Every ugliness and hidden hurt, the broken bits and pieces he carved his claim into. The monstrous parts that can shove aside the agony of my body to make room for cold purpose.

"Four hundred and sixteen," I tell him.

His brow lifts in a silent question.

"That's how many times an Oracle shoved a knife into my heart from ages five to twenty-one. How many times I spilled my blood on your altar, crossed into the Void, and told you to get fucked."

I slash my dagger across his chest. The blade parts fabric and flesh, leaving a thin crimson seam behind. And he lets me, standing there without so much as blinking—as if I'm beneath his notice.

"No one taught me how to be brave," I hiss, hacking at him again. Graceless. Brutal. "No one asked if I was okay. No one held my hand through the pain or told me to be strong. I did it because my people needed me to. I did it even as you used me up and threw me away like garbage."

Slash. Slash. Stab.

My blade carves into his skin. I hurl all my strength and impotent fury against him like waves crashing against stone.

And he heals and heals and heals.

"You think I haven't proven myself?" My voice echoes through the quiet arena. Hundreds of eyes are riveted on me.

On us. "I proved it every single day I woke up in a world that wanted to butcher me on the altar. That saw me as someone to carve into."

I force myself to keep going. If these are the last words I ever say, I'm going to make them count.

"I proved it by walking into your palace with my head high while everyone here waited for me to break. I went to Nyholm and played games with a fucking death god to be with Evander." An exhale shudders out of me. "I can't change what my ancestors did. I can't bring back the people they butchered any more than you can resurrect everyone who died in the war."

Alexios goes rigid. His face gives nothing away.

"But I'm done paying for the sins of a dead dynasty with my pain." My eyes fall on Evander, this god I've learned to love more than anything. "I just want him. I love him. And that doesn't change whether I'm breathing or a corpse on the pyre. So you can rip me apart or put me back together, but it won't make a difference. He's mine, and I'm his. That's the only truth that matters."

I let my dagger hit the sand. My chest heaves with each breath, but I won't bend or kneel.

"So do your worst, you bastard."

Alexios smiles, and the bottom drops out of my stomach. Then his hand closes around my throat.

"Then prove it. Give your life for his freedom."

57

BRYONY

"So that's the deal?" I breathe. "I die, and you take him off the leash?"

"That's right." Those burning eyes bore into mine. "One final death, and the Wolf gets to rule his territory."

His grip on my throat isn't crushing—just firm enough to remind us both of who's really in control here. He could end me with a thought, a twitch of his fingers.

"Amalthea Devaliant didn't hesitate when I gave her this choice," he says. "She just drove the blade home. And that brought peace between realms and the Accords that have held our worlds in balance for centuries. Because she knew the truth." He leans in, whispering, "To sacrifice is an act of love."

His wild thunderstorm scent floods my senses. Petrichor and ozone, lightning and rain.

"So what's it going to be, Princess? Ready to give up everything for him?" He tilts his head with a mocking smile. "Or do you only want him when there's power in it for you and a Scillarian throne to sit your pretty ass on?"

Evander yanks against his chains. "Bryony—"

"*Quiet.*"

An invisible force slams into Evander, choking the words into silence.

I don't look away from Alexios. I stare into those burning depths, and I let him see exactly who I am. What I'm made of. Because if there's one thing I've learned from a lifetime of prostrating myself at altars and spilling my blood for ancient oaths, it's how to bear a blade.

How to sacrifice.

"Give me your word," I say, and my voice doesn't shake. "Swear he goes free if I do this. On something that matters."

"On the blood of my sister," he says without hesitation, releasing me. "The Wolf knows what that means to me. No loopholes, no tricks. Just a simple transaction—your life for his freedom and everything that comes with it."

I nod, jaw clenched tight. "You have a deal."

Hundreds of demis watch in silence as I close the distance to where Evander kneels in the sand. Some whispers reach me from the stands. Do their hearts pound faster as they watch me work up the nerve to destroy myself? Are they hungry for it? Or maybe they understand this is the logical conclusion to my story.

The princess who opened her veins to the god-king who drank her dry.

It has a certain poetry, I suppose.

I cup Evander's face in my palm. Alexios' power must be gagging him, because his eyes scream the words his tongue can't seem to shape. They beg me not to do this. Not to leave him. Not to be one more thing he loves that turns to ash.

We want what we want. Even when we know it'll destroy us.

"I need you to listen to me," I tell him. "I know that after this is over, you won't forgive me for a long time, and that's okay." I blink back burning tears. "But you can't"—I fist my hand in his shirt—"spend another three centuries drowning in guilt and rage. You're a king, Evander. It's time to act like it and be what your people need. I promised you I'd keep fighting, but I also understand when I have to set down my weapons and kneel. It's shit, and it's not fair, but this is about more than us."

His chest shudders beneath my touch as he visibly struggles against Alexios' hold.

"Just promise me something?" The words barely make it past the lump in my throat. "When you think of me, remember that

I love you. And that if our positions were reversed, you'd make the same choice."

I lean down and press my lips to his in a kiss that feels like the end of worlds. Like galaxies colliding. Like two dying stars finally surrendering to the inevitable pull of gravity.

I kiss him with everything I have, every shard of my soul that belongs to him. I pour a lifetime's worth of feeling into the slant of my lips—*I love you and I love you and I love you.*

And then I wrench away.

I turn to Alexios and nod in a silent assent to get this over with.

He draws a blade from his boot. My hand shakes as I take it from him, its weight like a promise, an oath. This is my lineage, my birthright. House Devaliant was born and bred for this singular purpose.

It's only fitting that I return to it now—this time, on my terms. The death I choose.

"Remember," Alexios says. "You have to *mean it*. No half measures."

Drawing in a deep, steadying breath, I tighten my grip on the knife and lower myself to my knees, angling the point over my thundering heart.

My voice only trembles a little when I say, "I need your help to push it. I can't do it one-handed." The wrist he broke is numb now, hanging limply at my side.

Alexios kneels beside me, wrapping his hands over mine. "Look at him. Look at what you're dying for."

My eyes find Evander's again, and I let myself have this last moment to etch him into my memory. I think of all the times he held me. Laughed with me. All those sleepless nights and stolen kisses and bruising fingertips. I remember his smile. The softness of his wings under my palms.

I let the remembering fill me until there's no room for anything else—for fear or pain or regret. I wrap those moments around myself like armor and brace for impact.

"Ready," I whisper.

Alexios' stare meets mine, and we both shove the dagger into my chest.

Agony explodes through me. My vision flashes, narrowing down to the steel buried between my ribs, the bloom of scarlet spilling down my breastband.

"That's it." Alexios' voice. "Bleed for him."

So I do.

I fall back into the sand and yield to the darkness. Let it open its jaws and draw me into the drowning deep. There are no ledges to cling to, no handholds to scrabble for purchase, no way back. There's only the helpless surrender and the descent into the Void.

My life has been hundreds of deaths staring up at vaulted temple ceilings and marble statues. I know this hurt, the cold and nothingness of the vast, unyielding black. There's a terrible intimacy to this pain. Strange, how death feels the same as falling in love—all-consuming and terrifying. There's no great conflagration. Just the plunge. The fall.

Down.

Down.

Dow—

A scream shatters the nothing. I burst awake in agony, my spine arching as power sears through my veins, stitching me together. It fills every hollow space, every crack and crevice, until I'm burning from the inside out.

And then my back tears open.

The pain transcends anything I've ever known. It cleaves through muscle and sinew and bone, flaring wide to give way to—

Wings.

They explode from my shoulder blades in a spray of dazzling light. Pure white dappled with gold, resembling fresh snow touched by the first rays of dawn.

They're massive—and *heavy*. The muscles of my back strain as they struggle to compensate for the sudden weight.

I'm still trying to process—*being alive, these wings, this magic running through me*—when a familiar touch brushes my face.

Evander. Out of his shackles.

Awe fills his expression, breathless and full of quiet devastation as his gaze roams over me. Over my *wings*.

"I've got you," he murmurs thickly, tugging me against his chest. "I've got you, nemesis. Breathe for me, okay? Just keep fucking breathing."

I sag against him as the arena spins. As my body tries to reconcile the new shape of itself, to grapple with the reality of pinions and flight and *other*.

But Evander isn't finished with me.

His face hardens, and he grabs my shoulders to give me a small shake. "You reckless lunatic," he snarls. "What in the ever-loving fuck were you thinking?"

"I was thinking"—a cough rattles from my newly reformed lungs—"that I love you."

"Don't—" His voice cracks as he crushes me against him. "Don't you ever do that again. Do you hear me? *Never. Fucking. Again.*"

I'm spared answering by a pointed throat-clearing. Alexios fixes the assembled demis with a cutting look, and I swear the temperature plunges.

"I trust," he says, "that she's proven herself to you all? That Scillari claiming her is good enough to let her take her place at an Eternal's side? No further pound of flesh you'd like to extract?"

His gaze sweeps the arena, daring a single one of them to so much as breathe dissent.

No one makes a sound.

And then—movement. A demi with silver wings lowers his head, kneels, and places a hand over his heart. Another follows. Then another. They all fall to their knees one by one.

"*That's* for you, Princess," Alexios whispers.

For me.

I've been worshipped and exalted as the Princess of the Blood. The Anchor. The sacrifice. I've had my name screamed by crowds of faithful, been showered with priceless gifts, had poets write odes to my beauty.

And nothing—*nothing*—has ever felt as good as seeing these demis place their hands on their chests and go quiet for me. I didn't get this because I was born. I didn't get it through ancient oaths or bloodlines or traditions.

I *earned* this.

Alexios straightens. "You'll all have plenty of time to get acquainted with the Wolf's queen, but she needs rest now. Let him have her." He gestures upward with a jerk of his chin. "Go on. Out."

They rise into the air in groups, their wings catching the torchlight as they fly toward the open oculus. Power drifts across my skin, and my own wings twitch with an instinct I don't understand—something primal, a desire to stretch my limbs wide and follow.

"They want to fly with you," Evander murmurs, noticing my reaction. "It's tradition when an Eternal takes a Chosen. They'll wait until you're ready." He bumps my shoulder. "Told you they'd come to love you."

I watch until the last of them disappears from the arena into the night sky, and then it's only the three of us.

Alexios faces us. "Let's get one thing clear. This realm doesn't just hand out wings because you asked nicely. When a mortal bonds with a god, Scillari tests them. It needed proof you were worthy of its king."

Behind me, Evander's chest vibrates with a sound that's pure violence. "You could have fucking mentioned that."

"If I'd told her, it wouldn't have been real. The laws of our existence aren't suggestions I get to ignore when they're inconvenient." He spreads his hands. "Be grateful someone still remembers how this works. It's been thousands of years since one of us was stupid enough to soulbond with a human, and the realm rejected her. The last thing I needed was to put down another grieving, destructive Eternal."

He fixes me with an assessing look, gaze skating over my new wings. "One more thing." He holds out his hand, and the box I took from Nyholm materializes in his palm. "The seal inside releases the Wolf from his collar. Put the crystal right to his chest. When his power detonates, your bond is going to need attention."

"What kind of attention?" I ask.

"The kind that keeps you in bed for a week. So pick furniture you don't mind destroying."

Heat floods my cheeks. "*Oh.*"

"I'm sure you'll both have a lovely time." His red eyes flick between us. "One last piece of advice from someone who's lived a very long life: cherish what he's giving you. An Eternal doesn't bare their wings to just anyone. That's the kind of trust that can shatter realms. You fought for this. Bled for it. Died for it. Don't let anyone take it from you."

With a final nod, he turns and strides toward the towering double doors at the edge of the arena sands.

But Evander's voice rings out. "Wait."

Alexios pauses, glancing over his shoulder.

Evander pushes to his feet. "You gave me a gift I can't ever hope to repay." He closes the distance to Alexios. "A chance to keep my Chosen. To fly with her, to love her, to build a life with her in all the ways I never thought I'd get to have. And I owe you for that. More than I could ever put into words."

Then he seizes Alexios by the throat and slams him into the nearest wall. Stone fractures under the impact.

"But you *tortured* her." Evander's other hand draws back and punches straight through Alexios's stomach. The wet sound of tearing flesh echoes through the arena. "So if you ever so much as look at my woman again, I'll spend the next millennia finding new ways to rearrange your insides. Never speak to her again. Keep her name out of your *fucking* mouth."

A slow smile spreads across Alexios' face, and he lets his head fall back. "Message received, Wolf."

"Then get out."

Evander rips his fist free.

Alexios smirks, pressing a palm to the gaping wound in his abdomen. I watch as the flesh knits together beneath his splayed fingers.

Then he's gone, walking through the double doors without a backward glance.

For a moment, there's only the rasp of Evander's breathing. His hand and forearm are drenched in gore. The soft *drip-drip-drip* of blood hits the ground. He just stands there in the torchlight, chest rising and falling with each unsteady inhale as he stares at the red sand at his feet.

"Evander. Look at me."

Slowly, so slowly, he turns, and the expression on his face...

Stripped bare. Flayed open and vulnerable in a way I've never seen from him before.

"When I stood in the ruins of my home, a part of me died," he whispers. "There's no fixing that kind of grief. It just... hollows you out. Leaves you empty. But you got under my skin. You burrowed so deep that the thought of breathing without you was impossible. Because you're my heart."

He curls his fingers into his palm and shuts his eyes briefly. "I lost you." A broken whisper, so soft I have to strain to hear it. "For a minute there, I lost you, and it was like being in the wreckage. Like watching everything burn all over again. I didn't care if I lived or died because what's the point? What's the point of eternity if you're not in it?"

Something twists in me, sharp and painful. I've seen him angry. I've seen him vicious. But this... this grief is new. And it hurts.

He returns to my side, his clean hand trembling as it finds my face. "You can't do that again," he says. "You can't leave and expect me not to follow. If you die, I die. That's how this works now."

I kiss his palm, my vision blurring with tears. "I won't. Promise."

His attention drifts to my wings. Slowly, almost reverently, he reaches out to trail his fingers along the oversensitive arch of my wing, wringing a soft, involuntary noise from my throat. Too sensitive. Too much.

"Shhh," he soothes, continuing his exploration. "They're so beautiful, all white and gold. How do they feel?"

I blow out a slow breath. "Heavy."

"We'll train the muscles. Build your endurance and your pain tolerance." His head dips, and he presses an open-mouthed kiss to where my wings meet the skin. "I'll work this body until it sings for me."

"It already does," I whisper.

A helpless shiver rolls through me, and I know he feels it. We sway into each other, foreheads pressed together as we just breathe, relearning the shape of this. Of us.

After a small eternity, he withdraws, and his gaze strays to the box in my hand.

"Ready?" I ask him.

"Born ready, nemesis."

I lift the latch, and the lid falls open to reveal a glowing yellow crystal.

My attention cuts back to Evander's in a silent question. At his nod, I lift it free.

"So I just... put it on you?"

He laughs. "Just"—his hands close over mine, guiding the seal above his heart—"like this."

The crystal makes contact with a flare of light and sinks beneath his skin.

Searing light explodes around us. His power lashes against me, a concussive wave of energy that rattles the arena and sends fissures through the stonework.

But I barely register the destruction. Can't focus on anything beyond the way our bond fractures open, flayed nerve endings and endless hunger. A need so visceral that I feel it in every part of me.

That inhuman part of me, so newly woken, utters a soft purr of recognition. It knows this power, this wildness. The scent of him.

Then he lunges, crushing his mouth to mine in a kiss that tastes of blood and victory. Of possession. It's the drag of his tongue against mine and the sharp nip of teeth. It's wildfire singing through my veins.

His magic spreads beneath my skin. Power and life and

ancient, nameless things. Sensation and memory collide—the incandescent truth of it. Of him. Of this impossible, inviolable thing between us.

It feels like finally exhaling after a lifetime underwater. It feels like surfacing.

It feels like coming home.

58

EVANDER

I FIND BRYONY in the garden.

Her white and gold feathers catch the sun as she clears away the dead roses. Even after a few days, I'm still not used to her transformation, the proof that she's mine. Her skin glows differently now—softer, brighter. The old Devaliant sheen is gone, replaced by the crushed diamond luster of a demigoddess.

She hums as she moves. Though she's still a while away from flying long distances, her wings no longer drag on the ground. My girl is learning.

I bite back a groan as she kneels. She's wearing my shirt, leaving those long, muscular legs bare as she turns to toss a withered vine into her basket. I love seeing her in my clothes. That silent declaration—*she's taken, she's spoken for.*

This one is mine.

Our bond pulses. It's different since her death, a deeper link now that she has power of her own to Claim me. The eight-pointed star on my chest pulses in response to her nearness, to the way her magic reaches for mine, tangling together in that space where our souls meet.

The tension eases from her shoulders. "You're doing it again," she says without turning.

"Doing what?"

"The hovering." She glances at me through a tumble of silvery hair. "The lurking."

I flash her a grin. "Sweetheart, you bend over in nothing but my shirt, and I'm going to look. I'm only a male."

I close the distance between us. My hands find her hips, and her breath catches when I put my mouth to the curve of her neck.

My hands drift to the place where her wings join the muscles of her back. I stroke my fingers through the silken feathers, and she melts into me with a moan, her head tilting to the side. I take ruthless advantage, kissing along her throat.

I stroke her wings. There's an intimacy to touching her here, a rightness. It feels holy. Reverent. A gift I never thought we'd both share.

"Your control is getting better," I tell her. "You're not overbalancing anymore. The drag isn't as pronounced."

She snorts. "I destroyed three vases in the atrium yesterday."

A laugh rumbles out of me. "You'll get there. We'll train you up, get you nice and coordinated." I drag my teeth over her pulse, feeling her shiver. She smells like crushed petals and spring rain, like something wild and mine. "You left me alone in that big bed. For *gardening*."

"You're the reason my roses are dead. You should help me."

"You know you don't need to clear the roses with your hands anymore, don't you? You could magic it away."

"Just because I'm a demigoddess doesn't mean I want magic to fix everything." She leans into me. "Four days, Wolf. You've had me in that bed for four days straight."

"And the plan was seven days of making you scream my name before I had to share you with the rest of the world. You fucked up my schedule, nemesis." I lift her wrist to my mouth and let my lips drag over the glowing star. "Anything you want to talk about?"

For a moment, there's only the whisper of leaves overhead, the morning chorus of birds.

Then, "I miss my sister."

Ah. There it is.

"I know it's only been a week. But after everything that went down in Hellevig…" She swallows hard. "I hate thinking of her there alone."

"Elias is with her," I say. "He's one of Alexios' best warriors. And Bastien will be there in a few days for part of the rotation. They'll keep her safe."

Her glare could melt steel. "Right. Because what every woman needs when she's dealing with political shit and assassination attempts is Bastien 'I'd rather set myself on fire than smile' and some random demi guard instead of her sister."

I wince. Okay, yeah. Point taken.

"I'll take you to her. But I'll need to work something out with Alexios. He controls the Shroud, and now that I'm not his Enforcer, crossing between realms isn't as simple."

Her wings droop. "Oh."

"Hey." I tip her chin up. "I'll make it happen."

Her expression softens, and warmth floods the bond, that soothing sensation of our souls meeting down the tether like tangling tree roots. Over our eternity, those roots will spread, grow, deepen.

"You'd tear the world apart if I asked, wouldn't you?" she asks me.

A million times over, I think but don't say. She knows. She has to know.

What comes out instead is a low, rough, "Try me and find out."

I pull her more firmly against me, savoring how her breathing goes a little ragged. Then I capture her lips with mine, tentative at first, exploring. I've been doing this for days now—letting myself taste her, kiss her as if to relearn her. But then she pushes against me more insistently. A wordless demand.

So I slant my mouth over hers, kissing her slow and deep. The kind of kiss that says *mine* and *yours* and *always*. Her lips part with a sigh, and I savor the sweetness of her.

"I want you," I say when we break apart. "Tell me I can have you right now. Tell me you didn't bother with underwear under this shirt."

"No." It's barely more than a breath. "None at all."

Fuck.

A red haze takes over. My hands slide down to the backs of her thighs, and I lift her, pressing her to the tower wall. I keep one hand cupped under her ass to hold her in place as I work open the buttons of her borrowed shirt with the other.

"Five-day ban on gardening," I tell her.

"That seems excessive—"

Her words cut off on a moan as I close my mouth over her nipple.

"You left my bed empty." I punctuate the words with a sharp nip. "Actions. Have. Consequences."

I take my time with her. My lips map a burning trail down her throat, across her collarbones, between her breasts. Until she's making those little urgent sounds that drive me crazy. Need pulses between us, building with every touch. A feedback loop of *want* and *more* and *please.*

She unbuttons my trousers and grips my cock. My hips jerk into her fist, chasing more of that perfect friction.

"Keep that up," I grit out, "and this is going to be over embarrassingly fast."

"Then hurry up and *fuck me.*"

With a rough laugh, I notch myself against her pussy and push into her, relishing the tightness, the heat, her body yielding to mine. Her head thumps back against the wall, lips parting.

"Nemesis, you feel—" I break off, burying my groan in the crook of her neck. She feels like completion. Like everything I've ever wanted.

I start to move. A slow, deep grind that has our hips meeting on every downstroke. I refuse to rush this. I'll never get tired of seeing her mouth part on a gasp as I fuck into her. The snag of her teeth on her lower lip. The way her eyes glaze as she watches me. Her hips roll against mine, lifting with every thrust.

I've been careful with her these past few days. So mindful of her body's limitations after the transformation. But my queen has other ideas. Her thighs flex around my waist, using that new strength to urge me faster, harder.

"Stop treating me like I'm fragile," she pants.

If she wants to be ruined, I can do that.

I wedge my hand between her wings to grip the nape of her neck, yanking her in for a hard kiss. Then I'm slamming into her, driving up into her heat. Our bond floods with sensation—pleasure edged with a sweet ache as I give her what she wants. What we both need. She matches me, thrust for thrust, hands scrabbling at my shoulders, my wings, any part of me she can reach.

I slide my fingers to her clit and circle it until she's shaking. Nearly there. I work her higher, winding her tighter and tighter and tighter—

And then she *bites* me.

Her teeth close over the Claim on my chest, right on top of that star—*our* star—and pleasure whites out thought.

"Oh fuck," I groan. "Sweetheart, you can't just…"

She does it again, and my hips grind into her, seeking that liquid heat, that impossible rapture. Sensation bursts through me. She's everywhere at once—in my head, under my skin. Her pleasure bleeds into mine, building together until we're all tangled up.

Release crashes into me. For a suspended moment, I'm frozen, drowning in bliss so intense it hurts. I bury my face in her neck as I empty myself inside her, my hips rocking in shallow pushes. I dimly register her tensing around me as she joins me over the edge, her cries muffled against me. Her thighs squeeze my hips.

Fucking her has never felt so much like annihilation.

Her expression goes soft as she opens her eyes and kisses me. Because this is forever. This is eternity. My heart feels like it's going to beat out of my chest, like she's reached into my ribs and grabbed it, marked it as her own. I press my lips to her brow. Her cheeks. The corners of her mouth. I turn my face into her neck and just breathe.

"I love you," I rasp. They're too small, those three words. Too simple for the enormity of our souls brushing against one another. "I love you, I love you, I love you."

Later, as we're straightening our clothes, I see it.

Peeking out from beneath the tangle of dead vines, a glowing red rose opens its petals to the morning sun.

Alexios stands at the edge of the cliff, his wings spread wide, and his power building like a storm about to break.

"Come to threaten me again over your Chosen?" he asks.

The Shroud unfurls in a veil of stars, glimmering and vast, with colors bleeding together. Black lines of rot cut through it, eating the rest away.

"Tempting," I admit. "But no. I'm here to make a deal."

A sharp laugh. "Five days, and you're already crawling back for favors?" His red eyes cut into me, searching. "Give me one good reason why I should even consider it."

I breathe deep. *I can do this. For her.*

"Because I'll help you hold up the Shroud."

Alexios goes quiet, and I watch the calculations behind those garnet eyes. "Must be a big ask. Does the female whose name I'm meant to keep out of my fucking mouth know you're here bartering?"

Of course she does, you smug fuck. But temper has no place here. *Reason*, I remind myself. *Diplomacy.*

"She knows. Doesn't like it, but she gets it's my call."

He arches a brow. "How domestic of you. What do you want?"

"Permission to pass through the wards at will. Bryony wants to see her sister, and Theodora is bound to Hellevig until she births an heir to carry on their bloodline." I spread my hands in a silent, *There it is.*

The things we do for love. The monstrous bargains we strike.

Alexios just watches me, and I feel the weight of millennia in that hard red stare. The civilizations he ground to dust under his heel. Right now, he's the Eternal through and through— conqueror and god-king, the one who stitched the realms together using shreds of his own soul to do it.

"No," he says flatly.

I exhale through my nose, calling on every damn bit of restraint to keep from lunging for his throat. "You made me watch while you tortured my soulbonded mate," I say, my voice deadly soft. "By every Scillarian law, I'd be giving my judgment on your punishment. Instead, I'm volunteering to help hold up your barrier. Letting the Devaliant sisters see each other is a small fucking ask."

"It's not a 'small fucking ask,'" Alexios says. His power swells, pressure building, until a spark of lightning skitters over his cheek. "You want to parade a famous Devaliant through Vartena, where any idiot with functional eyes might notice their dead princess suddenly sprouted wings. Have you thought this through at all?"

My magic rises, snarling against his. The air thickens as our Eternal energies collide. "No one will see her. No one has to know." I take a step forward. "But Theodora needs her sister if you want her sane enough to anchor your precious Shroud. Let them have this, or I'll ally with Nyholm and leave you drowning under this burden alone. How long before it drives you completely insane, do you think? A century? Less?"

Electricity sparks between us and thunder rolls across the mountains, but I don't flinch. I've spent too many years watching him demolish things to fear his temper now.

Finally, he looks away. "Fine. She can go to Hellevig. Keep it brief."

"Thought you might see it my way." I roll my shoulders. "Now. How do we stitch my magic into this mess?"

"I'll bind you to a fifth of its weight to start. If you thought the collar hurt, wait until you experience the Shroud clawing into you."

"I'll hold. My Chosen bled for me. It's only fair I return the courtesy."

Something flickers over Alexios' face. Maybe a shadow of recognition, of what it means to destroy yourself for another. "Open a vein. Bleed onto the ground and let the Shroud drink deep. Let me handle the rest."

I unsheathe my blade and slice my left palm, watching as scarlet wells up and falls to the soil.

Alexios mirrors the action. His power unfurls and lashes my skin in a concussive wave of electric pressure. It sings through my veins and crackles over the Shroud in indigo lightning.

He cracks his neck. "Try not to scream too much."

Then he slams our bleeding palms together and—

Pain explodes through me. The Shroud tears through skin and bones, sinking claws into my soul and cracking me open. I'm lost. There's no gentle meld, no gradual coaxing of magic into new paths. Only a violent collision.

"Let it in." Alexios' voice is distorted and strange, filtering through layers of static. "Stop fighting, you stubborn fuck."

I squeeze my eyes shut.

And I fall.

I fall and fall and fall. Searing cold floods my senses, fills my nose and mouth and lungs until I'm suffocating from it. Submerged in the frigid rush burrowing into all the empty spaces.

Everything feels wrong. Like I've been torn apart and nothing fits right anymore and I'm wearing someone else's skin. My awareness stretches until I sense the pulse of the realms, the endless expanse of space between them.

And then ... it settles. Calms like a heavy weight pressing to my chest.

Distantly, I feel Alexios' hand on my nape. "Breathe through the pressure."

I drag in air and breathe, gulping greedy lungfuls as my body tries to reconcile this new shape. This peculiar tightness in my bones.

Slowly, I come back to myself. Light whirls behind my eyelids, and a strange ache pounds inside my skull.

Evander? A phantom touch skates my consciousness, soft as a sigh. *Are you okay?*

I send a surge of reassurance down the glittering tether that binds Bryony's soul to mine. *I'm fine. Just the Shroud getting comfortable.*

When my vision finally clears, I find Alexios watching me.

"Welcome back," he says. "You keep all your insides where they should be?"

"I feel like I got thrown off a cliff, then smashed to a pulp on the way down. How do you bear it?"

He smiles slightly. "Let it fill up your ribcage until you stop choking on it. You're not going to pass out, are you?"

The gall of this bastard.

I glare at him. "Not likely. What now?"

"I'll tell the sentries to let you pass. And Severin needs to know you're claiming Turpori until your brother gets his head out of his ass and takes his share."

I nod my thanks.

Silence falls between us, broken by the wind whistling over the mountains. I notice a subtle shift in the atmosphere, a prickling at my senses. The pressure in my chest tightens another notch.

"Does it ever stop feeling like this?"

Alexios clenches his jaw. When he finally speaks, his voice is softer than I've ever heard it. "No. It's always too much." He looks out over the rippling barrier, something weary bleeding through his careful mask. "But you learn to endure it and keep breathing even when it feels like your spine might snap."

I see him then—really see him. Not the god-king or the monster who hurt my mate, but the Eternal who's been bearing this responsibility for centuries. Who's felt it eating away at his sanity.

"This is the price we pay," he says. "When it's too much, go to your griefwood. Remember what you're stopping from happening."

Thunder rolls in the distance as storm clouds gather, and the heaviness of the Shroud presses harder against my chest. Testing my limits, waiting for me to crack.

But I won't. I'll carry this burden for her. For what she needs.

Lightning splits the sky, and then it begins to rain.

EPILOGUE

EVANDER

SHE'S GOING TO fall.

I watch Bryony move closer to the cliff, wings pulled too tight against her back. It's been fifteen days of watching her stumble and curse as she learns this new body. Fifteen days of pure torture. Because there's nothing worse than seeing your Chosen struggle and knowing you can't make it easier.

You're going to let me fall, Wolf. Then you're going to let me get back up and do it again.

I always keep my promises. So I keep letting her fall.

"You're thinking too much," Amara says, nudging Bryony. At the bottom of the cliffs, the waves of the Osbu Sea batter against the rocks. "Flying isn't about mechanics. It's instinct."

Bryony's wings twitch. "And exactly how long did it take you to master it?"

Amara smiles. "Years. But I wasn't an adult demigoddess, so you might as well put in some effort. Get your ass over there and jump."

Bryony inches her feet more. Her jaw's clenched so damn tight I can practically hear her teeth grinding. All day, she's been trying to wall up her emotions and pain from me, but her fear is bleeding through the bond.

Well. Can't have that. There's only so much I can take.

I rise from my perch on a rock and walk toward her. "You're too tense. You need to relax."

She whirls to face me. "Oh, I'm sorry. Is my learning curve not steep enough for you? Should I maybe try harder to overcome thousands of years of human nature telling me that jumping off cliffs equals death?" Her chin lifts in a way that makes me want to bite it. "Please, share your centuries of wisdom if you're such an expert."

I arch a brow. "If you'd rather figure it out yourself..." I turn as if to leave, counting down in my head.

Three... two... one...

Bryony lunges and seizes a fistful of my shirt, reeling me in until we're sharing breaths.

"Don't you dare," she hisses.

Without taking my eyes off her, I say to Amara, "Let me have a go, will you? I'll take over training."

A snort. "You sure you can keep our girl in one piece? Or are you just looking for an excuse to get handsy?"

"It's adorable that you think I need an excuse."

She barks a laugh. Then she's tipping backward in that effortless way of hers, those powdered dark wings snapping out to catch the updraft. She wheels once over our heads before disappearing beyond the jagged peaks of the mountains.

I let my gaze drag over my Chosen, mapping her hurts. The fresh cuts are already healing over. Good. Each day, her healing is swifter as her immortal body settles into itself.

"You're staring again," she murmurs.

"Can't help it." I brush my knuckles down her cheek. "You're the most beautiful thing I've ever seen. And I want to have you flying a tenth of the way to Hellevig next time. Why the hesitation?"

After a long moment, she whispers, "When I'm falling, it's like dying. I think I'll wake up, and this will all be a dream. And you'll be gone."

Oh, nemesis.

I hold her against me, wrapping my wings around us both. Everything else fades away. All I know is her—warm in my arms where she fits perfectly, her soul brushing mine.

"Feel this?" I breathe against her lips, pressing my palm flat over her chest. "The way your heart matches mine? The heat of my skin?" I graze my mouth across hers, not quite kissing. Just sharing air. "Can you taste me?"

Her lashes flutter. I duck my head and catch her in a proper kiss. As gently as I know how, I explore her soft lips with light grazes and lingering presses. She clutches my shoulders, pulling me closer. I delve deeper, licking into her mouth, swallowing her gasps, tasting how much she wants me.

"What about this?"

Slowly, so slowly, I walk my fingers up her spine, tracing the flex and bunch of new muscle shifting beneath her skin. I skim the downy place where flesh gives way to feathers, and *press*.

Bryony goes liquid against me, head tipping back on a broken moan. Pleasure pulses through the bond.

"What's the verdict, nemesis?" I breathe against the hammering pulse in her throat. "Real enough for you?"

She shudders, and I feel it travel the length of her and follow it with my palms. Slowly dragging up the curve of her hips, savoring each ridge and valley.

"Fuck me, please," she breathes.

"Impress me, and I might."

She gives me a look. "Since when are you such a tease?"

"Since I need to motivate you to use these wings." I nip at her lower lip. "Learn to fly, and I'll show you how immortals fuck in the sky. Agreed?"

"Yes."

"Very good," I murmur, satisfaction rumbling in my chest. "Now for your lesson. I know this body still feels foreign, but you have to trust it knows what to do. Let instinct override thought. When the wind shifts, there will be a tug low in your gut. Don't fight it. Lean into the pull and embrace the fall."

"You make it sound so simple."

"Simple and easy aren't the same thing." I press closer until there is no air between us. Until she has no choice but to breathe me in with each inhale. "Do you understand what being Chosen really means? What we are to each other?"

Bryony shakes her head, wordless.

"It means every cell in your body was crafted to complement mine. We're two pieces of the same whole." My lips graze her temple. "Your soul already knows the shape of the sky. Now you just need to close your eyes and fall."

I don't give her a chance to respond before I launch us off the cliff with a beat of my wings. She grabs my neck, and I hold her tight as we shoot upward. Up, up, past the Osbu Sea, through the clouds, higher than any human's ever dreamed of flying.

And it's glorious—this communion of air and excitement. The heat of her against me. I could drown in it, in the drag of her hair whipping across my skin, the salt-sharp scent of her exhilaration.

I slow our climb and level out until we're soaring over my new territory. Rivers of starlight dot the ground below, and I intend to build a new palace for us *right there*, where the red roses grow wild on the banks. A reminder of what it meant to nearly lose her once.

"We'll start with gliding," I tell her.

I take Bryony's hand and gently guide it back until her fingers brush the leading edge of her wing. "Feel that? The way your coverts blend into your scapulars? How the marginal coverts give way to secondary flight feathers?"

She nods.

"Good. Focus on that. Your body knows what to do." I press a kiss to her jaw, savoring the way she shivers against me. "And trust that I'll catch you if you need catching."

"I do. I trust you," she whispers. "Always."

Always. Not just for today, but for always. Something swells in my chest—raw and tender and too large for my body.

I let go.

She stops fighting the fall. Surrenders to the wind and…

Spreads her wings.

It happens slowly. A story measured in increments as instinct and new muscle memory war with panic. But inch by agonizing inch, those glorious feathers unfurl and catch the current.

And then she's soaring, wings spread wide, and a swell of pride and possession bursts through me.

My Chosen.

I pull up beside her and reach for her hand, threading our fingers together. She startles at my touch. I watch her nearly falter, wingtips dipping too low. I'm already lunging, ready to capture her back against me.

Hold, I remind myself. *Not yet. Catch her only when she needs catching.*

She recovers and rights herself in a beat of white and gilt feathers, throwing me a look of such fierce triumph that I'm breathless with wanting her.

Bryony's face is incandescent with joy. "I'm flying."

She is. Gloriously and inelegantly, with no art or artifice. But *flying*, nonetheless.

"What now?" she calls. Giddy with the thrill of it. "What next?"

I grin at her. "Everything."

I will never tire of chasing Bryony Devaliant across the sky. Of falling with her and *for* her, again, and again, and again.

Until the realms are ash and memory.

Glossary

Accords: The peace treaty brokered by the Devaliant family three hundred years ago to end the war between gods and humans.

Anchors: Individuals on both sides of the Shroud who maintain and hold the magical barrier in place. The Devaliants are the Anchors in Hellevig, and one of their bloodline must always remain in the city, or the veil will fall.

Asteria: Alexios' territory in Scillari.

Celestials: The primordial gods who came from the stars and created the realms.

Chosen: The soulbonded spouse of a god.

Claim: A visible, physical mark on a human's body that signifies the protection of an Eternal or demigod. Harming a Claimed individual is a direct challenge to the god who granted the Claim.

demigods/demigoddesses (demis): Powerful beings ranking below Eternals. They are the subjects of Scillari.

Devaliant: The ruling family of Luceni, whose bloodline brokered the Accords between gods and humans.

Enforcers: Assassins sent by Alexios to execute those who break their oaths to him.

Eternal: When the most powerful demigods ascend and gain their full power, they become Eternals. Most were killed during the god-human war. Every ascended begins as a demigod, but few become Eternals. "Eternal" is also a title for Scillari's rulers.

fleshtrade: The illegal trade of divine body parts and blood in Vartena. In the past, this was used to temporarily grant humans god powers in battle.

gods: A collective term referring to both ascended gods (Eternals) and demigods.

Hellevig: The capital city of Luceni and the seat of the Devaliants.

Luceni: The largest empire in Vartena, ruled by the Devaliants.

Lybräian: The formal dialect spoken by the Lucinian royal court and nobility.

Nyholm: The territory in Scillari ruled by the Dark King.

oathbreakers: Humans bearing the mark of Alexios' revoked Claim. They are marked for death and killed by Enforcers, existing on the lowest rung of society.

Oracles: The rare offspring of gods and humans, who reside in temples and act as the communication channel between Alexios and his Claimed. They collect blood tithes in temples all over Vartena.

Scillari: The realm of the gods.

the Shroud: The magical barrier that separates the realms of gods and humans. It was created as part of the truce to end the god-human war.

tithes: Blood offerings from Claimed humans to maintain Alexios' protection. Vartenans prick their fingers over the collection channels to shore up the Shroud's foundations. Devaliants alone give their lives for the tithe and are resurrected in the act of "anchoring".

Turpori weapons: Blades created by Bastien for demigod soldiers to enhance their abilities in battle. These godkilling weapons are contraband in Vartena.

Unclaimed: Humans without the protection of a god.

Vartena: The human realm.

Acknowledgments

The Wolf and the Crown of Blood has had such a wild journey. When I first started working on this book in 2022, fantasy romance was a little quieter in traditional publishing, so I wrote with the intention of self-publishing it. In hindsight, I was grateful for that process, which I think led me to write more fearlessly. And with fearlessness came an immense love for the manuscript, the characters, and the world.

I mentioned this book to Rosie de Courcy, my (now former) editor at Head of Zeus for my Katrina Kendrick romances. Rosie took it, and to my delight, Head of Zeus wanted it. So I am eternally grateful to Rosie for finding this book its US home, and to the team at Head of Zeus/Bloomsbury for their support and enthusiasm for my work, especially Aubrie Artiano, who is an absolute joy to work with.

This book's home in the UK is with the brilliant Daphne Press team, which I'm so thankful to continue collaborating with. I owe so much to Daphne Tonge, more than words can say. Many thanks to Davi Lancett and Cat Aquino, whose brilliant notes helped guide this manuscript in directions that made it so much richer and deeper.

All my love to my agent, Russell Galen, who has been so supportive of my pivot into romance. And, of course, Danny Baror, who has been such an incredible advocate for my work and doesn't blink when I surprise him with completed manuscripts.

I'm always so thankful for my husband, who does lovely things like making me coffee and bringing me chocolate when I'm in manuscript hyperfocus. I love you so much, and I'm the luckiest lady alive. And my readers, I love and adore each and every one of you. Thank you for joining me on this journey.

ABOUT THE AUTHOR

ELIZABETH MAY is the *Sunday Times* bestselling author of *To Cage a God*, the Seven Devils duology (co-written with Laura Lam), The Falconer series, and romance novels under the pseudonym Katrina Kendrick. Originally from California, Elizabeth holds a Ph.D. from the University of St Andrews. She currently resides in the Scottish countryside with her husband, three cats, and a lively hive of honeybees.

ALSO BY ELIZABETH MAY

The Falconer
The Vanishing Throne
The Fallen Kingdom

Thanks for reading!

Want to receive exclusive author content, news on the latest Aria books and updates on offers and giveaways?

Follow us on X @AriaFiction and on Facebook and Instagram @HeadofZeus, and join our mailing list.